Praise for Ben Bova

"Bova's fans and hard SF lovers should flock
to his latest novel."

—*Library Journal* on *Leviathans of Jupiter*

"A quick-paced space adventure."

—*Publishers Weekly* on *Leviathans of Jupiter*

"Bova proves himself equal to the task of
showing how adversity can temper character
in unforeseen ways."

—*The New York Times*

"Bova gets better and better, combining plausible
science with increasingly complex fiction."

—*Daily News* (Los Angeles)

"[Bova's] excellence at combining hard science
with believable characters and an attention-grabbing
plot makes him one of the genre's most accessible
and entertaining storytellers."

TOR BOOKS BY BEN BOVA

NEW
EARTH

BEN BOVA

A TOM DOHERTY ASSOCIATES BOOK
NEW YORK

NEW EARTH

Copyright © 2013 by Ben Bova

A Tor Book
Published by Tom Doherty Associates, LLC
175 Fifth Avenue
New York, NY 10010

www.tor-forge.com

Tor® is a registered trademark of Tom Doherty Associates, LLC.

ISBN 978-0-7653-6807-2

Tor books may be purchased for educational, business, or promotional use. For information on bulk purchases, please contact Macmillan Corporate and Premium Sales Department at 1-800-221-7945, extension 5442, or write specialmarkets@macmillan.com.

First Edition: July 2013
First Mass Market Edition: July 2014

Printed in the United States of America

0 9 8 7 6 5 4 3 2 1

To Bella Sue Martin and Jim Parsons,
for so many reasons

Nothing is so fatal to the progress of the human mind as to suppose our views of science are ultimate; that there are no new mysteries in nature; that our triumphs are complete; and that there are no new worlds to conquer.

SIR HUMPHRY DAVY

EARTH

Sufficient unto the day is the evil thereof.

MATTHEW 6:34

Chiang Chantao sat in his powerchair, floating high above the flooded city of St. Louis.

"This shouldn't be happening," he said, his voice barely more than a pained croak.

"But it is," said Felicia Ionescu, seemingly standing in mid-air beside him.

What had once been a thriving city was now a drowned disaster, buildings inundated, highways submerged, even the magnificent Gateway Arch's foundations awash in several meters of muddy water. Long lines of miserable refugees were plodding away from the city, automobiles, trucks, buses inching along, bumper to bumper, piled high with mattresses, bicycles, clothes washers, sticks of furniture; others were on foot, sloshing stolidly through the rain, the water knee-deep in some places, carrying babies and bundles of whatever they could salvage from their ruined homes.

"Kill the display," Chiang commanded.

The virtual reality simulation disappeared. Chiang was sitting in his powerchair in the middle of the VR chamber, a wizened, bald, crippled old man connected to the blinking, softly beeping heart pump and artificial lungs and other machinery that kept his emaciated body alive.

Felicia Ionescu was a tall, imposing figure, generously proportioned as an old-time opera diva, and just as imperious. At this moment, though, she did not look haughty or domineering. Despite her name, she looked unutterably sad.

"Demons and devils!" Chiang burst. "All my life we've been fighting the sea-level rise. We've built dams and levees and pumping systems all over the world! We had things under control! And now this."

He pointed a wavering clawlike finger at the satellite map of the world that covered one wall of the VR chamber. China's long rivers were now broad arms of the sea reaching a thousand kilometers inland, drowning villages and whole cities, killing hundreds of thousands, wiping out millions upon millions of hectares of productive farmlands.

Where once the Mississippi River had wound its peaceful way from the northern lakes to the Gulf of Mexico, a great inland sea was spreading, flooding Texas, Louisiana, Arkansas, reaching up into Missouri and still growing.

The Nile was inundating Egypt and the Sudan, drowning the Sphinx and lapping against the great pyramids. The swollen Orinoco River and mighty Amazon had virtually split South America into two separate subcontinents. Coastlines around the world were no longer recognizable: the sea was inexorably conquering the land.

"This wasn't supposed to happen," Chiang insisted, his voice a painful rasp. "We've stopped burning fossil fuels. We've removed gigatons of carbon dioxide from the atmosphere."

"Not enough," said Ionescu, mournfully. Like Chiang, she spoke Mandarin, but with a Romanian accent that was painful to the old man's ears.

"We're doing everything we can," he insisted.

"We started too late. Despite all our efforts, the global climate has tipped into a warm cycle. The Greenland ice cap is melting. So is Antarctica. And there's nothing we can do to stop it." She took a breath, then added, "We're paying for starting too late. We did nothing for more than a century, and now it's too late to prevent the floods."

Chiang craned his wattled neck to glare up at her. "And you're back again to wheedle me into approving a backup mission to Sirius? How many times do I have to tell you it's impossible?"

Ionescu closed her eyes, then said, as if reciting from rote, "As director of the International Astronautical Authority, it is my duty to remind you once again that the exploration program calls for several backup missions."

Waving his withered arm toward the satellite imagery again, Chiang demanded, "And what do I tell the people of Chongqing? And St. Louis? And Cairo and São Paulo and all the other cities that have been flooded? How do we feed the refugees? Where do we house them?"

Ionescu said, "We should have launched the first backup mission seventy-five years ago, long before either you or I came into power."

"Do you know what the Council would do if I recommended we send a backup mission to Sirius?" Chiang screeched. "They'd flay me alive and nail me to the gate of the Forbidden City!"

"You exaggerate."

"I've worked all my life to save our world from disaster. I've fought my way to chairmanship of the World Council. I'm not going to allow the IAA or any force on Earth to distract me from my purpose."

"It's less than two and a half billion kiloyuan for the first backup mission," Ionescu replied, her voice rising slightly. "We have all the basic facilities in place. We have the organizational infrastructure."

Chiang took a deep breath, while the life-support equipment on the back of his chair chattered angrily. "It's not the *amount* of money, woman, it's the symbolism. Here we're struck with the worst disaster since the original greenhouse floods five generations ago, and you want to spend badly needed funds on sending another team of pampered scientists to Sirius! It's impossible!"

Working hard to control her own volatile temper, Ionescu said, "The first team should have reached Sirius by now. They're only twelve people—"

"If they need help let them ask for it."

"Their messages take more than eight years to get here. They're effectively alone, isolated."

"Your predecessors knew that when they sent them, didn't they?"

"Yes, of course, but our original program plan called for a backup mission. Several of them, in fact."

"Those plans are canceled," Chiang snapped. "They're underwater. Drowned. Just like the village of my birth."

"It wasn't supposed to be this way," Ionescu said, almost pleading. "Twelve people, alone out there . . ."

"They're going to have to make the best of it," Chiang said. "Just as we are."

Ionescu turned from Chiang's age-ravaged, angry face and stared at the wall-sized satellite display. But in her mind's eye she saw the starship taking up its preplanned orbit around the planet Sirius C. New Earth.

ARRIVAL

We may prefer to think of ourselves as fallen angels, but in reality we are rising apes.

DESMOND MORRIS

AWAKENING

He opened his eyes slowly.

His eyelids felt gummy. Slowly he reached up with both hands to knuckle the cobwebs away. My name is Jordan Kell, he told himself. I've been asleep for eighty years.

He was lying on his back in the cryosleep capsule, looking up at the softly muted glow of the ship's ceiling panels. The coffin-sized capsule smelled like an antiseptic hospital room, cold, inhuman. A shudder went through him, his body's memory of the years spent suspended, frozen by liquid nitrogen.

Peering down the length of his naked body he saw that all the tubes for feeding and muscle stimulation had been removed. Nothing but faint scars here and there.

They'll fade away soon enough, he thought.

Well, we must have made it, he told himself. Eight point six light-years. Eighty years to reach Sirius.

Then a pang of doubt hit him. Maybe we're not there! Maybe something's gone wrong!

The robot slid into his view. It was a semi-anthropomorphic design, man-shaped except that it rolled along on tiny trunions instead of having legs. Its silicone-covered face had two glittering optronic eyes, a slit of a radiator where a human nose would be, a speaker grill for a mouth.

"Are we . . . ?" Jordan's voice cracked. His throat felt dry, raw.

The robot understood his unfinished question. "The ship has arrived in orbit around Sirius C," it said. Its synthesized voice was the rich, warm baritone of a noted dramatic actor back on Earth.

"Good," Jordan croaked. "Good."

"Diagnostics show that you are in satisfactory physical condition," the robot reported. "Your memories have been uploaded successfully from the central computer back into your brain."

"The others . . . ?"

"Their uploads are under way," said the robot. "You are the first to be revived, as per mission protocol."

Rank hath its privileges, Jordan thought.

The robot turned away briefly to the row of diagnostic monitors lining one wall of the narrow compartment. When it came back to Jordan's open capsule it bore a ceramic cup in one metal hand.

"A stimulant," it said, "and a lubricant for your throat."

Tenderly, the robot lifted Jordan's head with one silicone-skin hand and brought the cup to his lips, like a mother feeding a baby. He grasped the cup with both his trembling hands, grateful for its warmth.

Tea, Jordan realized once he'd taken a sip of the steaming brew. Tea with honey. Stimulant, lubricant, warmer-upper. Good old tea. He almost laughed.

"Do you feel strong enough to get to your feet?"

Jordan thought it over, then replied, "I can try."

The robot gently helped him up to a sitting position. Then Jordan swung his bare legs over the edge of the capsule and carefully, tentatively, stood up. He felt a little wobbly, but only a little. Not bad for a fellow who's a hundred and thirty-two years old, he thought.

The little cubicle's walls were bare, off-white. It was hardly big enough to contain Jordan's cryosleep capsule, a marvel of biotechnology sitting there like an elongated egg that had been cracked open. The life-support equipment and monitors blinked and beeped softly against the opposite wall.

Each member of the expedition had a cubicle of his or her own; the robots assisted with the reawakening process.

Staying at his side, the robot led Jordan three steps to the closet where his clothes were stored. He pulled the door open and saw himself in the full-length mirror inside the door.

He was a trim, well-built middleweight, standing almost 175 centimeters in his bare feet. Normally he weighed a trifle under seventy-five kilograms, but as he looked down at his bare body he saw that his long sleep had cost him some weight. The skin of his legs was still puckered from the freezing, but beneath the wrinkles it looked pink, healthy.

His face was slightly thinner than he remembered it, his arched aquiline nose a little more obvious, his cheekbones a bit more prominent, the hollows beneath them more noticeable. He saw that the neat little mustache he had cultivated so carefully over the years had grayed noticeably; it looked somewhat ragged. I'll need to attend to that, he thought.

Then, with a shock, he realized that his dark brown hair had turned completely silver.

They didn't tell us to expect *that*, he said to himself.

Back on Earth he'd often been called elegant, sophisticated. At this moment, farther from Earth than any human being had ever traveled, he felt shabby, weary, and strangely detached, as if he were watching himself from afar.

Jordan shook his head, trying to force himself to accept where he was and who he was. While cryonic freezing preserved the body, it also tended to degrade the synapses of the brain's neurons. All the members of the team had downloaded their memories into the ship's computer before they'd left Earth and gone into cryosleep.

With deliberate concentration, Jordan tested the upload. He remembered leading the team into the ship's luxurious interior. He remembered climbing into the sleep capsule, watching it close over him. Childhood memories floated before him: the Christmas he deduced that Father Christmas was really his parents; tussling with his brother Brandon; graduating from Cambridge; Miriam—he clenched his eyes shut.

Miriam. Her last days, her final agony.

My fault. All my fault. My most grievous fault.

It would have been good to have erased those memories, he thought.

Slowly, carefully, he pulled on cotton briefs, a turtlenecked white shirt, dark blue jeans, and comfortable loafers. Then he studied himself for a moment in the full-length mirror on the back of the closet's door, his steel-gray eyes peering intently. You don't look elegant and sophisticated now, he told himself. You look . . . bewildered, and more than a little frightened.

Then he realized, "I'm hungry."

The robot said, "A very normal reaction." It sounded almost pleased. "The wardroom is less than thirty meters up the passageway, in the direction of the ship's command center. The dispensers offer a full selection of food and beverages."

With a crooked smile, Jordan said, "You sound like an advertising blurb."

The robot made no reply, but it turned and opened the door to the passageway.

Jordan hesitated at the doorway.

"The wardroom is to the right, Mr. Kell."

Jordan tried to recall the ship's layout. The living and working areas were built into the wheel that turned slowly to give a feeling of gravity. Leaving the robot behind him, he walked carefully along the passageway. Although the floor felt perfectly flat, he could see it curving up and out of sight ahead of him.

The wardroom was empty as he entered it. Of course, he realized. I'm the first to be revived. I'm the team leader.

It was a pleasantly decorated compartment, its walls covered with warm pseudowood paneling, its ceiling glowing softly. Six small tables were arranged along its russet-tiled floor; they could be pushed together in any pattern the team wanted. At present they were all standing separately, each table big enough to seat four people.

Very comfortable, Jordan thought. Of course, crew comfort was a major goal of the mission designers. This far from home, a few luxuries help to keep us happy. And sane. Or so the psychotechs decided.

One entire wall of the wardroom was taken up by machines that dispensed food and drink. But Jordan's attention instantly was drawn to the wall opposite, a floor-to-ceiling display screen.

It showed the planet that the ship was orbiting. A lush green world with deeply blue oceans and fleecy white clouds, brown wrinkles of mountains and broad swaths of grasslands. Heartbreakingly beautiful.

Jordan marveled at the sight. It really is a New Earth, he thought.

ven while the massive floods, droughts, and killer storms of the greenhouse climate shift were devastating much of Earth, astronomers were detecting several thousand planets orbiting other stars. Most of these exoplanets were gas giants, bloated spheres of hydrogen and helium, totally unlike Earth. But a few percent of them were small, rocky worlds, more like our own.

One in particular raised hopes of being really Earthlike: Sirius C. It was almost the same size as Earth, and although its parent star was a fiercely blazing blue-white giant, much larger and hotter than the Sun, the planet's orbit lay at the "Goldilocks" distance from Sirius where its surface temperature was not too hot, and not too cold for liquid water to exist.

On Earth, liquid water means life. Beneath the frozen iron sands of Mars, liquid water melting from the permafrost hosts an underground biosphere of microbial life forms. In the ice-covered seas of Jupiter's major moons, living organisms abound. In the planet-girdling ocean beneath the eternal clouds of giant Jupiter itself, life teems and flourishes.

But Sirius C was a challenge to the scientists. The planet shouldn't exist, not by all that they knew of astrophysics. And it couldn't possibly bear life, Goldilocks notwithstanding, not sandwiched between brilliant Sirius A and its white dwarf star companion, Sirius B. The dwarf had erupted in a series of nova explosions eons ago. The death throes of Sirius B must have sterilized any planets in the vicinity, boiled away any atmosphere or ocean.

But there it was, a rocky, Earth-sized planet, the *only* planet in the Sirius system, orbiting Sirius A in a nearly perfect circle. Spectroscopic studies showed it had an Earthlike atmosphere—and oceans of liquid water.

Might there be a chance that the planet did harbor some kind of life forms? The astrobiologists worked overtime concocting theories to support the hope that the Earth-sized planet might indeed host an Earth-type biosphere. The popular media had no such problem. They quickly dubbed Sirius C "New Earth."

For nearly a full century, while governments and corporations all over the world toiled to alleviate the catastrophic results of the climate change, Earth's eagerly inquisitive scientists hurled robotic space probes toward Sirius C. Even at the highest thrust that fusion rockets could produce, the probes took decades to reach their objective, more than eight light-years from Earth. Yet once they arrived at the planet, what they saw confirmed the most cherished hopes of both the scientists and the general public.

Sirius C was indeed a New Earth. The planet bore broad blue seas of water, its continents were richly green with vegetation. There was no sign of intelligent life, no cities or farmlands or roads, no lights or radio communications, but the planet truly was a New Earth, unpopulated, virginal, beckoning.

Impatient to explore this new world in greater detail, the International Astronautical Authority asked the World Council to fund the human exploration of Sirius C. The Council procrastinated, citing the enormous costs of mitigating the disasters caused by the global climate shift. Then the lunar nation of Selene stepped forward and offered to build a starship. Shamed into grudging cooperation, the Council reluctantly joined the effort—meagerly.

They named the starship *Gaia*, after the Earth deity who represented the web of life. *Gaia* would travel to Sirius more slowly than the robotic probes, to protect its fragile human cargo. It would take some eighty years for the ship to reach Sirius C.

Men and women from all around the world volunteered for the mission. They were carefully screened for physical health and mental stability. As one of the examining psychotechnicians put it, "You'd have to be at least a little crazy to throw away eighty years just to get there."

But the crew of *Gaia* would not age eighty years. They would sleep away the decades of their journey in cryonic suspension, frozen in liquid nitrogen, as close to death as human bodies can get and still survive.

Gaia was launched with great fanfare: humankind's first mission to the stars. The explorers would spend five years mapping the planet in detail, studying its biosphere, and building a base for the backup missions to work from.

By the time the ship arrived in orbit around Sirius C, eighty years later, only a handful of dedicated scientists back on Earth were still interested in the mission. Most of the human race was struggling to survive the catastrophic second wave of greenhouse flooding, as the ice caps of Greenland and Antarctica melted down. The backup missions had been postponed, again and again, and finally shelved indefinitely by the World Council.

Even the eagerly waiting scientists saw nothing, heard nothing from the explorers, for it would take more than eight years for messages to travel from Sirius back to Earth.

ALONE

A lone in the wardroom, Jordan poured himself another cup of tea, then sat at one of the tables and stared in fascination at the planet sliding by in the wall screen's display.

It certainly looks like Earth, he thought. The data bar running along the base of the screen showed that the planet's atmosphere was astonishingly close to Earth's: 22 percent oxygen, 76 percent nitrogen, the remaining 2 percent a smattering of carbon dioxide, water vapor, and inert gases. The biggest difference from Earth was that Sirius C had a much thicker ozone layer high in its atmosphere: not unexpected, since the star Sirius emitted much more ultraviolet light than the Sun.

Jordan shook his head in wonder. It's like a miracle, he said to himself. Too good to be true. But then he realized that this was the first planet orbiting another star that human eyes had seen close up. What do we know about exoplanets? Perhaps Earthlike worlds are commonplace.

Enough speculation, he told himself. Get to work. Time to go to the command center and see what the mission controllers have to say to us.

Clasping his half-finished mug of tea in one hand, Jordan went back into the passageway and walked to the command center. It was a smallish compartment with a horseshoe of six workstation consoles curving around a single high-backed chair whose arms were studded with control buttons. Display screens covered the bulkheads, most of them showing the condition and performance of the ship's various systems; others offered views of the planet they orbited.

Jordan slipped into the command chair and frowned briefly at the keypads set into its armrests. He tried to remember which one activated the communications system. The symbols on each pad had always reminded him of children's sketches. The propulsion system's symbol was a triangle with wavy lines emanating from it. Life support a heart shape.

Communications was the headset symbol, he recalled. Touching that pad, Jordan called for the latest message from Earth. He reminded himself that the message he was about to see was sent from Earth more than eight years ago. It takes messages eight point six years to travel from Earth to Sirius.

A woman's face appeared on the main screen, above the row of consoles. She was a handsome woman, with dark hair pulled tightly back off her face. Strong cheekbones and a fine, straight nose. Her eyes were large and so deeply brown they looked almost black—and unutterably sorrowful.

"I am Felicia Ionescu, the newly appointed director of the International Astronautical Authority," she said, in a carefully measured alto register. "This message is being sent to reach you on the day that your ship attains orbit around the planet Sirius C."

Recorded more than eight years ago, Jordan repeated to himself.

"I hope that you have all survived the flight to Sirius and that you are well, and ready to begin the exploration of the planet."

Jordan thought her welcoming message was strangely heavy, bleak. Where's the congratulations? Where are the clichés about how all of Earth is thrilled that you've reached your destination?

"When you departed from Earth," Ionescu went on, "eighty years ago, we were recovering from the worldwide flooding caused by the global greenhouse warming." She took in a breath. "Unfortunately, now—eighty years later—a new wave of flooding has struck, caused by the continued warming of the global climate."

Her image disappeared, replaced by pictures of devastation: cities drowned, coastlines inundated, storms lashing fleeing refugees. Jordan stared in open-mouthed horror.

"Because of these calamities," Ionescu's voice said over the views of disaster, "the World Council has been unable to authorize the backup missions that were in the IA's original program."

The screen showed her face once more. She looked miserable. "I will work to my utmost to get the World Council to fund backup missions, eventually. But, for the present, you twelve members of the *Gaia* mission are alone in your exploration of Sirius C. I wish you well."

And her image winked off.

THE NEWS FROM EARTH

For long moments Jordan sat in the command chair, shocked beyond words. He could feel his heart thudding beneath his ribs, his stomach roiling.

Alone, he thought.

At last he pulled himself to his feet. Very well, then, he told himself. Alone. We have everything we need for a five-year stay at Sirius C. We'll do the best we can with what we've got and then we'll go home.

Yes, he thought. Now to break the cheery news to the rest of the team.

As resolutely as he could manage, Jordan marched back to the wardroom. Only one other person was there: Mitchell Thornberry, the roboticist, standing before the wall-screen display of New Earth.

"Hello, Mitchell."

Thornberry turned to face Jordan, a wide smile breaking across his fleshy face. "Top o' the morning to ya."

He was a solidly built man from the University of Dublin, just about Jordan's own height but thicker, heavier in the torso and limbs. His jowly face almost always displayed a quizzical little smile, as though the ways of his fellow humans amused him slightly. Or puzzled him.

Thornberry was wearing a loudly patterned open-necked shirt hanging over rumpled trousers. He looked as if he'd just come in from an afternoon picnic.

"And a very pleasant good morning to you, sir," said Jordan. And he thought, I'll wait until they're all here, the whole team together. No sense breaking the news eleven separate times.

"Well, we made it," Thornberry said, jabbing a finger toward the wall screen.

"It's uncanny, isn't it?" Jordan said. "It could be Earth's twin."

Thornberry shrugged. "It is what it is." Heading toward the dispensing machines, he added, "I'll let the scientists argue about how the planet could be so Earthlike. Me, all I've got to do is set up a working base down there on the surface and tend to me robots."

Pecking at the food dispensers, Thornberry pulled out a thick sandwich of beef cultured from the biovats, and a tall glass of chilled fruit juice.

"They should have packed some beer aboard for us," he grumbled as he brought his tray to the table where Jordan was sitting.

"No alcoholic beverages," Jordan reminded him. "The health and safety experts agreed on that."

"Ahhh," Thornberry growled. "A bunch of pissant academics with water in their veins."

Jordan smiled at the Irishman. Then he remembered that he too was hungry. He went to the dispensers and selected a salad from the ship's hydroponics garden. Then he returned to his cooling tea and sat down beside Thornberry.

"Wasn't your hair darker?" Thornberry asked, his thick brows knitting.

"It was," said Jordan, unconsciously fingering his mustache.

"Do you feel all right?"

"Yes. Fairly normal," Jordan replied as he sat down next to Thornberry. "A little shaky. I wonder how effective the memory uploading really is."

"Good enough," Thornberry said. "I can remember what we had for dinner the night before we left. And the Guinness that went with it." Then he sank his teeth into his sandwich.

"And you?" Jordan asked. "How do you feel?"

Thornberry swallowed before answering, "All right, more or less. Cold. Deep inside, I feel cold. I don't know that I'll ever feel warm again."

"Psychosomatic, I imagine."

"Oh? And who made you a psychotechnician?"

That stung. Of the dozen men and women on the ship, Jordan alone was neither a scientist nor an engineer. He was merely the head of the mission.

As brightly as he could manage, Jordan changed the subject. "The artificial gravity system seems to be working fine, after all these years."

Thornberry shrugged. "It's just a big Ferris wheel. Nothing exotic about it."

"No, I suppose not."

"Here we are!"

Turning, Jordan saw his younger brother, Brandon, entering the wardroom, together with Elyse Rudaki, the Iranian astrophysicist.

Brandon looked like an improved edition of Jordan: younger, taller, handsomer. Brandon's nose was thinner, nobler, his eyes a shade lighter. When he smiled he could light up a room. Like Jordan, he wore a turtleneck shirt and comfortable denim jeans.

Elyse looked like royalty: tall, slim, elegant, her sculpted face unsmiling, utterly serious. Her complexion was light, almost pale, a stunning contrast to her thick, lustrous dark hair, which she had piled high on her head, making her look even taller, more regal. Although she was wearing a casual blouse of light blue atop darker slacks, Jordan pictured her in a glittering red and gold sari.

But he thought she seemed somewhat uncertain of herself, as if slightly disoriented from drugs or drink. The upload, Jordan told himself. It's not perfect. Then he thought, Perhaps she's frightened. We're a long way from home. Or perhaps you're just projecting your own fears.

Getting to his feet again, Jordan smiled as he held out a chair for her. "Welcome to Sirius C, Elyse."

Before she could reply, Brandon gasped, "My god, Jordy, your hair's turned totally white!"

Forcing a smile, Jordan replied, "I prefer to think of it as silver. Rather becoming, don't you think?"

"I guess so," Brandon said uncertainly. "Are you . . . do you feel okay?"

"I feel fine," Jordan assured him.

Still looking doubtful, Brandon turned toward the wall display and called to the voice-recognition system, "Display screen, show us news broadcasts from Earth."

"No, wait . . ."

"Don't get huffy with me, Jordy. We can look at the planet any time. I want to see what's happening back home, don't you?"

With a resigned nod, Jordan replied, "I suppose so."

Elyse still stood beside him while Jordan held her chair. The wall screen broke into a dozen separate pictures. *The IAA is beaming news and entertainment vids to us,* Jordan remembered. *It's all automatic, preprogrammed. And it's all eight years old.*

The screens showed cities that looked unfamiliar to Jordan, women dressed in strange styles, newscasters wearing what looked like uniforms, sports matches that looked superficially like football and cricket and even tennis, but not quite right. Distorted. Changed.

Where's the flooding and disasters Ionescu showed me? Jordan wondered. Then he realized that newscasts and entertainment vids carefully avoided such unpleasantries.

"Palm trees in Boston?" Brandon marveled.

Elyse said, "The fashions are very revealing."

"Must be summertime," said Thornberry.

"Everywhere?"

"Eighty years have passed on Earth," Jordan pointed out. "Everything is slightly different. It's not the same world that we left behind us."

Thornberry wiped his mouth with his napkin and commented, "That's the way things were back home some eight years ago. It's taken eight and a half years for those signals to get from Earth to here."

"Eight point six years," Jordan murmured.

"Ah, who's counting?" Thornberry wisecracked.

But Brandon did not smile. "Look at them. Going about their lives perfectly normally."

"There doesn't seem to be any war," said Elyse, her voice hushed, subdued. "No violence."

"Or the news nets aren't showing any," said Brandon.

"Or mission control decided not to let us see any," Jordan said.

"Saints alive!" Thornberry pointed at one of the scenes. "Look! There's people scuba diving through a drowned city."

They all stared at the underwater scene.

"It looks like Sydney," Thornberry muttered. "Look! There's the opera house, half underwater."

"But not a word about us," Brandon grumbled.

"That newscast is eight years old," Thornberry pointed out.

Brandon insisted, "They knew we'd have arrived at our destination. But there's nothing in the news about it."

"I think I know why," Jordan said.

Thornberry looked up at Jordan from beneath his shaggy brows. "Do you, now?"

"What is it?" Brandon demanded.

"Let's wait until the others get here," Jordan said. "I'll explain it to all of you at once."

Thornberry looked curious, Elyse worried. Brandon put on the irritated look that Jordan had seen all his brother's life: half sulking, half impatience.

One by one the other members of the team filtered into the wardroom: three more women, five men. They all looked uncertain, a bit shaky. Only to be expected after an eighty-year sleep, Jordan thought. You didn't look too peppy yourself, those first few minutes.

How will they feel once they've heard the news I have to tell them? he asked himself.

The others helped themselves to food and drink, then slowly sat at the tables and watched the screen displays from Earth.

Brandon sat himself beside Elyse and said, "All right, Jordy. We're all here. What is it that you've got to tell us?"

Jordan stepped in front of the wall screen and looked at the eleven of them. Four women, seven men, their eyes focused on him.

"I'm afraid I have some disappointing news," he began. "There isn't going to be a backup mission."

"What?"

"No backup? But the IAA—"

"What do you mean?"

"There's been a second wave of greenhouse flooding," Jordan tried to explain. "Even worse than the original floods, five generations ago. The World Council has reneged on the backup missions, they've got too much reconstruction and resettlement to do."

"But we've seen nothing about such flooding on the news vids," said Harmon Meek, springing to his feet.

The team's astrobiologist, Meek was a scarecrow of a man, tall and almost painfully thin, all bones and gangling limbs. He was dressed almost formally, in a starched white shirt and a dark brown ascot, no less, with neatly creased trousers of charcoal gray. His thick mop of sandy blond hair looked as if it hadn't seen a brush in eighty years; his eyebrows were so pale they were almost invisible, and the cold blue eyes beneath them looked terribly perplexed.

"I'm afraid the vids were edited by the IAA," Jordan said.

"Nonsense!" Meek snapped. "I don't believe you."

Jordan smiled wanly at the astrobiologist, so full of righteous indignation. He commanded the communications system to show Ionescu's message.

Meek sank back into his chair and the team watched the message from Earth, with its scenes of devastation, in shocked silence.

"That's Volgograd," said Tanya Verishkova, in a choked whisper. "Flooded."

"Look at the refugees."

"Miles of 'em."

"So that's the situation," Jordan said, once the images winked off. "It doesn't change our circumstances, really. But it means that when we leave, there won't be a backup team to take over from us, or on its way."

Geoffrey Hazzard, the astronautical engineer and nominal captain of their ship, muttered, "Just like Apollo."

"What do you mean?" Elyse Rudaki asked.

Hazzard was an African-American from Pennsylvania, tall and rangy, his skin the color of mocha, his long-jawed face slightly horsy-looking, although his dark eyes were large and expressive.

"The first missions to the Moon," he explained. "They put a dozen men on the Moon inside of a few years, then stopped altogether. It was more than half a century before anybody went back."

"Well," Jordan said, trying to put up as good a face as possible, "we all knew we'd be pioneers in exploring New Earth. Now we're even more so."

From his seat beside Elyse, Brandon gave out a bitter laugh. "Pioneers, are we? We're all outcasts, that's what we are."

"Outcasts, is it?" Thornberry snapped.

Pointing to the wall-screen displays of the news vids from Earth, Brandon said, "Outcasts. Gone and forgotten. Twelve people, sent to explore a planet—a whole world! Just the twelve of us."

Mildly, Jordan said to his brother, "Bran, we're merely the *first* twelve to be sent here. There will be others, you know. In time."

"You think so."

"Sooner or later. There's got to be."

Thornberry said, "We've got robots, remotely controlled roving vehicles, all sorts of sensors and satellites. There's more than just the twelve of us."

"Think about it," Brandon replied, almost sneering. "Think about what we're doing. We've spent eighty years getting here. Eighty years. We're supposed to explore this planet for at least five years. Then we head back to Earth, another eighty years."

"But we haven't aged," Elyse said.

"What of it? When we get back home, damned near two hundred years will have passed. Two hundred years! We'll be strangers in our own world. We're already strangers. Outcasts."

As mildly as he could manage, Jordan said, "No one forced you to join this mission, Bran. We're all volunteers. We all knew the risks."

"Oh, sure, volunteers," Brandon retorted. "I *volunteered* because my department head made it clear that if I didn't I wouldn't get tenure; I'd be an assistant professor for another ten years or more."

"I volunteered willingly," said Elyse. "I considered it an honor."

"Very noble of you," Brandon muttered.

"Come to think of it," Thornberry said, rubbing his jaw, "the university's president didn't ask me if I wanted this mission. He told me I was the only man on the faculty who could do the job."

"Well, that's quite an honor," Jordan said.

"Maybe," Thornberry replied, drawing out the word. "But I got the impression that what he meant was that I was the only man on the faculty that he could spare."

"You see?" Brandon said. "We're expendables. Outcasts."

"Who's an outcast?" Meek demanded angrily. "I'm certainly not."

"Aren't you?" Brandon countered. "We've thrown away everything we knew back on Earth to take part in this mission, this fool's errand. When we get back to Earth—*if* we get back—we'll be strangers in our own world."

Jordan started to say, "Bran, why don't you—"

But Brandon plowed on, "Don't you see? They picked us for this mission because we're expendable. If we don't get back it'll be no loss to anyone."

"Expendable?" Meek snapped. "I'm not expendable. Young man, I'll have you know that I was selected over the top people in the field of astrobiology. The very top."

Brandon gave Meek a condescending smile. "Are you married?"

"I don't see what that's got to do with anything."

"You're single. Lifelong bachelor, aren't you?"

"Well, yes, but—"

"Any dependents?"

Frowning, Meek replied, "No direct family, no. I have a couple of distant cousins."

"I don't have any direct family, either," said Brandon. "Except for my big brother, here."

Thornberry, with his curious little smile, said, "You know, Brandon me lad, you didn't have to come on this jaunt. You could've said no."

"That's not true," Brandon said, with some heat. "I wasn't really given a choice. Were you?"

Seeing their tempers rising, Jordan said, "I think we've beaten this subject into the ground, don't you?"

But Meek was nettled. "Now look here, Dr. Kell. You may think lightly of yourself, but I regard us—all of us, including your brother—as the cream of the crop. The absolute cream."

"Especially yourself," Brandon sneered.

"Now that's enough," Jordan said firmly. "We are here and we have a job to do. It's a big job, a huge job, and it's the most important mission human beings have ever undertaken. Enough said. The subject is closed."

Brandon glared at his brother, then finally shrugged, grudgingly. Meek still looked nettled.

Jordan commanded the display screen to resume showing the planet below them. Enough of eight-year-old newscasts and messages of regret, he told himself.

The wardroom fell silent as the twelve of them stared at the planet sliding past on the wall screen.

"It looks so much like home," Elyse breathed.

"Yes, doesn't it," said Jordan.

EXAMINATION

For long moments the twelve of them stared silently at the display screen and its view of New Earth sliding slowly below them.

Then Hazzard hauled himself to his feet. "I'd better go check out the ship's systems."

"The ship's perfectly fine," said Thornberry. "The automated safety program would've alerted us if anything was amiss."

Hazzard nodded slowly. "Yeah, I know, but after eighty years I oughtta scan the screens. Automated maintenance and self-repair are okay, but I'll feel better if I take a look for myself."

As Hazzard went to the wardroom hatch, the team's physician, Nara Yamaguchi, looked at her wristwatch and announced, "It's three minutes before ten A.M., ship time. If we start the physical exams immediately, we can get them finished before dinnertime."

Her announcement was greeted by moans and grumbles. But Jordan said, "Dr. Yamaguchi has the responsibility of checking our physical conditions. Let's cooperate with her, please."

Yamaguchi made a stiff little bow to Jordan and said, with an almost impish grin, "Mr. Kell, you are first on my list."

Rank hath its privileges, Jordan repeated to himself.

Yamaguchi was a stubby, chubby young Japanese physician, a specialist in internal medicine. Her face was round, with a snub nose and eyes almost the color of bronze. Her hair was dull brown, chopped short in pageboy style. She was no beauty, yet she radiated intelligence and good humor, and she had the reputation of being an excellent diagnostician.

Jordan followed her down the passageway to the ship's small infirmary: little more than an examination table, a desk bearing a trio of display screens, and diagnostic scanners built into two of the walls and the ceiling. There were a couple of cubicles with beds in the next compartment, he remembered. Sitting on the examination table, Jordan removed his belt and shoes.

"Anything metal in your pockets?" Yamaguchi asked.

Jordan pulled the phone from his shirt pocket and handed it to the physician, who placed it on her desk. Funny, he thought. This instrument links me with the ship's communications system, it's a computer, a camera, a personal entertainment system, and a lot more, yet we still call it nothing more than a phone. The old name hangs on, despite all its varied functions.

Yamaguchi instructed, "All right, just lie back and let the scanners go over you."

Jordan looked up at the softly glowing light panels of the ceiling and listened to the soft hum of the machines behind them. He knew his body was being probed by X-rays, sculpted magnetic fields, positrons, and neutrinos. All in little more than the blink of an eye.

"It's a pretty soft life I've got," Yamaguchi said as she sat at her desk, studying her readout screens. "The scanners do all the work, the computer makes the analysis, and I take the credit."

"We're a healthy bunch," Jordan said. "Youngish . . . well, no one past middle age, physically. All of us are healthy. Or at least we were when we went into cryosleep."

"Maybe too healthy," Yamaguchi said.

"I beg your pardon?"

"Four women, eight men. It could cause problems."

Jordan felt surprised. He hadn't felt any interest in sex since Miriam died. And the others . . . "The psych team passed on the arrangement," he said.

"They won't be stuck here for five years."

"Do you think there might be problems?"

"Probably not with Dr. Meek; he's accustomed to bachelorhood. I don't know about you, though."

Jordan blinked with surprise. "I'll be all right," he said.

"Sure you will," she replied, with a mischievous grin. "Your brother seems to have paired up with Rudaki, and Verishkova followed Thornberry around all through our training classes like a puppy dog."

"I didn't realize," Jordan admitted.

"That leaves Hazzard, Zadar, de Falla, Longyear," Yamaguchi ticked off on her fingers. "All young and physically fit. I'll bet even I start to look good to them before very long."

"There's Trish Wanamaker."

Yamaguchi nodded. "I can always put saltpeter in the drinking water."

"Seriously?" Jordan gasped.

She laughed. "We have much more effective medications. But I hope I won't have to use them."

Jordan nodded, wondering what would happen if the need to calm down some of the men arose.

Yamaguchi returned her attention to her display screens. "You can sit up now."

"Passed with flying colors?" Jordan asked as he bent down to reach for his shoes.

"Almost," Yamaguchi replied, peering at the readouts. She looked up at Jordan. "You've lost the pigmentation in your hair."

"Yes. A bit disconcerting."

"It's not a problem, except cosmetically. But it is kind of strange."

"I think it looks rather distinguished."

Yamaguchi smiled minimally, but then she turned back to the screens. "There is something that concerns me, though."

The virus, Jordan thought. It's still detectable.

He got to his feet, pulled on his belt, and took his phone from Yamaguchi's desktop. The physician was intently studying her computer screens.

"You were exposed to a bioengineered virus when you were in India," Yamaguchi said, her eyes still on the screens.

Jordan sagged back onto the exam table. "The biowar," he said. "There were lots of gengineered bugs in the air."

Yamaguchi nodded, then finally looked up at Jordan. "This one's nestled in your small intestine."

"It's harmless," said Jordan, with a confidence he did not truly feel. "The medics back on Earth concluded that it's dormant and will remain so."

"For how long?"

"Indefinitely, they told me."

Yamaguchi said nothing, but her face had tightened into a concerned mask.

"After all," said Jordan, "I passed all the physical exams Earthside. They allowed me on this mission."

Pointing at the central computer screen, Yamaguchi said, "Your record shows that your wife died of a similar virus."

Jordan felt his face flame red.

"Her immune system had already been compromised by a different infection," he explained. "Mine wasn't."

"I'm sorry," said Yamaguchi.

"I'm really in fine health," Jordan insisted.

"Yes, so the scans show," Yamaguchi admitted. "But your little hitchhiker worries me."

"It's dormant," Jordan repeated.

"For how long?" Yamaguchi asked again.

"It's been several years—not counting our time in cryosleep."

"Cryogenic temperature didn't harm it," the physician muttered. "According to your file, the medical team back on Earth was hoping that the virus wouldn't survive freezing."

With a sardonic little smile, Jordan replied, "They used me and my hitchhiker for an experiment—to see what long-term cryonic immersion would do to the virus."

"Didn't bother it a bit," Yamaguchi murmured.

"Look, we have all sorts of bacteria and viruses in our bodies constantly, don't we? Most of them don't affect us at all. Some of them are even beneficial, aren't they?"

"This one isn't. It was designed to kill people."

Like it killed Miriam, Jordan admitted silently. Aloud, he said, "Well, it hasn't killed me."

Yamaguchi didn't reply, but the expression on her face said, *Not yet.*

"So what do you want to do, send me home?"

Yamaguchi almost laughed at the absurdity of that. "No," she said. "As long as you're asymptomatic there's nothing we can do. Except . . ."

"Except?"

"Let me study the literature and see how much I can learn about these engineered viruses. Maybe there's some way to destroy them."

"Perhaps they have a built-in limit to their life spans," Jordan suggested.

Yamaguchi shook her head hard enough to make her hair swish back and forth. "No, no, no. They're not nanomachines, with off-switches built into them. They're viruses, alive but dormant. Not even stem-cell therapy can deal with them."

"Perhaps nanomachines?" Jordan suggested.

With a nod, Yamaguchi said, "Specifically designed to attack the virus and nothing else. That could work—if we had the nano-tech facilities aboard ship."

"Which we don't," Jordan said.

"We can't. Safety regulations. We can't run the risk of having nanomachines infecting the ship."

"Yet they use nanotechnology on the Moon. Out in the Asteroid Belt."

"But not on Earth," Yamaguchi said. "And not on this ship."

"I suppose not," Jordan sighed. "I'll just have to live with the virus, the way I have been."

Yamaguchi said, "I want to check you on a weekly basis. Make certain your little bugs are remaining dormant. And in the mean-time I'll see if there's anything in the ship's medical library that might help us get rid of them."

"I'd appreciate that," said Jordan. And he remembered Miriam's final days. The pain. The unbearable pain.

BROTHERS

When Jordan returned to the wardroom, most of the men and women were still there, sitting around the tables, deep in conversations.

"Who wants to be next?" Jordan asked.

They all looked up at him, standing just inside the hatch.

Geoffrey Hazzard, back from the command center, got to his feet. "Might's well get it over with."

As he brushed past Jordan and stepped out into the passageway, most of the others got to their feet, as well.

"I suppose we should get to our quarters and settle in a bit," said Harmon Meek.

"I know it's a bit daft," said Thornberry as he headed for the hatch, "but I feel like I need a nap."

Meek looked down his nose at the beefy engineer. "That's ridiculous. You've been sleeping for eighty years, man."

"Yes. A bit of strange, isn't it?"

Brandon started to leave too, but Jordan touched his sleeve to hold him back. "Wait a moment, Bran, will you?"

With a glance at Elyse, who looked back over her shoulder at him, Brandon leaned his rump on the edge of the nearest table. Jordan waited until Elyse and the others left the wardroom, then turned to his younger brother.

"Bran, do you really feel so . . . so . . . alienated?"

"Alienated?"

"What you said earlier, about us being outcasts, expendables."

Brandon didn't reply. Jordan looked into his brother's light bluish gray eyes and thought, It's almost like looking into a mirror. A very flattering mirror.

"Well?" he prompted.

Brandon turned away slightly, but he answered, "It's true, isn't it? None of us are the best and brightest of their professions, are we? I'm certainly not. There are a dozen planetary astronomers who are better than I: better reputations, recognized leaders in the field. I'm just an also-ran."

"But the IAA picked *you* for this mission! Of all the people in the field they picked you."

"Because I'm expendable," Brandon repeated stubbornly. "Because nobody's going to miss me for a century or two."

Shaking his head, Jordan countered, "But the honor of taking part in the first human mission to another star! Surely—"

"Bullshit," Brandon snapped. "They picked us because we're expendable. Look at us, Jordan. Aside from you, none of us are leaders in our fields. We're all expendables. No family ties. Nobody's going to miss us, whether we come back or not. That's why they picked us. That's why we've been given this *honor*."

Before Jordan could reply, Brandon added, "And now they've hung us out to dry. No backup mission. The damned politicians got their glory by sending us out here, they don't give a damn if we get back or not."

"You really feel that way?"

"Yes. Don't you?"

Miriam's death flashed in Jordan's memory once more. I killed her, he thought all over again. If I hadn't insisted on that doomed mission to Kashmir she'd still be alive.

"No," he lied. "I really do feel it's an honor to be picked for this mission. Especially for a non-scientist, a mere administrator."

For the first time, Brandon smiled. "Mere administrator," he said. "One of the world's most distinguished diplomats. And now head of this mission. They should have given you a whip and a chair. You're going to need them."

Jordan smiled. "Riding herd on eleven scientists and engineers shouldn't be that difficult, really."

"You don't think so?"

"I hope not."

Gazing straight into Jordan's eyes, Brandon asked, "Tell me the truth now, why did you agree to come on this mission?" Before Jordan could think of a reply, Brandon added, "And don't tell me about the honor. You've already had honors enough for any man."

"It will look very impressive on my résumé."

"Your résumé's already damned impressive," Brandon said. "Come on now, the truth."

To get away from the memories, Jordan knew. To get as far away from the Kashmir and Miriam's death as humanly possible.

"Well?" Brandon persisted.

Jordan shrugged. "The truth? Why, I came along to be with my baby brother. Somebody's got to keep you out of trouble."

The sour expression on Brandon's face told Jordan what his brother thought of that excuse.

"You're a diplomat," Brandon said, "a troubleshooter, an administrator—"

"You mean a bureaucrat," said Jordan.

"What you accomplished in South America wasn't bureaucracy. You stopped a bloody war."

Jordan dipped his chin in acknowledgment.

"And China," Brandon went on. "And the Sahel drought."

Don't mention Kashmir, Jordan begged silently. Not India and the Kashmir.

"I just don't see what made you agree to come on this operation."

Forcing a smile, he said to his brother, "Adventure. Romance and adventure."

"Bull."

"And family ties," Jordan added.

"More bull."

Getting away from the memories, Jordan added silently. Getting as far away from anything connected with Miriam as I can. Away from the emptiness and the remorse. Away from the guilt. He ran a hand through his hair, wondering what he could tell his brother.

He decided to change the subject, instead. Jordan pointed to the wall screen. "Look, there's the terminator coming up. We're moving into the night side."

Darkness swallowed the view. In a moment, though, false-color infrared imagery filled the screen. Still, there was nothing much to see, only endless forests.

But then a pinpoint glow of light appeared in the midst of the darkness.

A GLOW OF LIGHT

What the hell is that?" Brandon yelped.

"A light," said Jordan, staring at the screen. "A light in the midst of all that darkness."

"That shouldn't be there," Brandon said.

"Maybe it's a fire," said Jordan.

"It's not flickering."

"Volcano?"

Brandon shook his head. "Too small. Too steady."

Without another word they both scrambled toward the ship's command center, the bridge, where all the system controls were.

"I'd better call the others," Jordan said as they hurried along the narrow passageway between the wardroom and the command center.

The command system's screens showed that the ship's systems were humming along without human intervention or guidance. Four of the screens displayed the planet below them.

The natural-light display showed the pinpoint of light on the planet's dark side, sliding off toward the horizon now. The other screens showed an infrared view, atmospheric conditions, gravitation measurements.

Jordan slipped quite naturally into the command chair and pressed the communications stud. "Intercom," he spoke firmly, "connect me to all team members."

In an instant the communications console showed he was connected.

"This is Jordan. The sensors show a spot of light down on the planet's night side. We're trying to determine what's causing it. I'd like the planetary field team and the sensor engineer to come to the bridge, please."

They all came, every one of the group, jamming the compartment, making it stuffy with their body heat.

"What on Earth could it be?" Meek asked, his eyes fixed on the light.

"We're not on Earth," someone snapped.

Thornberry replied, "On Earth it might be a village. Or maybe a roadside fast-food joint."

"One light," murmured Patricia Wanamaker, Thornberry's aide, the sensor engineer. Of the twelve men and women in the group, she was the only one not from Earth: she had been born in a space habitat orbiting the planet Saturn.

Trish was almost Jordan's height, heavyset, with a strong jaw set in a squarish, chunky face. Her ash blond hair was chopped mannishly short. Staring at the glow intently, she plumped herself down at one of the consoles.

"We'd better put up a surveillance satellite to cover the area," Jordan suggested.

Wanamaker nodded without taking her eyes from her console's screens. "I'll deploy one of the minisats. Synchronous orbit, so it can hover over the area."

"Good," said Jordan.

Geoff Hazzard, standing beside Jordan, said, "I'd better stay here for a while, keep an eye on things."

Jordan caught his meaning. "Of course," he said, getting up from the command chair. "I didn't mean to usurp your seat."

Hazzard smiled, almost embarrassed. "It's not *my* seat, Jordan. Not particularly."

Still, he settled himself quite naturally into the command chair, his long slim legs stretched out.

Sitting at her console, Wanamaker clipped a communicator over her left ear and began speaking into it in a whisper. The consoles all had voice recognition circuitry, but with six of them jammed in side by side, all the team members had been trained to keep their voices low, so that their commands would not be accidentally picked up by a neighboring console. Even so, while she murmured into the communicator, her stubby fingers twitched involuntarily, as if she were using a keyboard.

At last she looked up and announced, "Satellite launched. It'll take eighty-six minutes for the bird to attain synchronous orbit."

Jordan looked around at the team. "Any other suggestions? Anything more we should be doing?"

"Get a spectrum of that light as soon as you can," said Brandon.

"Put together a team to go down there and look firsthand," said Silvio de Falla. He was Brandon's geologist, short, solidly built, usually easygoing. But now he looked intense, eager as a greyhound who had just spotted a rabbit.

"Right away," Brandon agreed.

"Now wait," cautioned Meek. "We ought to scout the terrain first, see what we'd be up against."

"See what kind of topography that area has."

"Check for gravitational anomalies."

"I agree," said Jordan. "I'd like to know what the area is like before we go barging into it."

"But what if the light disappears before we get there?" Brandon countered.

Jordan spread his hands. "Now listen. We've just arrived here. It's night down where the light is shining. We haven't even begun to map the surface—"

"The robotic orbiters have mapped the whole planet," de Falla pointed out.

"But none of the orbiters detected that light," said Jordan.

"Because it wasn't there, most likely," Brandon said.

"Well, it's there now, and—"

"For how long?" Brandon insisted.

"We have no control over that," said Jordan, patiently. "But we do have control over our own safety. I don't want us—any of us—to go blundering into the unknown."

"For god's sake, Jordy, that's why we're here—to delve into the unknown!"

"And that's what I intend to do, Bran," Jordan said. "But it won't hurt to be a little cautious about it."

"For what it's worth," Hazzard added, "mission protocol calls for a robotic reconnaissance of any area we intend to send humans into."

Brandon's expression was somewhere between hurt and sulky, but he said nothing more.

"I think caution is a wise policy," said Meek. "We're on our own here. If anything goes wrong, we'll get no help from anyone else."

From her console, Trish Wanamaker said, "We could at least send a robot down there."

G ood thinking," said Jordan. Turning to Thornberry, he asked, "Can you arrange that, Mitch?"

With a happy grin, Thornberry replied, "By god, I'll send two rovers. There's safety in redundancy." And he pushed through the crowded compartment to one of the consoles.

"Can anyone think of anything else?" Jordan asked. "Something we should be doing?"

"I still have to examine more than half of you," said Yamaguchi. "One at a time."

"After the exams are finished we should have dinner," said Meek. "We need to get on a regular schedule sooner or later. I suggest sooner."

Jordan chuckled. "Yes, I suppose you're right. Still," glancing at the display screens, "it's been an exciting first few hours."

"With more to come," Brandon added.

Most of the team went back to their individual quarters, although Hazzard, Wanamaker, and Thornberry stayed at the command center. Paul Longyear, the lead biologist, headed for the infirmary with Yamaguchi. Jordan started back toward the wardroom with Brandon, Meek, and Elyse Rudaki.

"A spot of light," Jordan mused as he sat at one of the tables, facing the wall screen. The light was clearly discernable against the darkness of the planet's night side. "What could it be?"

"There aren't any other lights anywhere on the planet," said Brandon, sitting beside him.

"None that we have seen," said Elyse, who brought a mug of coffee from the dispenser and sat on Brandon's other side.

From the dispensing machines, Meek said, "Whatever it is, I suppose it's some natural phenomenon. A lava puddle, perhaps."

"Do you think that's likely?" Jordan asked.

"We don't know what's likely and what's not, not yet," said Meek, as he carried a tray bearing a teapot, a cup, and a plate of cookies to the table. Carefully arranging them on the table, he sat down and added, "This is a new world, after all. It might look superficially like Earth, but we shouldn't expect it be precisely like our planet."

"I suppose not," Jordan agreed.

Elyse shook her head. "Everything about this planet is strange, unexpected."

Brandon said, "Of course."

"How can it be here? How can it exist and bear life?"

"That's what we're here to find out," said Meek.

"But it shouldn't be here at all," Elyse continued. "Not with an atmosphere and oceans. They should have been boiled away when the Pup went through its nova phase."

"The Pup," Meek groused. "Astronomer's humor."

With a glance at Elyse, Brandon countered, "Sirius has been known as the Dog Star since ancient times."

"In the constellation Canis Major, the Big Dog," said Meek. "I'm not totally ignorant."

Undeterred, Brandon went on, "So when Sirius B was discovered, a dwarf star accompanying the Dog Star, naturally it was called the Pup."

"Naturally," said Meek, scornfully.

"The point is," Elyse said, totally intent, "when the Pup exploded it should have scoured that planet clean."

"But it didn't."

"Perhaps it did," Jordan said, "but the planet has had enough time to regenerate its biosphere."

"That would take billions of years," Elyse countered. "Sirius itself can't be more than five hundred million years old, and its companion must have been formed at the same time. The Pup couldn't have gone nova more than a few tens of millions of years ago."

"You're certain of that?" Meek challenged.

"Within a factor of ten or so," said Elyse.

"That's a pretty big margin of error," Meek sniffed.

"Not bad for an astrophysicist," said Jordan, smiling at her.

"Even so," Elyse insisted, "the planet hasn't had time to recover from the Pup's nova explosions. It's impossible."

"But there it is," Meek said, jabbing a finger toward the wall-screen display. "You can't deny that it exists."

"But how can it be?"

Mildly, Jordan replied, "That's what we're here to find out, isn't it?"

"Yes," she murmured. "Of course."

"Another thing," Brandon said.

Jordan groaned inwardly. Bran won't let the argument stop. Is he trying to impress Elyse or just trying to top Meek?

"Sirius C is the *only* planet in the system," Brandon pointed out. "There's nothing else. No other planets, not even asteroids or comets. The Sirius system is totally clean, except for this one planet."

"A planet very much like Earth," added Meek.

Elyse said, "Between Sirius's gravitational pull and the Pup's, all the minor bodies must have been swept away." Then she added, "Perhaps."

"Do you really think so?" Jordan asked.

Elyse smiled a little. "No, not really. It's the only explanation I could think of."

"The system's totally clean, except for that one Earth-sized planet," Brandon murmured.

"It is very strange," said Elyse.

"Scary, almost," said Brandon.

The four of them fell silent, each wrapped in their own apprehensions. Inexplicably, Jordan flashed back to the hell of Kashmir and Miriam wasting away from the man-made toxins of the biowar.

With a force of will he raised his eyes to the display screen and said, "Well, strange or scary or whatever, we're here to find out what this planet is all about, and by heaven that's what we're going to do."

As if on cue, Trish Wanamaker's voice came through the speaker set into the overhead. "The minisat will reach synchronous orbit in fifteen minutes."

With heartiness he did not truly feel, Jordan said to his companions, "Let's get back to the command center and see what the surveillance satellite has to show us."

"But I haven't even started my tea!" Meek bleated.

With Meek grumbling about his tea, the four of them trooped back to the command center. The ship was over the daylit side of the planet once again.

But one of the screens showed what the surveillance satellite was seeing: the darkness of the night side, broken by that single unblinking point of light.

Trish Wanamaker turned slightly in her console chair as they filed into the command center. "Starting a spectroscopic analysis of the light," she said, over her shoulder.

"Good," said Jordan, standing beside Hazzard, who was still slouched nonchalantly in the command chair.

Brandon and Elyse stood close to each other; Meek remained by the hatch, a skinny scarecrow with narrowed, searching eyes. Thornberry was nowhere in sight.

"Here's the spectrum," Wanamaker said, tapping at the console's touchscreen.

One of the smaller display screens on the console showed a graph with a sharply peaked curve rising steeply against the grayish background.

"That can't be right," Hazzard muttered.

"Put it on your main screen," Brandon told Wanamaker.

She whispered into her microphone, and the single, sharp-peaked curve appeared on the console's central screen, like a steep mountain rising out of a jagged plain.

"That's the spectrum of the light down on the nightside?" Elyse asked, her voice hushed, awed.

Wanamaker nodded once.

"Jesus Christ," Brandon said, also amazed. "It's a laser beam!"

That's a laser shining down there?" Jordan asked, unbelieving.

"A single wavelength," Wanamaker said, sounding just as stunned as Jordan felt.

"Not a single wavelength," Brandon corrected.

"A damned narrow set of wavelengths," Wanamaker admitted. "But they're bunched together. That's the signature of a laser beam, nothing else."

Jordan couldn't take his eyes off the display screen. The sharp peak twinkled, glittered against the background.

"Lasers occur in nature, don't they?" he asked.

"In interstellar nebulae," said Elyse. "Not in the middle of a forest."

Hazzard said, "I remember seeing a paper about a natural laser in a planetary atmosphere."

"Speculation," Wanamaker said. "Never been proven. Or observed, for that matter."

"It's artificial," Brandon said tightly, no doubt in him. "Man-made."

"Not *man*-made," Meek corrected.

"Better get Thornberry back here," said Jordan.

Once Thornberry entered the command center he gaped at the display and immediately started asking Wanamaker how much the minisat could tell them about the terrain in the vicinity of the light.

"The area'll be in daylight in another six hours," Wanamaker responded. "We'll be able to see it a lot better then."

"I'm going to dinner," Meek said. "I never got to finish my tea, you know. I'll be back in two hours."

Jordan watched him go, bemused slightly by Meek's cool insistence on feeding. The rest of them stayed in the command center, swapping theories and speculations until the region where the laser was slid into the daylit side of the planet. Meek rejoined them, but kept silently aloof from the guessing games.

The area turned out to be a high plateau, heavily wooded. None of the surveillance satellite's sensors could make out a building or roads or any signs of civilization or even a rough camp.

"Nothing but that damned spot of light," Brandon muttered.

Thornberry shook his head, scowling at the displays. "I've already set up a scouting team: a pair of rovers that can get through wooded terrain. They'll be ready to go in an hour or so."

Jordan glanced at his wristwatch. "Wait. I suggest we have dinner and then retire for the night. We can continue this in the morning, when we're fresh, and the area is in daylight."

"Go to bed?" Brandon yelped. "How do you expect any of us to sleep with that going on?"

"It's getting late," Jordan said calmly. "We're all tired. I know I am. You make mistakes when you're tired."

"But—"

"That light will still be there in the morning." Before Brandon or anyone else could object, Jordan added, "And even if it's not, we know its exact location and we can investigate the area thoroughly."

"I vote we stay at it and launch the rovers without delay," Brandon said.

Jordan smiled at him. "I didn't ask for a vote, Bran. Get some dinner and then go to bed. We'll all feel sharper, stronger, after a good night's sleep."

"We've been sleeping for eighty years," Hazzard said mildly, an ironic curve to his lips.

"I'm tired," Jordan said. "I assume the rest of you are, too."

"Not me!" Brandon snapped.

A flash of memory raced through Jordan's mind: six-year-old

Brandon kicking and struggling as their father carried him upstairs to bed, yowling that he wasn't tired, that he didn't want to go to bed, that he wasn't the least bit sleepy—then falling asleep the instant his head hit the pillow.

"All of us," Jordan said gently. "The planet will still be there when we wake up tomorrow morning."

"You're right," said Thornberry. "By the time the rovers are ready to land down there, it'll be dark again. I'm not happy with the idea of landing me rovers in the dark, night-vision sensors or no." He went to the hatch and stepped through.

"I've set the sensors on the minisat," Wanamaker said, pushing her blocky body up from the console chair. "If anything changes the system will alert us."

Hazzard shrugged. "Might's well eat and then catch some zees. The ship can take care of itself without us."

Elyse glanced at Brandon, then wordlessly followed the others through the hatch. Brandon gave Jordan a resentful glare, then he too went to the hatch.

Jordan stood there alone in the control center for a few silent moments, listening to the electrical hum of the instruments, the hushed whisper of the air circulation fans, staring at the display screen that showed the laser's sharp-peaked spectrum.

It can't be a laser, he said to himself. Even though he knew that it couldn't be anything else.

Jordan's quarters were identical to all the other living spaces aboard the ship: a fairly spacious compartment partitioned into a bedroom/lavatory and a sitting room that held a desk, a sofa, and two armchairs with an oval coffee table between them, and wall screens that were glowing with a faint pearly luster. There was a minikitchen in one corner, stocked with a refrigerator, freezer, and microwave oven. The bachelor's friend, Jordan thought as he eyed the microwave. Then he went past the shoulder-high partition, sat on the bed, and began pulling off his shoes.

The wall screens were blank, although they could be programmed to show anything from the art collection of the Uffizi Gallery in

Florence to the latest entertainment or game vids. Or any of the ship's sensor displays, as well.

Jordan felt very tired. Strange for a man who's only been awake for a few hours and done nothing more strenuous than lifting a salad fork. But emotional stress can be just as exhausting as physical, and he recognized the demands that his body was making. Or is it a form of fear, he wondered, fear of the unknown. Fear of what we're going to find down there.

Fear of what's going on in your own body, a voice in his head reminded him. Fear that the virus lying dormant in your gut will wake up and begin to slowly, painfully kill you.

He pulled the bedcovers over him, expecting to stare wide-eyed into the darkness after all the excitement of the day. Instead he quickly fell asleep. His last waking thought was that it couldn't be a laser down there. It couldn't be.

Well before 7 A.M., with nothing more than a quick cup of coffee in him, Jordan strode from his quarters toward the command center. As he expected, Brandon was already there, standing behind Thornberry, who was seated at the same console as the evening before.

"Good morning, sleepyhead," Brandon greeted.

"Good to see you at work so early," Jordan replied. "Did you sleep well?"

"Hardly at all."

Over his shoulder, Thornberry said, "I slept like a rock, I did. A trick I learned when I served with the disaster teams in Africa. Never stand when you can sit, never stay awake when you can sleep, and never pass a latrine without using it."

Jordan laughed politely. Brandon made a face behind Thornberry's back.

The command chair was empty; Hazzard had not risen yet, Jordan surmised. Still, he stepped past the chair to stand beside his brother.

"I presume the light is still shining," he said.

Brandon nodded tightly. "Bright and steady."

"Are you ready to launch your rovers?" Jordan asked the roboticist.

Thornberry pointed to the center screen of his console and explained, "Got them loaded into a rocketplane and found a good landing spot for them, an open glade less than five klicks from the spot where the light's emanating from. Be ready to launch in half an hour, we will."

"Good."

Slowly the command center began to fill with people. Hazzard slid into the command chair. Elyse came in and stood silently beside Brandon. Meek and Wanamaker and all the others jammed into the compartment, buzzing with low, tense conversations.

We should have made this area bigger, Jordan thought. Perhaps we can enlarge it. Then he told himself, No, that probably won't be necessary. After all, we're going to spend most of our time here down on the surface of the planet. At least, that's what the mission plan calls for.

"Launch in thirty seconds," Thornberry announced.

The digital clock in the corner of his console counted down: twenty seconds, ten, five . . .

"Launch," said Thornberry.

Jordan felt the ship shudder slightly. Launching the minisat had been no big deal, he realized, but launching a rocketplane bearing two sizable rover vehicles makes a noticeable jolt.

Thornberry turned in his console chair. "They're away. It'll take nearly an hour for them to enter the atmosphere." Then he smiled and added, "I'm going to grab some breakfast while I've got the chance."

Jordan and most of the others headed for the wardroom. Brandon, Elyse, and Hazzard remained in the command center.

"Call me if anything . . . happens," Jordan said to his brother. He realized he was going to say, *if anything goes wrong*. He had caught himself just in time.

In the wardroom, while Jordan and Thornberry both took merely juice and coffee, Trish Wanamaker loaded her breakfast tray with muffins, reconstituted eggs, faux bacon, juice, and hot tea.

Harmon Meek was already sitting at one of the oblong tables, his breakfast of cereal, toast, and tea neatly arrayed before him. Jordan led Wanamaker and Thornberry to the same table. Once they were all seated, Jordan marveled at how Trish could stow away so much food so quickly. Her chubby little hands were moving like a concert pianist's.

"What d'you think that light might be?" Thornberry asked, between sips of juice.

"Laser," said Trish, despite her mouth being stuffed with food.

Shaking his head, Thornberry argued, "How could a laser be there? There's nobody down there, no signs of any people—"

"No signs we recognize as human," said Meek, with a slightly superior air. "But then whoever put that laser down there wouldn't be human, would he? Or it, I mean."

"But there's no sign of *anything* artificial," Thornberry insisted. "Nothing down there but trees and rocks."

"No sign that we can detect," Meek countered. "That's why we're sending your rovers down there, isn't it?"

"Yeah," Thornberry admitted grudgingly. "Right."

"Somebody's down there," Meek said firmly. "That laser didn't get there by itself."

Trish looked up from her half-demolished breakfast and asked, "But who could it be? I mean, who put that laser down there in the middle of the forest? And why?"

Jordan murmured, "Sherlock Holmes."

"Sherlock Holmes?"

"I believe it was Holmes who said that it was useless to speculate in the absence of facts."

"Hah," said Meek. "Excellent point. We're just wasting our time until the rovers start to transmit some useful information to us."

"Which they should be doing in another hour or so," Thornberry said, with a glance at his wristwatch. "The rocketplane ought to be hitting the atmosphere in a couple of minutes." He pushed his chair back and got to his feet.

Jordan rose, too. Trish kept gobbling her breakfast and Meek pointed to the wall screen. "You'll pipe the imagery here, won't you?"

"Of course," Jordan said. Then he and Thornberry headed for the command center.

Brandon and Elyse were still standing close enough to touch, Jordan saw. Is there a romance going on? he wondered. Brandon's always been a fast worker, but even for him this would be something of a record. Then he recalled, Of course, they knew each other all through the training period and embarkation, before we went into cryosleep.

Hazzard had put the imagery from Thornberry's console onto the command center's main screen, but all it showed was hash.

"Blackout," Hazzard said. "Atmospheric entry plasma sheath blocks transmissions." Then he added, "Temporarily."

The screen suddenly cleared and Jordan saw a world of jagged peaks and thickly leafed trees scudding past as the rocketplane skimmed above a heavily forested chain of mountains. Thornberry hurried to his console chair, then turned back with an almost apologetic expression on his fleshy face.

"Entry and landing's automated," he said.

From his command chair, Hazzard said, "I've set up the override program. If we need to, I can fly the bird."

Thornberry nodded.

"It'll be fine," Jordan assured him.

Still, they were all tense as they watched the ground rushing up toward the camera. The rocketplane's speed slowed noticeably, but still there was nothing to see but an endless forest stretching to the horizon in every direction.

"The sky is blue," Elyse said, in a half whisper.

"Those trees are damned tall," said Brandon.

"Final retroburn," muttered Thornberry. The rocketplane seemed to hover in midair momentarily.

"There's the clearing," Hazzard called out, pointing.

"Ah, she's gliding in like a blessed angel," said Thornberry.

Jordan watched as the open, grassy glade expanded to fill the display screen, tilted slightly, then straightened out and rushed up. The ground looked smooth, covered with green grass. The view bumped once, twice, then all motion stopped.

"She's down," Thornberry sighed, as if a gigantic weight had just been taken off his shoulders.

Hazzard flexed his fingers, then recited, "Log entry: oh-eight-forty-two hours, this date, spacecraft one landed on Sirius C. Fill in geographical coordinates."

Jordan let out a gust of breath that he hadn't realized he'd been holding. She's down, he told himself. The craft has landed safely.

The camera atop the landing craft slowly revolved, showing a broad grassy glade surrounded by tall, straight-boled trees, darkly green. Mountains in the distance, their peaks bare rock. The glade was flat and smooth, not a rock or boulder in sight, as if the area had been specifically cleared for the rover's touchdown. The sky above was turquoise blue, dotted with puffy white clouds.

The first view from the surface of New Earth, Jordan thought.

"Send this view to Earth right away," he said to Hazzard.

"Won't get there for more'n eight years," Hazzard replied.

"Yes, but send it. Send it now."

"Right."

For the next three-quarters of an hour they watched as the rocketplane automatically checked all its internal systems and activated its sensors. Meek and the others filtered into the command center and watched with Jordan as the numbers scrolled along the bottom of the main display screen: atmospheric pressure, temperature, composition—all were well within the limits that had already been recorded for New Earth by the earlier robotic probes.

We can breathe that air, Jordan told himself. Then he added, If it's not full of dangerous microbes.

"Activating rovers," Thornberry said, in the flat, almost mechanical tone of a mission controller. The command center fell completely silent, but Jordan could sense the excitement vibrating among the onlookers. He felt it himself.

The view switched to show the shadowy interior of the rocketplane. One side swung open and down, turning into a ramp. Brilliant, glaring sunlight streamed in.

"Rovers check out," Thornberry reported tersely. "Out you go, lads."

His console's main screen split to show two views, from the cameras mounted atop the two rovers. Hazzard flicked his fingers across the keyboard built into his chair's armrests and two of the wall screens above the consoles lit up to show the view from each of the two rovers. The machines trundled down the ramps and out onto the smooth grassy ground.

"Over the river and through the woods . . ." somebody singsonged. Brandon, Jordan thought.

"There's no river." Elyse's voice, clearly.

The rovers plunged into the forest, at ten kilometers per hour. Jordan watched, fascinated, as the thick-boled trees glided past. There was precious little foliage between the trees, hardly any bushes at all. The woods looked almost like a well-tended park.

"Look," said Brandon. "There's a little stream."

"A babbling brook."

"Look out for animal life," said Meek. "The equivalent of squirrels or other arboreal forms."

His biologist, Paul Longyear, hurried to one of the unused consoles, muttering, "The sensors should be taking bio samples of the air."

Longyear was a young Native American with a complexion the color of dried tobacco leaf, dark hair braided halfway down his back, and deep onyx eyes.

"Can't those pushcarts go any faster?" Brandon demanded.

Thornberry shot him a grim look over his shoulder as he replied, "Sure they can. But not over territory we haven't mapped yet. I don't want these darlings bumping into trouble."

"Maybe there's tiger traps down there," somebody snickered.

"We don't have any idea of what's down there," Jordan said, loudly enough to stop the chatter. The terrain had been mapped from orbit, of course, but the forest covered the ground too thickly to see details smaller than a few meters.

Onward the rovers trundled, among the sturdy trees, maneuvering around rocks and boulders, some of them big as houses.

"Should be getting to the spot where the laser is," Thornberry muttered. "Any minute now."

And at that precise moment, all the screens went blank.

FRUSTRATION

What the hell?" Thornberry exclaimed.

Jordan stared at the suddenly dark screens. What's gone wrong? he asked himself.

While Thornberry growled into his microphone, Longyear announced from his console, "Bio sensors have crapped out, too."

"Everything's down," Thornberry said, bewildered. Then he added a heartfelt, "Damn!"

"What's the problem?" Brandon wondered.

"Run the diagnostics program," Hazzard suggested.

"I'm trying," said Thornberry. "No response. They're dead as doornails. Both of 'em."

"Can't you do something about it?"

Shaking his head, Thornberry said, "The down side of making machines smart enough to operate on their own is that they operate on their own. They're clever enough so that when they sense something down there that's out of their database, they protect themselves by going into hibernation mode until we can restart 'em."

"So restart them."

"I'm trying, dammitall!" Thornberry roared. "But the little toothaches don't respond."

"Some anomaly down there."

"A black hole, maybe."

"Be serious!"

Jordan said to himself, Very well, you're supposed to be the leader of this group. Show some leadership.

"Mitch, would you keep on trying to reestablish contact? Geoff, lend him whatever help you can." Turning to the others, Jordan said, "The rest of us should clear out and let Mitchell and Geoff try to sort this out."

They reluctantly began to shuffle out of the command center. Brandon took Elyse's arm and led her toward the hatch.

Jordan looked back at Thornberry. The roboticist was poking away at his console's touchscreen, muttering darkly. But his console's displays remained stubbornly blank.

There's nothing you can do for him, Jordan told himself, except let him do his work without the rest of us breathing down his neck. He followed his brother and Elyse down the passageway to the area where the living quarters were.

Brandon stopped in front of the door to his quarters. "What now?" he asked Jordan.

"I don't know about you, but I intend to sort out my clothing and personal supplies. I have a hunch that we'll be going down to the surface much sooner than we had planned to."

Elyse looked worried. "What could have made the rovers go blank like that?"

With a shrug, Jordan said, "Malfunctions happen. Mitchell will figure it out. He's a good man."

"And if he doesn't?" Brandon challenged.

Jordan said, "Then we'll have to go down to the surface and see what's wrong with them."

"See what's happened to them, you mean."

"Yes, perhaps."

"I'm going down to the hangar deck to check out our landing craft," Brandon said.

"Good idea," Jordan said. "But let's give Mitchell a chance to reestablish contact with the rovers. No need to jump into the unknown just yet."

"The hell there isn't! Something's going on down there and we've got to find out what it is."

"Bran, whatever's *going on* down there, have you considered the possibility that it might be dangerous?"

Elyse looked suddenly alarmed. "Dangerous?"

"Apparently the rovers think so," Jordan said.

Impatiently, Brandon said, "There's always a certain amount of danger when you're dealing with the unknown."

"That's true," said Jordan. "And it's my responsibility to see to it that we minimize the danger as much as we can."

"So we just sit up here in orbit with two dead rovers on the surface and a laser beacon shining at us?"

"You think it's a beacon?" Elyse asked.

"What else?"

Jordan made himself smile as he said, "Bran, there's a difference between what you want it to be and what it actually is."

"Do you want to bet?"

Now Jordan's smile turned genuine. "No thank you. For what it's worth, Bran, I agree with you. I think it's probably a beacon, too. But that doesn't mean we should go barging down there before we've considered all the possibilities."

"Meaning?"

"Meaning that I intend to do what all bureaucrats do when they face a new problem: call a meeting."

By midafternoon Thornberry had given up in exasperation his attempts to reestablish contact with the two rovers.

When Jordan returned to the command center, Thornberry was alone at his console, sagging wearily in its spindly, wheeled chair, his rumpled shirt stained with sweat. He looked thoroughly defeated.

Jordan sat at the next console, beside him, and said softly, "You've done all you can, Mitch. Go get something to eat."

Thornberry didn't move. Instead he muttered, "I am maintaining a kindly, courteous, secret, and wounded silence as a gentle reproof against those two knock-kneed, goggle-eyed, outrageously obstinate machines."

Chuckling at the Irishman's wry humor, Jordan repeated, "Get something to eat. And then come over to my quarters at fifteen hundred hours. We've got to plan out what we should do next."

Once Thornberry shambled out of the control center, Jordan

called Brandon, Elyse, Meek, and Hazzard to join him in his quarters at 1500.

They all arrived promptly and sat around the coffee table, the expressions on their faces ranging from apprehensive to frustrated to downright worried.

Pulling the wheeled chair from his desk up to the little glass coffee table, Jordan said, "The five of you represent the chief technical groups of our team. We need to plan out what our next step in exploring New Earth should be."

"Send a team down to see what happened to the rovers," Brandon said immediately. He was sitting tensely on the sofa, next to Elyse. Hazzard sat at her other side, Meek and Thornberry in the armchairs, facing each other across the coffee table.

"And find out what that laser is all about," added Elyse.

Turning to Meek, Jordan asked, "How much biological data did we get before the rovers blanked out?"

"Air samples," said Meek. "Nothing startling. There are single-celled creatures in the air, the equivalent of bacteria and protists. A few insect analogs. Dust, of course. Some pollen."

"Anything harmful?"

"I don't have enough data to determine that. Yamaguchi's looking over what we've got so far. If you send a team to the surface they should wear biohazard suits, to be on the safe side."

Turning to Thornberry, Jordan asked, "Mitch, do you have any idea at all of why the rovers died?"

The roboticist shrugged his heavy shoulders. "As far as I can tell, they just shut themselves down. They must have encountered something beyond the limits of their programming."

"Maybe somebody shut them down," said Brandon.

"Somebody? Who?"

"Whoever's shining that laser at us."

"But there's no sign of intelligence down there," Thornberry argued. "No radio signals, no buildings, no roads . . ."

"There's the laser," Jordan pointed out.

Hunching forward in his chair, Brandon ticked off points on his fingers. "Whoever built that laser is using it to attract our attention. They disable the rovers before the machines can get close enough to the laser for us to see what's there. Isn't it obvious? They don't want machines, they want *us*. They want us to come down and meet them."

"So they can cook us and eat us," Hazzard muttered, half-joking.

"I doubt that cannibals use lasers," Jordan said.

Meek pointed out, "But they wouldn't be cannibals, not at all. We're a different species from them."

"Like beef cattle are different from us," Hazzard maintained.

No one laughed.

They debated the situation for another hour, but Jordan realized that there was only one decision they could reasonably make.

"All right, then," he said at last. "We can send another rover or two down, or we can send a team of people. Which should it be?"

"People!" Brandon snapped.

Thornberry countered, "I'd like to send a couple of rovers to different places around the planet and see what happens to them. See if they operate normally."

"That would mean the area around the laser beacon is a special place," said Meek.

"A dangerous place," Jordan said.

Brandon shook his head. "I think they're making it abundantly clear that they want us to come down and meet them. In person."

"Meet who?" Jordan asked. "If there are intelligent aliens down there, capable of building a laser and disabling our rovers, why are they being so coy? Why not try to contact us? Send us a radio message. Blink the laser, use it as a communications beam."

"Yeah," Thornberry agreed. "If they're intelligent they could send up a spacecraft of their own to greet us properly."

Meek shook his head. "It's obvious that they don't think the same way we do."

"Is it?" Brandon countered. "Seems to me they're very deliberately trying to get us to go down there and meet them."

"Luring us in," Jordan muttered.

"But why?" Elyse asked. "Why are they behaving this way?"

Jordan looked around the table at their faces, then said, "There's only one way to find the answer to that question. We'll have to send a team down to the surface."

"Right!" said Brandon.

DECISIONS

t took another whole day to get a landing party assembled and checked out. Jordan gathered the entire group in the wardroom and had them push all six tables together. Once all twelve of them were seated, he began to announce his decisions.

"As you know," he began, "I try to manage our group on a consensus basis. We're not a hierarchical organization, not like a university department. While we have leaders in the various fields of interest, such as astrobiology—"

Meek dipped his chin in acknowledgment.

Jordan went on, "All of you have been cross-trained in different specialties."

Thornberry interrupted, "And we have a squad of robots to help us."

Nodding, Jordan resumed, "That's right. The robots are going to be of enormous help."

"Like the two rovers dozing down on the surface," Brandon sneered.

Thornberry shot him a dark scowl.

"Now, about the landing team," Jordan said, hoping to forestall an argument. "I've decided to go myself. Bran, you're our planetary astronomer: I think you're an obvious choice. And you, Harmon, you're our astrobiologist."

"I could go," said Paul Longyear, the biologist. "Professor Meek could stay in real-time link with me."

"No, no, no," Meek said, wagging a forefinger vigorously. "I'll go to the surface myself. You stay here and monitor the biosensors, Paul."

Longyear looked crestfallen, but said nothing.

Rank hath its privileges, Jordan repeated to himself, a little surprised that Meek was so insistent on going himself. His estimation of the man rose a notch.

"I want to go, too," said Elyse. She was sitting beside Brandon, as usual.

Gently, Jordan said, "I'm afraid we won't need an astrophysicist on this jaunt. Later, once we know more about what's going on down there, we'll set up a permanent base and we'll all go to the surface."

Elyse was obviously unhappy with Jordan's decision, but Brandon looked relieved.

Jordan decided to keep Thornberry on the ship; the roboticist had launched two additional rovers to different points on the planet's surface, and they were performing perfectly well, sending up reams of data. The two defunct rovers near the laser site remained quite dead, to Thornberry's exasperated disgust.

"Mitch, you'll be our mission controller," Jordan told him. "Our contact with the ship."

Thornberry's heavy-jowled face contorted into an apologetic frown. "I hope I can keep in touch with you better than those two blasted deadbeats."

"What about me?" Hazzard asked, from the far end of the table. "Why can't I go with you?"

"We need you to run the ship, Geoff," Jordan told him. Hazzard nodded acquiescence, but his expression was far from pleased.

He pointed out, "I could fly the plane that's already down there back to the ship. Maybe recover the rovers while I'm at it."

"You can do that from here, remotely," said Jordan, "once we've reactivated the rovers."

"Guess so," Hazzard muttered.

"If something should . . . go wrong down on the surface," Jordan added, "you'll be in charge of the ship, Geoff. You'll have to make the decision about what to do next."

Dead silence. None of them wanted to face such a possibility.

Pointing to Silvio de Falla, the geologist, Jordan said, "We'll need you on the team, Silvio."

De Falla, short, swarthy, with a trim dark beard tracing his jawline, and large brown eyes, nodded wordlessly. But his smile spoke volumes.

"That's it, I think," Jordan said. "The four of us. Any questions? Suggestions?"

There were plenty, and Jordan patiently let everyone have his or her say. Finally, when the comments became patently repetitious, he concluded, "Very well, then. This afternoon we check out the landing vehicle and tomorrow we go down to the surface."

His dreams that night were confused, jumbled, yet somehow menacing. Jordan saw himself in the beautiful, deadly Vale of Kashmir once again, but he was all alone, none of the team that should have been with him were there, not even Miriam. He was toiling down a dirt road that seemed endless, alone, not another soul in sight. Slowly, as gradually as summer wasting into autumn, the air began to thicken. It grew darker and harder to breathe. Jordan was choking, gasping, staggering as he tried to catch his breath, coughing up blood . . .

He snapped awake and sat up in bed, soaked in cold perspiration.

"Nerves," he told himself. "You'll be all right once you get down to the planet's surface." Still, he felt cold despite his compartment's climate control. His hands were trembling.

He lay back on the bed and tried to think if there might be something he'd forgotten in his preparations for the landing. Four of us, he recounted. Planetary astronomy, astrobiology, and geology. Plus me. Their fearless leader. Four will be enough. If something goes wrong, if we die down there—he squeezed his eyes shut and tried to remember a quote from Shakespeare. What was it? From *Henry V*: something about, "If we are marked to die we are enough to do our country loss; and if to live, the fewer men, the greater share of honor."

Honor. We're not going down there for honor. Then for what? He almost laughed. For curiosity. To poke into the unknown.

No, it's more than that, he realized. Brandon's right. Something— or some*body*—is down on that planet and whatever or whoever it is, it apparently wants to meet us. And I want to meet it, whoever or whatever it might be.

There's nothing down there that could kill us. At least, I don't think there is. Nothing we know of. The sensors haven't shown us anything dangerous. But what conked out the rovers? The unknown can be dangerous, he reminded himself.

Briefly he thought about taking a tranquilizer, but instead turned resolutely on his side and commanded himself to sleep.

He felt dreadfully alone.

DEPARTURE

Put on a good air, Jordan told himself as he showered. Exude confidence. Keep your fears to yourself. They're unreasonable, anyway. Whenever you have nothing to do, the memories gang up on you. Get out there and get to work. Summon up the action of the tiger.

He gave a cheerful greeting to the handful of people already eating their breakfasts in the wardroom. Brandon was nowhere in sight. Nor Elyse.

Meek came in, smiling happily. "Good morning, all," said the astrobiologist. "It's a good day to go exploring, isn't it?"

Jordan wondered if Meek was putting on a false optimism, too.

Breakfast finished, Jordan and Meek made their way down to the bowels of the ship, to the hangar deck where the landing vehicles were housed. The feeling of gravity was noticeably lower here, closer to the ship's centerline.

Three sleek, silvery, delta-winged rocketplanes stood side by side inside the big, metal-walled hangar space. One side of the hangar was an air lock large enough to accommodate a rocketplane. Jordan saw that one of the four parking spaces was empty, where the plane that had already been sent to the surface had once been.

One of the planes gone, he thought. And this is only our third day here.

Their footsteps echoed off the metal deck and the bare hangar walls as Meek and Jordan approached the nearest rocketplane. Jordan could see his brother's face through the windscreen of the vehicle's cockpit.

Eager as a puppy, Jordan thought. If it were up to Bran, we would have flown down to the surface yesterday or even the night before, ready or not.

Clambering through the plane's hatch, Jordan made his way toward the cockpit, hunching slightly because of the low overhead. Meek, gangling right behind him, had to duck even lower. The plane's interior smelled new, unused. That will change, Jordan told himself.

They squeezed through the cargo bay, where a spring-wheeled excursion buggy big enough to carry six people was stowed, together with a pair of inert robots. I hope they work better than the rovers, Jordan thought.

The cockpit had six reclinable chairs. Brandon was already ensconced in the pilot's seat, and the central screen of the control panel showed Geoff Hazzard's dark, unsmiling face.

"I'll be standing by at the remote control panel here in the bridge," Hazzard was saying. "Your vehicle's programmed to land itself, but I'll be right here in case there's any problems."

Brandon nodded briskly. "How much of a lag time is there between you and this ship?"

Hazzard's eyes flickered once, then he answered, "Microseconds. If I have to take over, you won't even notice a lag."

"Good."

"Ready to go?" Jordan asked.

Brandon turned around in the chair and broke into a big smile. "Now that you two are here, Jordy."

Meek, hunched over so much that his hands were clasping his knees, asked, "Where's de Falla?"

"Back in the equipment bay, checking out our biosuits and the other gear. Thornberry's going over the buggy remotely, from the bridge."

"Shouldn't de Falla be here when we take off?" Meek asked.

"He will be," Brandon said.

As if on cue, Silvio de Falla ducked through the hatch, his dark liquid eyes large and round, his teeth flashing as he smiled brightly. "Field equipment checks out," he reported. "Thornberry says the buggy's ready. We're good to go."

"All right, then," said Brandon. "Everybody sit down and strap in."

Jordan slipped into the right-hand seat beside his brother. A tiny control yoke poked out from the instrument panel in front of him, and a console studded with levers and switches sat between the two seats. As he pulled the safety harness over his shoulders he wondered if he should remind Brandon that he shouldn't touch any of the controls. The ship flies itself, he knew, and Geoff can take over if he has to.

He decided not to mention it. Brandon seemed happy as a kid in a toy store. Why spoil his fun?

Turning slightly in his chair, Jordan saw that Meek and de Falla were in the two seats behind him, fastening their safety harnesses.

Eagerly, Brandon said to Hazzard's image on the display screen, "You can start the countdown, Geoff."

Hazzard nodded gravely, then said, "Jordan, mission protocol says you have to give the word."

Jordan waved one hand in the air. "By all means, start the countdown."

"Okay," said Hazzard, "countdown clock is started. You launch in three minutes. And counting."

Jordan sank back into the chair's padding and squirmed a little to make the safety harness clasping his shoulders more comfortable. He glanced at Brandon, who was staring straight ahead. Pretending to be a spaceship captain, Jordan thought, smiling inwardly. Bran will never grow up, not completely. That's my department. I'm the sober brother, all grown up and serious; he's still something of a boy.

"Pumping out hangar deck," Hazzard's voice stated flatly.

Inside the cockpit they barely heard the clatter of the pumps sucking the air out of the hangar. Jordan felt himself tensing, though: excitement, fear, wonder, worry—all of them bubbling inside him.

"Rotating," said Hazzard.

The rocketplane turned slowly toward the air lock hatch. Out of the corner of his eye, Jordan saw his brother lick his lips.

"Opening air lock hatch," Hazzard announced.

The massive hatch slid open silently. Jordan saw the infinite darkness of space, speckled by bright unblinking stars. Where's the planet? he wondered.

"Launch in fifteen seconds."

As the synthesized voice of the automated countdown system ticked off the seconds, the rocketplane rolled to the edge of the open hatch. Despite himself, Jordan tensed in his chair. Then the rocket engine roared to life and Jordan felt a hard, firm push against his back. The rocketplane flung itself out of the hangar and into empty space.

THE MOON

Then mighty Achilles prayed to his mother, Thetis the Silver-Footed, "Mother, my lifetime is destined to be so brief that ever-living Zeus, sky-thunderer, owes me a worthier prize of glory."

HOMER,
The Iliad

ANITA HALLECK

Given the choice between long life and glory, Anita Halleck chose long life. She was more than halfway through the second century of her life as she stood beneath the glassteel dome of the observatory atop Mt. Yeager, staring wistfully at the Earth.

The observatory was an empty shell now, a tourist attraction instead of a working astronomical facility, little more than a transparent dome and a set of plush couches ringing the circumference of the circular chamber, with virtual reality rigs for tourist visitors dotting its floor. Almost all of the astronomical studies undertaken on the Moon were done at the Farside observatory, which Halleck had been briefly involved with many years earlier.

The lunar nation of Selene lay buried beneath the worn, slumped mountains that circled the giant walled plain of Alphonsus. Above the barren, airless, pockmarked plain hung the glorious blue-and-white globe of Earth, more than half full at the moment, a glowing beacon of life and warmth set in the dark and sterile depths of space.

Halleck sighed inwardly. Nearly a century earlier she had opted to have her body filled with therapeutic nanomachines, virus-sized mechanisms that destroyed invading bacteria and viruses, cleansed her blood vessels of dangerous plaque, rebuilt damaged cells, acted as a superhumanly efficient immune system to protect and preserve her body.

The result was long life. Despite her years, Halleck was as tall and youthful as she had been a century earlier, slim waisted and long legged with a long sweep of chestnut hair draped dramatically over one shoulder and falling halfway down to her belt.

But the cost was to be exiled from Earth, never permitted to set foot on the planet of her birth, the world of humankind's origin. Nanotechnology was totally banned on Earth. No one carrying nanomachines in her body was allowed even to visit.

More than twenty billion people crammed in there, Halleck thought. How many crazies, how many fanatics, how many idiots who could turn nanomachines into an unstoppable plague that would destroy everyone and everything? No wonder they banned nanotech.

And now the second phase of the greenhouse warming was sweeping across the world, drowning cities, reshaping continents, killing millions and driving still more millions into refugee camps or aimless migrations across what was left of civilization.

"It's beautiful, isn't it?"

Startled, she turned to see Douglas Stavenger smiling at her. Like her, Stavenger's body was filled with nanomachines. Like her, he appeared strong and youthful, a handsome man of middle years, broad of shoulder and flat in the middle. Unlike her, Stavenger had filled his long life with service to the city-state of Selene, first as head of its governing council, later as the éminence gris who gently but firmly pulled the strings behind the scenes.

"I don't know why I torture myself staring at it," Halleck admitted.

Stavenger cocked his head slightly to one side, his version of a shrug. "It's home," he said. "It always will be, no matter how long we stay away."

She knew that he had not made his way to this observatory and bumped into her by accident.

"Felicia Ionescu called on me this morning. She's come here, to Selene," she said.

Stavenger said, "So I heard."

"She wants to get the second mission to Sirius C funded."

With the ghost of a smile, Stavenger said, "I wish her well, but . . ." He let the thought dangle, unspoken.

"Chiang is dead set against it," Halleck said, knowing that she was telling Stavenger a fact he already knew.

"He has a lot of responsibilities on his hands," said Stavenger.

"I don't know what Ionescu thinks I can do," Halleck said. "I haven't been active in IAA affairs for years. Decades."

For a couple of heartbeats, Stavenger said nothing. Then, "Maybe she thinks you could help."

Halleck shook her head. "It'd be foolish to send the backup mission before we hear from the first team. And that won't happen for another eight years."

"Still," Stavenger said mildly, "it would take eight years or more to get the next mission ready to go."

Halleck walked across the observatory's empty floor, her steps clicking on the concrete, and sat wearily on one of the couches. Stavenger followed her, almost silent in his softboots.

"Scientists," she said, almost scoffing. "They're always pushing for more."

"It's a big universe," said Stavenger.

"But what good is it?" she demanded. "What does it accomplish? So they explore another planet. Does that help anybody? Does that solve any real problems?"

Stavenger looked amused. "Strange question to ask, here, in this place."

"You mean on the Moon? So what? So we're living on the Moon. What of it?"

"We wouldn't be here if scientists hadn't pushed to explore."

She looked into his handsome, fine-boned face and saw that he was amused—and dead serious.

"You think they should start the backup mission now? With all the problems on Earth? The flooding and all?"

"There are always problems on Earth. And here in Selene, too. That shouldn't stop our push to explore."

"Where will it end?"

"It won't end. We keep on exploring, keep on learning. That's where new knowledge comes from, the frontier. And new knowledge always leads to new wealth, new benefits for everyone."

"Very philanthropic."

"Very practical," Stavenger corrected.

"Ionescu will never be able to convince Chiang and the others."

"That's why you've got to help her."

"Me?"

"You. You know the political ropes. You have the energy and the drive. Do you have the guts to get back into the fight?"

Halleck stared at him.

Stavenger added, "What good is long life if you don't work for something worth doing?"

ENCOUNTER

It's only fully modern humans [not Neandertals] who start this thing of venturing out on the ocean where you don't see land. Part of that is technology, of course; you have to have ships to do it. But there is also, I like to think or say, some madness there. You know? How many people must have sailed out and vanished on the Pacific before you found Easter Island? I mean, it's ridiculous. And why do you do that? Is it for glory? For immortality? For curiosity? And now we go to Mars. We never stop.

SVANTE PÄÄBO
Max Planck Institute for Evolutionary Anthropology
Leipzig, Germany

All feeling of weight dwindled away as the winged rocket-plane established a tight orbit around Sirius C. Jordan's eyes flicked from the windscreen to the displays on the control panel while he struggled to keep his stomach from floating up into his throat. Sirius C loomed huge and lushly green outside, sliding majestically below them.

"We're approaching the night side," Brandon said. Needlessly, Jordan thought.

"Copy night side," said Hazzard, from the display screen in the center of the control panel.

The planet disappeared in darkness. Not a light to be seen. Not even the laser, which was over on the daylit side now. It was as if the planet had been swallowed by some monstrous dragon, Jordan thought. Then he realized, There's no Moon! New Earth doesn't have a moon, not even a tiny speck of rock orbiting it. That's a major difference from Earth. Funny I hadn't thought of that earlier.

For more than half an hour the four men sat in silence while the control panel's displays beeped and winked at them. Utter darkness outside, as if the planet had disappeared. Then they crossed the terminator into the daylit side. As the blazing star Sirius rose above the curved horizon they stirred into conversation again.

"It's all forest, from pole to pole," Meek said.

"That's what Earth would be like," said de Falla, "when the full effect of the global warming takes hold."

"If it weren't for us," Brandon said.

Yes, Jordan thought. The human race has altered the face of Earth far beyond nature's strictures. Even the tropical rain forests that were once thought to be untouched Edens have been shaped and transformed by human tribes for long millennia.

Looking past the curving rim of the planet, with its sliver of bright blue atmosphere, Jordan squinted at distant Sirius, this world's sun, glaring a hot blue-white against the darkness of space. Not far from the star was a smaller sphere, little more than a brilliant dot, but almost as bright as Sirius itself. The Pup, Jordan realized. Sirius's dwarf star companion.

"Retroburn in one minute," said Hazzard, all business.

"Copy retroburn," Brandon answered, aping the astronaut's clipped manner.

One of the screens on the control panel lit up to show Thornberry's jowly face. "Good luck, lads," he said, his usual grin replaced by utter seriousness.

"Thank you, kind sir," Jordan replied, trying to mask his own inner tension.

The retrorockets fired and the sudden feeling of weight was welcome. Jordan watched through the windscreen as the heavily forested planet came up to meet them. He remembered the first time he had flown an airplane solo, how suddenly menacing the trees around the airport became.

"Plasma blackout coming up," Hazzard warned.

They were entering the planet's atmosphere now, dipping into the upper fringes of the air at hypersonic speed. Lights flickered out there, Jordan saw, dancing little fireflies at first but within moments the ship was engulfed in the blazing reds and yellows of air heated to incandescence. He heard the ferocious roar of wind even through the heavy insulation of the cockpit as the ship began to shudder and buck.

It's all right, Jordan told himself, gripping the edges of his seat. Perfectly normal. We're using atmospheric friction to slow us down to a safe landing speed. Still, the craft bounced and rattled as the wind screeched into a long wailing banshee whine. Jordan felt perspiration beading his brow and upper lip. He glanced at Brandon, who sat rigidly, his fists clenched in his lap, fighting the temptation to grab the controls.

The air cleared and the ride smoothed out. No engine noise now; the air rushing past reminded Jordan of the soarplane flights he had taken. The forest was gliding by beneath them, coming nearer, nearer.

"You're through the blackout," Hazzard said. The wide smile on his face told Jordan that Geoff had been uptight, too.

"We're going straight down to the glade," Brandon said, his smile looking a little forced.

Hazzard nodded once. "Almost. You'll make one forty-degree turn to get her nose into the wind, and then in you go. No sweat."

Not much sweat, Jordan amended silently.

"There it is!" Meek called out, his long skinny arm pointing between Jordan and Brandon to the open glade where they were to land.

It looked like a green postage stamp to Jordan. As it grew bigger, closer, he could make out the other rocketplane sitting smack in the middle of the field.

"Wheels down," Hazzard announced as the sudden rush of air filled Jordan's ears.

He swallowed hard as the ground rushed up to meet them. Not all that much room for us, he thought.

The ship hit the ground hard, bounced, then settled onto its landing gear and rolled bumpily along the grassy ground. Jordan saw the earlier plane flash past.

"Plenty of room," Brandon said shakily.

"Braking," said Hazzard.

Jordan felt his body strain slightly against his shoulder straps. Then everything stopped. No sense of motion. No noise. No vibrations.

"We're down," Brandon said, almost in a whisper.

"Copy landing," said Hazzard. "You stopped eleven point six meters from the calculated stopping point. Not bad for a bunch of amateurs."

Meek blew out a gust of breath somewhere between a sigh and a snort. De Falla grinned weakly.

"Checking ship's systems," Hazzard said. "Nobody get up yet."

"Everything's fine," said Brandon, scanning the control panel. "All green lights."

After a few seconds Hazzard agreed. "You're clear to leave your seats."

Thornberry spoke up from another of the display screens. "The ship's sensors are sampling the air. Looks grand, so far."

"Let's suit up and go outside," said Brandon.

"By all means," Meek agreed.

He and de Falla unbuckled, got out of their seats, and headed aft. Jordan thought they made an almost laughably odd couple: Meek bone thin, all gawky arms and legs, so tall he had to bend over; de Falla barely as high as Meek's shoulder, built as solidly as a little truck.

Brandon swung around and got up from his seat before Jordan could. With a placating smile, Jordan made a sweeping gesture and said, "After you, little brother."

They clumped down to the cargo hold, where their six-wheeled excursion buggy waited. Two humanform robots, gleaming metal, sat silent and inert on the rearmost seats. De Falla handed out the nanofabric transparent biohazard suits, which looked to Jordan like plastic raincoats that included leggings, booties, gloves, and inflatable bubble helmets. They began to pull them on, over their clothes.

As he closed the neck seal on his suit, Brandon asked, "When do we decide that we can breathe the air out there?"

Meek said, "Not until we've done a thorough analysis."

"The ship's sensors are sending data up to Longyear," de Falla added. "He'll analyze the data and give us a decision as quickly as he can."

As he picked up one of the air cylinders, Meek said, "It will be far better to be cautious about breathing the local air. Far better to err on the side of caution."

Jordan took the cylinder from his hands and helped Meek to worm his arms through the shoulder straps.

"Damned inconvenient, these suits," Brandon complained.

"Better inconvenient than dead," said Meek, as Jordan connected the cylinder's air hose to the plug in the biosuit's neck ring.

"Besides," said Jordan, picking up another cylinder and gesturing Brandon to turn around, "these suits aren't all that bad. They're flexible, easy to move around in. They even smell rather flowery, don't you think?"

Brandon, his back to his brother, grumbled, "I don't like them, perfumed or not."

Jordan helped de Falla get his air tank connected, then let Brandon connect his for him. At last they were all ready.

De Falla scrambled into the driver's seat of the buggy; Jordan sat beside him while Brandon and Meek took the next two seats, in front of the stolid robots. The rear deck of the buggy was already packed with sensors and field equipment.

While de Falla checked out the buggy's drive motors, Jordan turned on the communications link. Thornberry's face took form on the control panel's central screen.

"All your buggy's readouts are in the green, Jordan," the roboticist reported.

"Good," said Jordan. "Thanks." Turning to the others, he asked, "Everyone ready?"

"We're ready!" Brandon exclaimed.

"Mitch, we're ready to go outside," Jordan said into the microphone built into his suit's neck ring.

"Godspeed, lads," said Thornberry's tiny image on the display screen.

De Falla pressed a gloved thumb against the keypad that controlled the air lock. The hatch swung slowly open. The four men saw a beautiful green swath of grass and, beyond its edge, tall straight-boled trees swaying gently in a slight breeze. Through the trees, in the distance, rose steep mountains, green with forest growth almost to their bare, rocky peaks. A waterfall tumbled brightly down the sheer flank of one of the mountains.

"Here we go," de Falla breathed. Then he nudged the buggy's throttle and the cart lurched forward. It bumped over the edge of the hatch and down the ramp that extended to the ground of New Earth.

INTO THE FOREST

t's like a park," Brandon marveled as they drove toward the edge of the glade. "A beautiful, well-tended park."

Jordan agreed. The glade was wide and level, no large stones or knolls to mar its smoothness. As if it had been prepared to be a landing field.

Meek echoed Jordan's thoughts. "Well tended by whom?"

Brandon laughed. "Mother Nature."

Thornberry broke into their conversation. "I've laid out the track of the two rovers on your navigation screen, Silvie."

De Falla glanced at the screen. "I see it."

Brandon leaned over the side of the buggy. "I can see their tracks on the grass!"

"Good," said Thornberry. "Follow them right along."

"Right," de Falla said.

The trees looked vaguely like pines, Jordan thought. Tall straight trunks with foliage high above. The kind Native Americans used to build their dwellings. What were they called? Then he remembered, lodgepole pines. Good for construction.

De Falla followed the tracks of the robotic rovers as they rolled into the forest. The way was easy, the trees were spaced widely enough to allow ample passage through them. Not much foliage between the trees, just a few clumps of bushes here and there.

"Butterflies!" de Falla called out. Jordan followed his outstretched pointing arm and saw a dozen or so bright yellow creatures flittering around the bushes at the base of a tree.

"We should have brought a net," Brandon joked.

"A mature forest," Meek observed primly. "The trees' canopies shade the ground, which makes it difficult for smaller shrubbery to grow."

"There was a war here," said de Falla. Before anyone could react, he went on, "A war of different forms of plant life, all competing for the sunlight they need to live. The trees won, and the other forms died out."

"Not entirely," Jordan said, pointing to a clump of bushes off to their right.

De Falla nodded, but replied, "If we'd been here a few thousand years ago, this whole region would be entirely different. Lots of different species, wouldn't look anything like this."

"Life evolves," said Brandon.

"Ecologies evolve," de Falla amended.

Meek h'mphed. Jordan smiled to himself: Harmon resents having a geologist making comments about biology. Territorial imperative, academia style.

A massive boulder loomed up ahead. Jordan could clearly see the tracks of the rovers swinging off to the right to get around it. Glancing at the navigation screen, he saw the rovers' tracks marked in bloodred.

De Falla turned in the same direction to skirt the boulder.

"Look!" Meek shouted. "A squirrel!"

Jordan saw a tiny blur of gray scampering up one of the trees. It stopped, chattered angrily at them, then scooted farther up.

"It couldn't be a squirrel," Jordan heard himself say.

"It certainly looked like a squirrel," Brandon said.

"Convergent evolution," said de Falla, with awe in his voice. "Similar environment evolves similar species."

"That's not what we have here," Meek said.

With a grin, de Falla replied, "Isn't it? Sure looks like it to me. Grow a forest and you get squirrels."

"Stick to your geology, man," Meek asserted, "and leave the biological questions to those who know something about the field."

De Falla shrugged good-naturedly.

"Haven't seen any birds," Brandon pointed out.

"You will," de Falla assured him. Then he added, "Probably."

"They won't be the same as birds on Earth," said Meek. "I can assure you of that."

De Falla looked as if he wanted to argue about it, but he kept his mouth shut.

Meek shook his head. "All the life forms we've found in the solar system are completely different from anything on Earth."

"Different environments," said de Falla. "None of those worlds is anything like Earth."

"What about those things in Europa's ocean?" Brandon asked. "Beneath the ice. Aren't they like terrestrial algae beds and kelp?"

"Outwardly," Meek said, "but their biochemistries are very different."

"Do you think there might be predators in these woods?" Brandon wondered. "You know, something like bears or wolves?"

Before Meek could reply, de Falla said, "That's why we brought the stun guns with the rest of the equipment."

"Maybe we ought to take them out and have them handy," Brandon suggested.

Meek said firmly, "Predators will be wary of us, they've never seen anything—"

De Falla tromped on the brakes so hard they all jolted forward in their seats.

"The rovers," Jordan said, pointing.

The two rovers were sitting about a hundred meters ahead of them, parked side by side among the trees, squat oblong shapes on multiple little wheels. They looked unblemished, factory-new, gleaming in the sunlight filtering through the trees' canopies high overhead.

"Mitch, are you still there?" Jordan called.

"Right here," Thornberry replied, his face filling the control panel screen.

"We see the rovers."

"Yes, I've got them on camera."

Brandon started to get up from his seat. "Let's go see what's wrong with them."

Jordan half-turned and gripped his brother's wrist. "Let's scout the area a little first." To de Falla he said, "Silvio, can you get us a little closer?"

De Falla nodded once and nudged the throttle. The buggy edged forward, slowly.

"I don't see anything," Brandon said.

"No footprints," said Meek. "No sign of tracks in the ground. Except the rovers' own, of course."

When they got to about twenty meters' distance, Jordan asked de Falla to stop. He stood up at his seat, gripping the seat back in front of him for balance, and scanned the ground around the rovers. Meek was right, he saw. The grass was undisturbed except for the tracks of the rovers themselves.

They were flat, ungainly vehicles resting on springy wheels designed to traverse over rough territory. Sensor pods and antennas studded their tops. Powered by a self-contained miniature nuclear electric system, they had a design life of six months. But they hadn't lasted six hours on the surface of New Earth.

Cautiously, the four men got out of the buggy and approached the rovers. Both were silent, unmoving. Jordan laid a hand on the cover of the nearer rover's miniature nuclear power plant. Cold. That shouldn't be, he thought. The power plant should be warm, if it's still functioning.

Jordan realized he couldn't get to his shirt pocket for his phone with the biosuit covering him. Feeling slightly annoyed, he trotted back to the buggy and slid into his seat.

"Mitch, the rovers are cold, as if their power systems have shut down."

"I'll activate the robots," Thornberry said. "They'll do a diagnostic."

The two robots suddenly stirred to life, got up from the rear of the buggy, and rolled across the grassy ground toward the rovers.

"Now we'll get to the bottom of this," said Thornberry's image.

An hour later, as Jordan sat in the buggy, Thornberry's face looked bitterly unhappy.

"They're just dead," he growled. "As if somebody drained the deuterium out of their reactors."

"How could that be?" Jordan asked.

"How should I know?" Thornberry snapped.

"Should we fly a pair of new fusion reactors in to replace the dead ones?"

"I suppose so. But I just can't understand what would conk out their power systems. It's uncanny, it is. Downright spooky."

Jordan tried to smile at the puzzled roboticist. "You'll figure it out, Mitch, sooner or later."

Thornberry shook his head and began to mutter his mantra, "I am maintaining a kindly, courteous, secret, and wounded silence—"

"Hey! Look!"

Jordan snapped his attention to his brother, who had walked a little way farther among the trees.

Standing again, Jordan called, "Bran, what is it?"

"I thought I saw somebody out there." He pointed deeper into the woods.

"Somebody?"

Meek and de Falla both strained to look in the direction Brandon was pointing.

"A man, it looked like," said Brandon.

CONTACT

All three of them hurried to where Brandon was standing, gazing into the trees.

"A man?" Jordan asked, a little breathless.

"A figure," Brandon said, still looking. "I thought it was a man. In some sort of a robe."

"An optical illusion," Meek sniffed.

"Dammit, Harmon, I know what I saw!"

"You know what you *thought* you saw," replied Meek. "The mind plays tricks on us sometimes. I remember once, when I was a graduate student—"

Brandon strode off in the direction he'd been pointing.

"Bran! Wait!" Jordan shouted after him.

"He must've left footprints," Brandon said over his shoulder.

Meek shook his head. "Nonsense," he huffed.

De Falla flailed his arms. "I don't know if he really saw a man, but there are surely insects here."

"Really?" said Meek.

Jordan strode to his brother's side. Brandon was peering at the ground, searching.

"It was right about here," he murmured.

The ground looked undisturbed to Jordan. No footprints except their own.

"I could've sworn I saw him."

"It doesn't seem all that likely, Bran," Jordan said gently. "Perhaps it was an animal of some sort."

"Standing on its hind legs?"

Jordan shrugged. "This is all new territory. We don't know what to expect."

"Maybe we'd better get those guns."

"Not a bad idea," Jordan agreed. The two brothers went back to the buggy and pulled out a pair of slim dart-firing rifles.

"Do you think these things could stop a bear?" Brandon asked, heading back toward the spot where he thought he'd seen someone.

"They do on Earth," Jordan said, hefting the rifle in one hand. It felt light, more like a child's toy than a weapon that could protect them.

De Falla shouted, "Look! Birds!"

They looked up as a flock of brightly colored birds swooped past, wings glittering in the sunlight. They certainly look like birds on Earth, Jordan thought, no matter what Meek thinks.

"Squirrels, insects, birds," Brandon said. "Why not people?"

Turning slowly, Jordan looked all around him. He saw de Falla and Meek gazing at the birds as they flew off into the distance. The two inert rovers, with the robots bent over them. Their own buggy. And Brandon standing beside him with that sullen, stubborn look he'd known since childhood, cradling the rifle in his arms.

"There's absolutely no sign of intelligent life on this planet, Bran. You know that."

"I know what I saw."

Gripping his brother's shoulder, Jordan smiled and said, "Well, if you're right, we'll run into him again, I imagine."

"You're humoring me, Jordy."

"Perhaps I am," Jordan admitted. "What else can I do?"

"Help me look for him!"

"I don't think we should get too far away from the others. And the buggy."

"Keeping your line of retreat open?"

"It's the sensible thing to do, don't you agree?"

"Sensible," Brandon said. "But wrong."

And he started off deeper into the forest.

"Bran, wait," Jordan called, trotting after him.

"I saw a man," Brandon insisted. "A man in a long robe. It was sort of bluish."

Jordan grabbed for his brother's arm again and dragged him to a halt. "All right. You saw a man. But there's no sign of him now."

"That doesn't mean—"

"If he exists, we'll see him again, no doubt. In the meantime, I think it's foolish to go crashing off into these woods before we know more about what this place is like."

Brandon stood there glaring at his brother for several silent moments. Then, very deliberately, he clicked open the neck ring of his biosuit and lifted up the edge of his bubble helmet. The helmet deflated into a sagging lump of nanofabric and Brandon pulled it off his head entirely. Jordan was so shocked he didn't know what to do, what to say.

"There," Brandon said. "I'm breathing this world's air. It's not harming me."

Jordan had to swallow hard before he could say, "How do you know that? There could be microbes, viruses, all kinds of—"

"Good morning, sirs."

They whirled around toward the sound of the softly melodious voice. Standing fifteen meters before them was a tall, lean, totally bald, vaguely oriental-looking man in an ankle-length pale blue robe, holding a small furry creature in the palm of one hand and gently stroking it with the other.

ADRI

am Adri," the man said, his voice soft, almost a whisper. "Welcome to New Earth."

Jordan stared at the man, blinked once, twice, then gaped at him again. Standing beside him, Brandon was equally goggle-eyed.

The man smiled gently. "I hope I haven't shocked you. The question of a first meeting is always very delicate, don't you think?"

His face was spiderwebbed with age, Jordan saw. He was quite tall, a few centimeters taller than Meek, and appeared to be very slim beneath his long robe. His eyes were almond shaped, pale blue. The hue of his skin was faintly brownish yellow, almost gray. His cheeks were gaunt, hollow. His hands were thin, with long talonlike fingers that slowly stroked the furry thing he was holding.

Meek and de Falla came running up to them.

"Well, I'll be damned," said Meek. De Falla said nothing, he simply stared.

"I am Adri," the man repeated, with a gentle smile. "I hope you'll forgive the somewhat dramatic scenario we've concocted to produce this first meeting."

"It was a surprise," Jordan admitted. Then he said, "My name is Jordan Kell. This is my brother, Dr. Brandon Kell, Dr. Harmon Meek, and Dr. Silvio de Falla."

"You said *we*," Brandon snapped, almost accusingly. "There's more of you?"

"Oh, my, yes. Of course. There would have to be, wouldn't there?"

Jordan asked, "Who are you? How many of you are there?"

Looking slightly embarrassed, Adri replied, "Oh, there's a

goodly number of us here. I'm afraid we've kept ourselves hidden from your orbiting cameras."

"You look human," Jordan said, his voice hollow with awe. "You speak English."

"Yes. We thought it best to make our first meeting as comfortable for you as possible. There's no way to entirely avoid the shock, of course, but we do want to make it as easy for you as we can."

"Then you're not really human?" Meek asked.

"Oh yes, I'm as human as you are."

"Convergent evolution," de Falla said, his voice awed.

Adri shook his bald head. "Not quite. It's a bit more complicated than that." He slid the little pet into the folds of his robe, then clasped his long fingers together, as if in prayer.

But only for a moment. Pointing to the rifle still in Jordan's hands, Adri said softly, "If those are weapons, you won't need them here. There are no dangerous animals in this forest."

Ignoring that, Brandon asked, "This is your home world? You live on this planet?"

"Yes. Of course," said Adri. "I would be pleased to show you our community."

"By all means!" said Brandon.

"Wait a moment," Jordan said. "We should report this to the others."

"Your colleagues aboard the ship. Of course. I'll be happy to greet them." Adri started toward the buggy, the four men following him. Brandon rushed ahead, dumped his rifle in the back of the buggy, then slipped into the driver's seat. Jordan heard him speaking excitedly over the communications link.

Jordan moved beside Adri, who paced along leisurely. The glossy-furred animal peeked out from the robe, big round eyes glittering, then ducked back inside again. Meek came up on Adri's other side, and de Falla trailed a few paces behind.

"By the way," Adri said, "you really don't need those protective coverings you're wearing. There's nothing in the air here that can harm you."

Jordan felt his brows knitting. "How can you know that? How can you be so sure?"

Pointing to Brandon, still jabbering excitedly with Thornberry, Adri replied, "He's breathing the air."

"He's an impetuous young man," said Jordan.

"But he's unharmed."

Jordan stared at the alien for a long, wordless moment, thinking, Can we trust him? Does he know what he's talking about? Is he telling us the truth?

Turning to Meek, Jordan asked, "Harmon, what do you think? Would it be all right to get out of the biosuits?"

Glancing toward Brandon, Meek answered, "Let your brother be our guinea pig. He's volunteered for the honor."

Jordan asked Adri to sit beside Brandon so that Thornberry and the others aboard the ship could see him. On the smallish display screen their expressions were almost comical as they crowded around Thornberry: wonder, surprise, open-jawed awe. That must be what I looked like a few minutes ago, Jordan thought.

They were all talking at once. Thornberry began to look irritated as the rest of the team jostled him.

"I am pleased to meet you all," Adri said, his voice suddenly strong enough to cut through their jabber. "I am delighted that you made the journey here, and I wish you well."

Literally pushing the others away, Thornberry admitted, "To say that we're surprised would be a grand understatement."

"I understand," said Adri.

Standing outside the buggy at Adri's side, Jordan wondered, "Why aren't you surprised? You seem almost to have been expecting us."

Adri turned to him with his patient smile. "We've been observing you for a long time: watching your video broadcasts, monitoring your radio emissions. We detected your ship taking up an orbit around this planet. We projected a laser beacon to inform you of our presence. You quickly grasped its significance and sent your pair of machines here."

"And you conked them out," said Thornberry's image on the comm screen, almost accusingly.

Adri looked slightly embarrassed. "Yes, I'm afraid we did disable them. We wanted you to come here yourselves. Making our first contact through your machines would have been . . . awkward."

"Can you turn the rovers back on?" Thornberry asked.

"Oh yes, of course. You'll find that they are both in perfect working order now."

Thornberry glanced down; Jordan concluded he was working his console screen.

"Well I'll be dipped in sheep droppings," he muttered. "They're both humming as if they'd never been off."

"It's been a pleasure to meet all of you," Adri said, in his gentle, genial tone. Then he slipped out of the seat to stand beside Jordan. "Now, if you're willing, I would like to show you our community." Pointing deeper into the forest, Adri said, "It's only a few kilometers, in that direction."

"Why don't you sit up front, with Brandon," said Jordan.

"Oh, that's not necessary. I can sit behind you."

"No, no. I insist. You know the way. You can be Bran's navigator."

Adri seemed to think it over briefly, then made a polite little bow. "Thank you."

He climbed into the right-hand seat. Jordan stashed his rifle, then sat with Meek in the second row while de Falla climbed into the rearmost row, empty since the robots were still with the reactivated rovers.

As the buggy started up, Jordan marveled at how fantastic this all was. *It's impossible,* he told himself. *I must be dreaming.*

Yet he opened the neck seal of his biosuit and pulled the deflated plastic helmet down off his head.

THE CITY

Brandon drove a good deal faster than de Falla had, pushing through the forest at Adri's direction along what appeared to be a fairly well-defined track that wound among the trees. Jordan leaned between them and asked for a report from Longyear on the quality of the air.

The biologist's lean, somber face appeared on the comm screen. "The bio program's still analyzing the sampling data you've beamed up. Nothing toxic, apparently. But the analysis isn't finished yet."

Jordan nodded. "Brandon and I have removed our suit helmets."

Longyear's dark eyes widened. "That's premature, Jordan. There could be—"

"We've volunteered to be experimental subjects. So far, so good."

Looking unhappy, the biologist muttered, "What's done is done."

"Can't argue with that," Jordan said, feeling somehow cheerful, buoyant.

They rode on for another few minutes, and then Jordan saw stone buildings standing among the trees. Large buildings, several stories high, with flat roofs green with lush gardens. A small crowd of people was clustered in front of the nearest building.

"It's a regular city!" Brandon cried out.

And indeed it was. Adri directed them down a central street, flanked on either side by handsome stone buildings. Brandon drove slowly now, gaping at the buildings and people they were passing. There were animals among the people, too: four-footed creatures that looked vaguely like miniature horses, about the size of a Shetland pony. Apparently they were used as beasts of burden. He could see no vehicles of any sort, not even a bicycle. Most of the ponies were a plain dun color, although a few of them were deeper shades of brown.

At the end of the street, Jordan saw, stood an imposing multistoried structure with a long stone stairway leading to a veranda that seemed to run completely around the building.

How could our sensors have missed all this? Jordan asked himself. All right, the roofs might appear to be natural greenery and the stone is probably local material, so the cameras and multispectral sensors might have concluded it's all natural formations. But the straight streets? That should have been an immediate tipoff that this is artificial. Straight lines don't appear in nature. Not gridworks of city streets.

As if he was reading Jordan's thoughts, Adri turned slightly in his seat and said, "I'm afraid we disguised our little community from your orbiting cameras."

"How could you do that?" Jordan asked. "And why?"

"We were very fearful of shocking you, you must realize. We wanted our first contact to be as gentle as possible. As nonthreatening as possible."

"Nonthreatening," Jordan echoed.

"Despite the guns you were carrying," Adri chided softly.

The people walking along the streets were perfectly human-looking men and women. Some wore ankle-length robes, as Adri did, but there were plenty of other styles of clothing, some of them very colorful. Small doglike animals scampered among them, apparently free to scurry wherever they wished. Many of the people turned to stare in curiosity at their buggy rolling past, although others seemed to ignore it. New Yorkers, said a cynical voice in Jordan's head.

As they approached the broad stairway at the end of the street, Adri said to Brandon, "You can stop at the bottom of the stairs."

Jordan tapped his brother's shoulder. "Are we beaming all this up to the others?"

Nodding without taking his eyes from his driving, Brandon said, "Automatic feed. Thornberry's getting everything our cameras see."

"Good," said Jordan.

They glided to a stop at the base of the stairs. A dozen or so people were coming down the stairs toward them.

"A reception committee?" Jordan asked as he swung his legs over the side of the buggy and got to his feet.

"A welcoming committee," said Adri. He got up too, more slowly, stiffly. "We have decided to speak English to you. I hope that is agreeable."

"That's fine," said Jordan.

As Brandon, Meek, and de Falla got off the buggy, Adri went on, "I believe that English is the lingua franca of your people."

A pun? Jordan asked himself. A multilingual pun from an alien?

The others came down the steps and arranged themselves around Adri and the four men from Earth. Looking them over, Jordan saw that there were six women and six men, their hair and skin coloring ranging from pale Nordic to dark African. It's as though some politician put together a group to represent every possible type of human being on Earth.

But we're not on Earth, he reminded himself. These people may look human, but they are aliens.

One of the women, a pretty, pert redhead with short-cropped hair and smiling brown eyes, took a step forward and said, "Welcome to our city. We hope you make yourselves comfortable here." She was wearing a short-sleeved light tan blouse and dark brown slacks.

"Thank you," said Jordan, with a suggestion of a bow. "My name is Jordan Kell. You are . . . ?"

She looked puzzled for a moment, then seemed to grasp what Jordan was asking her. "Oh! My name is Aditi."

"A charming name," said Jordan. "And may I ask, what do you call your city?"

Again she looked perplexed. Adri said, "We merely call it the city."

"And this planet?" Brandon asked. "When we first met you, you called it New Earth."

"Yes," said Adri. "Isn't that what you call this world?"

"That's right. But what do *you* call it?"

"And how did you know that was the name we used?" Meek added.

Adri smiled placatingly. "This planet's name in our language is very similar to your term, New Earth."

Meek's lean face took on a suspicious scowl. "And just what is your language, may I ask?"

Adri stood silent for a moment, then uttered an indecipherable sound, a combination of a fluting whistle and an undulating low moan. Meek's jaw dropped open and Jordan fought down an urge to laugh at the astrobiologist's consternation.

"I'm sorry," Adri said. "Our language has very different roots than yours. I believe it will be much easier if we communicate in English. At least for the time being."

"I agree," said Jordan. "At least for the time being."

Aditi gestured toward the stairs and said, "Would you like to see our . . ." She hesitated, looked at Adri.

"Our administrative center," Adri finished for her.

"City hall?" Jordan asked, with a smile.

"Oh, it's more than that, Mr. Kell. Much more."

THE ADMINISTRATIVE CENTER

With Aditi on one side of him and Adri on the other, Jordan climbed the steps of the impressive building. He felt somehow eager, excited by these strange yet familiar surroundings. It's as though I've come home, he thought. Home, to a place I've never been to before.

Brandon, Meek, and de Falla were behind him, Brandon chatting with the welcoming committee as they made their way up the stairs, while Meek and de Falla kept a guarded silence. Jordan opened the front of his biosuit and fished his phone from his shirt pocket.

Hazzard's dark face appeared on the tiny screen. "We're tracking you, Jordan, no problem," said the astronaut.

"Where's Thornberry?" Jordan asked.

"He's running the remote console, packing the rovers into the ship they flew in on," Hazzard replied. "Wants to move them to other regions now that they're working okay."

"And the robots?"

"They're back at your plane, standing by."

Nodding, Jordan said, "We're going into what appears to be their main building. Reception might not be so good once we're inside."

Lowering his voice, Hazzard asked, "You trust these aliens?"

Jordan glanced at Adri, climbing the stairs beside him, then Aditi, on his other side. "Yes," he answered. "I do. At any rate, we won't learn much by keeping our distance from them."

"Maybe," Hazzard granted. "Just stay in touch with me."

"Of course." He flicked the phone shut and stuffed it back in his pocket.

Adri said, "I'm afraid I couldn't help overhearing your conversation."

Jordan shrugged. "That's all right."

"You'll find that electromagnetic reception inside our buildings is quite clear."

"Good."

"I can understand your teammate's concern. Xenophobia is a survival trait that must have been important in your earlier evolution."

"I suppose it was," said Jordan. "But I think it's time we got past it."

"Oh yes," Adri agreed, beaming. "Long past time, I should think."

Adri led them through an imposing entry, high double doors of some dark wood, and into the building. Out of the corner of his eye, Jordan noticed Aditi eying him curiously. This must be just as exciting for her as it is for us, he realized. And he felt glad of it.

Escorted by the little band of aliens, Jordan and the three other Earthmen followed Adri through stately corridors and large rooms that appeared to be offices where men and women sitting at desks were working away industriously. He felt impressed with the size of the offices and the apparent efficiency of these people.

"Just what are they doing?" he asked Adri.

"Oh . . . administrative tasks, for the most part. We have a sizeable community here."

"I can see that."

They entered a smaller room, where a long table was set with dishes and glassware.

"You must be hungry," said Adri. "We've prepared something of a luncheon for you. I hope—"

Brandon interrupted, "You've prepared food we can eat?"

Again that patient smile curved Adri's thin lips. "You and we can digest the same foods, I assure you. We're just as human as you are."

"That's not possible," Meek objected. "By all we know of biology, it's impossible for two species from two different star systems to share identical biochemistries."

"By all you know of biology," Adri retorted, patiently. "You are about to learn much more than you currently know."

Trying to stop an argument from developing, Jordan said, "Well,

I'm rather hungry, aren't you? If Adri says we can digest the food, why not take him at his word and give it a try?"

"That's a good way to poison ourselves," de Falla blurted.

Adri extended a hand to his shoulder but the geologist flinched back.

"Please," said Adri, "we have no wish to harm you. And we do know something of your biology. After all, we've been watching and listening to your broadcasts for many years. And your Internet is a cornucopia of information on all sorts of subjects."

Before de Falla or anyone else could respond, Adri added, "But if you wish, you can have your robots carry the food you brought with you and eat it."

"We don't mean to offend you," Jordan said.

"No offense is taken," Adri replied. "We understand how strange this must be for you. Strange and perhaps more than a little frightening."

Glancing at Aditi, Jordan said, "It's certainly strange. And rather wonderful, actually."

De Falla asked Jordan, "May I borrow your phone?"

Jordan handed it to the geologist, wondering how the man was going to eat if he remained sealed inside his protective suit.

De Falla walked off to a corner of the room, speaking in low, urgent tones to Hazzard up in the ship.

"He's not usually so . . . tense," Jordan apologized to Adri.

The alien smiled once more. "It's understandable. What I find remarkable is how you and your brother have thrown caution to the winds."

Jordan glanced at Brandon, who was in earnest conversation with Aditi. He noticed how nicely she filled the clothes she was wearing. "My brother's the impulsive type."

"And you?" Adri probed. "You don't strike me as impulsive."

Jordan had to think a moment. At last he said, "I suppose I trust you. I'm hoping that we can be completely frank with one another. We both have a lot to learn."

Adri's smile widened. "Yes, that is quite true. A lot to learn."

HOSPITALITY

Most of the welcoming committee left the dining room, rather reluctantly, Jordan thought. Adri bade the four men from Earth sit at the oblong table, which was set with eight places.

Jordan looked across the room to de Falla, who was still on the phone, deep in intense, serious conversation. Adri, standing beside Jordan, was also gazing toward the geologist. This is getting awkward, Jordan thought. They've prepared a meal for us and Silvio's holding up the proceedings.

But how could they possibly have produced food that we can eat? Jordan asked himself. Adri says our biochemistries are similar, but how similar can they be? We're from different stars, different worlds. This planet seems very much like Earth, but it can't be identical. Even the smallest difference could be potentially dangerous, fatal.

With those thoughts whirling through his mind, Jordan excused himself to Adri and walked across the room toward de Falla.

"You're absolutely certain?" the geologist was saying into the phone, in a tense, urgent whisper.

De Falla glanced up at Jordan as he approached, nodded once, and said tightly, "All right. I'll tell him."

He clicked the phone shut.

"What did they have to say?" Jordan asked as he accepted the phone from de Falla.

De Falla's normally cheerful expression was gone. He looked worried, suspicious.

"They're all over the place," he complained. "Longyear says the air's okay to breathe—he thinks. Thornberry's sending one of the robots here with food packets from the plane. Hazzard thinks we ought to go back to the plane and stay there overnight. Or maybe go back to the ship in orbit."

"Is there any reason why we shouldn't eat the food that these people have prepared for us?" Jordan asked.

"They're all agreed on that. No way. It can't be suitable to our bodies. We shouldn't touch it."

Jordan said, "They're entirely right to be cautious." He turned back to the table, where Adri and the others were seated and waiting for them. Brandon had seated himself beside Aditi, Jordan noticed.

"How long will it take the robot to get here with our food?"

"It's already on its way," de Falla answered. "Maybe another fifteen, twenty minutes."

Jordan gripped the geologist's arm and started toward the table. "Let's continue the experiment, then. Brandon and I will try the food they've prepared. You and Meek can wait until the robot arrives."

De Falla looked appalled. "You could be killing yourselves!"

"They don't look like poisoners to me," Jordan said, gazing toward Aditi, who was chatting amiably with Brandon.

"They might not want to harm us," said de Falla, "but if their biochemistry is even an eyelash different from ours . . ."

Trying to appear unconcerned, Jordan said, "We'll soon find out, one way or the other."

De Falla shook his head. "This is crazy."

"Perhaps," Jordan admitted. "But no matter what you eat, you'll have to open your biosuit."

As the geologist fumbled with his suit seals, Jordan sat down at the empty chair between Adri and one of the other women. At last de Falla took the only other empty chair, down the table across from Meek. A door in the sidewall opened and human servants—at least, they looked like humans to Jordan—began to bring in trays of food and drink.

"I'm afraid we don't have any intoxicating refreshments for you," Adri said as the service began. "Only water . . . or milk, if you prefer."

"Water will be fine for me," Jordan said.

"You don't produce any wine?" Brandon asked.

With a slight shake of his head, Adri replied, "Oh, yes, we do. But we rarely drink it, especially during the daytime."

Brandon looked puzzled by that, but Jordan thought, Different customs. Our biochemistry may be the same, but our social customs aren't.

Adri cocked his head, as if listening to something that only he could hear. Then, looking down the table at de Falla and Meek, he announced, "Gentlemen, your robot has arrived with food from your supplies."

At that moment, the chamber's main door opened and the humanform robot rolled in, bearing a knapsack slung over one shoulder. It headed directly toward Jordan.

Pointing, Jordan told the robot, "Deliver to Dr. de Falla, please, and Dr. Meek."

The aliens watched interestedly as the robot brought containers of food and bottles of water out of the knapsack and laid them before Meek and de Falla. Then it rolled back to the door and left the room.

Rising to his feet at the head of the table, Adri said, "Well, now that we all have been served, I suppose we can begin." Raising his glass of water, he proclaimed, "Welcome to New Earth, gentlemen. May your stay with us be pleasant and instructive, for both of us."

"Hear, hear," said Jordan.

The food was excellent, Jordan thought. A salad of greens, a main course that looked and tasted like roast beef. Darkish bread, something like rye. Jordan saw that Brandon ate with relish.

Aditi, sitting between Brandon and de Falla, asked the geologist, "May I try a taste of your food?"

De Falla looked surprised. He glanced at Jordan, who nodded an okay, thinking, Our thin sandwiches aren't as tasty as their beef. Nutritious, yes, but not haute cuisine.

Sure enough, Aditi took a bite from the half sandwich de Falla had handed her, made a smile for him, and left the remainder on her dish.

As the servants began clearing away the dishes, Meek yelped and jumped out of his chair. "A rat!" he shouted. "Look, it's a rat! Two of them!"

De Falla hopped up from his chair, too. Brandon half-rose.

Jordan saw a dark furry creature about the size of a rat scurrying along the floor. It dashed under the table and out the other side. None of the aliens seemed in the least bit perturbed, although Adri rose to his feet.

"I must apologize," he said. "These creatures have been developed to clean the floor. They are not vermin, they are rather like the machines you use to sweep your floors. Vacuum cleaners, I believe you call them."

Jordan chuckled. "Bioengineered floor sweepers?"

"Yes," said Adri. "They are not harmful, I assure you."

Meek and de Falla sat down, shakily. The astrobiologist looked distinctly leery.

Trying to explain further, Adri said, "You see, where you have invented machines for certain tasks, we have developed biological means."

Jordan remembered that he hadn't seen any vehicles of any type on the city's streets: only those horselike creatures.

After everyone calmed down, Adri said, "We've taken the liberty of preparing quarters for you. Assuming you wish to stay, that is."

From down the table Meek said, "That's very kind of you, but I think we'd better return to our plane."

Jordan felt torn. He knew that returning to the ship was the safer thing to do, the more practical course. Yet he felt fascinated by this adventure: Intelligent, humanlike aliens, with a city that's obviously the product of a significant technology. There's so much to learn! So much to discover!

He realized that everyone's eyes were on him, waiting for his decision.

Why not carry the experiment to the next step? he asked himself.

"My brother and I will be happy to stay here," he announced, almost surprising himself. "Dr. Meek and Dr. de Falla will want to return to our plane, I'm sure."

Meek looked relieved. De Falla looked . . . angry.

FEARS

ordan walked down the broad stairs with Brandon, Meek, and de Falla. Their little buggy was sitting exactly where they had left it, with the robot that had brought their food sitting obediently inert in the rear row. Most of the aliens had dispersed after lunch, but Adri and Aditi stood at the top of the stairs, waiting for Jordan and his brother to return.

"You're crazy!" de Falla hissed, lowering his head and hunching his shoulders as if trying to prevent anyone from reading his lips.

Jordan replied, "For god's sake, man, we've made physical contact with an intelligent alien race! I, for one, intend to learn as much about them as I can, as quickly as I can."

"They're not going to disappear if you come back to the plane with us."

"And they're not going to murder us in our beds if Bran and I stay here overnight."

De Falla looked as if he wanted to keep on arguing, but instead he pressed his lips into a hard, unhappy line.

As they reached the buggy, Brandon asked Meek, "Harmon, what do you think?"

"Think?" Meek looked alarmed, like a student unexpectedly called on by his professor. "Think about what?"

"About all this," Brandon said, sweeping his arm in a wide gesture.

Meek ran a hand through his shaggy hair. "I think Silvio is correct. But he doesn't go far enough. We should go back to the ship."

"You mean, in orbit?" Jordan snapped.

With a vigorous nod, Meek said, "Why spend the night here when you could be safe and sound, up in orbit."

Jordan said, "You may be right, both of you." Before either man could say anything, he went on, "And yet I simply can't turn my back on all this."

"I think you're being foolish," Meek said. "Emotional."

Jordan glanced up the stairs at Aditi standing there, waiting. "You're probably right about that," he muttered.

"Come on," de Falla said to Meek. "Let's get going, before they change their minds about letting us leave."

He climbed into the driver's seat and Meek got in beside him, the knees of his long legs poking up awkwardly.

"I'll give you a call first thing in the morning," Jordan said.

"If they don't slit your throats first," de Falla muttered darkly.

Jordan watched the buggy trundle down the street, then turned and started up the stairs again, Brandon at his side.

"Silvio's gone off the deep end," Brandon said. "He used to be a fun guy, but he's turned hostile."

"This is a lot for him to swallow," said Jordan. "A lot for each of us, actually."

"But it's turned him into a paranoid."

"He'll adjust."

Brandon said, "Maybe it's better that he goes back to the ship. I got the feeling he was pretty close to cracking up."

So much for all the psych testing before we took off, Jordan thought. But then the psychiatrists never expected us to meet intelligent aliens. None of us expected that.

As they approached the top of the stairs, Jordan saw that the sky was darkening. Thick clouds were rolling in.

"It looks as if it's going to rain," he said as he reached Adri and Aditi.

Squinting up at the sky, Adri said, "Yes. Rain has been predicted."

"But it won't bother us," said Aditi. "We're protected."

"By going indoors," Jordan said.

"No, the entire city is protected," she corrected.

"The whole city?" Brandon asked.

Adri replied, "The city lies beneath a protective dome."

"I didn't see any dome."

"It's not material," Adri explained. "It's a dome of energy. That's why your orbiting sensors didn't see our city: the dome blocked their view."

"A dome of energy?" Jordan asked, intrigued.

"Yes," said Aditi. "We don't really need these buildings at all. We could live completely out in the open, if we wished. Protected by energy shields."

Adri pointed out, "The material buildings are more energy-efficient. And, of course, we learned how to build structures long before we learned how to generate energy shields."

"Of course," Brandon said, his voice hollow.

Adri gestured toward the building's entrance. "Would you like to see the quarters we have prepared for you?"

"Certainly," said Jordan. Then he added, "I presume they're inside a building."

Adri laughed. "Yes, yes, of course they are."

"If you'd prefer to stay outside," Aditi said, "we could provide energy shelters for you."

Jordan glanced at Brandon, then answered, "No, thank you. We're accustomed to living inside structures with solid walls and roofs, just as you are."

Adri led them back into the building, down its central corridor, out the rear into a long rectangular courtyard bordered with small flowering trees. At the end of the courtyard stood a smaller, two-storied building. Jordan walked between Adri and Aditi; Brandon stayed on Aditi's other side. The sky above had grown ominously dark, thick clouds scudding past. Lightning suddenly flashed and almost immediately thunder boomed, jarringly loud. Yet no rain fell on them, although Jordan felt a strong breeze gusting through the courtyard, making the little trees sway.

Totally unconcerned about the storm, Adri pointed to the building ahead and explained, "This is what you would probably call a dormitory." He cocked his head slightly to one side, then added, "Or perhaps a hotel."

"You must have other cities here and there," Jordan said. Another flash of lightning and an immediate peal of thunder.

"Oh no, this is our only community. We have no need for more."

"Farms, factories? That sort of thing?"

Nodding, Adri replied, "Yes, they are all here, on the edge of our city. The farms are enjoying the rain, I should think."

"Everything we need is here," Aditi said.

"You mean to say that the rest of the planet is empty?" Brandon asked, unbelieving.

"Not empty," said Adri. "This world is teeming with life."

"I mean human life," Brandon said.

Adri smiled at him. "Our entire human population lives here, in the city. The rest of the planet is for the other living species."

Jordan thought a moment, then asked, "That means you must keep your own numbers at a stable level."

"Yes, certainly."

"We have to," said Aditi. "Otherwise we would put a strain on our natural resources."

With a sigh, Jordan said, "I wish our people on Earth were that wise."

"It is necessary," said Adri. "We must live in balance with the planet's resources."

Brandon said, "Back home we use the resources of the rest of the solar system."

"And our numbers keep growing," Jordan added.

"Yes, that may be so for you," said Adri, "but as you can see, we have no other planets to exploit. We must live within the resources that this single world can provide."

With that, they approached the main door to the dormitory building. It opened for them automatically.

The interior of the building was richly decorated with swirling, colorful abstract murals.

"Each corridor is color-coded," Adri explained. "The predominant tone in this main corridor is orange, as you can see. Side corridors are in cooler tones: blue, green, lilac."

"Impressive," said Jordan. "And delightful."

"I'm so pleased you enjoy it."

Brandon asked, "Do you sleep here? In this building?"

"Yes, we do," Aditi answered. "On the upper floor."

Adri stopped at an intricately carved door. It slid open at the touch of his fingertip.

"I hope this suite will be comfortable for you," he said, ushering Jordan and Brandon in with a sweep of his arm. "It has two separate bedrooms connected by the sitting room, here."

Aditi remained out in the corridor.

"Aren't you coming in?" Jordan called to her.

She broke into a bright smile and stepped into the sitting room.

Jordan looked around the room. It was handsomely furnished with a long, low sofa, several armchairs, two desks on opposite walls. The walls themselves glowed slightly, a pearly gray. Wall screens, he realized. He noticed a faint trace of a floral scent. Jasmine? he wondered.

"If this is a dormitory room," Brandon said, grinning, "I can't imagine what your luxury hotel suites must look like."

Jordan saw that the doors leading to the bedrooms were both open. The bedrooms looked identical: large, comfortable, attractively appointed. He caught a glimpse of a small gray creature that scurried beneath the bed in one of the rooms. Startled for an instant, he recovered his composure. Vacuum cleaner, he reminded himself.

"You can communicate with your ship," said Adri, "using the wall screens."

Aditi said, "The closets contain robes in your sizes. We were uncertain as to what you would prefer for clothing, so we merely provided the robes. I hope they're satisfactory."

"Perfectly satisfactory," Jordan said.

Brandon joked, "I hope whoever's in the room above us isn't a flamenco dancer."

Adri's expression went so perplexed that Jordan had to stifle an urge to laugh.

"Flamenco dancer?" Aditi asked, also obviously puzzled.

"It's a form of entertainment," Brandon explained, and he stomped his feet a few times while snapping his fingers.

"I see," said Adri, still a bit uncertain.

But Aditi broke into laughter. "It's a joke! You were being humorous."

"I was trying," Brandon said.

Quite seriously, Adri said, "I can assure you, whoever is residing above this suite is not a flamenco dancer."

Jordan said, "We're glad to hear that." And he studied Aditi's vivacious, happy face, reveling in the sound of her laughter.

Adri said, "If you don't mind, we'll leave you two to familiarize yourselves with your quarters and relax awhile. Shall I call for you for dinner in a few hours? Will that be all right?"

"That'll be fine," Brandon said.

To Aditi, Jordan asked, "Will you join us for dinner?"

"If you like," she said.

"I'd be very pleased if you did."

With a smiling nod, Aditi said, "I'll be happy to."

Once they were alone in the sitting room, Jordan flipped his pocketphone open and called Thornberry. To his surprise, the roboticist's face appeared on the wall screen opposite the sofa, slightly larger than life.

"All is well," Jordan reported. Swinging the phone slowly around the room, he went on, "As you can see, they've set us up in very comfortable quarters. We'll be having dinner with Adri in a little while."

"We've been monitoring you through your phone," Thornberry said, his heavy brows slightly knitted. "Glad to get visuals, though. Now what was that business about energy domes?"

Jordan felt mildly annoyed. They're eavesdropping, he thought. We'll have to turn the phones off if we want any privacy.

"I'll ask Adri for more details," he replied. "When you come down here, perhaps you can meet with their technical people."

"I'd like that," said Thornberry.

"What about Meek and de Falla?" Jordan asked. "Are they coming up to the ship or staying down here?"

Hazzard came into the picture, behind Thornberry's shoulder. "They're coming up here. I pointed out to them that they'd just have to go back tomorrow, but they insisted on returning to the ship. They're really spooked, especially Silvio."

"I'm afraid so," Jordan agreed.

"How are the aliens treating you?" Hazzard asked.

"Very well indeed," said Jordan. "You can tell de Falla to relax."

"You're in uncharted territory, Jordan," Hazzard said. "Be careful."

"Thanks for the advice. I'll call you first thing in the morning."

"Or sooner, if you need to."

"Yes, certainly. But for now I'm going to turn off our phones."

"No!" Hazzard snapped. "We need to be in constant touch with you."

Frowning slightly at the oversized image on the wall screen, Jordan said, "I don't feel comfortable having you listening in on every word I say."

"We need to know what's going on," Hazzard insisted. Thornberry agreed with a tense nod.

Jordan saw that his brother was grinning at him. To Hazzard, he said, "Geoff, I'm going to pull rank on you. I'm going to turn off our phones after dinner. If they murder us in our sleep you'll find out about it soon enough."

"I don't like it," said Hazzard.

"I understand," Jordan replied. "Your objection will be noted in the ship's log."

Once the wall screen went blank, Brandon said to Jordan, "You want some privacy when you're with Aditi."

Jordan tried to stare his brother down, failed, and at last admitted, "Wouldn't you?"

The four of them had a leisurely meal in a sizeable dining room down the corridor from their suite. Several dozen tables were filled with couples and larger groups. Human—or rather, alien—waiters served trays laden with steaming soups, crisp salads, and savory meats. There was no wine, but Adri introduced them to a pungent drink that somehow seemed to go well with each course.

Jordan chatted with Aditi, for the most part, leaving Brandon to talk with Adri.

"I take it that Adri heads your government here," he prompted.

"Government?" Aditi asked, as if the term was new to her.

"He's your leader," Jordan said. "He makes the final decisions about things."

"Oh! You mean chief of the administration. Yes, you could say that's Adri's position."

"And you? What do you do?"

Again Aditi looked briefly at a loss, but then her expression brightened. "I'm a teacher."

"A teacher? Really?" Jordan realized that he hadn't seen any children in the city. Not one.

"Yes."

"Can you teach me your language?"

She smiled. "It's very different from yours. We use different tones, different parts of the vocal organ."

"Would it be very difficult to teach me?"

"It might be," Aditi said, her face growing serious. "The most arduous part of learning is preparing the mind to accept new knowledge."

"I never thought of it that way."

"Would you like to see more of the city? The farms, the orchards, they're quite lovely."

Jordan felt she was changing the subject, but he nodded readily. "I'd be happy to have you show them to me."

"Good," said Aditi. "First thing tomorrow."

At last they finished the meal with cups of a brew very much like coffee. Jordan bade a reluctant good night to Aditi and Adri, then he and his brother made their way back to their quarters.

"No dessert," Brandon noted.

"So they're not trying to fatten us up for the slaughter," said Jordan.

"From what Adri told me, they don't slaughter meat animals. The grow their meat in biovats, just as we do on the ship."

Jordan nodded. "Makes sense. Why raise an animal just to kill it when you can grow the same meat from a culture of a few cells?"

They entered their suite. Jordan popped his phone open and called up to the ship. Trish Wanamaker's chunky face appeared on the wall screen.

"Where's Thornberry?" Jordan asked.

"Sleeping, I guess. He's been at this station all day, just about. I've taken over the night shift."

"I see. Well, we've had a pleasant dinner with our new friends and now we're going to retire. I'll turn off the phones, but I'll call you when we awake."

Wanamaker looked troubled. "Geoff won't like that."

"I know. We've been through all that. Geoff will just have to accept it."

With a shrug, Wanamaker said, "You're the boss."

"Good night, Trish."

"Good night, boss."

Her image winked off and Jordan clicked his phone's power button. Brandon pulled his phone from his shirt pocket and did the same.

"No alcoholic beverages," Brandon observed as he went to the sofa and plopped down on it.

"That drink they served with dinner wasn't bad, though," he said to his brother.

"I wonder why they didn't serve us the wine that Adri told us they make?"

Jordan shrugged. "Perhaps they didn't want us to get sloshed our first night here."

Brandon grinned at him. "It's been a helluva day, hasn't it?"

"Indeed it has."

"Do you think Hazzard's right? Are we in any danger here? Should we be on our guard?"

Jordan eased himself down onto the armchair nearest the sofa. "We're in the lions' den, Bran. If they harbor evil intentions we'll know about it soon enough."

"They've got a high technology. Higher than ours, with their bioengineered animals and energy domes."

"And a lot more, I'm sure."

Leaning forward intently, Brandon said, "I get the feeling that they expected us. They knew we were coming."

"Well, they did set up the laser beacon to attract us."

"No, I don't mean that. I think they expected us to send a ship here. They probably tracked us all the way from Earth."

"Really?"

"They've been studying us, Jordy. For god knows how long. They've learned our language, they know where we've come from. It's like they expected us."

"They could have learned a lot by tapping into our radio and video broadcasts, I suppose. And the webs, of course."

"Why? Why would they do that?"

"Why not? They're as intelligent as we are. We sent probes to this planet before our mission was launched. Of course they knew about us, expected us."

"But why didn't they try to contact us? If they can pick up our radio and video, why didn't they call us?"

"I'll have to ask Adri about that."

Brandon shook his head. "It's all just too damned convenient. A planet just like Earth. Human beings. We can breathe their air and eat their foods. It's uncanny. It gives me the creeps, kind of."

Jordan said nothing.

"Tell me the truth, Jordy: doesn't all this bother you? Doesn't it worry you?"

Jordan thought about it as he looked into his brother's troubled eyes, and found that the truth startled him. "Bran, the truth is that I feel as if I've just arrived home."

REBELLION

Jordan awoke and stared at the ceiling for long, languorous moments. Morning sunlight slanted through the room's one window. A bird—a winged creature about the size of a hummingbird with feathers gleaming like jewels—was flitting back and forth up near the ceiling. Bug catcher? Jordan wondered.

His bed was one of the most comfortable he'd ever slept in; it seemed to mold itself to his body shape. He knew he had dreamt, but he couldn't remember what his dreams were about. Probably better that way, he thought.

He rose, showered, then shaved with implements neatly laid out on the bathroom cabinet top. His pencil-thin mustache seemed a bit less ragged than it had appeared a few days ago.

Three ankle-length robes hung in the bedroom closet, all in the same bluish gray tone. Underwear in the bureau drawer, together with slipper socks that had padded soles. They all fit reasonably well, although the underpants felt looser than Jordan would have preferred. So they know my approximate size, he thought, but not my precise preferences.

Brandon was already in the sitting room, wearing his own slacks and wrinkled shirt from the day before, in thoughtful conversation with Paul Longyear.

"It's just plain impossible," the lean-faced biologist was saying. "I spent half the night running a statistical analysis of the likelihood of a biosphere being so exactly like Earth, and the program kept blowing up in my face. Everything goes to infinity! It's just impossible!"

Brandon made a sour face at the image on the wall screen.

"Paul, you know there are lies, damned lies, and statistics. It doesn't matter what the computer program says, the planet is here. It exists."

"How can it be so much like Earth?"

"Maybe Earthlike planets are commonplace. For all we know—"

"Come on, Brandon," Longyear interrupted. "Out of the thousands of exoplanets that have been discovered, this one individual planet is a duplicate of Earth. An exact duplicate!"

"Not entirely exact," Brandon said.

"With human beings living on it!"

Jordan had never seen the normally imperturbable, stolid Longyear so worked up. His hair, normally braided in a neat queue, looked frayed, hanging down over his shoulders in careless disarray. His dark eyes glittered with suspicion. Or is it fear? Jordan asked himself. Fear of the unknown. Fear that we're finding ourselves pretty ignorant, compared to Adri's people.

"It exists," Brandon repeated. "It's real, no matter what the theories or the statistics may say."

"Have you considered," Longyear said slowly, as if trying to calm himself, "that everything you're seeing is an illusion? A trick? Maybe they can manipulate your senses so that you see what they want you to see."

Brandon rolled his eyes toward the ceiling. Then, "Listen, Paul. The food I ate last night wasn't an illusion. It gave me a gas attack. I've been burping and farting all damned night."

Jordan laughed aloud as his brother abruptly ended the link and Longyear's image on the wall screen winked off.

"Really? The food gave you gas?"

Brandon grinned slyly. "A little. Not as bad as I made out to Paul." He shook his head. "He thinks they're manipulating our minds, that all this is just an illusion."

"It could be. Gas and all."

"Get real, Jordy."

"Is that possibility any less real than the idea that this planet is a natural duplicate of Earth? Down to an intelligent race that exactly resembles us?"

Before Brandon could reply, a fluting musical tone filled the room. Turning, Jordan saw that their front door was glowing with a pulsating light.

"Doorbell?" he wondered as he rushed to the door.

It slid open at the touch of his finger. Aditi stood in the corridor, smiling at him. She wore chocolate brown shorts and a lighter short-sleeved blouse. Her hair, the color of autumn leaves, was nicely tousled.

"Welcome!" said Jordan, delighted. Then he noticed an orange-furred catlike creature slinking around Aditi's ankles, looking up at him with big, bright, saucer-shaped curious eyes.

"Welcome to both of you."

Aditi glanced down at the animal. "Sleen is a pet. She's very quiet. You don't mind if she accompanies us?"

"Not at all. Come on in."

"The robe fits you," she said as she stepped into the sitting room. "I'm relieved. I wasn't certain we had the right measurements for you. We only had an hour or so, and the remote measuring system can be . . . well, less than exact."

"The system worked beautifully. The robe is very comfortable," Jordan said, ushering her in with a sweep of his arm.

Aditi said, "I thought we'd have some breakfast and then go to see the farms."

"Fine," he said, "although I should speak with the people on the ship first. Why don't you and Brandon go to the restaurant and I'll join you in a few minutes."

She looked slightly disappointed, but said, "Very well."

Brandon offered his arm and gallantly led her out of the suite. The furry pet trailed after them, tail held high. Jordan stood in the middle of the sitting room, wondering if he'd just made a grievous mistake.

The wall screen was wide enough to show Thornberry, Hazzard, and Meek sitting side by side at one of the wardroom tables. They looked grim, like three judges about to pronounce a death sentence.

"We've reviewed the mission protocol," Hazzard said, without preamble. "There's nothing in it that covers the situation we're in."

With an amused smile, Jordan said, "I should think not."

"But we can't all go down to the surface, Jordan. The protocol specifies that there has to be at least a skeleton crew aboard the ship at all times."

"That could be handled by robots, couldn't it, Mitch?"

"It could," said Thornberry.

But Hazzard said, "The protocol says crew members, not robots."

"How many would constitute a skeleton crew?"

"Three, at least," said Hazzard.

"So seven of you can come down and join Bran and me here."

Meek spoke up. "Not there, where you are. Not in their city."

"Why not?"

Thornberry said, "We thrashed this out last night, Jordan. We've come to the conclusion that we should set up a base camp for ourselves, just as we planned to do before we knew that the aliens existed."

Jordan felt slightly nettled. "But why go to the trouble of setting up a camp when you can live here in comfort? Even luxury."

"Mission protocol," said Hazzard, rigidly.

"But—"

Meek pointed a lean finger and said, "We've decided it will be much safer for us to set up our own base and not be in the hands of these strangers."

"Don't you think that's a little . . . well, overly cautious?" Jordan asked.

Thornberry smiled placatingly. "Look, Jordan. These folks may be grand and wonderful people. But we don't know that for certain, now, do we?"

"They've certainly treated Bran and me very handsomely."

"Yes, surely they have. But there's nothing wrong with being just a teeny bit careful, is there?"

Before Jordan could answer, Meek blurted, "Safety first! Fools rush in, but we're not going to be foolish. No matter what you say!"

Good lord, Jordan thought. I have a rebellion on my hands!

Hazzard looked grimly adamant. "Look, Jordan, we're on our own here. The messages we're sending back to Earth take more than eight years to get there. And another eight years for them to respond. We'll get no help from home."

"But we're not under any threat. Adri and his people have been more than kind to us."

"We have no idea of what their motivations are," Meek said, almost vehemently. "Or their intentions. I, for one, have no desire to live among them. Not until we learn much more about them. *Much* more."

"We've decided that's our best course of action," Hazzard said.

"I see," said Jordan. Trying to buy time so he could think the situation through, he asked, "Have you decided where you'll set up your camp?"

"In the clearing where the rocketplanes put down," Hazzard replied. "It's close enough to their city to be convenient and—"

"And far enough away to give us a measure of safety," Meek added.

Jordan saw that Thornberry wasn't wearing his usual slight smile.

"Mitch, do you feel the same way?"

Looking uncomfortable, Thornberry spread his hands and said, "It's for the best, Jordan."

Is it? Jordan wondered. But aloud, he replied only, "Perhaps it is."

And he thought, When faced with a rebellion, join it so that you can lead it.

THE FARMS

A fter breakfast, Brandon returned to their apartment, eager to talk with Elyse, back on the ship. Aditi, with her pet slinking alongside her, led Jordan along a street faced with low buildings to the edge of the city and the stone walkway that seemed to circle its perimeter.

Beyond them stood large cultivated fields, rows of green crops poking their heads above the neatly tilled soil. The catlike Sleen bounded into the field and was quickly lost to sight in the greenery.

"Don't worry about Sleen," Aditi said. "She always finds her way home. She's just out hunting for a while."

Jordan nodded.

"You're very quiet this morning," said Aditi.

"I have a lot to think about," Jordan said.

"Such as?"

"Well, this is all rather overwhelming. To find a planet so much like Earth, peopled by creatures who look exactly like human beings—"

"We *are* human beings," Aditi said, a smile dimpling her cheeks. "Just like you."

"Really?"

Her smile faded. "Our studies showed that you are xenophobic. I was hoping you wouldn't be. Adri told me you were carrying weapons when he first met you."

"We were in a strange environment," Jordan tried to explain. "Possibly hostile . . ."

She smiled at him. "But now you know better?"

"It's just that . . . well, as I said, it's rather overwhelming. Please give me a little time to get accustomed to all this."

Aditi looked at him thoughtfully for a moment, then said, "You can have all the time you need."

Turning, she began to explain that the farms were outside the energy dome that protected the city from weather. Jordan saw heavy-looking deep brown animals moving slowly along the rows of crops, with long snouts and flicking red tongues.

"Do those beasts tend the farms entirely on their own?" he asked.

"Mostly on their own," said Aditi. "They behave almost entirely by hardwired instinct. They have a very low order of intelligence."

"Like some of our politicians," he muttered.

"Politicians?" Aditi asked. Then, before Jordan could reply, she said, "Oh, you mean your leaders of government."

"Yes," Jordan said. Changing the subject, he asked, "The weather. Do you ever have serious storms? Storms strong enough to damage the crops?"

Aditi looked at him quizzically for a few heartbeats, as if she were searching her memory for the right answer. At last she replied, "Severe storms are very rare at this latitude. If one develops, we extend the energy shield to protect the fields."

"I see."

Aditi led him out into the farm. Jordan felt a tingle flicker through him as they stepped from the paved walkway onto the bare ground.

"We're outside the energy dome now, aren't we?" he said.

Aditi nodded. "Yes. Out in the open."

Squinting up at the sun, Jordan saw Sirius glowing a hot bluish white. And a smaller blaze of light not far from it. The Pup, he realized. Sirius's white dwarf companion.

"It must seem strange to you," Aditi said, "to see two suns in the sky."

"Everything here is strange," said Jordan. "Yet somehow . . . familiar."

They walked down the row of what looked to Jordan like newly sprouted cabbage. The sky was dotted with puffy white clouds. The earth at his feet looked soft, warm. He saw a beetle scurrying between sprouts.

"How old are you?" Aditi asked.

Surprised, he replied, "Fifty-two, if you must know."

"Oh! Was I impolite?"

"Only a little."

"I became one year old sixty-seven days ago," she said.

"One?"

Aditi laughed at his consternation. "Our orbit around Sirius takes thirty of your years."

"Oh. Of course."

Jordan looked in the direction they were walking. The cultivated fields seemed to end well short of the wooded hills that rose before them. Beyond the hills, craggy mountains rose, green with trees almost to their rocky crests. Darker clouds were building up above them.

"Our calendar is different from yours," Aditi said. "We have no moon, so we don't count months the way you do."

Jordan replied, "That's a shame. No beautiful moonlit nights."

"When the Pup swings in its orbit farther away from Sirius we have practically no nights at all. Just a sort of dim twilight."

"Moonlight can be very romantic," said Jordan.

"'The orbèd maiden, with white fire laden, whom mortals call the Moon,'" Aditi quoted.

"You know Shelley?"

"I love his poetry."

"You know so much about us," Jordan said, "and I know so little about you."

"We've been studying your world for a long time. More than nine years." Then she added, "Our years."

"Nearly three hundred Earth years. That goes back to before we invented radio."

Aditi nodded.

"Did you know that we existed . . . the human race, I mean?"

"We saw that your world seemed to be a duplicate of ours," she said.

"So naturally you studied it."

"Naturally."

"Yet you never developed space flight? No satellites, no astronauts?"

Aditi seemed to think about his question for a few heartbeats. Then, "There are no other planets in our system. And the other stars are so far away."

"So you were born here, on this planet?"

"I've lived here all my life," she replied, looking directly into his eyes. "I've never been anywhere else."

Jordan realized her eyes were very beautiful, a soft delightful brown.

"And Adri and all the others," Jordan heard himself asking, almost like a prosecutor questioning a witness, "they were born here too? They didn't come from another planet, another star system?"

She shook her head. "No. How could they?"

"I . . . I was just curious," he stammered.

She glanced up at the sky and Jordan looked up too. The clouds over the mountains were thickening.

"We'd better go back," Aditi said. "It looks like it's going to rain."

Jordan took her arm and pulled her to him and kissed her. Aditi looked surprised, startled even, her eyes wide and searching.

Then fat drops of rain began to spatter around them and, laughing like children, hand in hand, they ran back toward the shelter of the city's energy dome.

GUILT AND FEAR

Jordan spent the next two days almost constantly with Aditi. For the first time that he could remember, he put aside his duties and left it to Brandon to deal with the people on the ship while he spent every waking moment with the woman he found to be so delightful, so fascinating.

Fully human, he found himself thinking. I wonder how fully human she really is.

And Aditi seemed to enjoy his company. She showed him every corner of the city, and they took long walks out into the countryside.

He found himself unburdening his soul about Miriam.

"It was all my fault," he confessed one afternoon, as they sat on the grass beneath a spreading shade tree. "I was burning to stop the fighting in Kashmir."

"You wanted to prevent more people being killed in the war," Aditi said, very seriously. "Your motives were noble."

"My motives were very noble," Jordan answered bitterly. "I saw visions of the Nobel Peace Prize before my eyes."

"That wasn't your real motivation," she said.

"Wasn't it?" Jordan shook his head at the memories. "Whatever, I dragged Miriam into that hellhole with me, and it killed her."

"The monsters who used biological weapons killed her. Not you."

Leaning his head against the rough bark of the tree, Jordan said, "Yes, perhaps so. But I brought her there. I knew it would be dangerous, but I brought her there anyway. I should have protected her, cared for her. Instead . . ."

He saw that she was waiting for more, her gentle brown eyes focused on him, patiently waiting for him to finish the story.

"I loved her so much," Jordan choked out. "And she loved me. That was the wonder of it. She loved me. Loved me so much she let me lead her to her death."

Aditi leaned toward him and patted his tear-streaked cheek.

"The pain," he moaned. "Those last days . . . so terrible. I was so helpless . . . there was nothing I could do."

"Jordan," she whispered, her lips close enough to brush his cheek, "you are a good man. A very lovable man. Please don't be sad. Don't dwell on the past. Think of the future. Think of what you can accomplish."

He took a deep, shuddering breath and nodded once again. "We can't undo the past. But does it ever let go of you?"

"In time it will. In time."

Jordan's pocketphone chirped. He flinched at the interruption, thinking that he'd ignore it. Whatever it is, it can wait, he told himself.

Yet he reached into his shirt pocket and pulled the damned phone out and flipped it open.

Brandon's face appeared on the little screen.

"Time to get back to work, Jordy," his brother said, a crooked grin on his handsome face. "Hazzard's bringing the first group down in an hour."

Time to get back to work, Jordan repeated silently. He looked up at Aditi, who held her hand out to him. Together, they got to their feet and headed back to the city.

Jordan, Brandon, and Adri walked through the cool forest to the glade where Thornberry would set up the expedition's prime base. To his surprise, Jordan saw that both rocketplanes that had landed there days earlier were gone.

"Hazzard flew them back to the ship," Brandon explained before Jordan could ask. "Remotely, from the ship. Meek and de Falla rode one of them."

Brandon's phone chirped. As he flicked it open, Jordan looked over his brother's shoulder and saw Thornberry's heavy-browed face.

"We're on our way down to you," said the roboticist, grinning happily. "Hazzard's flying the bird in person, he is."

"Great," said Brandon. "Jordy and I are here at the glade, waiting for you."

"Be with you shortly," Thornberry said. Then the phone's little screen broke into hissing static and went blank.

"Plasma blackout," Brandon muttered.

Adri, standing on Jordan's other side, said, "I would like to invite your friends to stay in our city. We have adequate facilities to take care of them all."

Jordan smiled doubtfully. "I'm sure they'll appreciate the offer—and reject it."

"I don't see why," Adri said.

"A variety of reasons," said Jordan. "Adherence to the mission protocol, for one. Our mission plan made no provisions for finding a friendly native city on New Earth."

"But surely now that you know we are here, your plan can be altered, adapted."

Jordan shook his head. "Perhaps later, when the others get to know you better, get accustomed to you."

"Ahh," Adri said, understanding dawning on his face. "Fear. That is the greatest reason of them all, isn't it?"

"I'm afraid it motivates almost everything we do," Jordan admitted. "Almost everything."

CAMPING OUT

A double clap of deep thunder pealed across the grassy glade.

"They've gone subsonic," said Brandon.

"There they are!" Adri pointed a long arm. At first Jordan saw nothing, then the swept-wing shape of the rocket-plane came into his focus, trailing clean white contrails from its wingtips.

His eyesight must be considerably better than mine, Jordan thought.

"What a beautiful machine," said Adri, in an awed near-whisper.

Jordan tried to see the rocketplane through the alien's eyes. Yes, it is beautiful, he realized. Graceful as a swan, purposeful as an eagle.

The plane made a wide sweeping turn as it swooped lower, put down its landing gear, then came in over the trees at the far end of the glade and touched down smoothly on the grass. Jordan watched it roll across the glade, bumping gently on the slightly uneven ground, and finally come to a halt less than a hundred meters from where they stood.

Brandon started running toward the rocketplane, but Jordan called to him, "No rush, Bran. Hazzard will wait till she cools down before popping the hatch." Turning to Adri, he explained, "The plane will still be hot from its entry into the atmosphere."

Adri nodded. "The air friction generates considerable heat, I suppose."

Nodding back at him, Jordan thought, He understands physics. Or at least, aerodynamics.

He saw that Brandon was talking into his pocketphone.

". . . outside, waiting for you to pop the hatch and come out,"

Brandon was saying. Jordan thought his brother sounded impatient. As usual.

"Give us ten minutes." Hazzard's voice.

Brandon turned to Jordan and Adri, a big smile lighting his face. "Elyse is on board. She's here."

Jordan suppressed a chuckle. Bran wears his heart on his sleeve, he said to himself. Then he thought, Well, what have you been doing the past two days, old boy?

The hatch opened at last and the ship's ladder extended to the grassy ground. Hazzard was the first one to appear in the hatchway. He hesitated a moment, looked around, then clambered down the ladder in an easy, long-legged jog.

Thornberry came next, then Meek, Longyear, and at last Elyse Rudaki. Brandon rushed to her, as Silvio de Falla and Thornberry's assistant, Tanya Verishkova, followed down the ladder. Nara Yamaguchi, the last of them, blinked at the lip of the hatch, raised a hand to shield her eyes from the bright sunlight, then started down the ladder.

Thornberry eyed Jordan's gown with an impish grin. "So you've gone native, have you?"

"It's actually quite comfortable," Jordan said.

Once all seven of them were standing beside the ship, Adri said in a surprisingly powerful voice, "Welcome to New Earth."

Meek took one step forward and replied, "Thank you." Turning slightly to the others, he said, "This is Adri, the, eh . . ." His face contorted into a puzzled frown. "Eh, just what *is* your title, sir?"

Adri smiled placatingly and said, "We don't put much store in titles, I'm afraid. Just call me Adri."

"But what do you do?" Meek insisted. "What is your job here, your position?"

Spreading his hands slightly, Adri replied, "My task at the moment is to welcome you to this world, and to offer you accommodations in our city."

"Oh no!" Meek snapped. "No, no, I'm afraid we can't accept such an invitation. We're here to build our base of operations right here, at this location."

Jordan stepped in. "It's close enough to the city for easy visits back and forth."

"I see," said Adri. "I understand."

"We appreciate your offer of hospitality," Jordan went on. "In fact, I would like to remain in your city for at least a little longer."

Brandon smirked at his brother. "Now why am I not surprised at that?" he murmured.

Hazzard strode up. "The second rocketplane's due in a few minutes. I'll control it remotely from the bird we came in on." And he turned and trotted back toward the plane he had piloted.

BASE CAMP

Thornberry stood in the late-afternoon sunshine, his beefy arms folded across his chest, a satisfied smile on his face. Four large hemispherical shelters stood on the grassy glade, eggshell white, interconnected by metal mesh walkways laid across the grass. A half-dozen humanform robots had erected the bubble tents, and were now busily transferring equipment and supplies from the rocketplanes to the bubble tents' interiors.

Jordan and Adri stood with Thornberry while most of the other humans carried their personal effects into the shelters. They look like a column of worker ants, Jordan thought, intently busy. He noticed that Brandon and Elyse Rudaki walked together, their arms loaded with packages.

At least Bran will have some clean clothes, Jordan thought. He won't have to wash his underwear and socks in the bathroom sink anymore.

"We'll be able to live and work here indefinitely," Thornberry was telling Adri, "with resupplies from the ship, up in orbit."

"Your ship produces food for you?" Adri asked.

Nodding vigorously, Thornberry said, "Fruits and vegetables from hydroponics tanks, meatstuffs cultured from the biovats."

"We have extensive farms," said the alien. "Perhaps we could provide you with a wider variety of vegetable products, if you like. Meat, as well."

Thornberry glanced toward Meek, who was leading a robot laden with a heavy crate of equipment. "Perhaps later on," he said. "For now, our mission plan calls for us to stay independent of indigenous potential foodstuffs."

"I see. Of course."

"And we'll be making virtually zero impact on the local environment," Thornberry added, with some pride in his voice. "All our systems are closed-loop. We recycle practically everything."

Jordan watched Adri's spiderwebbed face, wondering if Thornberry's *virtual* and *practically* registered with him.

Meek came gangling up to them. "Well, we're almost finished. Our prime base is just about ready for occupation."

"May I invite all of you to dinner?" Adri asked. "A welcoming celebration."

Meek frowned mistrustfully. "I believe it would be better if we stayed in our own base, for now. Much better."

"You are suspicious of us, Dr. Meek."

"Yes, quite frankly I am," Meek replied. "I have no intention of hurting your feelings, sir, but I feel very strongly that we should follow our original mission protocol and begin to live as independently on this planet as we can."

Very seriously, Adri asked, "Do you intend to post guards while you sleep?"

Meek blinked at him. "The robots can fill that function, I suppose." He looked to Thornberry for confirmation.

"Oh, they make wonderful guards, they do," said the roboticist. "They never sleep, they're always on alert."

"Yet they can be deactivated," Adri said, with just a hint of mischief in his almond eyes.

Meek gaped at him.

Thornberry said, "I've been meaning to ask you about that, Adri. How did you shut down me two rovers, back when they first landed here?"

With a wintry smile, Adri said, "I'm afraid I'm not an engineer, as you are, sir. You'll have to speak with some of our technical specialists about that."

Thornberry looked decidedly unsatisfied.

Paul Longyear strode up to them. "We're finished unloading," the biologist reported. "The base is ready for business."

"Good," said Meek.

Jordan raised his voice to tell them, "I'm very proud of you, all of you. You've established the first human outpost beyond our own solar system."

"Well, that's what we're here for, isn't it?" said Meek.

Glancing at the westering suns, Adri said, "I'm afraid I must leave you now. I am truly glad that you've come here and I hope that you are comfortable in your independent base. Again, welcome to New Earth."

Jordan said, "I'll spend the night here with my companions, Adri."

"Understandable," the alien replied. "I'll tell Aditi."

Jordan felt his cheeks redden. "Yes. Thank you. Please tell her I'll see her tomorrow."

"I will," said Adri. Then he turned and began walking toward the trees and the path back to the city. Jordan saw him pull his pet from his robe and fondle it as he walked.

"Strange fellow," Thornberry murmured.

"What do you expect?" said Meek. "He's an alien."

Longyear watched Adri's retreating back for long moments, then finally said, "He doesn't seem worried about our coming here to his world."

"Should he be?" Jordan asked.

With his dark eyes fixed on Adri's departing figure, Longyear said, "I don't know. If an alien starship took up orbit around Earth and a team of aliens came down and started to build a camp, wouldn't we be worried about them? Suspicious of their motives?"

"For heaven's sake, they know our motives," Meek snapped. "They've been listening to our radio and television broadcasts for years."

"Centuries," Jordan corrected.

"I don't know," Longyear said slowly. "He just seems so . . . so cool about it all. Gives me the creeps."

"That's your Native American heritage talking," said Thornberry. "Adri's people have never been invaded and conquered by strangers."

"How do you know?" Longyear wondered.

Jordan said, "I don't think it's got anything to do with history or heritages."

"You don't?" Meek challenged. "Then what?"

"I think that Adri's people have a technology that's superior to ours. Much superior. They have no reason to be afraid of us because they know that we can't hurt them."

Thornberry rubbed his jaw. "Maybe we should be afraid of them."

WHAT'S IN A NAME?

The interiors of the plastic bubble tents were divided by two-meter-high partitions into cubicles that served as quarters for individuals, and wider areas for workshops and laboratories. The largest open area was for dining, and all nine of the landing team assembled there at the end of the day.

Jordan looked down the table at the eight of them. Hazzard had returned to *Gaia*. He, Trish Wanamaker, and Demetrios Zadar, the team's astronomer, planned to remain aboard the ship.

The dining area felt strangely cold to Jordan. It smelled new, unused. The dome of the bubble tent curved high above, lost in shadows. The tall partitions were bare, undecorated. Well, that will change over time, he told himself. This is our first night; after we've been here a while this place will start to feel more lived-in. More like home.

Two robots stood passively against the far partition of the dining area, awaiting the order to begin serving the meal. The nine people around the table were quiet, talking to each other in hushed whispers. They looked pensive, Jordan thought, uncertain, almost frightened.

He got to his feet and raised his glass of carbonated water. "Here's to our first night on New Earth. The first of many. We have a grand adventure ahead of us."

All the others raised their glasses, but without any real fervor.

"You may begin serving," Jordan said to the robots as he sat down. Both machines turned and went through the open doorway to the kitchen.

Brandon, on Jordan's right, asked, "Is that how you think of our mission: a grand adventure?"

"Why, don't you? We're on a new world, we've encountered intelligent humanlike people and their civilization. Just think of what's ahead for us!"

"That's what I wonder about," said Meek, sitting a few chairs farther down the table.

"This Adri is a pretty slick fellow," Thornberry said. "He answers our questions, but the answers don't seem to tell us anything."

"Do you trust him?" asked Elyse, who was sitting beside Brandon.

"If we trusted him," Brandon said, "we'd be having dinner in his city, instead of here."

Jordan said, "Bran, you and I have stayed at the city, we've partaken of Adri's hospitality. No harmful effects. Nothing sinister."

"It's just too confoundingly pat," Meek grumbled. "Too good to be true."

Longyear and several others nodded.

"Harmon," said Jordan gently, "perhaps you're looking a gift horse in the mouth."

"Beware of Greeks bearing gifts," Longyear muttered.

The robots glided into the room and began to place bowls of steaming soup before each person.

Jordan looked down the table at their suspicious faces. "Very well, you don't trust Adri and his people. What do we do about it?"

Brandon replied instantly, "We try to find out as much as we can about them. Who they really are. Where they come from."

"Adri says they were born here; they're natives of this planet," said Jordan.

"How can they be exactly like us?" Meek argued. "It's beyond the realm of belief."

Longyear countered, "They evolved on a planet just like Earth. Maybe it's convergent evolution, or parallel evolution, if you want to call it that. I mean, this is the first really Earthlike planet we've found. Maybe wherever the conditions are the same, the results are the same, too. Inevitable."

"I can't believe that," said Meek. "It goes against everything we know about biology. And statistics."

"Maybe it doesn't," Longyear replied. "I mean, we have two

examples of Earthlike environments and both of them have produced a human species."

De Falla spoke up. "That's another thing. How could this planet have survived the Pup's explosions? How could it possibly bear any life at all?"

"Zadar told me that Sirius can't be more than five hundred million years old," Meek chimed in. "That's not enough time for a planet to evolve such a complex biosphere."

"Especially if the Pup went through a nova phase and showered this planet with lethal radiation," said Meek.

Elyse said, "And this planet has no moon."

"What does that have to do with it?" Jordan asked.

"Earth's Moon acts as an anchor," she explained. "It keeps our axis of rotation from tipping over too far. Without a big moon serving as an anchor, this planet should wobble wildly, its climate should swing back and forth every few tens of thousands of years."

"Which would destabilize its ecosystems," Longyear said. "Ice ages and global warmings, one right after another."

"You see?" Meek said, almost triumphantly. "None of this adds up."

Jordan raised both hands. "All right. All right. We have a lot of questions to be answered. But for the moment, let's dig into this soup before it cools off."

Meek dipped his spoon into the soup, then looked up and said, "We should set up a systematic investigation. Paul, you start examining the local plant and animal life. Sylvio, you and Elyse should dig into the geology, see if there's evidence of damage from Sirius B's nova explosions."

Brandon said, "That's my area, too."

"Then you work with them."

"And Zadar can compute the range of the planet's axis shifts," Elyse suggested.

Jordan said, "Good. Let's put together an agenda for study. I'll question Adri about his people's history."

"We should've brought a cultural anthropologist with us," Brandon said.

"Who knew we'd need one?" said Thornberry, with a crafty grin.

Soon they were all firing questions back and forth, creating agendas, working out a map to be explored.

Jordan watched them at it while he quietly spooned up his soup. Hardly tasting the brew, he smiled inwardly. Now they're working instead of fretting, he told himself. They've replaced their suspicions with curiosity. Good.

And he thought that he would like to ask Aditi several thousand questions about her people, her society, her customs, herself.

The following morning, Jordan dressed in his own clothes, which had been brought down from the orbiting ship along with everyone else's. He could hear others coughing or splashing in the common lavatories. These partitions leave a lot to be desired as far as privacy is concerned, he thought.

He started for the dining area, but stopped at the open doorway to Brandon's cubicle. His brother was sitting at his desk, his phone open on the desktop, long lists of words scrolling down the big flat screen affixed to the desk.

"Hard at work this early?" Jordan called from the corridor. "I'm impressed."

Brandon looked up, the expression on his face dead serious.

"Come and look at this, Jordy."

Jordan stepped through the doorway and went to his brother's side. The screen showed lists of what seemed to be proper names, with definitions beside them.

"Elyse thought Adri's name sounded vaguely familiar to her. She thought she'd heard it somewhere before. So this morning I started poking through our files on names from various cultures."

"She thought she'd heard Adri's name before? Back on Earth?" Jordan asked.

"Take a look." Turning to the computer, he commanded, "Show name Adri."

The words on the screen dissolved, replaced by *Adri*, and a definition:

Minor god in Hindu mythology who protected mankind and once rescued the sun from evil spirits who were trying to extinguish it. Modern Hindu name meaning "rock."

Jordan blinked at the screen. "It must be a coincidence of some sort," he murmured, trying to convince himself. "A wild coincidence."

"Is it?" Brandon asked, his voice flat and hard. "Another coincidence? Aren't these coincidences getting beyond the realm of belief?"

Jordan said nothing.

"A completely Earthlike planet. Peopled by creatures who are totally like us. Now one of them has a Hindu name. That's way beyond coincidence, Jordy."

"Look up Aditi," Jordan said.

Brandon commanded the computer, and the screen instantly showed:

Aditi: Archaic mother goddess, Hindu (Vedic). Wife of Kasyapa or Brahma. Mother of rain god Indra, and of Hari and the Adityas. Perceived as a guardian goddess who brings prosperity and who can free her devotees from problems and clear away obstacles.

Jordan stared at the screen.

Brandon said, "That's no coincidence, Jordy. None of this is a coincidence. It can't be."

EXAMINATION

Jordan called Meek and Thornberry to Brandon's cubicle. They crowded the narrow space, bumping against the bed, the desk. There were no chairs; they had to stand and lean in behind Brandon. Once they looked at the names and their definitions, Meek said heatedly:

"I knew it. I knew it! They're not what they claim to be. None of this is natural. It can't be."

Jordan shook his head as he sat on the unmade bed. "An entire planet made to exactly resemble Earth? It beggars the imagination."

Thornberry shook his head. "Maybe what we're seeing is an illusion. Maybe we're being tricked."

"How could that be?" Jordan demanded.

"How could any of this be?" Brandon countered, still seated at his desk.

Meek stood hemmed in by the desk, the expression on his face radiating suspicion. "Things are not what they seem," he said, tapping the forefinger of his right hand into the palm of his left. "We're being tricked. Hoodwinked."

"But why?" Jordan asked, almost pleading. "Why would anyone go to all this trouble?"

"That's what you've got to find out," Meek said.

"Me?"

"You're on friendly terms with this Adri person. You should confront him, tell him that we know he's up to something."

Jordan ran a hand through his silver hair. "I suppose so," he said, reluctantly. To himself he added, I'm supposed to be the leader here. It's time for me to lead.

As he started down the path toward Adri's city, Jordan marveled again at how Earthlike the trees and shrubbery were. A squirrel-like creature scampered up one of the stately tall trees, a blur of gray fur. Then a dark buzzing little ball of purposeful energy, very much like a bee, zoomed past his ear, making him flinch. Birds glided through the foliage high above. Sunshine filtered through the forest canopy.

Meek and the others are right, Jordan thought. This is all too good to be true. Maybe it actually is an illusion, maybe Adri and his people have some way of reading our minds and then showing us what we want to see.

Suddenly Adri was on the path, walking slowly toward him, wearing his usual ankle-length grayish blue robe. Jordan noticed that it bore an intricate design, fine threads making delicate loops and curves.

"Good morning," Jordan called to the alien.

"And a very pleasant good morning to you, friend Jordan," said Adri, with a warm smile.

He seems so friendly, Jordan thought. So happy to see me.

"I was going to the city to find you," said Jordan.

"I was going to your camp to find you," Adri said.

"I have a lot of questions to ask you."

Nodding, Adri said, "I'm sure you do. I hope I can answer them all to your satisfaction."

They started walking side by side, through the rich green foliage and the warm dappled sunlight, toward the city. Adri reached into the folds of his robe and pulled out a tiny creature, no bigger than the palm of his hand. He stroked its dark fur soothingly.

He noticed Jordan staring at the animal. "Pets can be a very good relaxation implement," he said, almost apologetically.

Is he nervous? Jordan wondered. Worried?

"What is it that you want to know?" Adri asked.

"All this is not what it seems, is it?" Jordan began.

Adri blinked. "I don't understand you."

With a wide sweep of his arm, Jordan said, "This planet, your city, you yourselves . . . it's all an illusion that you're producing to make us feel comfortable about you."

"Oh no. No, no, no," Adri said, his voice soft but the expression on his face troubled, distressed. "I assure you, this is how I look. I'm as human as you are, truly."

"It's so very hard to accept."

Smiling gently, Adri said, "I believe you have a saying, 'What you see is what you get.'"

"How can you have exactly the same form as we do? It goes against everything we know."

Adri's smile widened slightly. "Then you are learning something new. That is progress, isn't it?"

Jordan stopped and planted his fists on his hips. "Adri, my friend, I'm afraid that I don't believe you. I *can't* believe you."

Adri stood in silence for a few heartbeats, stroking his furry pet, apparently thinking it over. "Would it help if I went back to your camp with you and allowed your people to examine me?"

Surprised by his offer, Jordan said, "Yes, I believe it would."

"Then let's do that, by all means." Adri turned around and started heading for the camp.

Jordan caught up with him in a few strides and walked alongside the alien, who slid his pet back inside his robe.

"I appreciate your willingness to let us examine you," Jordan said, almost apologetically.

Adri murmured, "Doubting Thomas."

"From the Bible."

"Yes."

Suddenly embarrassed, Jordan stammered, "I . . . I don't mean to call you . . . I mean, well, it's only natural for us to doubt such coincidences."

"You've been to so many worlds that you know that this one is anomalous," Adri said, almost seriously.

"No, this is the first—" Then Jordan realized that Adri was bantering with him. He laughed and the two of them walked side by side back to the humans' camp.

Adri patiently allowed Meek and Longyear to examine him. X-rays, magnetic resonance imaging, tissue samples, neutrino scans: all revealed a completely human body. Even his tiny pet, which Adri clutched in both hands through the examination, closely matched a species of miniature terrestrial prairie dog. Scans of Adri's brain were strikingly similar to scans of the humans in the computer files.

The alien seemed to take all the prodding and scanning with good grace. He accepted lunch with Jordan, Brandon, and Elyse while Meek and Longyear studied the results of their tests. His furry pet remained hidden inside his robe.

"Aditi was asking about you," Adri said as they sat in the dining room, munching on sandwiches.

Jordan felt his heart leap.

"About your name," Brandon said, his face showing suspicion. "And hers."

"They are from your Hindu culture," Adri replied easily. "I'm afraid you would find our names, in our own language, impossible to pronounce."

"We seem to have the same vocal equipment," Brandon said, almost accusingly.

Adri acknowledged the point with a dip of his chin. "Yes, of course. But it would take you quite a bit of time to learn how to make the sounds we make quite naturally."

"You learn your language in childhood, of course," said Jordan.

"Of course," Adri said.

They spent the afternoon in more examinations, more tests. Dr. Yamaguchi gave Adri a standard physical exam, testing his reflexes, muscular coordination, even his eyesight. Adri accepted it all with an accommodating smile. Through it all his little pet sat in a corner of Yamaguchi's cubicle, silent and still, its bright eyes watching.

At last, late in the day, they had gone through every test they could think of.

"If there's nothing more," Adri told Jordan, "I should return to the city now."

Jordan walked with him partway along the trail through the forest.

"You must come to the city tomorrow," Adri said, once Jordan stopped. "Aditi would like to see you again."

"I would very much like to see her," Jordan heard himself admit.

With a smiling nod, Adri said, "Tomorrow, then. Perhaps you would be good enough to let our people examine you."

Surprised, Jordan burst into laughter. "Certainly! Turnabout is fair play."

Adri laughed too. Then he turned and started along the trail once more. "Until tomorrow, then," he called to Jordan.

Once Jordan got back to the base he found Meek, Longyear, and Thornberry waiting for him at the entrance to the main shelter. They looked grim.

"Well," said Jordan, "Adri's as human as you or I, isn't he?"

Meek said, "More than you know."

"What do you mean?"

"Come with us," said Meek.

They led Jordan to Longyear's biology lab. The biologist called up the scans he had done on Adri's DNA.

Jordan peered at the screen's display. "It looks perfectly normal to me. Of course, I'm no expert—"

"It is perfectly normal," said Longyear, almost in a growl. "That's human DNA. From Earth."

EARTH

———————

Whoever fights monsters should see to it that in the process he does not become a monster. And when you look long into an abyss, the abyss also looks into you.

FRIEDRICH WILHELM NIETZSCHE

The president of the United States turned to the sweeping painting that covered one wall of the Oval Office and angrily called out: "Show Honolulu!"

The painting—portraits of all the presidents of the twentieth century, from Theodore Roosevelt to Bill Clinton—dissolved into an aerial camera's view of a city devastated by an immense typhoon. Streets were flooded, roofs torn away, windows smashed, the line of luxury hotels along Waikiki Beach empty and dark while waves surged up the broad beach to smash through shattered glass partitions and into their lobbies.

The television's sound was muted, but the president and his visitor both winced as if they could hear the roar of the waves, the howl of the wind, the crashing, ripping sounds of destruction.

"That's my home," said Kaholo Newton, from behind his gleaming broad desk. His voice choked with a mix of misery and anger, he added, "I grew up there, right there, in Waikiki. Now it's all gone. All gone."

"Mr. President," said Felicia Ionescu, in a hushed voice, "I know there are many demands on you—"

"But you're here to add one more, aren't you?" Newton said, practically sneering at the woman.

The two of them were alone in the Oval Office: no aides, no secretaries, no one to record what they said. Kaholo Newton was a native Hawaiian, a small brown-skinned man with luxuriant thick dark hair and iron-hard eyes of ebony. He seldom got up from behind his desk when visitors arrived in the Oval Office: to do so would have revealed his diminutive stature. He was especially wary of standing in the presence of Ionescu, who towered over him.

"Mr. President," Ionescu began again, "there are twelve men and women on the exploration team at New Earth. They are alone, farther from Earth than any human being has yet gone. They expect a backup mission to be sent to help them."

President Newton scowled disdainfully. "Don't try to con me, Felicia. We both know that those twelve people don't expect any help from us. They volunteered for their mission, knowing they'd be completely on their own."

"But we owe it to them—"

"Owe? We *owe* them?" the president fairly shouted. "What about the people of Honolulu? What about the people of Hawaii? What about my family, my mother and three sisters? They're all missing!"

"I didn't know," Ionescu admitted, her voice low.

President Newton closed his eyes and pulled in a deep, calming breath. It was a technique he had used many times: give a visitor the impression that you are struggling masterfully to control yourself.

"What do the Chinese say about this backup mission?" he asked.

Ionescu squirmed slightly in her chair in front of the president's desk. "They . . . they haven't committed themselves, as yet. I believe they are waiting to see what the United States will do."

"And Chiang? As head of the World Council he must have considerable influence on the people in Beijing. They wouldn't hang him out to dry; it would be a terrible loss of face for one of their own."

"Chairman Chiang is . . . reluctant to commit himself."

"Ah! So there you are."

"I thought," Ionescu said haltingly. "I thought . . . that if America announces it will support the mission . . . if America would lead the way . . ." Her voice trailed off.

The president shook his head. "Impossible. We can't take money away from reconstruction and recovery projects to send another gaggle of scientists out there."

"But—"

"Maybe when the people already there send in their reports about what they've found," the president offered.

"We won't receive any word from them for eight years," Ionescu said.

The president spread his hands and almost smiled. "All right, eight years. Maybe by then the climate situation will have calmed down somewhat. Maybe by then we can think about sending out another mission. Especially if the news from New Earth is interesting enough."

What the president did not say was that by then, eight years into the unguessable future, he would be safely retired and some other person would have to face the responsibility of paying for another mission to New Earth.

DISCOVERIES

Whatever nature has in store for mankind, unpleasant as it may be, men must accept, for ignorance is never better than knowledge.

ENRICO FERMI

TURNABOUT

The following morning, as Jordan left his cubicle and headed for the camp's dining hall, Brandon fell in step beside him.

"Good morning, Jordy."

"Morning, Bran."

"Going to the city this morning?"

"That's my intention."

Brandon said, "I was talking with Thornberry and Meek last night. They think it would be a good idea if you kept your phone on, so we can record what Adri and the others say to you."

Jordan felt his brows knit. "Record . . . ?"

"I think it's a good idea."

"Do you?"

Brandon broke into one of his boyish smiles. "Oh, you can turn it off when you're alone with Aditi."

Jordan did not smile back at him.

As he walked the trail through the forest toward the city, Jordan felt the phone in his shirt pocket weighing like a guilty conscience.

Bran's right, he told himself. We should be recording everything. Still, he felt it was somehow a sneaky thing to do, a betrayal of trust.

Then he saw Aditi standing on the stone walkway that circled the city, smiling warmly at him, and he forgot about the phone.

"Good morning," he called, hurrying his steps toward her.

"Good morning to you," she called back. And all Jordan's doubts and fears about these aliens and their intentions melted away in the warmth of her greeting.

He resisted the urge to take her in his arms. Instead he simply extended his hand. She took it in her own.

"Adri told me about his physical examination," she said as they began to walk down the city's broad central avenue. The street was busy with men and women, some strolling idly, others striding purposefully, as if on some important business. Aditi's pet feline was nowhere in sight.

"Today it's my turn to be poked and prodded," Jordan said, trying to make it sound light, pleasant.

Very seriously, Aditi replied, "No one is going to touch you. All the tests are noninvasive."

"Of course," he said. The irony in his voice was lost on her.

"I will be in charge of your examination," Aditi said, rather proudly.

Somewhat surprised, Jordan asked, "You're a medical technician, as well as a teacher?"

She hesitated, then replied, "I've had the training. All of us are capable of many tasks."

They were heading for the main building, Jordan saw. Behind it was the dormitory where he and Brandon had been housed.

As if she could read his mind, Aditi asked, "Will you be staying here tonight?"

"I'd like to," he admitted. "I'll have to call back and tell the others first."

"Of course," she said.

As they neared the main building's stately flight of entrance steps, Jordan asked, "And Adri, what tasks is he trained for?"

Again that little hesitation, as if she were checking through her memory for the correct answer. Or waiting for instructions. At last Aditi said, "Adri is our . . . historian. I think that is the best way to describe his duties."

"Historian?"

"He deals with the past," she said. Then she added, "And the future."

"I don't understand."

Her lovely face puckered into an almost troubled frown, as if she were struggling to find the right words to explain it to him.

"I think that's the best way to describe it," Aditi said. "Adri studies the past of our people, and yours, and makes projections of what the future might be like."

"The future of my people?"

"Yes. Naturally."

"I'd like to see what he has to say about that," Jordan said.

"I'm sure he'd be happy to discuss it with you."

They walked the rest of the way in thoughtful silence. As they started up the stairs of the main building, Jordan asked, "How far back does your history go?"

"Millions of years," Aditi answered. "Our years. We have existed for a very long time."

"Back on Earth we wonder how long the human race can survive. You give me hope."

"An intelligent race can survive almost indefinitely. Especially if it is intelligent enough to adapt to changing environments."

"Ah," said Jordan. "That's the key, then, isn't it? How intelligent are we?"

Very seriously, Aditi said, "The key is the ability to give up outworn concepts, modes of behavior that no longer work for survival."

"What do you mean by that?"

"Your people back on Earth have survived ice ages and pandemic plagues and your own aggressive, xenophobic nature. The question before you now is whether the strengths that have helped you to survive have become countersurvival in the face of new dangers."

"You mean the greenhouse climate shift?"

"That's part of the problem you face. You seem to have overcome the move toward authoritative governments—dictatorships. But there are new challenges that face you."

"New challenges? Beyond the climate shift?"

"Yes."

"What are they?"

Aditi did not answer for several heartbeats. At last she said, "You should speak to Adri about that. He's the expert in that field, not I."

They had reached the top of the stairs, and Aditi led him through the building's central corridor to a set of rooms that looked to Jordan like a clinic. The area smelled faintly of antiseptics. People spoke in whispers.

She led him confidently through the warren of hallways to a room that looked to Jordan like a laboratory: the walls were lined with consoles that hummed softly. In the middle of the room stood a tall glass-walled booth. No one else was in the room; they were alone.

Pointing to the booth, Aditi said, "If you'll step in there, I can scan your body."

With a slightly mischievous grin, Jordan asked, "Should I take off my clothes?"

She actually blushed. "No, not at all. That won't be necessary."

Jordan stepped into the booth.

"Close the door, please," Aditi said as she walked to the equipment set along the wall.

Jordan pulled the glass door shut.

"Please stand still for a moment."

He did. He even held his breath. He heard a brief buzz, felt nothing. Aditi had her back to him, studying the gauges and display screens.

"Good," she said. "You can come out now."

"That's it?" he asked.

"That's it," she said, still intently peering at the readouts. "We have a complete picture of you, down to the molecular level."

"That was easy."

But Aditi said, "The scans show you had a virus in your lower intestinal tract that could potentially be dangerous—even fatal."

"It's dormant," Jordan said. Still, he couldn't suppress the shudder of fear that went through him.

Then he realized that she'd said "had."

Before he could ask her, Aditi said, "I eliminated it."

His knees went weak. Jordan squeaked, "Eliminated it?"

"Actually, the equipment automatically destroyed the virus," Aditi said. "I should have asked your permission first, I know. I hope you don't mind."

Jordan laughed shakily. "I don't mind. I don't mind at all."

She eliminated the virus, Jordan said to himself over and over. Just like that, a tap of the finger and the virus is gone. The idea whirled through his thoughts as Aditi led him up a winding stairway, toward Adri's office.

"Your technology is quite impressive," he said, walking alongside her. "Far ahead of ours."

"In some ways, yes," Aditi murmured.

"Yet you've never developed space flight. I find that rather odd."

With a sidelong glance, she said, "We develop technology to solve problems. Disease has been a problem for both our peoples. It's that simple."

Is it? Jordan wondered silently.

Adri's office turned out to be a spacious, sunlit, airy room on the top floor of the building, with long windows that looked out on the city's stone buildings and busy streets. Not a vehicle in sight, Jordan noticed. Pedestrian traffic only. And genetically engineered animals.

Like the building's corridors, the walls of the office were covered with graceful swirling abstracts. There was no desk, no sign of hierarchy; merely comfortable-looking furniture scattered about the room.

Adri was seated on a long, curving couch when they entered the room. He rose gracefully to his feet and went toward Jordan, arms extended in greeting. In his floor-length robe he seemed to be gliding across the smoothly tiled floor.

"My friend Jordan," he said, in his thin, whispery voice. "It's good to see you again."

"It's good to see you, too, Adri," said Jordan.

"I'm glad that Aditi was able to remove a potentially life-threatening virus from your body," Adri said as he pointed Jordan toward the couch where he'd been sitting.

Jordan turned to Aditi. "How in the world did you—"

Before she could answer Adri said, "The readouts of your medical examination were transmitted to me here automatically. I hope you don't mind."

"No, I suppose not." Jordan looked around the room but he saw no display screens, no communications equipment of any kind.

Gently taking Jordan's arm with one hand, Adri pointed toward the ceiling with the other. "Holographic projectors," he explained. "All the hardware is out of sight."

Jordan allowed the alien to lead him to the couch. He sat on it, and Aditi sat beside him. Adri crooked a finger at a plush armchair and it rolled across the floor to him. He sat in it, facing Jordan.

Suddenly a medical diagnostic console appeared before Jordan's startled eyes, beeping softly, its screens showing glowing curved lines.

"A hologram," Adri said, with a nonchalant shrug.

"I see," said Jordan.

Just as suddenly, the hologram winked out.

"Your people are comfortable in their base camp?" Adri asked.

With a nod, Jordan replied, "Reasonably so. I'm sorry that they seem so . . ." he searched for a word, "so apprehensive about you. Suspicious."

"That's quite natural, I suppose."

Aditi said, "It's one of those survival traits that has become countersurvival."

"Perhaps so," Jordan granted. "But you must admit, all this is a lot to swallow."

"Yes, I suppose it is," Adri said. "What can I do to make the situation better?"

"You can start by telling me more about yourselves. Aditi tells me you've existed for millions of years."

"Our civilization has, yes. Our culture."

"And you've never developed space flight?"

Adri glanced at Aditi, then said, "We live on this planet. We have no need of space flight."

"Yet you've apparently been studying Earth for some time."

"Many of your centuries."

"From here, on the ground."

"We have optical and radio telescopes. We've listened to your radio and watched your television broadcasts. We've tapped into your digital webs. We've mapped and measured your planet. You exist in a very rich solar system: it's filled with planets of astounding variety. And moons, asteroids, comets. No wonder you went into space. We have nothing here but our one lonely world."

"But if you have telescopes of such sensitivity, why didn't you try to contact us? Why didn't you tell us you're here?"

"Fear," said Adri, quite flatly.

"Fear?"

"Your people are still decidedly aggressive. And xenophobic. You still have racial tensions among your own kind. The sudden announcement of an equally intelligent species would create severe problems for you."

"So you waited for us to find you."

"Yes, we did."

Jordan shook his head. "That must have taken enormous patience. How long have you known of our existence?"

"We observed your cities and the pollution you poured into your atmosphere. We heard your earliest radio transmissions."

"And all that time you waited."

Aditi said, "We waited in hope that you would find us and reach out to us."

"Which you have done," said Adri. "And we have welcomed you."

"Yes," said Jordan. "The question now is, where do we go from here?"

MOTIVATIONS

Without an instant's hesitation, Adri replied, "Why, we try to help one another, of course."

"Help? In what way?"

Aditi said, "We can offer you medical technology that is far advanced over your own."

"And the energy shields," Adri added.

"Yes, they would both be welcomed. But what can we offer you?"

"Understanding," said Adri.

Jordan felt puzzled. "Understanding?"

Adri nodded. "Yours is a large, aggressive species. How many people are there on Earth now?"

"Something like twenty billion. The recent spate of flooding has apparently killed a good many, of course, but the latest census figures I remember put the total in the twenty billion range."

"Twenty billion," Adri murmured.

"We are only a few thousand," said Aditi.

"Thousand?"

"Yes," Adri said. "Our numbers are very small. Frankly, we've been afraid of you. You could swallow us up in one gulp."

"That's why you haven't contacted us," Jordan realized.

"Your history is filled with the unfortunate consequences of contact between one group of people and another. The Neanderthals, for example. The Native Americans."

Jordan suddenly understood Paul Longyear's hard-eyed suspicions.

"So you waited until we reached out to you."

"It seemed the best course of action for us," Adri said. "Now that we have made contact, our future is in your hands."

"Yet you could have remained hidden," Jordan said. "You shielded your city from our ship's sensors. We had no idea you were here."

"If we had stayed hidden, what would have happened?" Adri asked. "You would have landed and started to explore this planet. Sooner or later you would have stumbled upon us."

"And destroyed us," Aditi said glumly.

"No! Why would we do that? How could we do it?"

Smiling gently, Adri said, "Friend Jordan, not every human being is as civilized as you. Twenty billion of you! How many would come here, to this world? How quickly would they turn it into a replica of the disaster they have created on their own home world?"

"We would be wiped out," Aditi repeated.

Jordan said nothing for a moment, his thoughts spinning. Then, "And now that we've found you, that danger exists."

"It does indeed," said Adri.

"What are you going to do about it?" Aditi asked.

Her face was unutterably sad, Jordan saw. As if I've just condemned her entire race to extinction.

"What can I do about it?" he wondered aloud.

Adri said, "That is one of the problems that face us."

"One of the problems? There are others?"

"Oh, yes. But let us deal with this first problem first."

"You are a test case for us," Aditi said. "If we can make you understand, then perhaps there is a chance that contact between our two peoples can be beneficial."

"And if not?"

Adri sighed heavily. "You are slightly more than eight light-years from Earth. Your transmissions of information back to your home world will take eight-some years to reach their destination."

Jordan nodded.

Looking slightly guilty, Adri said, "Your messages to Earth are not getting through. I'm afraid we've blocked your transmissions."

"Blocked them? How?"

"It's only temporarily, until we decide whether we should proceed with you."

"And if you decide not to proceed?"

"Then your messages back to Earth will be permanently blocked. Earth will decide that your mission somehow met with disaster."

"They'll think we're all dead," Jordan realized.

"You will not be allowed to return," said Adri. "You will have to stay here."

"With us," Aditi said.

Jordan sat there for long, silent moments, trying to digest it all. *If we don't measure up to Adri's standards we won't be allowed to return to Earth. The people back home will think we've been killed.*

Yet he found himself thinking, *Well, would that be so terrible?* He looked at Aditi's young, lovely face: so earnest, so caring. And he thought, *Earth's a madhouse, filled with self-seeking egoists who've wrecked the planet. What do I owe them? They killed my wife. They did nothing while the global climate spiraled out of control. Why not stay here and live with these people? With Aditi.*

At last he rose from the couch. Aditi stood up beside him.

"I'll have to talk this over with the others. They've got to know what's at stake."

Adri slowly, stiffly got to his feet. "By all means. Tell them that we would be happy to have them stay here and join us."

Jordan smiled bleakly. "You would be happy, I can believe that. But they won't be."

REACTIONS

hey'd force us to stay here?" Thornberry's beefy face twisted into an angry scowl.

"We're their prisoners!" Meek wailed.

Jordan had returned to the base camp and called a meeting of the entire team. Aditi had wanted to accompany him, but Jordan decided that it would be better for her to remain in the city.

Now they sat around the long table in the dining area, looking just as angry and fearful as Jordan had expected. At the foot of the table a display screen showed Geoff Hazzard, Trish Wanamaker, and Demetrios Zadar, still aboard the orbiting ship. Hazzard looked grim, hostile. Trish and the astronomer seemed puzzled, confronted with a problem they had never expected.

Standing at the head of the table, Jordan spread both arms to quiet them down. "You can understand how afraid of us they are," he said.

"They're afraid of us?" Meek said, incredulous. "Hah!"

Longyear shook his head doggedly. "I say we go back aboard *Gaia* and drag our tails out of here."

"Would they try to stop us?" Elyse wondered.

Thornberry said, "If they could deactivate my two rovers, I imagine they could conk out our rocketplane."

Looking more alarmed than ever, Meek said, "You mean they could keep us here against our will?"

"I suppose that's better than killing us," Brandon said with a sardonic grin.

"I knew it!" Meek shouted. "I knew it. We're all going to be murdered in our beds."

"Don't be an ass," Brandon snapped.

"Now look here, young man—"

"Stop it!" Jordan commanded. "Settle down and stop bickering, both of you. This is exactly the kind of reaction that Adri fears from us: emotion instead of rationality."

Brandon smiled crookedly at his brother. "All right, Jordy. What's the rational approach to this?"

Before Jordan could reply, de Falla said, "The first thing to do is to see if the ship's systems will work."

"Everything's working so far," said Hazzard, from the display screen. "'Course, we haven't had to fire up the fusion drive."

"Could you check out the propulsion system without lighting it off?" Longyear asked.

"Sure. That's what I'll do."

"Fine," Jordan said. "That's a reasonable first step. But it doesn't get to the heart of our problem."

"Which is?" Brandon prompted.

"How do we convince Adri and his people that Earth is not a threat to them?"

That silenced them. Even Meek looked thoughtful. But the silence lasted only a moment.

Thornberry said, "Seems to me our real problem is how do we counter their ability to knock out our vehicles. If we learn how to do that, we'll be able to leave whenever we want to."

Jordan nodded. "A good point. And there's only one way to learn that: by working with Adri's people. By letting them show us their capabilities, teach us their technology."

Elyse objected, "Do you think they'd be naïve enough to tell us anything useful?"

"Perhaps not," Jordan admitted. "But for the present, I think our best course of action—perhaps our *only* course of action—is to play along with them, show them we harbor no enmity toward them, show them that we're eager to learn from them."

"And we can offer to teach them our technology," Brandon added. "After all, they don't have space flight."

"They don't seem to have any transportation vehicles at all," Jordan said.

"That's very odd," said Thornberry. "If they don't have vehicles of their own, how do they know enough to deactivate ours?"

Longyear piped up. "I'd like to find out how their DNA matches ours. Was there some contact between us and them in the past?"

"But they don't have space flight," said Dr. Yamaguchi. "How could there have been any contact?"

"There must have been," Longyear insisted. "You can't get identical DNA without contact of some kind. Maybe both our races come from some third species."

"An interstellar pollinator?" Brandon scoffed. "Like Arrhenius's panspermia theory? Get real, Paul."

Longyear frowned.

"Be that as it may," said Jordan, trying to maintain control of the meeting, "we have an agenda of goals to reach for."

"We do?" asked Meek.

"Yes, we do," Jordan replied. Pointing to Hazzard, "Geoff, you check out the ship's propulsion system. We might decide to leave here right away."

Hazzard nodded.

"I've got to return to the city and tell Adri that we've decided to work with him and his people. Who's willing to join me?"

"Not I," Meek snapped. "I'm not going to set foot in their city, not willingly."

"I'll go," said Brandon. "And I'll ask Adri to put me in touch with whatever passes for a geologist among his folks."

"I'll go, too," Elyse said.

Jordan felt mildly surprised. He surmised that she wanted to be close to Brandon, but he had to ask, "What can an astrophysicist accomplish—"

Before he could finish the sentence Elyse said, "You mentioned that they have advanced telescopes. I would like to see them, study them. This could be an unprecedented chance to study a white dwarf up close."

"I see," Jordan replied, trying not to smile at her. "Of course." And he thought, I want to be close to Aditi; she wants to be close to Bran. From the look on Brandon's face, he saw that his brother wanted to be close to Elyse, as well.

"I want to go," Thornberry said. "There's a lot for us to learn, there is."

"I'll go, too," Longyear added, although he didn't look very happy about it. "You'll need a biologist, and I want to figure out how their DNA can be so much like ours."

"Five of us, then," said Jordan.

Meek wagged his head from side to side. "I don't like it. I don't like it at all. I tell you, you're putting yourselves into the lions' den."

"Perhaps so, Harmon," Jordan replied. "But I seem to recall an old adage, 'Behold the lowly turtle: he only makes progress when he sticks his neck out.'"

The others around the table laughed feebly. Meek made a sour face.

As soon as the meeting broke up, Jordan and the four others headed for the city. It was nearly sunset when they left the base camp. The shadows of twilight lengthened as they marched along the forest trail. Jordan realized he didn't know how to contact Adri with his pocketphone, yet he had the feeling that Adri knew perfectly well that he was coming.

Sure enough, the alien was standing at the edge of the city, on the stone walk that circled the buildings, practically beaming at the five approaching humans.

But Aditi was not with him.

"Welcome, my friends," said Adri, extending both arms to them.

"We're here to begin the process of learning to get along together," Jordan said. In his own ears, the pronouncement sounded slightly pompous.

But Adri's aged face smiled at him. "Very good. But let's have dinner first."

Aditi joined them for dinner, and Jordan felt happy and relaxed at last.

Jordan woke up the next morning feeling truly rested. His bedroom in the city was almost like home to him: he felt comfortable in it, at ease. The room wasn't spacious, yet it felt pleasantly airy. Its only window looked out on a charming courtyard, colorful with blossoming shrubbery and a stately tree at its center. Even the hummingbird buzzing overhead seemed familiar, friendly.

He hoped that Brandon felt the same way, then wondered if Bran were in his own room or down the hall with Elyse.

Staring up at the high ceiling, he thought of Aditi. Except for that one quick kiss in the rain a few days earlier, Jordan had not made any romantic moves on her. He wanted to, the physical urge was definitely there, but thoughts of Miriam rose in his mind. Her ghost separated them.

For her part, Aditi had seemed pleasant enough through dinner, a warm, happy young woman who laughed easily and sparkled with intelligence. Yet she seemed content to be a friend, a companion, and nothing more. There was a limit to her friendliness, he could feel it, like an electric fence.

While the dessert was being served, Jordan asked her about her people's customs regarding marriage and family.

"I've never been married," she said, as if surprised by his question.

"But your people do marry," he pressed.

She glanced at Adri, seated beside her. "Yes," she said slowly, almost reluctantly. "Marriage is rare among us, though. Our birth rate is so low that there is little need for marriage and child rearing."

"But you do marry."

She finally understood. "Yes," Aditi answered with an amused smile. "But marriage isn't necessary for a couple to have a sexual relationship."

And suddenly Jordan felt tongue-tied. He turned his attention to his dessert and hoped none of the others noticed his burning cheeks.

Lying in his bed, Jordan remembered the moment and his embarrassment. Like a pimple-faced teenaged bumpkin, he said to himself. Like a foolish—

His phone chirped, interrupting his musings. He sat up and reached for it on the bedside table.

Geoffrey Hazzard's face filled the little screen, dark, unsmiling.

"Good morning, Geoff," Jordan said. "You're up pretty early, aren't you?"

Hazzard broke into a sardonic little smile. "You've slept pretty late, haven't you?"

The clock readout at the bottom of the phone's screen showed it was precisely 8 A.M. New Earth's spin rate was almost exactly the same as Earth's, to within a few milliseconds. Another coincidence that seemed too good to be true. But there it was, coincidence or not.

"I'm getting lazy, I admit it," Jordan said, suppressing a yawn. "How's everything aboard the ship?"

"That's what I'm calling about."

Jordan felt a pang of alarm. "Something wrong?"

"Not with the ship," said Hazzard. "All systems check out solidly in the green. Nothing wrong with the fusion drive."

"Then why are you calling?"

"Half an hour ago our sensors detected a major flare on the Pup. It's putting out a lot of energy. Looks like we're going to be hit by a major radiation storm."

"Is it dangerous?"

"Could be. I've stepped up the power for our magnetic shielding. It'll stop the protons, they're the biggest danger, but a lot of gamma and X-ray radiation's going to zip right through the magnetic field."

"You'll have to spend a few hours in the storm cellar, then."

Hazzard frowned slightly. "More like a couple of days."

"I see."

"I was thinking maybe we could come down to the surface for a day or so, stay at the base camp."

"And be protected by the planet's atmosphere."

"Beats sitting in the damned coffin for hours on end."

"What about the ship's systems? Will they be damaged?"

"They're hardened. Should be okay. If there's damage we could repair it afterward."

Jordan thought swiftly. "All right, come on down, then. I'll alert Thornberry and the others."

The astronaut broke into a big, bright smile. "Thanks, Jordan. I'll tell Trish and Demetrios."

Hazzard's image winked out. Jordan put in a conference call to the others in the city and asked them to meet him in his quarters immediately.

"A solar storm?" Elyse said, suddenly excited. "I'll have to get to the observatory! I can observe the planet's magnetosphere and its interaction with the plasma cloud. This is wonderful!"

She and Brandon were in the sitting room that connected Jordan's bedroom with his brother's. It was obvious that she had spent the night with Brandon.

Thornberry, slumped on one of the armchairs, was less excited about the impending storm. "Could be trouble for the ship's electronic systems," he muttered, rubbing his stubbled chin.

"What about the propulsion engines?" Jordan asked.

Thornberry made an elaborate shrug. "Might fry the electronic controls, but it shouldn't hurt the engines themselves. They see plenty of radiation when the fusion reactor's burning, they do."

Longyear looked thoughtful as he sat in the other armchair, leaning his chin on his fists. "Hazzard and the others ought to be safe enough in the storm cellar," he mused.

"He's asked to come down to the base camp," said Jordan. "And I agreed."

"Then there'll be nobody in the ship?" Thornberry asked.

"For a day or two," Jordan said.

Thornberry chuckled. "I can just hear Meek shrieking when he finds out about that."

"What would Meek have to complain about?" Brandon asked.

"He'll say this flare was caused by Adri, to get us to abandon the ship, so he can have all of us in his grip here on the ground."

The others laughed, weakly. Jordan wondered if Meek would be right.

SHIELDING

The little meeting broke up. Elyse—with Brandon at her side—left to go to the astronomical observatory on the other side of the city. Thornberry and Longyear hurried out to the buggy that the roboticist had parked at the city's edge and headed back to the base camp, to inform Meek and the others that Hazzard, Trish Wanamaker, and Demetrios Zadar were on their way to join them.

Standing alone in his suddenly emptied sitting room, Jordan decided he'd better talk to Adri and see what he knew about the upcoming solar storm.

He called out to the room's communications system, "Contact Adri, please."

Almost instantaneously the wall screen showed Adri. He looked up from where he was sitting, apparently slightly surprised. Adri appeared to be in conference with a half-dozen younger men and women, sitting on the chairs and couches scattered about his spacious room.

"Oh, yes, the radiation storm," Adri said, nodding slightly. "I was just informed of it by our astronomers."

"So they're aware of it."

"Of course." Adri hesitated a moment, then went on, "Why don't you come to my quarters, where we can discuss the situation?"

"I'll be there directly," said Jordan.

The airy penthouse room was empty when Jordan got there, except for Adri himself. The people who had been there before were gone.

"Welcome, friend Jordan," said Adri, rising slowly from the couch where he'd been sitting. "Have you had breakfast?"

Jordan crossed the big room swiftly and grasped both of Adri's outstretched hands in his own.

Without preamble, Jordan said, "The three people who were aboard our ship in orbit are coming down to the base camp, for the duration of the storm."

"A wise precaution," said Adri. "This is going to be a severe storm, from what I'm told, and they will be much safer beneath our protective blanket of air than aboard your ship in orbit."

Adri sat back on the couch; Jordan took one of the armchairs facing him. Somehow Adri looked older than ever before, weary, bent with age. Off in a corner of the room, the alien's furball pet seemed to be curled up, asleep.

"I was just about to order breakfast for myself," Adri said. "Would you care for something?"

Jordan shrugged. "Some buttered toast, perhaps. And tea."

"Of course." Adri called to one of the wall screens and ordered breakfast for two.

"So it will be a very severe storm," Jordan said.

Looking quite serious, Adri replied, "Very. The Pup throws off flares every now and then, but this one is among the largest we've ever recorded."

"Will it cause much damage?"

"Here on the ground? No, no: the atmosphere protects us to a great degree, and our energy shields will absorb whatever radiation reaches the ground."

"But our ship in orbit?"

"It may suffer some damage, I'm afraid."

"I see," Jordan said.

"We could provide an energy shield for your camp," Adri suggested. "It would be the prudent thing to do."

Thinking how Meek would react to that, Jordan still said, "Thank you. I'll ask Dr. Thornberry to work with your people to set it up."

"Very good," said Adri. "I'll tell Aditi to direct the installation."

With a knowing smile, he added, "She'll be glad of an excuse to be near you again."

Jordan forced himself to concentrate on business. "Could you provide an energy shield for our ship, as well?"

Adri looked away for a moment. At last he said, "That might be feasible, but we won't have time to do so before the radiation storm strikes."

"But if you can set up a shield for our base camp, why not the ship?"

"It would have to be lifted to your ship."

"We can do that easily enough."

"And then integrated with your ship's systems," Adri went on, "to make certain it would not interfere with their operation. That would take a day or so of testing and adjustments, I fear."

"Oh. I see." But despite himself Jordan wondered if Adri was telling him the truth.

As Jordan prepared to leave the city and return to the camp, he was surprised to see Brandon enter their sitting room, looking downcast.

"I thought you were staying with Elyse," he said to his brother.

Dejectedly, Brandon replied, "She's talking technobabble with the astronomers. I'm just in the way."

"Feeling left out?"

"Totally."

"Your first lovers' quarrel," Jordan teased.

"No quarrel," said Brandon. "She wasn't paying enough attention to me to have a quarrel."

Suppressing a chuckle, Jordan offered, "Well, you can come back with us to the camp."

"Yeah, I guess that's what I'll have to do."

Jordan couldn't help telling him, "Aditi's coming with us."

Brandon looked surprised. Quickly recovering, he said only, "Good for you, Jordy."

As they trudged through the woods toward the cluster of hemispherical shelters that comprised the base camp Jordan stayed alongside Aditi. Behind them, a minihorse carried an electronics black box the size of a shipping crate, the generator for the energy dome. Brandon and the others walked up ahead.

"Does the Pup burp out flares very often?" Jordan asked Aditi.

She looked puzzled. "Burp?"

Jordan rummaged in his mind for a definition. "Like when you've gobbled down your food too fast." And he pantomimed a burp.

"Ah!" Laughing, Aditi said, "You mean 'expel forcibly, belch, erupt, explode.'"

"You sound like a dictionary."

"I'm quoting from a dictionary."

Surprised, Jordon blurted, "You have a dictionary memorized?"

Again she laughed brightly. "No, but I can call one up when I need to."

He understood. "You have a communications system? Built in?"

Aditi tapped her short-cropped red hair. "Inside the skull. We all do. It's installed in childhood."

Impressed, Jordan muttered, "That beats carrying a phone around, I suppose."

When they reached the base camp, Meek eyed the minihorse and the equipment it was carrying with unconcealed hostility.

"I don't like this," he told Jordan. "I don't like this at all."

Taking the astrobiologist by the arm and leading him away from Aditi and the stolid beast, Jordan said, "Harmon, it's for your own protection."

"How do we know that?"

"The city is protected by an energy dome."

Undeterred, Meek insisted, "We have no idea of how it works or what it actually does. I'm against—"

"What it does," Jordan interrupted, "is protect you from any excess radiation caused by the storm."

Meek's long, craggy face was a picture of suspicion. "The Pup just happened to emit a flare. Hazzard and the others just happen to prefer leaving the ship and coming down here. Adri just happens to offer what he claims is a protective energy shield for our camp."

"And I just happen to accept his offer," Jordan countered, "and order the energy shield to be set up here. That's all there is to it, Harmon."

"I'm against it."

"Your objection will be noted in the expedition's record."

"Fine."

Jordan didn't tell Meek that the expedition's record was not being transmitted to Earth. Adri was blocking all their transmissions. He smiled to himself grimly. Harmon would go ballistic if he knew that.

Then he thought, perhaps I should go a little ballistic, myself.

But he kept his doubts to himself.

Hazzard and the two others arrived aboard a rocketplane that glided in smoothly to a picture-perfect landing. The astronaut looked happy to be back with everyone else.

"The ship'll be okay," he said, once Jordan asked him. "If there's damage from the storm we should be able to repair it."

"It's just we fragile human beings that have to be protected," Thornberry added, cocking a derisive eye at Meek.

Thornberry and Brandon helped Aditi to lift the crate of equipment from the back of the minihorse and place it squarely in the middle of their encampment. Once they uncrated it Aditi bent over the generator and tapped several switches on its top.

Jordan felt a momentary tingle through his body. Aditi peered at the readouts flickering along the top of the shield generator, then turned to Jordan and announced, "The shield is on. We are protected now."

Jordan decided it would be best for everyone to remain at the camp until the radiation storm abated. Meek and de Falla disappeared into the bubble tent that housed the geology lab, to pore over rock samples. Longyear joined them, together with several others, including Dr. Yamaguchi.

Thornberry bent over the shield generator, eager to learn how it worked. He quizzed Aditi, who apparently knew only how to turn the generator on and off, not its principles of operation. Hazzard, with nothing to do, walked around the camp, seemingly pleased to be free of the confines of the ship.

Jordan went from one group to another, checking on their needs, their findings.

Then he called Elyse, who was at the city's astronomical observatory, where she was watching imagery of the Pup's seething, boiling surface. She looked totally rapt as she stared at the screen, barely paying attention to Jordan. One of the city's astronomers stood beside her, intently watching the readout that displayed the steeply rising level of radiation up above the atmosphere.

Jordan nodded to himself, satisfied that he had made the right decision to allow Hazzard and the others to come down to the camp, and to accept Adri's offer of a protective shield.

When he reached the bubble tent that housed the geology lab, Meek and Longyear were sitting on folding chairs at the far side of the lab, heads together in whispered conversation. The instant Jordan stepped in, they both stiffened like naughty little boys caught raiding the cookie jar.

Jordan merely smiled and asked de Falla, who was sitting at a bench closer to the entryway, "How's the work going, Silvio?"

"Interesting," said the geologist. "I'm dating the rocks. You know, argon/potassium ratios, uranium/lead ratios, that sort of stuff."

"Calculating their age from the amount of radioactive elements in them," Jordan said.

De Falla nodded, and cast a glance at Meek and Longyear, who were sitting silent and unmoving across the lab.

"What have you found so far?"

With an almost boyish grin, de Falla said, "Confusion. Most of the samples we've chipped out are a lot younger than I expected. Younger by hundreds of millions of years."

Puzzled, Jordan asked, "Younger? What does that mean?"

"I don't know. Not yet." Scratching at his neat little beard, he added, "But if these rock samples are typical of the planet, then this planet is somehow much younger than Earth. A whole lot younger."

"Well, Elyse says Sirius itself can't be more than half a billion years old."

"I know. But how could this planet have evolved such a complex biosphere in so short a time? On Earth, it took more than a billion years before life crawled out of the oceans and colonized the land."

"So this planet isn't an exact duplicate of Earth, after all," Jordan said.

"No, it's not," said de Falla. But there was little conviction in it. He seemed more doubtful of his discovery than proud of it.

Jordan left the lab tent and went to find Aditi. She was still with Thornberry, by the shield generator. Jordan asked her, "What do you know about the geology of your world?"

"Not very much, I'm afraid. Ask Adri about it; he can put you in touch with our geologists."

He nodded and took her arm and started to walk with her among the bubble tents. Looking back at Thornberry, who was still peering intently at the generator, Jordan said, "I wonder if it's a good idea to leave Mitch alone with your equipment."

Aditi asked, "What do you mean?"

"I get the distinct feeling that he'd like to take the thing apart to find out how it works."

She laughed. "He won't be able to do that. The equipment is self-protective."

"It resists tampering?"

"Yes, of course."

"How?"

"I don't know how it works, but if you try to open it up without tapping in the proper security code, it will give you a mild shock."

"Really?"

"We have curious tinkerers among our people, too," Aditi said.

Jordan found himself saying, "I think it would be best if you stayed here tonight. No sense walking back to the city in this radiation storm."

She looked up at him. "It wouldn't be dangerous for me, not really."

Shaking his head, Jordan said firmly, "No. I want you to stay here tonight." Then he laughed lightly and added, "If you don't mind."

Aditi didn't answer. But she didn't reject the idea, either.

Late in the afternoon, as Jordan walked with Aditi back toward the communications center, he saw Brandon step out of the biology lab's bubble tent.

"Bran," Jordan called to his brother. "How goes it?"

Stepping quickly toward Jordan, Brandon said, "Radiation level's peaked. It's starting to go down. Slowly."

"I wonder how the ship made out?"

"Hazzard's been checking on it remotely. She answers his queries, and the diagnostics don't show any major damage."

"That's good. I get the feeling that Meek thought the radiation storm was cooked up by Adri to destroy our ship."

Brandon glanced at Aditi, then said, "That's not a joking matter, Jordy. You know there's a cabal simmering along?"

Jordan felt mildly surprised. "A cabal?"

"Meek. He and Longyear and several others. They've formed a faction that's not happy with your leadership."

"Oh, that."

"It's more serious than you think, Jordy."

"How serious can it be?"

"They're talking about pulling up stakes and heading back to Earth," said Brandon. "I think maybe Hazzard agrees with them."

"Nonsense," Jordan scoffed.

"They're serious, Jordy. Meek is scared shitless of Adri and this whole situation. He says it can't be natural. Everything we're learning about this planet points to the conclusion that what we're seeing isn't natural."

"He's overreacting," said Jordan, with a glance at Aditi. "He'll get over it, in time."

"I don't know, Jordy," Brandon said. "I just talked with Elyse, over at the observatory. She's found out that this planet doesn't have a magnetosphere."

"No planetary magnetic field?"

"None."

"Another difference from Earth," Jordan murmured.

"Considering the radiation flux from the Pup's flare, we ought to be getting fried here on the ground, without a magnetic field to deflect the charged particles."

"That's why Adri gave us the energy shield."

Shaking his head, Brandon said, "Elyse told me that something's absorbing the radiation, stopping most of it from reaching the planet."

"Something? What?"

"Damned if I know. If there's no magnetic field, then what on Earth is protecting this planet?"

"The energy shield," said Aditi.

Both the brothers turned to her.

Brandon demanded, "You mean the shield protecting this camp is strong enough to deflect the flux from the flare?"

"No, it's not. This little shield merely absorbs the residual amount of radiation that gets through the big shield."

"The big shield?" Jordan asked.

Aditi nodded. "The planetary shield. The energy screen that protects the whole planet."

Brandon gaped at her. "You mean you've got an energy shield strong enough to handle the flux coming in from the flare?"

"Certainly," Aditi replied, as if it was the most normal thing in the world. "We don't have a natural magnetic field, so we had to set up an energy shield to protect ourselves."

For several moments neither brother spoke, as they tried to absorb what Aditi was telling them.

A man-made energy screen that protects the entire planet, Jordan marveled. And she takes it for granted; it's perfectly normal to her.

But Brandon said, "Wait till Harmon hears about *this*. He'll want to hightail it out of here today!"

Jordan stared at his brother, thinking, We can't leave! We just got here. And there's so much to learn, so much to explore.

He glanced at Aditi, who stood patiently at his side, looking as if she were wondering what all the fuss was about.

Framing his words carefully, Jordan said to his brother, "Bran, I can understand Meek's fears. I worry about all this myself. I mean, it's just too good to be true. But we mustn't run away from it. We've got to learn about it. There's an enormous amount to be learned, I'm certain of that. And I intend to stay and learn, not run away like a frightened little boy."

Brandon smiled tightly. "That's just about what I thought you'd say. Now tell it to Meek."

Taking in a deep breath, Jordan said, "I'll do that. In the morning. I'll call a breakfast meeting and we can thrash this out, with all of us present."

Nodding, Brandon said, "Okay. I'll tell Meek and the others."

"Good. Do that."

As Brandon hurried away, Aditi asked, "Will this be trouble for you?"

"Perhaps," said Jordan. "But I'm supposed to be this group's leader, so I'm going to have to lead them."

And he remembered an old dictum from another leader of an earlier century: The secret of being a successful manager is keeping the five guys who hate you away from the four who haven't made up their minds.

The evening was more than a little awkward. He had to find a space for Aditi to sleep. Very hesitantly, he phoned Elyse Rudaki at the observatory again to ask if Aditi might spend the night in her cubicle.

Elyse smiled knowingly. "Of course. I'm not using it."

"I . . . ah . . . well, since you're still in the city . . ." Jordan stammered.

Elyse seemed amused by his consternation. "Even if I were in the camp I wouldn't be using my own cubicle. Not as long as Brandon is there."

Jordan mumbled a thank-you and cut the connection.

He did not want to eat dinner with everyone else. No sense starting a debate with Meek and his clique over dinner, he told himself. We'll have it out in the morning.

So he picked up a pair of dinner trays and met Aditi outside, where her minihorse was placidly munching on the grass. They sat upwind of the animal, with their backs against the sloping, slightly yielding wall of a bubble tent, laid the prepackaged meals on their outstretched legs, and opened them. They instantly heated themselves.

"Rather romantic, actually," said Jordan as the aroma of their steaming meals wafted up to them. "Dining out in the open, under the—"

His voice caught in his throat. Up above them, the sky was glowing with colors. Long gossamer sheets of delicate green, red, blue, white shimmered and danced across the heavens, almost blotting out the stars.

Aditi gasped. "Aurora," she breathed.

Jordan found his voice. "From the radiation storm," he said softly. "Some of the radiation got through your screen and it's lighting up the ionosphere."

"It's so incredibly beautiful," she said.

"Overwhelming."

Without thinking consciously about it, Jordan impulsively reached for Aditi and pulled her to him. His dinner slid off his legs and onto the grass as he held her tightly in his arms and kissed her.

FACTIONS

Aditi and Jordan never finished their meal. They never even started it. They clung to each other for hours, caressing, kissing, speaking to each other in low, breathless voices.

"I had to travel eight and a half light-years to find you," Jordan said. "To come alive again. To feel love and warmth again."

Nestling her head on his shoulder, Aditi said, "I never realized how overpowering an emotion love can be. It . . . it simply sweeps you away."

"It does that," said Jordan. Looking up at the aurora again, he added, "Of course, we had a little help from the stars."

She giggled. "Yes, we did."

He looked down at her beautiful face, lit by the flickering aurora, and kissed her again.

"It's getting late," she said. "You have your meeting tomorrow morning."

"I don't want this night to end."

"But it must," Aditi said. She picked up her forgotten dinner tray and climbed to her feet.

Jordan got up beside her, slowly, reluctantly. "The aurora seems to be fading away."

"The storm must be ending."

"And our storm?" he asked.

She smiled gently at him. "It's just beginning."

"Will you come to my cubicle?"

"I can't. It wouldn't look right to the others."

"I don't care about the others! Let's—"

Aditi silenced him with a fingertip on his lips. "Do you want Dr. Meek and the others who are frightened of us to think you've been seduced by an alien Madame Butterfly?"

He burst into laughter. "I think you mean Mata Hari."

"She was the spy?"

"Not a very good one, I'm afraid. She got caught. And executed."

"Oh." Aditi's face, half hidden in shadows, broke into a contrite smile. "You know what I mean."

"Yes," he said. Reluctantly. Very reluctantly.

They all met the next morning in the dining area for breakfast. After a pair of robots served the prepackaged food trays, Jordan got to his feet and said, "You're probably wondering why I asked you all here this morning."

No one laughed.

"Seriously," he continued, "we seem to have a difference of opinion about what our course of action should be."

Everyone turned to Meek, who was bringing a forkful of scrambled faux eggs to his mouth. He froze for an instant, put the fork down, and looked squarely at Jordan.

"I think we're in over our heads here, and we should leave immediately and head back to Earth."

"But we've made the greatest discovery in the history of the human race," Jordan said. "Should we run away from it?"

"As fast as we can," said Meek.

"But why? What are you afraid of?"

Meek glanced at Aditi, who was seated at Jordan's side. He pushed his chair back and got to his feet. "What I have to say may offend you, Aditi. But I've got to say it."

"Please go ahead," Aditi replied. "Speak your mind."

"Very well. This planet shouldn't be here. These people shouldn't be here. Everything we've learned about Adri and his people leads to colossal contradictions."

"Such as?"

"Adri's DNA is identical to ours," said Longyear. "That's not possible, not natural."

De Falla spoke up. "The planet's geological structure is much younger than it should be."

Meek resumed, "They have technology that's far superior to ours."

"But they don't have spacecraft, not even satellites," Hazzard added.

"Now wait," said Jordan. "Adri and his people have treated us quite well. They've welcomed us—"

"Like the spider to the fly," Tanya Verishkova muttered.

"He's not being honest with us," Meek went on. "He isn't telling us the truth."

Turning to Aditi, Jordan asked, "Is Adri being honest with us?"

Aditi said in a clear, calm voice, "Everything Adri has said to you has been the truth. He has never lied to you."

"Ah, you see?" Meek said, waggling a finger at her. "They speak like lawyers."

"What do you want to know?" Aditi asked.

"Why are you here? Why did you lure us to you?"

She looked genuinely perplexed. "We have lived here all our lives, just as you have lived on Earth. And we didn't lure you, you came here to us."

Longyear said, "Our ship's sensors couldn't detect your city."

"Because of its energy shield."

"But you sent out a laser beacon to attract us."

"We observed your ship in orbit, just as we observed the earlier ships that had no people aboard them."

"How did you know the earlier ships were uncrewed?" Meek demanded.

She shrugged. "No one came down to the ground, as you did."

"Why'd you shine that laser beacon?" Thornberry asked.

"To attract your attention."

"Aha!" Meek snapped.

Jordan said, "Harmon, turn the situation around. If an alien spaceship arrived in orbit around Earth, what would your reaction be?"

"Blow it out of the sky," Thornberry said, without an instant's hesitation.

"Be serious."

"Well . . ." Meek hesitated, then answered, "I suppose I'd want to meet whoever was aboard it."

"And ascertain if they were dangerous or not," de Falla said.

"And examine them medically," Yamaguchi added.

Longyear asked, "But what would be the chances that they were human? Down to their DNA?"

"We don't know," Jordan said. "This is our first experience with alien life." Before anyone could reply, he added, "Intelligent alien life."

"What about those whales in Jupiter's ocean?" Verishkova asked. "The leviathans?"

"They're not intelligent," said Longyear.

"Aren't they? I've read papers that say they are."

"Whether they are or not," Jordan said, "Adri and the people here on New Earth are fully intelligent."

Meek insisted, "I say we go back to Earth and report what we've found."

"And leave all these questions unanswered?" Jordan challenged. "The biggest discovery in human history, and you want to run away from it?"

Meek slowly sank back onto his chair. "I think they're dangerous," he grumbled. "I can't help feeling that we're in danger here."

"Have they done anything harmful to us?" Jordan asked. "Have they been anything but helpful, generous?"

"They're not telling us the whole truth about themselves. They know a lot more than they're telling us."

"Then we should dig into the matter and learn more about them," Jordan said.

A stubborn silence filled the tent.

"We're here to discover, to learn," Jordan pleaded. "You're all scientists and engineers. You've dedicated your lives to exploring, to uncovering new knowledge. Why run away from the opportunity of a lifetime?"

"To save our lives," Meek answered.

Jordan looked around the table. "How many of you feel we're in real danger here?"

Meek's hand shot up. After a moment's hesitation, Longyear, Wanamaker, and de Falla raised theirs also. Hazzard looked uncertain, uncomfortable, but his hands remained in his lap.

Suppressing a satisfied smile, Jordan said, "The nays have it. We're staying."

Meek shook his head. "This is a mistake, I tell you. A fatal mistake."

"The mistake, Harmon," said Jordan, with some steam behind it, "would be to pull up stakes. Instead of running away, we've got to learn all we can about this world and its people. We have a whole new world to explore! Let's get on with it!"

But even as he spoke so positively, Jordan wondered how much he was being influenced by Aditi, sitting there and beaming prettily at him.

TRANSITION

Jordan looked at his team, their faces all turned toward him. You're their leader, he reminded himself. Show some leadership.

"Very well," he told them, "I'm going back to the city. I'll talk to Adri and try to get some of our questions answered. Who wants to come with me?"

Not a hand went up.

"Mitch, don't you want to talk to their engineers? Find out how these energy shield generators work?"

"I do," said Thornberry, "but . . . maybe later. Not just now."

Hazzard said, "I'd better get back to the ship, check out all the systems."

"Make certain the propulsion engines are working," Meek muttered.

Turning to his brother, Jordan asked, "Bran, you want to come to the city, don't you?"

"When Elyse is finished with their astronomers," Brandon replied, looking uneasy. "Right now she wouldn't have time for me." Before Jordan could object, he added, "Besides, I've got plenty to do here."

Jordan shook his head. "I see. All right, then, I'll go alone and have a talk with Adri."

"He'll tell you anything you want to know," said Aditi. "Or he'll put you in contact with specialists who have the information you want."

Nodding, Jordan said, "Good. Then my task will be to set up a series of conferences for each of you with specialists in your different fields."

"That'll be grand," Thornberry said, without enthusiasm.

"Fine by me," said Brandon.

Meek said nothing.

Walking back toward the city with Aditi, Jordan couldn't keep his mind on Meek and the growing fears that all the others seemed to have. His mind refused to dwell on it. Instead, he marveled that the forest seemed more alive than he'd ever found it before. Birds twittered above, little animals scampered across the ground, butterflies fluttered among the colorful flowers.

I've never noticed all this before, he said to himself. I never saw how beautiful and vibrant it all is.

And then he understood. It's because I'm with Aditi. She makes the world wonderful. She makes me alive again.

He recognized that he had at last let go of the past. Not forgotten it. Not dismissed it. But he had stopped clinging to it, stopped going over it, again and again, endlessly. He had let go. He had opened his heart to life again.

A miracle has occurred, he told himself. This beautiful, intelligent, warm, and loving woman truly cares for me.

It wasn't that he forgot Miriam. For a moment he felt almost guilty about Aditi. But he finally understood that love is not finite, not a zero-sum game. The love you feel for one person does not lessen the love you feel for someone else. Love can expand to encompass the whole world. A man can fall in love all over again, marveling at his good fortune, and this doesn't diminish his love for the woman he had lost.

Eight point six light-years, he kept telling himself. I had to travel eight point six light-years to find her. I'm not going to let her go.

Once they reached the city, Jordan went through the day almost in a trance. He and Aditi met with Adri, who promised to help the team members meet specialists in their fields. He had dinner with Adri and Aditi.

Then he walked Aditi to his suite, grateful that Brandon had stayed at the camp.

As he ushered her into the sitting room, he stammered, "Ah . . . would you care for something? Is it possible to get an after-dinner drink?"

Aditi stepped close enough to brush against him. "We don't need an alcoholic beverage, do we?"

He felt flustered, almost embarrassed. "Sometimes it helps . . . that is . . ."

"Jordan, darling," Aditi said, twining her arms about his neck, "I love you. You love me, don't you?"

"I do."

"Then let's go to bed."

He gulped, but managed to say, "By all means!"

RACING TOWARD EXTINCTION

The days seemed to fly by. Jordan split his time between the base camp and the city.

Activities at the camp settled into a busy, productive routine. Brandon and de Falla, accompanied by two robots, took off on a geological expedition, flying halfway across the planet in a rocketplane piloted remotely by Hazzard, who had returned to the orbiting *Gaia*.

"I might as well go out in the field," Brandon groused. "Elyse has practically taken up residence at the observatory. She spends more time talking with Zadar than me."

Jordan suppressed a grin. He said, "It's a good thing Demetrios is up on the ship. Otherwise, I think you might get jealous of her fellow astronomer."

Brandon's answer was a sour grimace.

Jordan made a point of having lunch with Elyse in the city the next day.

"Bran misses you terribly," he told her.

"I miss him, too," she said. "But no one's seen a white dwarf this close! We're breaking new ground here."

"What about this planetary energy shield?" Jordan asked her. "Have you discussed that with the observatory's astronomers?"

Elyse frowned slightly, as if annoyed by a question from a layman, team leader or not. "I'll get to that, Jordan. But we've got all these observations of the Pup to make!"

Jordan nodded. She's deeply into her studies and she doesn't want to be sidetracked, he knew. I wonder how much she misses Brandon, out in the woods halfway across the planet?

"One day our Sun will become a white dwarf," Elyse pointed out. "We're looking at the future of our own star."

There's no sidetracking her, Jordan realized.

After several days of hesitation, Longyear and Yamaguchi accompanied Jordan into the city and began examining not only the people, but their beasts of burden and their pets. Yet they returned each night to the camp.

The biologist grew more and more mistrustful. "It's terrestrial DNA, all of it. Every species we've examined carries an almost exact duplicate of Earth-type DNA."

Yamaguchi seemed happy enough about it. She began to write a research paper titled, "Convergent Evolution: Earth and Sirius C." Longyear grudgingly helped her with it.

Jordan worried about Meek, who seemed to be lost in his fears, accomplishing nothing as the days wore on, staying in the camp and never setting foot in the city.

Adri came to visit the camp, and Jordan showed him through the labs and workshops. When they came to the biology laboratory, Meek was sitting at the workbench on a stool, his heels hooked on one of its rungs, the knees of his long legs almost reaching his squared-off chin.

"Hello, Harmon," Jordan called. "We have a visitor."

Meek nodded warily.

"Dr. Meek," said Adri, smiling amicably. "How can I convince you that we are not dangerous to you?"

Meek's brow furrowed. At last he said, "You could answer my questions truthfully."

Adri nodded. "Of course." Jordan saw his brow arch slyly as he added, "Would you like to test me with a lie detector?"

Looking annoyed, Meek said, "I wish I had one."

"Perhaps you could construct one."

Hiding his amusement, Jordan said, "I'm sure that won't be necessary. Will it, Harmon?"

Meek didn't answer.

Without being invited, Adri pulled up one of the stools lining the workbench and sat next to Meek. "Ask me anything you wish, sir."

Jordan stood off to one side, scrutinizing the expression on Meek's face. He saw fear, and sullen resentment. Yet something more, as well: there was human curiosity tucked in among his apprehensions.

"Where do you come from?" Meek started.

"Why, from here. This planet. New Earth."

"You were born here?"

"I've lived here all my life."

"How old are you?"

"Twelve."

Meek's eyes went wide.

Jordan chuckled and said, "Twelve New Earth years. Each orbit of this planet around Sirius takes thirty Earth years."

"Which means," Meek said, "that you're . . . three hundred and sixty years old?" His eyes went even wider.

Adri smiled modestly. "Yes, your arithmetic is correct."

"Three hundred and sixty years old?" Meek yelped.

"I'm afraid so."

"Do your people regularly live such long lives?" Jordan asked.

Adri nodded solemnly. "Yes. So can you. Your biological sciences are steadily increasing your life spans, are they not?"

"Yes, but three hundred and sixty years," Jordan marveled. "We haven't reached that yet."

"We can help you," said Adri. Then he added, "Although, with your enormous population, I wonder if extending your life spans would be a good thing."

Meek recovered from his surprise. "How old is your race?"

"Our civilization goes back many millions of years."

"And you've existed on this one planet all that time?"

Adri spread his hands. "My race has lived only on this planet. We have never lived elsewhere."

Jordan said, "What we find remarkable—unbelievable, almost—is that you're so much like us. This entire planet is so Earthlike. It's uncanny."

"Yes, I suppose it is."

"It's more than uncanny," Meek grumbled. "It's unbelievable. To find a planet exactly like Earth, and intelligent beings exactly like humans—"

"Not exactly," Adri pointed out.

"Down to your DNA," said Meek.

"Yes, biologically we are very similar," Adri admitted. "But socially, culturally, we have significant differences."

"You control your numbers," said Jordan.

"We live in harmony with our environment," Adri responded. "We are not xenophobic. We are not competitive, not aggressive. We have welcomed you to our world, while you are distinctly suspicious of us." Before Meek could reply, Adri amended, "Perhaps I should say, you are *instinctively* suspicious of us."

Meek said, "You disapprove of our instincts?"

Smiling gently, Adri replied, "It's not a matter of my approval or disapproval. Your instincts served you well, long ages ago. But now you must outgrow them."

"Why? Because you say so?"

"Because they are destroying you. You have devastated your planet with overpopulation, with environmental degradation, with famines and wars and hatreds. You are teetering on the brink of extinction, whether you realize it or not."

"You sound like one of those overzealous eco-activists," Meek said.

"Forgive me," Adri immediately apologized. "I should not be telling you how to live your lives."

"Someone should," said Jordan.

"It's just that . . ." Adri hesitated, seemingly gathering his thoughts. At last he said, with infinite sadness in his voice, "It's just that to witness the destruction of an intelligent race is a terrible, terrible thing."

"Do you really feel that we're so close to destroying ourselves?" Jordan asked.

"Indeed," said Adri, his aged face showing grave concern. "You are heading for extinction. Racing toward it, I'm afraid."

Meek seemed thoroughly chastened as Adri sat on the stool beside him, his expression bleak. Jordan himself felt unutterably sad at the thought of the human race's extinction.

Rousing himself, Jordan said, "Well, we're not dead yet. We can overcome our problems, if we want to."

"If you want to," Adri agreed. "That's the question. Can you alter your modes of behavior, your ways of thinking, soon enough and well enough to avert the catastrophe that's facing you?"

"We can try," said Jordan.

"We will help you all that we can, of course," Adri said. "But your people will have to make some wrenching changes in their fundamental attitudes."

Meek said nothing. He seemed lost in thought.

Adri got up from the stool. "I must return to the city now. Dr. Meek, I hope I have given you the information you sought."

Meek nodded wordlessly.

Jordan said, "I'll go with you to the edge of the camp, Adri."

"No need for that, friend Jordan. I can find my way." He turned and headed for the lab's door in his seemingly effortless gliding walk.

As soon as Adri was out of sight, Meek stirred to life. "I don't trust him. Despite everything he says, I don't trust the man."

"Perhaps," Jordan said, "you don't trust him *because* of everything he says."

To Jordan's surprise, Thornberry took up residence in the city. He spent his days in happy conference with young men and women who were fellow engineers.

"It's unbelievable, the things they can do," he said to Jordan and Aditi over dinner one evening. "I mean, they've developed quantum computers, for god's sake. No bigger than a grain of sand, yet more powerful than anything we've got. They implant 'em in their skulls at birth!"

"I know," said Jordan, looking at Aditi.

"I mean, we've been talking about quantum computers for damned near a century now, and we're nowhere near making one work. These people carry them around inside their heads! If I could bring one of 'em back home, I'd become a billionaire overnight, I could."

Aditi said, "We can show you how to build them."

Thornberry nodded eagerly. "I'm talking to your bright young folks about just that, I am."

"Good," Jordan said.

The three of them were sitting at a small table in the dining area of the dormitory building. The place was filled with Aditi's people, young and old, men and women. Conversations in their fluted musical language and laughter drifted across the room. Human servants carried trays of food and drink to the tables.

But they're not human, Jordan thought as he listened to Thornberry with half his attention. They're human in form, but they belong to a different race, a different civilization. They're aliens.

"And these energy shields," the roboticist went on, "they take 'em for granted, they do. It's ordinary engineering, as far as they're concerned."

Aditi said to Thornberry, "The shield generators are ordinary engineering. After all, we've used them for many generations."

"I know," said Thornberry. "But what I can't figure out is how they work."

"The engineers haven't explained it to you?" she asked.

"They explain to me for hours, they do," Thornberry said, "but for the life of me, the more they explain the less I understand."

Jordan snapped his attention to the roboticist. "What do you mean, Mitch?"

"They're talking about physics and principles that're beyond me. Maybe a quantum physicist could understand them. More likely a string theoretician."

"The closest we have to a physicist would be Elyse Rudaki," said Jordan.

Thornberry nodded. "Maybe I should ask her to listen to 'em. Maybe she could understand the math."

Aditi looked troubled. "Do you mean that the engineers are not answering your questions?"

His beefy face contorting into a troubled frown, Thornberry said, "Oh, they answer my questions, they do. But their answers are beyond me."

"Then we must find someone who can explain it to you more clearly," said Aditi.

Jordan smiled slightly. "Mitch, perhaps you've got to go to school and learn more physics."

Thornberry conceded the point with a nod. "Maybe I should. Maybe what I need is a patient teacher."

Jordan turned to Aditi. "You're a teacher, aren't you?"

"Yes, that's right," she said.

"Could you help Mitch? I realize that advanced physics is probably beyond you, but perhaps you could find one of your fellow teachers who could help."

She looked thoughtful for a moment, then smiled and said, "I'll ask Adri about that in the morning."

As they turned their attention back to the dinners before them, Jordan marveled all over again at how closely the New Earthers' cuisine resembled Earth's. The meat on his plate certainly looked and tasted like veal. Grown in a biovat, but cooked to perfection with a tangy sauce that was tantalizingly familiar yet slightly different from anything Jordan could remember.

They were finishing their desserts when Jordan spotted Paul Longyear walking past their table.

"Paul," he called, "join us for coffee?"

Longyear stopped, looked over their table, and pulled out the empty chair.

"It's not coffee," he said as he sat down. "Tastes almost the same, but it doesn't have any caffeine at all."

"You've tested it?" Jordan asked.

"I've been analyzing all their foodstuffs," said the biologist. Holding up a thumb and forefinger a mere millimeter apart, he went on, "They're all this close to Earth normal. Nothing in them that's harmful to us, but just a tinge different."

Aditi said, "I'm pleased that you find our food satisfactory."

"More than satisfactory," Jordan said. "It's delicious. And I find the slight differences to be rather exotic."

Thornberry pouted. "I haven't found a decent potato here. I miss them, I do."

Aditi looked troubled.

Then Thornberry added, "But we don't have decent potatoes at our camp, either. Nor aboard the ship, by damn. The nearest honest potato is back on Earth, more'n eight light-years away."

Jordan murmured, "The rigors of exploration."

Thornberry broke into a hearty laugh. Looking around at the busy dining area, he guffawed, "Right you are. It's hell out here on the frontier."

Longyear didn't laugh. Jordan thought he looked uptight, preoccupied by something that was bothering him.

When the waiter brought their coffee the biologist sipped at his cup minimally.

"So what have you and Nara been up to?" Jordan asked him, trying to shake him out of his dour mood.

"Cataloging the various species of animals here," Longyear replied. With a shake of his head, he added, "It's amazing what these people can do with biological engineering."

Jordan glanced at Aditi. The "these people" phrase didn't seem to bother her a bit.

"I mean," Longyear went on, "they use genetic engineering the way we use mechanical engineering. Instead of inventing machines for labor-saving jobs, they gengineer animals."

"And plants, too," Aditi said. "Most of the fruits and vegetables we eat have been genetically modified."

"We've done that on Earth," Longyear said to her.

"We have?" Jordan asked.

"He means genetically engineered crops," said Thornberry. "Frost-resistant wheat, grains that resist insect pests. It's a big business."

But Longyear said, "We've been doing genetic engineering for a long time, Mitch. Centuries. Millennia."

Aditi said, "I had no idea your biological sciences were that advanced so long ago."

With a hint of a smile, Longyear said, "They weren't. The genetic engineering we did back then was done the old-fashioned way."

"What do you mean?" Jordan asked.

"Well, take corn for instance. When my ancestors first came to what we now call Mexico, corn ears were no bigger than my thumb. But by consistently planting kernels from the biggest ears, over many generations we produced the kind of corn we eat today."

"Selective breeding," Jordan said.

"That's right. The old-fashioned method of genetic engineering. We took wild cattle and pigs and bred them generation after generation to carry more meat. And to be docile. We fattened them up and dumbed them down."

"And then we figured out the double helix," said Thornberry. "Now we can do inside of a year what it took centuries to achieve before."

Longyear nodded tightly. Then he turned to Jordan. "I need to talk to you. In private."

Something's in the wind, Jordan thought. With a glance toward Aditi, he replied to the biologist, "Will tomorrow morning do?"

"Fine," said Longyear, tight-lipped. Then he repeated, "In private."

CONUNDRUM

T he following morning, Jordan left Aditi sleeping in his bed, showered, shaved, and dressed as quietly as he could, then went to Longyear's quarters. To his surprise, Meek was there, standing uneasily by Longyear's desk.

"Harmon! I didn't know you had come to the city."

"I came early this morning," said the astrobiologist. "I was up at the crack of dawn, the very crack of dawn."

Longyear's apartment was a single room, partitioned into a bedroom area, kitchen, and a sitting room furnished with a small sofa, a pair of armchairs, and a sleekly curved desk. The walls were covered with display screens that glowed pearly gray.

"I hope you had a pleasant walk through the forest," Jordan said as he went to the sofa.

"I drove a buggy," Meek replied. He dropped his lanky frame onto one of the armchairs.

"I see." Turning to Longyear, who got up from his desk and went to the other armchair, Jordan said, "I gathered from the way you asked for this meeting that you didn't want Aditi present."

"That's right," the biologist said. Frowning slightly, he said, "It's not that I don't . . . um, trust her. It's just that I think it's better if we thrash this matter out among ourselves before talking to Adri or any of the others about it."

"All right," Jordan said, leaning back on the sofa's plush cushions. "What's the problem?"

"It's not a problem so much as a conundrum."

"A conundrum?"

Meek said, "A puzzle. A riddle."

"Thank you, Harmon," said Jordan, dryly.

Longyear's lean face was entirely serious. "I've been thinking about this planet's ozone layer."

Jordan felt surprised.

"It's much thicker than Earth's," Longyear said.

"Well, it has to be, doesn't it? Sirius emits much more ultraviolet radiation than our Sun does. The ozone layer screens out the UV, protects life on the planet's surface."

"Exactly right," said Meek.

Longyear leaned closer and asked, "But how did the ozone get there, in the first place?"

Jordan blinked at him. "As I understand it, the ultraviolet light coming in creates a reaction that turns some of the oxygen molecules high in the atmosphere into ozone: oxygen-three, isn't it, where regular oxygen is a two-atom molecule."

"Right," said Longyear. "But how did the oxygen get into the atmosphere?"

Feeling as if he were taking a high school science exam, Jordan answered, "From living plants that give off oxygen as a result of photosynthesis."

"Aha!" Meek pounced. "And how could plant life arise in the face of the heavy ultraviolet radiation reaching the planet's surface?"

Jordan was puzzled by that. "Why . . . how did photosynthetic plants arise on Earth? In the oceans, wasn't it? Single-celled bacteria in the water."

"That's what happened on Earth, true enough," said Longyear. "The so-called blue-green algae—"

"Cyanobacteria, actually," Meek interrupted.

A frown flashed across Longyear's face as he continued, "Those single-celled creatures lived deep enough in the water so that the Sun's UV didn't reach them."

"The water protected them," Jordan said.

"Right. And over many eons, they pumped enough oxygen into Earth's atmosphere to allow an ozone layer to build up. The ozone layer protected the planet's surface from killing levels of ultraviolet and life could eventually evolve on land."

Jordan spread his hands. "So the same thing has happened here, obviously."

"Not so obvious, Jordan," Longyear contradicted. Ticking off points on his stubby fingers, the biologist said, "One, Sirius puts out so much UV that it's tough to see how life could have arisen in the first place."

"Really? Even in the oceans?"

Raising a second finger, Longyear went on, "Which brings us to point number two: time. It took billions of years for life to evolve in the oceans of Earth. Billions of years for those cyanobacteria to generate enough oxygen to change the atmosphere and form an ozone layer."

"This planet can't be that old," Meek said. "Sirius itself can't be more than half a billion years old, from what Elyse Rudaki's told me."

"That's not enough time for a thick ozone layer to be built up," Longyear resumed.

"So how did it get there?" Meek demanded.

"How did life evolve on the ground without an ozone layer to protect it from lethal levels of UV?" Longyear added.

Jordan looked at them: Longyear earnest, serious, troubled; Meek burning with righteous indignation.

"Life couldn't get started on the ground without a strong UV shield, a thick ozone layer high in the atmosphere," Longyear repeated. "But the ozone layer couldn't get created until life spent billions of years producing oxygen."

"And this planet can't be more than half a billion years old," said Meek, almost triumphantly.

Jordan sat up straighter. "Are you certain of this, Paul? Or is it unproven speculation?"

"I've run the numbers through the computer. Considering the level of ultraviolet that Sirius emits, and the time scale involved, there's no way that such a thick ozone layer could have been built up."

"That's . . . odd," Jordan said, weakly.

"And then there's this energy shield they've put up to protect against solar storms," Longyear went on.

"That's because there's no planetary magnetic field, as on Earth," said Jordan.

"Uh-huh. And how did Adri's people evolve to the level of high technology without a geomagnetic field to protect them?"

Jordan blinked at him.

"Adri's been lying to us," Meek insisted. "There's no way that these people could have originated on this planet."

"That's hard to believe," Jordan protested. "I mean, they're *here*, they exist. Together with all the other life forms we've seen."

"Planetary engineering," Longyear said. "Terraforming."

"The idea of reshaping an entire planet to make it like Earth? That's ridiculous!"

"Is it?" Meek snapped. "Look around you. It's been done."

"But the energy it would require," Jordan argued. "The resources. The time."

Meek said, "They're a much older race than we are. They have a much superior technology. Look at those energy shields, their technology is light-years ahead of ours."

"But to transform an entire planet . . ."

"That's what they've done," said Longyear, totally certain.

Meek insisted, "And we've got to find out why."

CONFIRMATION

Jordan's first thought was to go to Adri and ask him about Longyear's conclusion. But he hesitated. Instead, he decided to call his brother, still out in the field with de Falla, halfway across the planet.

Leaving Aditi in the city, Jordan joined Meek and Longyear in the buggy that the astrobiologist had driven to the city. All the way back through the shadowed, softly quiet forest, Jordan wrestled with his conscience. He found that he didn't want to believe that Adri was lying to him, that Aditi was part of a scheme to deceive him and the other humans. It can't be, he told himself, over and over. It can't be.

And yet, if Longyear was right, Adri and his people were carrying out a massive deception. And Aditi was part of it. Mata Hari indeed, he thought. More like Delilah.

Then a new worry hit him. Can Adri tap into our phone conversations? What if he can listen to everything we say to each other?

By the time they reached the camp and Jordan had walked to the barracks tent, he had decided that there was nothing he could do about the possibility of Adri's eavesdropping. If he can listen to our phone conversations, he surely must have overheard what Longyear and Meek told me this morning.

Once he reached his own cubicle, Jordan reluctantly sat on the springy, narrow cot and flipped open his pocketphone. Brandon answered immediately, looking sunburnt, his hair tossed by a fresh breeze, smiling like a man happy with his work. In the phone's small screen, Jordan could see that his brother was up in the mountains:

bare slabs of jagged rock rose behind him, and wisps of clouds threaded through the craggy peaks.

As he explained what Longyear and Meek had told him, Jordan could see his brother's face grow somber, grave.

"They might be right, Jordy," Brandon said. "What we're finding out here is that this planet is much younger than Earth. A lot younger."

"Geologically speaking," said Jordan.

"Right. Half a billion years old, at most."

"That would still give it enough time to develop indigenous life, wouldn't it? Enough time for life to evolve into an intelligent species."

"It took more than four billion years for an intelligent species to arise on Earth," said Brandon.

"But that doesn't mean it couldn't happen sooner, elsewhere."

"Maybe, maybe not," said Brandon. "We just don't know. We're trying to make valid conclusions with just two examples. Hard to draw a curve with only two data points."

Jordan sank back on the cot and stared at the domed ceiling of the bubble tent.

"How can we tell for sure?" he asked.

Brandon shook his head. "Jordy, if I knew, I'd tell you."

Jordan understood the unspoken message. Ask Adri. He knows. The question is, will he tell me the truth?

And he realized that, before confronting Adri with his suspicions, he had to face Aditi.

Dreading what he had to do, Jordan walked through the mid-afternoon heat back toward the city. Sunshine filtered through the high canopies of the trees. Birds swooped above and butterflies flitted through the foliage. Furry little animals scampered and chittered. He saw it all but paid no attention. His thoughts were entirely on Aditi.

And there she was, standing alone on the stone walkway that circled the city's perimeter, as if she were waiting for him.

"Hello," he called. Then he couldn't help adding, "Been waiting long?"

"No," she answered. "I . . . I had a feeling you'd be coming."

"Woman's intuition?" he taunted as he stepped next to her.

Aditi looked slightly puzzled. "No . . . not intuition . . ."

"Have you been tracking me?"

She smiled at him. "Yes, of course. We track the emanations from your phone. Even when you've turned it off there's enough residual radiation to be detected."

He did not smile back. "And you listen to our phone conversations."

"I don't," she said, totally serious now. "The communications technicians do."

"So we have no privacy."

"I'm afraid not. Adri says we need to know what you're thinking, how you're reacting to finding us."

"I see." A part of Jordan's mind was telling him that Adri's eavesdropping was perfectly natural. We'd listen to his chatter if we could, he thought. Two intelligent races bumping into each other. There's a lot to learn, a lot to find out, a lot to be afraid of.

Aditi said, "You're not angry, are you?"

He looked into her bright brown eyes and saw that she was worried. Or acting, he couldn't help thinking.

"Are you?" she repeated.

"Aditi, dear, we're lovers. We shouldn't have secrets between us." Then he added, "Do you really love me?"

"Oh, Jordan," she gushed, and flung her arms around his neck. "Of course I love you! I never thought this would happen, but I do love you, truly I do."

"And I love you, Aditi my darling. But . . ."

She pulled away from him slightly. "But you're suspicious. I can't say I blame you."

"It's just that, the more we learn about you, the less it all adds up."

She nodded. "I know."

Pointing to a stone bench a few meters from where they stood, Jordan said, "Why don't we sit there and you can explain it all to me."

"I'll explain as much as I can," she said, sitting on the bench.

Jordan sat down beside her. The stone was warm from the afternoon sunlight.

"Contact between two intelligent races is a very delicate matter," Aditi began. "Especially when one of the races is so much younger than the other."

"I understand," he said. "But you—Adri, that is—he hasn't been entirely truthful with us."

"Oh no!" she blurted. "He's been completely honest with you. He's never told you anything that's not true."

"But he hasn't told us the entire truth, has he?"

Aditi fell silent for a moment, and Jordan recognized that she was using her implanted communicator to ask for instructions.

Grasping her by the shoulders, he demanded, "Don't ask Adri how to answer me. You tell me, yourself."

Strangely, she smiled at him. "Very well, that's what I'll do."

"Adri can hear us?"

"Not now. I've turned off my communicator."

"Just like that." Jordan snapped his fingers.

So did Aditi. "Just like that. It's controlled by the brain's electrical fields."

"So we're alone."

"Yes. Completely." Looking almost impishly pleased with herself, Aditi asked, "So what do you want to know?"

"Why has Adri been so . . . so deceptive with us?"

"It's not deception, Jordan. Not in the least. Adri and the others decided that we would answer all your questions completely truthfully, but only the questions that you actually ask. Nothing more. No additional information."

"Why would—"

"You're like schoolchildren, Jordan. We didn't want to give you more information than you could handle. So we decided to answer your questions truthfully, but to go no further than your questions. As you learned more about us, learned to ask deeper questions, we would answer them."

"Like schoolchildren," he murmured. "And you're our teacher."

"One of them."

"That makes me teacher's pet, I suppose," he said, surprised at how bitter it sounded.

Aditi didn't seem to notice the sharpness of his tone. With a smile, she murmured, "Much more than a pet, dearest. Much more."

"You were . . . assigned by Adri to educate me?"

Her eyes went wide with surprise. "As a teacher, I was asked to be part of the committee of welcome." Lowering her eyes, she went on in a near-whisper, "I had no idea that I would fall in love." She hesitated a heartbeat, then asked, "You did fall in love with me too, didn't you, Jordan?"

His heart melted. "Yes, I did, Aditi. Hopelessly, helplessly in love."

She beamed happily at him.

So they sat on the stone bench in the warm afternoon light as the sun dipped lower and the shadows lengthened. Aditi explained Adri's rationale for dealing with the visitors from Earth.

"We didn't want to swamp you with too much information about ourselves. We decided to let you find out about us and our world at your own pace."

"You're a teacher, but I haven't seen any children in your city. None at all. Do you have schoolchildren?"

"I teach adults," Aditi replied. "Children are rare among us."

"I see."

"We don't have the same kind of family relationships that you do," she said.

"You told me that you do have marriages," he recalled.

"Rarely."

Suddenly he felt himself smiling. "So if I were to ask for your hand in marriage, would I have to get your parents' consent?"

"My parents?"

"Your mother. Your father."

Aditi shook her head slightly. "I have no parents."

"You're an orphan?"

"No. You don't understand. I wasn't gestated in a woman's womb. I wasn't born, the way you were. None of us were."

Jordon felt his insides quake. "What do you mean?"

"I was created from genetically engineered cell samples. All of us were."

"Created . . ." Jordan's mind reeled. "You mean, in a biovat? Like meat?"

"More sophisticated than your biovats," she replied. "An artificial womb. All of us were produced in such devices."

"Even Adri?" Jordan heard his voice squeak.

"Yes, even Adri. Every one of us has been generated in a laboratory facility."

MARS

Far-called, our navies melt away,
On dune and headland sinks the fire.

Rudyard Kipling,
"Recessional"

TITHONIUM BASE

ithonium Chasma is a part of the great Martian rift valley, which stretches nearly four thousand kilometers across the frozen rust-red desert of Mars. The rugged multihued cliffs of its south face rise some two kilometers above the valley's dusty floor. The cliffs of the north face are not visible from where Tithonium Base stands; the valley is so broad that they are beyond the short horizon.

Wearing a transparent nanofabric pressure suit, Jamie Waterman stood before the flat inscribed stone that marked his wife's grave. Not that Vijay's remains were there. On Mars you couldn't bury a person: her decaying remains would contaminate the Martian ecology. No, Vijay had been cremated, as she had wished, and her ashes carried into space and jettisoned there by one of the rockets returning to Earth. Her spirit became a cloud of ashes, drifting eternally in space.

Looking back at Tithonium Base, Jamie saw that the structures looked timeworn, weary. Just as he felt. Old. Tired. The Navaho part of his soul felt that death was coming. Looking up into the clear, butterscotch sky of Mars, he felt that soon his spirit would be a cloud wafting up there, looking down upon a long, arduous lifetime's work.

Jamie had spent his life striving to keep human explorers working on Mars, uncovering the buried villages of the long-extinct Martians, translating their prayer tablets, helping the struggling Martian lichen to survive the pitiless harsh environment.

And working to keep the million-year experiment going.

Now it was all in danger again. Funding from Earth was drying up, evaporating like a puddle of water in the thin Martian atmosphere.

His son, Ravi, walked out to meet him, full of youthful energy. He was almost half a meter taller than his stocky father, his skin darker than Jamie's copper hue. But he had his father's easy smile, his father's clear brown eyes, his father's broad cheekbones and unbending perseverance.

"Y'aa'tey," Ravi said. The old Navaho greeting. *It is good.* "I figured you'd be here."

"Y'aa'tey," Jamie replied, his voice reedy and rasping, like the thin Martian wind.

"The L/AV lifts off in half an hour," said Ravi.

Jamie nodded. "I know. I'll be there to see you off, don't worry."

Ravi grinned at his father. "I got that shitload of messages you want me to deliver: Dex, Dr. Ionescu, all the others."

"In person. I've been talking to them from here, but you've got the chance to see them face-to-face."

"I don't know about President Newton," Ravi said slowly. "He might not want to see me."

"You've got to get to him."

"I'll do my best."

"I know you will, son."

Almost mischievously, Ravi said, "I'm surprised you didn't put Chairman Chiang on the list."

Jamie shook his head inside the bubble helmet of his nanosuit. "Chiang's an old hothead. We've got to work around him, get all the others to agree to continue our funding. Then he'll come around. Not before."

An uncomfortable silence fell between them. Jamie turned his back on the stone marker and started walking slowly back toward the base and the rocket vehicle that would take his son to the ship waiting in orbit.

At last Ravi asked, "Dad, what if I fail? What if they absolutely refuse to continue funding us?"

Jamie didn't hesitate an eyeblink. "Then we'll go down to a

shoestring operation. Most of the people will go back home, but a handful of us will remain. We'll keep the work going."

"But—"

"We're just about self-sufficient. We'll get along. We've been through lean periods before and survived."

Ravi didn't say what he was thinking: Mom didn't survive. She didn't make it through the last time you had to live on a shoestring.

"The important thing," Jamie went on, leaning a hand on his son's shoulder, "is to keep the experiment going."

Ravi knew what his father meant. The million-year experiment. They had excavated several pits deep enough to expose the Martian extremophiles that lived under the permafrost layer. They had domed over the excavations and kept them warm despite overnight temperatures that plummeted to a hundred degrees below zero or lower.

The hardy bacteria were surviving, thriving, in fact. At one of the pits they had even begun to clump together in cooperative aggregations—the first step toward evolving true multicellular organisms.

It was an experiment to see if Mars could be returned to life, its own indigenous Martian life, an experiment that would take millennia to complete. Biologists were stunned by its boldness. Religious fanatics worried that it might prove that evolution is more than a theory.

Father and son walked side by side through the base's scattered buildings and out to the concrete slab where the spindly, spraddle-legged landing/ascent rocket was being loaded.

Ravi turned to his father and said, "I won't let you down, Dad."

"I know you won't."

"But if . . . if those flatlanders don't come through with more funding, I'll come back here anyway."

"Now wait," Jamie said, suddenly alarmed. "Just because I'll stay here doesn't mean you have to. You've got to find your own path, Ravi."

"I know where my path leads, Dad: back to Mars."

Jamie tried to reply, but his throat was suddenly choked with tears.

One of the crew loading the rocket called, "Hey Ravi, you coming or not?"

Ravi waved to him, then said to his father, "I've got to go, Dad."

"Go with beauty, son."

"But I'll be back. One way or the other. I'll be back."

"Go with beauty," Jamie repeated.

REVELATIONS

Most men, when they think they are thinking, are merely rearranging their prejudices.

KNUTE ROCKNE

THE BIOLAB

Jordan stood dumbfounded, staring at Aditi, thinking, She wasn't born naturally. She was created, built out of cell samples, gestated in an artificial womb, a machine. She's not natural, not real . . .

Yet she was sitting beside him on the stone bench, her beautiful face looking concerned, worried that his innate fears and prejudices would destroy their loving relationship.

Jordan squeezed his eyes shut momentarily. She *is* real, he told himself. She's as real as I am. She's warm and loving and—alien.

He opened his eyes and Aditi was still there, beside him, close enough to touch, close enough to catch the delicate floral scent she wore, close enough to see that her eyes were troubled.

"Have I shocked you?" she asked, her voice low.

He had to pull in a breath before he could answer, "It's . . . a surprise. I never thought . . ."

"Would you like to see the facility where we were created?"

"I'm not so sure," he said. "I don't know if I'm ready for that."

Aditi got to her feet and reached a hand out to Jordan. He rose, took her hand, and numbly followed her as together they walked into the city.

People were strolling along the streets, together with the pony-sized animals they used as beasts of burden. Smaller pets scampered among them, unhampered by leashes. Many of the people smiled and said hello.

He asked her, "All of these people were . . . ?"

"Created in the biolab, yes," Aditi answered easily. "So were the ponies and all the other animals you have seen here in the city."

"And the animals in the forest?"

She shook her head. "They procreate among themselves, of course."

"Of course," he said weakly.

As she walked purposefully along the street, Aditi said, "Jordan, it's merely another way for a species to reproduce. We use our technology. We can control every aspect of gestation. It allows us to produce babies that are healthy, intelligent, and empathetic."

He said nothing, but his mind pictured hordes of identical clones being mass-produced like automobiles or robots. He knew it was nonsense, that Aditi was not a mindless zombie, that every one of Adri's people was as individual as humans. Yet the picture remained in his mind. Things that looked like human beings being stamped out in a factory assembly line.

Aditi sensed his inner turmoil. "Jordan, dearest, the end product of our way is the same as the end product of your way: a baby. A squalling, gurgling, dribbling baby. Just the same as your babies. Just as human."

They were at the entrance to a smallish building. Its door opened at Aditi's touch and they went into the biolab.

Jordan followed Aditi through rows of equipment, all silent and still. She pointed out the microscopes and specimen containers, the glassware for cell cultures, the reactors where egg and sperm cells were united.

Like our biovats for meat, Jordan thought. Smaller, though. Much smaller.

"And here are the gestation chambers," Aditi said, gesturing to a line of small spheres that looked to Jordan like gourds made of plastic with half a dozen flexible pipes connected to them.

"They enlarge as the fetus grows, of course," Aditi said.

"I see," he murmured. Then he realized, "None of the equipment seems to be functioning."

"Not now. We don't need any more people for the time being. When the need arises, we can gestate newborns."

"And where do the eggs and sperm come from?" he asked.

"From us," she replied. "We donate ova and sperm cells when they are needed."

Rather cold-blooded, Jordan thought. But he said nothing.

Going down the line of artificial wombs, Aditi stopped at one. "This is where I was gestated," she said. "Number six."

The writing on the bench's top was indecipherable to Jordan, but he looked from it to her face, smiling hopefully.

"It did a good job," he said, smiling back at her.

Aditi broke into tears. Leaning her head against his chest, she sobbed, "You don't think I'm a monster?"

"I know you're not."

"You can accept me, knowing how I was created? How different I am?"

Folding his arms about her, Jordan said, "I love you, Aditi. I don't care how you were created; that doesn't matter."

He wasn't being entirely truthful. Jordan felt a slight shiver of apprehension as he looked past her tousled head to the row of artificial wombs standing silently on the bench, waiting to be used again to create new aliens.

RETURN TO CAMP

've got to go back to the camp, tell the others about this," Jordan said, as they walked back toward the entrance of the biolab.

"I understand," Aditi said.

The door opened again at her touch and they stepped out into the sunshine and bustle of the late-afternoon street. The slanting rays of sunlight felt warm, soothing, on Jordan's shoulders. Squinting against the brightness, he felt a cooling breeze that rustled the trees planted along the sidewalk.

"Will you come back tonight?" she asked.

As they walked along the street, back toward the city's perimeter, Jordan shook his head slowly. "I don't think so. This will be a lot for Meek and the others to digest. I'll have to stay with them, I'm afraid."

"I understand," she repeated. Reluctantly, Jordan thought.

"Will you come with me?" he asked. "Spend the night in my cubicle?"

Without hesitation, Aditi replied, "I'd like to, Jordan, but I don't think it would be best. I don't want them staring at me as if I'm a freak."

"I understand," he said. "I should have known."

They walked to the city's edge in silence, each wrapped in their own thoughts. Jordan knew that Aditi was right. Let Meek and Longyear and the others absorb this new information. It'll stun them, I'm sure. I don't want Aditi to be there when they find out about it. I don't want them staring at her, whispering about her. Let her stay here in the city, where she'll be safe.

Safe? He wondered why he thought about it that way. Surely

she'd be safe in our camp. No one's going to harm her. Not Long-year and certainly not Meek. They're frightened of her, but they wouldn't harm her. Yet he had instinctively felt concern for her safety.

And he realized that what men are frightened of, they often lash out against. It was a very human reaction.

By the time Jordan reached the camp, Sirius was setting, turning the sky into a blazing bold vermillion and painting the low-lying clouds deep violet. Higher above he saw the pinpoint of the Pup, bright as a laser, riding above the horizon-hugging cloud deck.

To his surprise, Brandon and de Falla had returned. They were at the rocketplane they had traveled in, out at the edge of the camp, while a pair of robots unloaded their gear. De Falla was watching the robot; Brandon stood nearby, all smiles, with Elyse clutching his arm happily. Jordan thought that she must have come in from the observatory once she learned that Bran was returning.

"Finished your survey so soon?" he asked de Falla, as one of the robots drove their tractor down the plane's cargo bay ramp and out onto the grass.

"That sector, yes," the geologist replied. "We've mapped it down to a centimeter scale and sampled its rocks and soil."

"We ran out of clean clothes," Brandon joked.

Jordan said, "Bran, I want you and all the others to gather at the dining area at seventeen hundred hours. I have some important new information to share with you. Tell the others, will you?"

Brandon nodded. "Okay, Jordy, I'll spread the word." He started off toward the cluster of bubble tents, Elyse at his side, leaving de Falla and the robots to finish unloading the rocketplane.

Jordan personally told Meek about the meeting, then went look-ing for Longyear and Thornberry.

Precisely at seventeen hundred hours Jordan stepped into the bubble tent that housed the camp's kitchen and dining area. All eight of the others were there, sitting at the longest table in the place, heads together in buzzing conversations. On the wall-sized display screen at the end of the table, Hazzard, Trish Wanamaker, and Demetrios Zadar looked on from the wardroom of the orbiting *Gaia*.

Jordan went to the head of the table. The talk stopped and they looked at him expectantly.

"I've learned something about our aliens that's both very interesting and . . . well, frankly, rather unsettling," he began.

"They're evangelists and they want to convert us to their religion," Brandon wisecracked.

A few titters ran along the table. Meek shot Brandon an annoyed glare.

With a tolerant smile, Jordan said, "No, it's not that bad."

"Then what is it?" asked Yamaguchi.

Jordan hesitated a heartbeat, then plunged, "They aren't born naturally. They aren't conceived and carried in a woman's womb. They're gestated in apparatuses in a laboratory."

Absolute silence for almost half a minute. Then Meek said, "I knew it! They're not real. They're constructs. Biological constructs."

"They're as real as you and I, Harmon," Jordan countered. "They simply were created in a different way."

Brandon asked, "Adri, too? All of them?"

"All of them."

Yamaguchi said, "But they're fully human. For all intents and purposes, they're identical to us."

"Down to their DNA," Longyear added.

"They were *constructed*," Meek insisted. "By whom? And for what purpose?"

"Yes," said Elyse. "If they were constructed in a laboratory, who built the laboratory?"

"Earlier generations, I suppose," Jordan answered.

"No, no, no," said Meek. "This is all part of a plan. A consistent plan of deception. Those people, their city, this entire planet . . . they're all part of a gigantic scheme."

"A scheme to do what?" asked Hazzard, from the screen. "What's the point behind all this? What are they after?"

"There's no deception," Jordan said firmly. "They've been completely honest with us."

"You'll pardon my saying so," Meek retorted, "but it seems to me that you've been sleeping with the enemy."

Jordan felt his innards turn to ice. He smiled coldly at the astro-biologist. "They're not our enemy, Harmon. And I can tell you that, no matter how they're created, they're as human as you or I."

Meek looked as if he were going to retort, then thought better of it and closed his mouth. Jordan looked to his brother for a word of support, some sign of understanding, but Brandon was silent, and he avoided Jordan's eyes.

"Contrary to any conspiracy theory," Jordan went on, trying to sound more certain than he felt, "Adri and his people have answered all our questions."

Thornberry spoke up. "Without telling us much at all. I've never had such lovely runarounds as their engineers have been giving me."

"Adri's policy," Jordan tried to explain, "is to answer our questions with absolute honesty, but not to go any further than our questions require."

"Now what kind of mischief is that?" Meek complained.

"He feels that contact between two alien races is a very delicate matter. He wants to be open and aboveboard with us, but he won't feed us more information than we're ready to accept."

"So how in blazes do those energy shields work?" Thornberry demanded.

Almost grinning at the roboticist, Jordan answered, "When you know enough to ask the right questions, they'll give you the right answers."

"Ahh, it's all malarkey, that's all."

"No, it's not, Mitch. You should be seeking out their physicists and learning the basics on which their technology is built."

"I'd have to be a PhD physicist to understand 'em!" Thornberry bleated.

"Then you'll have to learn physics from them," said Jordan.

"Back to school, then. Is that it?"

"I think it is," said Jordan. "For all of us. We have a lot to learn, and the first thing we must learn is how to ask the proper questions."

Turning to Meek, he added, "That goes for you, too, Harmon. Instead of being afraid of these people, you should be trying to learn from them."

Meek grumbled, "They won't like the questions I ask."

"But they'll answer them," Jordan replied.

UNANSWERED QUESTIONS

With obvious misgivings, Meek and Thornberry agreed to accompany Jordan back to the city the next morning. To Jordan's mild surprise, Brandon and Elyse asked to go, too.

Jordan felt briefly uncomfortable, until Brandon said, "I'm the planetary astronomer, remember, Jordy? I've got a lot of questions to ask about this planet's formation and composition."

"And there's a lot of astrophysics for me to learn," Elyse added. "No human being has seen a white dwarf this close. It's the opportunity of a lifetime for me!"

Jordan agreed with a good-natured shrug, then looked down the table toward Longyear. "What about you, Paul? Do you want to come with us? There are still lots of biology questions to be answered."

Before the biologist could reply, Meek said, "I'll ask the biology questions. It would be best if Paul remains here in camp. I'll stay in touch with him."

Longyear tried to hide his frown of disappointment, without success.

"And you, Silvio?"

De Falla answered, "I've got plenty to do, sorting out all the samples we took and integrating our detail map into the general planetary map we put together from orbit."

Yamaguchi said, "I'd certainly like to see their medical facilities."

"Later," said Jordan. "There'll be time for that later."

Tanya Verishkova sat in silence, her pale blue eyes on Thornberry. The roboticist felt her stare and said to her, "Tanya, my dear, you stay here and mind the robots. I'll check in with you regularly."

She nodded glumly.

Five of us go to the city, Jordan said to himself, and four remain here in camp. In time, we'll all move into the city. But we have to build trust first.

He glanced at Meek, sitting next to Longyear. Funny fellow, Jordan thought. He's suspicious of Adri, filled with fears of a conspiracy against us, yet he won't let Paul go with us. He wants to tackle the biology questions himself. Is it curiosity that's driving him, or the old academic cutthroat competition?

As the meeting broke up and Jordan started back toward the barracks tent, Brandon grabbed his arm.

"Jordy, we need to talk."

Elyse was leaving the dining area with all the others. The two brothers were alone. Brandon looked utterly serious, almost solemn.

"What is it, Bran?"

Resting his rump on the corner of the nearest table, Brandon said, "Meek and the others are worried about your fitness to lead."

"My fitness?"

Looking unhappy, Brandon said, "About your judgment. You know, with you sleeping with Aditi . . ." He left the rest of the thought unsaid.

Jordan felt his innards turn cold once again. "My sleeping with the enemy, as Harmon put it?"

"Well . . . yeah."

"She's not our enemy. None of them are."

"How do you know, Jordy?"

"What harm have they done to us?"

"What are they planning to do?" Brandon countered.

"Go to the city and ask them. They'll answer you truthfully."

"But not with the whole truth."

"They will, in time."

Brandon shook his head. "Jordy, I think you should step down. Let Hazzard or one of the others be in charge."

My own brother! Jordan thought. He's against me!

"Jordy, if you don't step down voluntarily, Meek's going to call for a vote and you'll be forced out."

"And once Meek's in charge he'll pack us all up and head back to Earth with his tail between his legs," Jordan said. "Is that what you want?"

"No, of course not. But . . ."

"But what?"

"Don't let them humiliate you, Jordy. Step down voluntarily."

Jordan held his temper, barely. With deliberate calm he replied, "Very well, Bran. I'll step down. On one condition."

"One condition?"

"That you take my place as leader of this Neolithic band."

Brandon's jaw dropped open.

A NEW REGIME

Jordan marched off to his own cubicle, steaming inside. Brandon's gone over to Meek's side, he growled to himself. My own brother has helped Meek and the others kick me aside.

He was too angry, too hurt, to even think of having dinner. Not in the dining area. Not with all those others. Instead, he stripped off his clothes and flung himself on the bunk. Briefly he thought of returning to the city to be with Aditi, but he realized that would only confirm the asinine fears of Meek and his ilk.

As he lay on his cot, staring up at the shadowed dome of the tent, he wondered if he should let it come to a vote. Instead of obediently stepping down, why not have it out in the open? Who's for me and who's against?

Then he realized that such a move would be foolish. Divisive. It would tear their little team into two antagonistic groups. Unless they *all* vote against me, he thought. The idea almost made him laugh. Yes, it could be a unanimous vote against me. Even Brandon.

Well, he told himself, at least I'll be free to be with Aditi and Adri and leave the rest of these noble explorers to their own devices.

But that's just what you've been doing all along, isn't it? he asked himself. You've been staying with Aditi and living in the city and ignoring the people you were supposed to be leading. No wonder they want you out! It was inevitable.

Strangely, he smiled to himself. I can't blame them, he thought. They're actually doing the right thing.

His last thought before falling asleep was, *And now I can be with Aditi full time.*

Jordan woke early and went to the communal lavatory to shower and shave. Thornberry was already there, standing by one of the sinks, washing his hands. He looked sheepish.

"Jordan," he began, "I'm sorry about last night."

"What did you decide?"

The roboticist's guilty expression morphed into a puzzled little frown. "Your brother took over, by god. He told us you would step down and he would step up. Just like that." Thornberry snapped his fingers.

"And Meek accepted that?"

"He did. He didn't like it much, but he accepted it when the rest of us started congratulating Brandon."

With an almost pleased smile, Jordan said, "Harmon expected to be elected the new leader."

"That he did," said Thornberry. "But your brother saved us from that, thank the saints."

"Good."

Almost reluctantly, Thornberry asked, "Are you still planning to go with us to the city this morning?"

"Why not?" Jordan asked. "What else do I have to do?"

After breakfast the five of them clambered aboard one of the buggies and headed for the city. Brandon drove, with Elyse sitting beside him. Meek and Thornberry sat together and Jordan contented himself with the last row. They rode in an awkward silence through the cool, bright morning.

Jordan sat back and admired the stately trees of the forest, for a while.

Then Meek turned toward him and asked, "Do you plan to stay in the city?"

"For the time being," Jordan replied easily. "I have a lot of questions to ask Adri and the others."

With obvious discomfort, Meek said, "What we did last night isn't a reflection on how we feel personally about you, Jordan. I hope you understand that. It's not a personal reflection at all."

"Of course, Harmon," Jordan said cordially. "I understand completely."

Meek looked puzzled as he turned back and stared straight ahead for the rest of the ride.

Adri stood waiting for them at the city's edge, looking like a modernist statue, tall and willowy slim, in his ankle-length blue-gray robe. Jordan wondered what Meek would do if he knew that Adri could track their movements. Run back to the ship and flee back to Earth, most likely. Brandon's going to have his hands full controlling him.

Aditi was not there. Jordan felt disheartened. Have I hurt her? Disappointed her with my reaction to her revelation about the biolab?

Brandon pulled the buggy over to a stop and they all piled out.

"Greetings, friends," said Adri, his spiderwebbed face creasing into a warm smile. "Welcome."

"And the top o' the day to you, sir," said Thornberry, smiling genially. "We've come to attend school with your people."

"School?"

Meek, almost as tall and lean as Adri, said, "We're here to learn, sir. We've come to find the answers to many, many questions."

"Good!" said Adri. "We are here to answer your questions, whatever they may be."

Jordan let out a sigh of relief. We begin well, he thought.

"Won't you get into our vehicle, Adri?" he said. "You can ride into the city with us."

"With pleasure," said Adri. Brandon slid behind the wheel again and the others resumed their seats. Jordan extended a hand to Adri, who looked bemused as he climbed into the buggy's last row.

"Aditi asked you to forgive her for not coming out to greet you. She's busy arranging for our best scientific and technical experts to meet with you."

"That's good," said Jordan, as his pulse thumped happily. Then he realized that Adri already knew why they had come to the city, and was making preparations before they had told him of their intentions. None of the others seemed to notice this, not even Meek.

They drove to the administrative center, where Aditi was waiting at the foot of the stairs with a handful of young men and women. Several of them wore robes of various colors, although most of them were dressed as Aditi was, in comfortable shorts and blouses. Within minutes, Meek, Thornberry, Brandon, and Elyse were all engaged in deep conversations with their tutors—that's how Jordan thought of them. Soon enough, they each strolled off to separate parts of the city, humans and aliens, talking animatedly. Even Meek looked pleased with the two biologists Aditi had gotten for him: a young man and a slightly older-looking woman.

Adri excused himself and headed up the stairs by himself. Jordan stood at the base of the stairs, alone with Aditi.

There were too many people strolling along the plaza for him to take her in his arms as he wanted to. Instead he asked an innocuous, "How are you?"

"Better," she said, with a pert smile, "now that you're here."

He smiled back at her. "Did you sleep well?"

"Undisturbed."

Jordan felt his cheeks redden. "I . . . uh . . . I've been relieved of my duties as leader of our group."

Aditi looked stricken. "Because of me?"

He shook his head. "Not really. It was my own fault."

"It was because of me," she said. Jordan realized that it was true, at least in part. And he didn't give a damn.

"We'll both sleep better tonight," he said.

Aditi laughed, like the ringing of a little silver bell. "Perhaps. Or perhaps we won't sleep at all."

DINNER

Jordan and Aditi had dinner that evening with Brandon and Elyse. Thornberry and Meek were each eating with their respective tutors. Adri begged off when Jordan asked him to join them.

"I have much to do," he said. "Besides, I eat very little, and it's difficult to maintain my diet when I dine with you hearty youngsters."

Jordan felt mildly surprised to be considered a youngster, but then he remembered that Adri was nearly four centuries old.

Over dinner, Brandon was strangely silent. His new responsibilities are weighing on him, Jordan thought. Handling Meek and his cohorts isn't going to be easy. Then he said to himself, Good! It's about time Brandon grew up.

Elyse bubbled with enthusiasm over her chance to study the Pup. "To observe a white dwarf star close up," she said. "To watch its flares, measure the fusion reactions still simmering along its photosphere. I'll be the most envied astrophysicist in the world!"

Brandon teased, "Until the next batch arrives here."

Jordan asked, "How's the planetary astronomer faring, Bran?"

"Plenty to do, plenty to find out. De Falla and I are working up a geological history of this planet. It's a lot younger than Earth, if what we've sampled so far is typical of the whole planet."

They chatted as they ate, until abruptly Brandon said to Aditi, "Jordy told us about your way of reproduction."

Jordan felt a flash of anger.

Aditi began, "I know it must seem strange to you, but we—"

"Not strange," said Jordan. "Different."

Brandon said, "There's something to be said about not having to get pregnant, I suppose."

"Or not worrying about becoming pregnant," Jordan heard himself say.

"I don't know," Elyse murmured, looking straight at Aditi. "For many women, pregnancy is a very special thing."

"All I've ever heard is complaints," Brandon said. "Backaches and morning sickness and all that."

"How many women have you gotten pregnant?" Aditi asked.

Brandon's eyes went wide. "Me?" he squeaked. "None!"

Smiling at his brother, Jordan corrected, "None that you know of, Bran."

"None," said Brandon, firmly. "Zero."

"So far," said Elyse.

They all burst into hearty laughter, except Brandon.

Reddening slightly, Brandon tried to change the subject. "You know, Aditi, your method of reproducing yourselves reminds me of an old, old joke."

Oh no, Jordan thought. He's not going to try to make a joke out of this.

"The only jokes you know are old ones," Elyse teased.

Ignoring her, Brandon explained, "Back in the early days of space flight, astronauts from Earth landed on this planet that was populated by a race of intelligent robots."

Elyse rolled her eyes toward the ceiling as she took a forkful of the cakelike dessert before her. Aditi's attention was riveted on Brandon.

"The robots understand that their visitors are from another planet," he went on, "and they show the astronauts all through their city."

"Just as we're doing for you," Aditi said.

"Well, yeah, that's right. But at the end of the day the robots throw a big dinner party for the astronauts. A thousand robots fill the hall."

"They knew how to make human food?" Jordan asked. "Or did they feed the astronauts machine oil?"

Brandon frowned at his brother. "So, during the dinner, one of the robots gets up and says, 'We've shown you the factory where we make more robots. How do you make more humans?'"

"Oh-oh," said Elyse.

Brandon plowed on. "Well, the astronauts are embarrassed. They're rocket jockeys, not scientists. So they try to explain, stammering a lot, how humans make more humans."

"And?"

"And all the robots bust into uproarious laughter! The astronauts are stunned. They didn't expect laughter."

Brandon waited for a suspenseful moment, then went on, "One of the robots apologizes to the astronauts. 'I'm sorry. We shouldn't be laughing. But you see, what you just described—that's the way we make automobiles.'"

The table fell silent. All eyes turned to Aditi. Brandon's expression morphed from expectant to troubled. Jordan seethed. Of all the insensitive oafs . . .

And then Aditi broke into laughter. Delighted, tinkling laughter, like wind chimes at a mountaintop monastery Jordan had once visited.

"You make automobiles in factories," Aditi giggled, "the way the robots make robots."

"It's an old joke," Brandon said weakly.

"But it's still funny," said Elyse. "A little."

"I'm sorry if I offended you," Brandon said to Aditi.

"No, no," she replied. "I'm not offended."

Jordan thought that if she was hurt by Brandon's joke, she was being very gracious about it. More gracious than I'd be.

HOLLOW PROGRESS

he days rolled by. Brandon shuttled back and forth from the city to the base camp. Elyse spent most of her time at the astronomical observatory. Thornberry and Meek seemed quite contented with what they were learning. Delighted, even.

"The way they can manipulate force fields," Thornberry enthused one morning, as Jordan visited the laboratory where he spent most of his time, "it's incredible, it is. Simply incredible."

Half a dozen young physicists and engineers were in the lab, looking happy that the human roboticist was so impressed with their work.

Pointing to the disassembled components of an energy shield generator scattered across a lab table, Thornberry said, "They tap into dark energy as easily as you or I plug in an electrical appliance, they do."

"What you call dark energy," said one of the young men, "is merely another fundamental force, like the strong nuclear force."

Thornberry nodded impatiently. "Yes, so it is. But the energy shield you create with it absorbs not only charged particles, but neutral electromagnetic energy, as well. Hit it with a burst of gamma rays powerful enough to fry a rhinoceros and it merely soaks 'em up. It actually *uses* the incoming radiation to power itself!"

"It's pretty fundamental," said the physicist.

"To you it's fundamental," Thornberry said. "To me, it's a bit of black magic."

Jordan felt impressed, although he didn't fully understand the principles Thornberry was talking about.

Even Meek seemed pleased with what he was learning. His

suspicions were melting away—slowly—in the light of newfound knowledge.

"The things they can do with biology," he said over lunch one afternoon. "Not only do they manipulate DNA to produce new species, they can control genetic expression and suppress aging!"

Longyear, de Falla, Yamaguchi, and Verishkova visited the city in turn, each of them brimming with enthusiasm about what they were learning. Hazzard and the others aboard *Gaia* came down from time to time and got swept up in the new knowledge Adri's people were sharing so freely.

Jordan was pleased, very pleased. Especially since he and Aditi were living together now. He spent his days checking with the others, strictly informally, and talking with Adri about how well everyone was getting along. He spent his nights with Aditi.

"It's uncanny," Longyear told Jordan one afternoon. "Parallel evolution was just a far-out concept that nobody really expected to be real, but here's a whole planet full of parallel species."

The biologist's earlier suspicions seemed to be washed away by the new discoveries he was making.

Only de Falla remained puzzled. "Either my basic geology program is screwed up, or this planet doesn't make sense."

He was having dinner with Jordan, Brandon, Elyse, and Aditi, in the city's main dining hall. The spacious, high-ceilinged room was filled with whistling conversations and clattering dinnerware. Jordan heard laughter drifting from several tables. He saw Thornberry and Verishkova sitting at a long table with a dozen alien scientists. And Meek sitting amiably with Adri and a pair of other aliens. Meek! Jordan shook his head in wonder.

"What's wrong with your program?" Brandon asked the geologist.

De Falla's round, beard-trimmed face looked troubled. "It's giving me ridiculous results."

Brandon prompted, "Such as?"

"Well, you know that Adri's people have been feeding me all the geological data I've asked for. And Hazzard's been dropping seismological probes all across the planet."

Jordan nodded.

"When I feed the data to the computer for a geological profile I get impossible results," de Falla complained.

"What do you mean?" Elyse asked.

Looking almost embarrassed, de Falla said, "The model of the planet's interior that the program draws up shows that this planet is hollow."

Jordan blurted, "Hollow?"

De Falla nodded morosely. "It just doesn't make any sense."

"How could a planet be hollow?" Jordan asked.

Brandon laughed. "Maybe your computer was programmed by one of the Hollow Earth kooks back home."

"It's not funny," said de Falla. "I've gone over the damned program six ways from Sunday and I can't find the glitch in it."

"The planet can't be hollow," Jordan said. But he turned to his brother and added, "Could it?"

"No way," said Brandon, wagging his head. "If it were hollow it wouldn't have the mass to produce the gravity we experience."

"But the computer keeps saying it's hollow," de Falla insisted.

"Your program's got to be wrong," said Brandon. "Why don't you get Thornberry to take a look at it?"

"I already have. He and Tanya went over everything. They couldn't find the glitch either."

Brandon made a sour face. "Well, something's screwed up someplace. Hollow planets don't exist."

"Trouble is," de Falla went on, "the computer's model is so damned specific. It shows a shell a couple of hundred kilometers thick, and inside it—nothing. It's hollow."

"Can't be," said Brandon.

"I know," de Falla agreed. "But there it is."

Jordan said, "What can you do about it?"

De Falla broke into a sheepish grin. "What would any geologist do in a situation like this? Dig."

"Dig?"

"Get more evidence. Dig some deep cores and sample what they bring up."

"That sounds difficult," said Jordan.

With a shrug, de Falla replied, "It beats staring at a computer screen and wondering why the program's gone crazy."

"How many cores?" Jordan asked. "Where?"

"I've mapped out six locations, spread around the planet. I can show you, in my lab."

Brandon said, "Let's adjourn to your lab, then."

FIELD TRIP

he five of them stood before the display screen that covered one entire wall of the room de Falla was using as his geology laboratory. It was a fair-sized room, with a floor-to-ceiling window that opened onto one of the city's gracious, tree-lined plazas. Although it was well past sunset, the scene outside was clearly lit by the glow of the Pup, riding high above the silvery clouds.

Shelves filled with rocks, pebbles, containers of dirt lined the two other walls. The room had two long worktables covered with a spectrograph, microscopes, and other equipment, plus a sizeable desk that bore a humming computer. The ceiling lights were off, the lab was lit only by the wall screen, which showed a map of the planet, slowly rotating, garishly daubed in false colors and marked with a scattering of bright blue dots.

"The colors indicate different types of terrain," de Falla was explaining, "and the dots show where we've taken soil and rock samples."

"We?" Jordan asked.

"Robots, mostly. I've done a few quick field trips, but most of the work's being done by robots."

Jordan pulled up one of the stools lining the nearer worktable and rested his rear on it.

Brandon said, "So now you want to dig deep cores?"

De Falla nodded. "Six of them." To the computer he commanded, "Display deep core sites."

Three bright red dots began to flash on the sphere. Another one appeared over its northern rim as the image slowly rotated.

"I intend to drill these cores myself," de Falla said. "The robots can do the heavy work, but I'll have to be on-site to direct them."

Brandon said, "Suppose I help you? We could cut down the time it'd take."

After a moment's hesitation, de Falla agreed with an easy smile. "Sure. I could use all the help I can get."

Turning to Jordan, Brandon asked, "You want to come along, Jordy? See how science really gets done?"

He glanced at Aditi, then said, "All right. Providing it doesn't take too long."

"A few days," said de Falla. "Maybe a week."

"You can be away that long," Brandon coaxed. Looking straight at Aditi, he added, "You've got nothing else to do."

Jordan seethed inwardly, but said nothing.

Elyse spoke up. "I can't leave my work at the observatory. The Pup is entering an active cycle, from what the astronomers tell me."

Grinning at her, Brandon said, "You wouldn't like it out in the field, anyway. Jordy and I will have to rough it. Tents. Latrines. That sort of thing."

"I'll stay here in the city, thank you," Elyse said.

Aditi said, "We could provide you with energy shields. You wouldn't need tents."

Jordan could see that Aditi wasn't happy about being separated from him for a week.

Later, as they prepared for bed, he asked her, "You don't want to come out with us, do you?"

She countered, "You don't want me to come with you, do you?"

Stretching out on the bed, Jordan answered, "It might be a bit awkward, your being with me while Elyse stays here in the city."

She slipped into bed beside him. "You go with your brother, Jordan. I'll miss you, though."

"I'll miss you, too, darling."

"But not tonight. Tonight we're together."

"Together," he murmured, reaching for her. But in the back of his mind he realized that one day he would have to return to Earth. Will Aditi go with me? he wondered.

"I've got to learn how to fly one of these birds," Brandon muttered as they soared high above a mountain range in one of the rocket-planes.

"Hazzard seems to do the job quite well," said Jordan, sitting in the right-hand seat beside his brother. Hazzard's image filled the main screen on the control panel. He appeared to be quite happy controlling the plane from the bridge of *Gaia*.

Brandon shook his head. "It still kind of bothers me, letting Geoff pilot us remotely. No reflection on you, Geoff," he said to the screen.

"Any time you want to fly one of the birds yourself, just let me know," Hazzard said, with a malevolent grin. "Just tell me where you want the bodies sent."

"Thanks a lot," said Brandon.

Jordan watched the jagged peaks go past. There were patches of snow huddled in hollows that were sheltered from sunlight; otherwise the rocks were bare. Jordan thought he saw what looked like a herd of mountain goats peacefully negotiating the steep slopes.

Suddenly Brandon sat up straighter and pointed. "There's the sea!"

Jordan saw a broad expanse of water glittering beneath the afternoon sun. A rim of white beach ran along its edge, and the swells appeared to run up smoothly onto the sand without breaking. A gentle, peaceful sea, Jordan thought. No surfing, but the sparkling water looked warm, inviting.

De Falla had chosen this spot for drilling because his geology profile indicated the planet's crust was thinner here.

"If the damned planet really is hollow," he had told Brandon and Jordan, "then you might be able to break through the crust and prove it."

Brandon had laughed at the geologist. "It's not hollow, Silvio. You know that and I know that."

De Falla had nodded grudgingly. "But nobody's told the damned computer program."

Jordan couldn't help picturing in his mind what would happen if the planet really was hollow and they punctured its thin shell. He saw a balloon collapsing, whizzing every which way as the air inside it escaped.

Not very likely, he told himself. Still, he couldn't shake the image.

With Hazzard piloting remotely, the plane made a long, swooping turn out over the water, then glided in for a smooth landing on the hard-packed beach sand. Even before the engines had completely shut down, Brandon unbuckled his seat harness and headed for the hatch.

"Looks like a tropical paradise out there," he said over his shoulder. "We should have brought the women."

Fine time to think of that, Jordan grumbled silently as he got up from his seat.

He followed Brandon to the hatch. His brother swung it open and Jordan heard the murmur of surf. Looking past Brandon's shoulder, he saw that the waves lapping up on the beach were only a few centimeters high. Babies could play here, he thought. Then he remembered that Aditi's people had no babies, not at present.

The beach was as lovely as a video scene, with graceful palmlike trees fringing it, swaying gently in the warm breeze blowing in off the sea. Sirius was high in the brazen sky, bright and hot. Jordan welcomed its warmth on his shoulders, although he had to put on a pair of dark glasses to cut down the glare.

Turning, he saw a pair of humanform robots already at work, unloading equipment from the plane's cargo hatch. The crates looked big, heavy.

"What's that?" he asked as they walked toward the hardworking robots.

Brandon peered at the nearest crate. "Laser drilling equipment. For de Falla's deep core."

"How far down will it drill?"

"Tens of kilometers, unless there's a hitch."

"You mean, unless the beam strikes especially hard rock?"

Brandon shook his head vigorously. "No, Jordy. The beam's powerful enough to vaporize any kind of rock. The only problems we might encounter will be equipment breakdowns. Once we've got the laser running, it'll cut through anything like butter."

Jordan felt impressed.

With a wicked grin, Brandon punned, "Now we're going to get down to the core of the matter."

"Can we go deep enough to disprove that the planet's hollow?"

"Yes indeed, Jordy." Brandon couldn't suppress another pun. "We're going to knock the stuffing out of the hollow planet idea."

It's going to be a long week, Jordan told himself.

SOONER OR LATER

t took two days to wipe the confident grin off Brandon's face.

The afternoon that they landed was spent in setting up the laser drill. Brandon picked a spot away from the beach, up amidst the trees and ground foliage. With Jordan's help, he set up a pair of seismometers and a miniature radio transmitter that allowed the GPS satellites in orbit overhead to fix their position with nanometer precision.

While they were doing that, the robots erected their tent. Brandon had politely refused Aditi's offer of an energy shield.

"We won't need it," he said.

Jordan thought it might have been interesting to sleep out in the open, without a tent hemming in their view, but he went along with his brother's decision. *Bran's been on field trips a lot more than I have,* he told himself.

Once the tent was up and filled with their two cots and footlockers, Brandon led one of the robots, carrying a power shovel, to dig a latrine back in the brush and trees that fringed the beach. Adri and the city's biologists had assured them that there would be no environmental problem from the latrines. *Same DNA,* Jordan thought. *We won't contaminate anything here.*

They slept on side-by-side cots in the tent, but Jordan awoke in the middle of the night. Restless, he got up quietly from his cot and tiptoed out into the night. It was cool in nothing but his T-shirt and briefs; the breeze coming in off the sea chilled him.

Yet the sea itself was magnificently beautiful and he regretted not bringing Aditi with him to share it. No moon, but the Pup, low on the horizon, sent a stream of glittering silver across the softly murmuring sea. Stars twinkled in the sky. Jordan tried to make sense out of their configurations, but he couldn't recognize any of the constellations he knew from Earth.

Except—he peered into the dark sky and, yes, there was Orion, leaning lopsidedly above the sea horizon. Good old Orion! Jordan's heart leaped at the familiarity of it. Rigel, Betelgeuse, the Belt, and the Sword. Eight point six light-years from home, and there was Orion, friendly and familiar.

On an impulse, he ducked back into the tent and rummaged in the dark until he found his pocketphone. Then he went back outside and called Aditi. She was thickheaded with sleep at first, but as Jordan showed her the beach and the soft glow of the Pup she revived.

"It's beautiful," she said.

"I wish you were here," said Jordan.

"Well, we can share the view, at least."

He sat on the sand, his back against one of the gracefully bent trees, and held the phone so that Aditi could see the silvery waves running gently up the beach. They talked until he grew drowsy.

At last Aditi said, "You'd better get back to your bed, Jordan. You're half asleep."

"Good night, love," he said.

"Good night, darling," she replied.

"I wish you were here."

"So do I."

He went back to his cot and slept soundly until sunrise.

Drilling began with the morning. Brandon spent much of his time on the phone with de Falla, making certain that everything was just right, before turning on the laser. It rumbled to life, and a plume of smoke burst up from the ground.

"Won't the smoke block the laser's beam?" Jordan asked.

Standing with his fists on his hips like some old-time plantation overseer, Brandon replied, "De Falla says it won't. The beam is intense enough to burn right through the smoke. It just recondenses as the gases rise above the laser's output head. What you're seeing won't affect the laser at all."

And it certainly appeared so. All day long, Jordan watched the control console that the robots had set up next to their tent. It was linked to the laser equipment by a tangle of snaking cables. The laser growled away and the graph on the console's central screen showed a single bright green line heading straight down, deeper and deeper into the planet's crust. By sunset it had passed the eight-kilometer mark and was still blazing away, without stopping.

"Should we leave it running overnight?" Jordan asked.

"Why not? The robots can tend to it. If there's any problem they can wake us."

Over their prepackaged dinners, Jordan said, "So this is what field work is all about. The robots do the work and you take the credit."

Brandon frowned at his brother. "I gather the data. I make sense out of what the equipment is doing. I'm the brains of this operation."

"And the robots supply the muscle."

"Used to be grad students that provided the muscle. I put in my time as slave labor, believe me."

"I suppose you did," said Jordan.

They finished eating, did their ablutions, and got ready for sleep. Jordan could hear the laser growling away out in the darkness. It ruined the romantic aura of the place, he thought.

As he stretched out on his cot, hands cradling the back of his head, Brandon reminisced, "Grad students included women, of course. Field trips were a lot more interesting then."

"Perhaps Thornberry could rig one of the robots for you," Jordan suggested, grinning into the shadows.

"That's a filthy idea, Jordy. I like it."

"Ask Thornberry about it," Jordan joked.

"You think Mitch is making out with Tanya?" Brandon asked.

"Yes," Jordan answered without hesitation. "It's Longyear and de Falla I wonder about. They're both young and unattached."

"Maybe Yamaguchi's giving them something to dampen their sex drive."

"Then there's Yamaguchi herself. What about her sex drive?"

"She's Japanese. Terrific self-discipline."

"And Hazzard?"

"Trish."

"That's what I thought," Jordan said. "What do you make of Zadar?"

Brandon didn't answer for a moment. Then, "He's Greek, of course . . ."

"Don't be a lout!"

With a chuckle, Brandon said, "I don't know. Demetrios is a pretty quiet guy."

Jordan surprised himself by asking, "How serious are you about Elyse?"

"Pretty damned serious," Brandon replied without hesitation. "She means a lot to me, and I think I mean a lot to her."

"Good," said Jordan. "It's time you found someone."

"Approval from my big brother! That's a first."

Surprised, almost hurt, Jordan said, "I want you to be happy, Bran."

"Works both ways, Jordy. What about you and Aditi?"

Jordan sighed. "I didn't think that, after Miriam, I could ever fall in love again. But I have."

"It's a little tricky, her not being really human."

"She's as human as you or I, Bran. As human as Elyse."

Brandon didn't reply for several moments. Then, "But when it comes time for us to leave, Jordy, what then?"

"I don't know. We haven't discussed it. Neither one of us wants to look that far ahead."

"But you'll have to, sooner or later."

"Sooner or later," Jordan agreed. "Sooner or later."

SURPRISE

Jordan woke with sunlight glowing on the wall of the tent. Brandon's cot was already empty, though rumpled, unmade. Jordan could see him sitting outside on the folding chair in front of the console that was monitoring the laser's progress, wearing nothing but his skivvies. He dressed quickly, then went out to the latrine. He could hear the laser thrumming steadily.

God's in his heaven, he thought, and the equipment's working fine. All's right with the world.

But then he heard Brandon call, "Jordy, take a look at this."

Jordan walked to where Brandon was sitting and, peering over his brother's shoulder, saw that the bright green line depicting the depth of the borehole had flattened out.

"That can't be right," he said to his brother. "Can it?"

Brandon hunched forward in the rickety folding chair, scowling and muttering as he tapped keys on the console's control board.

"Damned thing hasn't gone a centimeter deeper since just after midnight."

"But the laser's still running," Jordan said.

"It is, but it's not going anywhere."

"How can that be?"

Shaking his head, Brandon muttered, "Damned if I know."

"It's hit something that it can't vaporize," Jordan mused. "Some particularly hard form of rock."

"Jordy, that laser is powerful enough to vaporize any kind of rock. Construction crews used lasers like that to dig the Moho shaft in Siberia, for chrissakes."

"Well, *something* has stopped it."

Brandon bolted out of the flimsy chair, knocking it over, and hurried to the generator that powered the laser. He looked more than a little ridiculous, Jordan thought, in nothing but his briefs and T-shirt, standing between the two silent and unmoving robots.

"Power output's at maximum," he called to Jordan as he scanned the generator's dials. "That beam's powerful enough to melt the Rock of Gibraltar."

"How long can the generator go on running?"

"Weeks. It's nuclear."

"And the laser is working?"

"Christ, Jordy, you can *hear* it running!"

Jordan realized how upset Brandon was; he only used language like that when he was distraught. There was no smoke blowing out of the borehole. The laser is running, but it's not vaporizing any of the rock down there.

How deep has it gone? he wondered. A glance at the console's screen showed him. The depth line flattened out at fourteen kilometers.

Brandon came back to the console, carefully picked up the chair, then leaned a thumb on a square red button on the control board. The laser abruptly turned off. The world went quiet. Then Jordan heard the sighing of the trees in the soft breeze, the murmur of the surf. A bird trilled, somewhere.

"What do we do now?" he asked.

"I'm going to get dressed," Brandon said, "after I instruct the robots to pull up the laser head."

"And then?"

With a grim shrug, Brandon replied, "Then we send a camera down the hole and see what the hell's stopped the goddamned laser."

They picked at their breakfasts while the robots methodically hauled the laser head back up to the surface.

Brandon said, "Well, it sure isn't hollow."

"Apparently not."

"Might be some weird form of matter. Some super condensate."

Jordan dipped his chin slightly. "Apparently this planet isn't an exact duplicate of Earth."

"Not below its crust, anyway."

"It only looks like Earth on the surface."

"Yeah."

Jordan could see that Brandon was despondent, deeply disappointed that the laser had run into a problem he couldn't understand.

"Well," he said, as brightly as he could manage, "perhaps you've run into a new kind of planetary structure. You might become just as famous as that fellow who discovered continental drift."

"Wegener," Brandon answered dully.

"You ought to call de Falla and see if any of the other drills have run into the same problem," Jordan suggested.

Cheering up a bit, Brandon said, "Good idea."

Jordan walked toward the borehole, where the two robots were working the equipment that was slowly hauling the laser head up to the surface. Fourteen kilometers, he recalled. It'll take several hours to get the laser up here and then a camera down again.

Brandon came over beside him. "De Falla says none of the other drills have gone as deep as we have yet."

"The perils of the pioneer," Jordan said, trying to lighten his brother's mood. "Being first and all that."

Brandon huffed. "Somebody once said that pioneering is just finding new ways to get yourself killed."

"Oh, come on now, Bran. You've run into something new, something unprecedented, perhaps. You should be elated. It's a chance to learn new things about planetary structures."

His brother nodded bleakly. "Maybe."

It was late afternoon by the time the robots got the camera down to the level where the laser had stopped. De Falla phoned to tell them that two of the other drilling rigs had stopped, as well.

"At what depth?" Brandon asked.

"Fourteen klicks," answered the geologist. "Give or take a dozen meters."

"Something's down there," Brandon said tightly. He was sitting at the console again. Its central screen showed a murky view from the still-descending camera. Jordan saw from the data bar alongside the screen that the camera had almost reached the depth where the laser had been stopped.

In the phone's screen, de Falla looked more puzzled than dejected. "Something's down there, all right," he agreed. "But what?"

"I'll call you back," Brandon said. "We're starting to get a camera view." He clicked the phone shut and tucked it into his shirt pocket.

Jordan looked over his brother's shoulder at the console's main screen. The two robots stood behind him, silent and still. Yet Jordan couldn't help feeling that they were peering over his shoulder, straining to see what was down there, just as he was.

The lights that accompanied the camera brightened to full intensity. Jordan blinked at what he saw. He heard Brandon grunt.

"It looks like metal," Brandon muttered.

"Smooth," said Jordan. "As if it were polished."

"It *is* polished," Brandon said. "And there isn't even a scorch mark from where the laser beam hit it."

"Polished metal?" Jordan wondered aloud.

"It's artificial," said Brandon, with absolute certainty.

CONFIRMATION

They sent the camera's view back to de Falla, at his digging site, and the geologist excitedly reported running into the same metallic barrier at the same depth.

Brandon looked sulky, almost angry. Jordan had seen that expression on his brother's face many times before: when Brandon couldn't get what he wanted, he pouted.

"A layer of polished metal at a depth of fourteen kilometers below the surface," Jordan mused. "That's . . ." He struggled to find a word.

"All across the planet," Brandon said, almost growling.

"Only six points," Jordan pointed out.

"Jordy, we could dig six hundred boreholes. Or six thousand, six million. We'll find the same thing in every one, guaranteed."

Jordan thought that nothing they had yet found on New Earth could be guaranteed.

"Come on," Brandon said. "Let's pack it all in and get back to the base camp. I want to talk to Adri about this."

"Yes," Jordan agreed. "He has some explaining to do."

It was twilight when their rocketplane touched down at the base camp. De Falla was already there, waiting impatiently as they came down the metal ladder from the plane's hatch.

"I left the robots to pack up," the geologist said. "Hazzard'll fly them all back here tomorrow."

"Why the rush?" Brandon asked.

Leading them straight to the bubble tent that housed the geology lab, de Falla said, "I wanted to run the data about this metal layer through the profile program, see what comes up."

Brandon nodded. "Makes sense."

Meek, Thornberry, and Elyse joined them as they practically trotted toward the tent.

Brandon reached out his hand to Elyse as he asked her, "You came back from the city?"

"Once Adri told me you were returning from your field excursion, yes," she said, smiling happily at him.

"What do you make of this latest finding?" Meek asked Jordan.

"Harmon, I'm merely an unemployed administrator. I don't make scientific judgments. That's your department."

"It can't be natural," Brandon said.

De Falla, leading their little parade, said over his shoulder, "That's my conclusion, too. A sheet of polished metal fourteen kilometers deep isn't natural."

Jordan expected Meek to be glowing with triumph. Instead, he looked worried, frightened. "How could there be a layer of polished metal fourteen kilometers below the surface?"

"We'll have to ask Adri," said Jordan.

"And if he doesn't know?"

"He knows," de Falla said, with grim certainty. "The question is, will he tell us?"

Jordan phoned Adri, who immediately agreed to come to the camp to answer their questions. Jordan wondered if Aditi would come with him, but hesitated to ask in front of all the others.

They ate dinner together while they waited for the alien, all nine of them, bouncing unanswerable questions around the table, making guesses, suppositions. Jordan listened to them in silence. Scientists, he thought; they can't simply sit and admit they don't know what's going on. They have to try to find an answer. Or invent one.

A scrap of poetry came to his mind. Robert Frost, he remembered: *We dance round in a ring and suppose, but the* secret *sits in the middle and knows.*

It was full night by the time Adri reached the camp, walking briskly in his usual befigured robe. Jordan's pulse quickened when he saw that Aditi walked beside him, looking fresh and happy in a knee-length skirt of dark green and a short-sleeved white blouse.

The night was lit by the Pup, casting a silvery moon glow over the tall, silent trees and the round white domes of the camp.

"Good evening, my friends," said Adri, his thin voice carrying through the shadows. "It's good to see you all once more."

As his brother had done with Elyse, Jordan held out a hand to Aditi. She came to him and clasped it warmly.

But Brandon said sharply, "We need some answers from you, Adri."

"Of course. I will be glad to tell you anything I can."

De Falla said, "Let's go over to the geology lab. The computer should be finished with the profile by now."

"By all means," said Adri.

As they started toward the tent, Jordan whispered to Aditi, "I missed you."

Her smile lit up the landscape. "I missed you, too."

De Falla led the little procession through the camp's bubble tents to the geology lab. Jordan noticed that Meek walked several paces behind Adri, with Longyear beside him. Both men wore tight-lipped expressions, taut with hostility. Brandon walked alongside Elyse, of course, chatting happily with her, nearly oblivious of the others.

Once in the geology tent, de Falla called up his computer's profile of the planet's structure while Adri sat on one of the stools lining the worktable. The others clustered around the table, looking expectantly at the computer's big flat display screen.

"As you know," de Falla said, his round, beard-fringed face utterly serious, "we've been digging boreholes at several locations."

"To determine the structure of this planet, I presume," Adri said.

De Falla went on, "And we've hit an anomaly."

A wisp of a smile appeared on Adri's age-creased face. "An anomaly?"

The display screen lit up, showing a graph that depicted a cross section of the planet's structure. The metal layer appeared in blazing red at the fourteen-kilometer depth. Below it was nothing but a dull gray, indicating that the deeper structure of the planet was unknown.

De Falla began, "There seems to be a layer of polished metal—"

"At a depth of fourteen kilometers," Adri interrupted. "Yes, that is correct."

"It can't be natural."

"It's not."

Jordan felt his breath catch in his throat. Meek looked like a prosecutor who's just heard his suspect confess. Longyear looked angry, almost, de Falla stunned, despite his previous attitude. Even Thornberry's usual quizzical smile was gone, replaced by a suspicious scowl.

Brandon snapped, "You know about this?"

"Yes, of course," said Adri.

They clustered around him, as taut and stressed as a lynch mob. All they need is a rope, Jordan thought.

Brandon asked, "There's a shell of metal fourteen klicks deep?"

"Yes."

"All around the planet?"

"Yes," said Adri, as if it was the most natural thing in the universe. "Of course. It's the structural base for New Earth's crust and biosphere."

Meek found his voice. "Look here, are you telling us that the upper layers of this planet have been . . . landscaped? You've deliberately shaped this upper section of the planet, this entire biosphere?"

In a placatingly calm voice, Adri replied, "New Earth has been constructed to resemble your world as closely as possible."

"Constructed?" Longyear squeaked.

Adri's smile turned slightly rueful. "We had no intention of deceiving you, my friends. Our policy has been to allow you to discover the truth at your own pace."

Jordan said, "Are you telling us that this entire planet has been built, deliberately constructed to resemble Earth?"

With a nod, Adri said, "And placed close enough to your world so that you would find us, and come to examine us."

Elyse gasped, "Red Sirius!"

"What?"

"Naked-eye observations of Sirius made more than two thousand years ago, around the time of Christ," she said, almost breathless. "They reported that the star had turned red."

Adri said, shamefaced, "I'm afraid that was due to the construction operation," he admitted. "I'm sorry if it confused your astronomers."

"You *constructed* this planet?" Meek asked, in obvious disbelief. "This entire planet? You *built* it?"

"Not I," said Adri. "Our Predecessors did."

Meek said, "But why? How?"

Adri glanced at Aditi, then turned back to Meek and explained, "Our race is much older than yours. Our technology, as you've seen for yourselves, is considerably in advance of yours."

"Then you do have spaceflight," Thornberry said. "You're not from this planet, you came from somewhere else."

"Our civilization does have the capability for spaceflight, yes," Adri said. "But we—myself, Aditi, all the others you have seen here on this world—we have lived on this planet since our conception. We have never been anywhere else."

"But to build an entire planet," Jordan objected. "It's fantastic!"

"Who built it?" Brandon demanded. "If you and your people have been born here, then who the hell built this planet?"

"Our Predecessors," said Adri.

"Your ancestors?"

"Our Predecessors," Adri repeated.

"Why would they do such a thing?" Meek demanded again. "What's the purpose of it all?"

"Why, to bring you here. To encourage you to make contact with us."

Frowning, Brandon said, "Wouldn't it have been easier for you to come to Earth and announce your presence?"

"And what would your reaction be if suddenly a starship appeared in your skies? Even if we beamed messages to you, instead of sending a starship, your world would be in turmoil, wouldn't it?"

Jordan almost chuckled. Glancing at Meek, he said, "There are plenty of people on Earth who'd be terrified, true enough."

"What would you do?" Adri repeated.

Meek answered, "Why, we . . . we'd try to ascertain who you are, of course. And what you want."

With a sad shake of his head, Adri replied, "The shock of such a meeting would be traumatic for you. Why, even now, on Earth there are people who claim there can be no other intelligent races in the universe!"

"So we have a few benighted fanatics," Thornberry said.

"They deny the possibility that the indigenous life in Jupiter's ocean could be intelligent," Adri pointed out.

"The leviathans," Elyse murmured.

Adri went on, "We have studied your history very thoroughly. We have seen the dreadful consequences of sudden contact between two of your own cultures."

Longyear muttered, "Wounded Knee."

"And a hundred other tragedies," said Aditi. "The Aztecs and Incas. The Polynesians. Even the Chinese went through centuries of exploitation and humiliation."

"That is why," Adri resumed, "we decided to make our contact with you as gentle as possible. We did not go to your planet and announce ourselves. Instead, we encouraged you to come here, to us."

"You lured us here," said Meek.

"If you wish to use that term," Adri replied gently. "The point is that only a small group of you has come here, as we expected. And we have allowed you to discover the truth about us in your own time, at your own pace." Turning once again to Meek, he added, "And even so, we face suspicion, hostility, and outright fear."

Jordan said, "You're telling us that we have nothing to be afraid of."

"Oh no," said Adri. "You have much to be afraid of. And so do we."

CULTURE SHOCK

What do you mean by that?" Meek demanded.

Adri hesitated, then replied, "Contact between two intelligent cultures is fraught with dangers."

"You've contacted other intelligent species?" Brandon asked.

"Not I personally," said Adri. "None of us has ever been beyond this planet. But our Predecessors, our progenitors, over the course of the millennia they have come into contact with many civilizations."

Jordan blurted, "There are lots of civilizations among the stars?"

Adri shook his head sorrowfully. "Intelligence is the rarest occurrence in the universe, I'm afraid. And even at that, in so many cases, an intelligent species destroys itself before it can attain true self-mastery."

Brandon said, "But we've seen no evidence of any intelligent races in the galaxy, until now. We've searched for almost two centuries, and our telescopes haven't turned up anything."

"As I said," Adri replied, "intelligence is very rare. However, the universe is very large, and there are many intelligent civilizations scattered among the stars."

"Intelligent species destroy themselves?" Jordan asked.

"Unfortunately, that seems to be the norm. It's very rare for an intelligent species to survive long enough to achieve true civilization."

Thornberry pushed to Adri's side. "So that's why you're here? To help us to survive our own shortcomings?"

Adri hesitated for several long moments, staring into Thornberry's questioning eyes. At last he answered, "Yes, that is part of our purpose."

Jordan caught the nuance. "But only part of it?"

"It's as much as I can tell you for the moment. Now you know something of who we are and why we are here. I think it best for you to absorb what you've just learned before we proceed any farther."

"There's more?" Meek asked.

"Oh, yes. Much, much more."

"But you're not going to tell us what it is," Brandon said accusingly.

"In time," said Adri. "For now, Aditi and I must return to the city. You'll want to discuss what I've told you among yourselves. Tomorrow is another day."

The humans stood mutely as Adri and Aditi made their way to the entrance of the bubble tent and went outside into the silvery shadows of the night.

Jordan followed them, like a man in a dream. Aditi turned back toward him, extended her hand to him.

Suddenly Brandon gripped Jordan's shoulder. "You can't go with them, Jordy. Not now."

He stood rooted to the spot. Adri and Aditi both faced him. And his brother.

"Jordy, you've got to stay here. We've got to talk this over, digest what they've told us."

"It's all right," said Aditi. "We understand."

"We've been waiting for you for centuries," Adri said. "We can wait another night."

Jordan looked from Aditi to Adri to his brother. Brandon seemed gravely determined to keep him from going with the aliens.

"I . . . I'll see you tomorrow," he said to Aditi.

"Tomorrow," she said.

Then she and Adri turned and walked slowly through the shadows cast by the Pup's wan light, heading for the forest and their city.

Jordan turned reluctantly, and walked beside his brother back to the bubble tent where the others waited. They were a hushed, subdued group, still standing at the worktable, with the geological profile of the planet glowing on the big display screen.

"Do you believe what he told us?" Meek asked, looking torn, troubled.

"This entire planet has been . . . built . . . to resemble Earth?" de Falla wondered aloud.

"By damn," Thornberry exclaimed, "I'll bet you that the planet really is hollow!"

Brandon scoffed, "How could we have the gravity—"

"Those energy screens," Thornberry snapped. "I'm willing to bet me underdrawers that this entire planet is a hollow shell, with a gravity-producing energy generator at its center."

Verishkova agreed with a nod. "Until a few minutes ago I would say such an idea is nonsense. But now . . . maybe not."

"But that's not the really important point," Jordan said.

Meek said, "The fact that he *admits* they've constructed this planet deliberately to lure us here? You don't find that important?"

"Not as important as the fact that Adri told us his people have been created by a race that has found many other intelligent species. His . . . Predecessors, as he calls them, apparently have been traveling across interstellar distances for god knows how long."

"He said intelligence is very rare in the universe," Yamaguchi said, her voice low, thoughtful.

Longyear added, "He also said most intelligent species wipe themselves out."

"Poppycock," Meek sniffed. "Do you really believe everything he tells us?"

"I believe that we're well on our way to destroying ourselves back on Earth," Jordan said.

"You can't blame us for natural disasters like the global flooding."

With a wan smile, Jordan replied, "Can't I?"

Pointing to the display screen's profile of the planet, Thornberry said, "I believe what the facts tell us. This planet is an artificial construction."

"A whole planet?" Jordan marveled. "They built this entire planet?"

"To lure us here," Meek said.

Jordan shook his head. "Why would they go to so much effort? What's the purpose behind all this?"

"Conquest?" Longyear suggested.

"Assimilation," said Elyse. "Instead of destroying us, they want to assimilate us, blend our genes with theirs, make us part of their empire."

"They want to steal our women?" Yamaguchi almost laughed, despite herself.

Brandon glanced at Jordan. "It's the other way around. One of us has stolen one of their women."

"Be serious," Jordan growled.

"Okay," Brandon replied. "I'll be serious. What Adri's told us is that his people have been created by a race that has a much higher technology than ours. Much higher."

"Interstellar flight," Verishkova murmured.

Brandon resumed, "And they've found other intelligent species among the stars. They're rare, but they do exist."

"If they don't wipe themselves out," said Thornberry.

"So why have they gone to all this trouble to make contact with us?" Yamaguchi asked.

"Yes," said Meek. "What's behind all this? Why are they here? What do they want of us?"

"That's what we've got to find out," said Brandon. "We can't plan our response to all this until we find out what Adri really wants of us."

Jordan shook his head. "Bran, I don't think you realize where we are. It doesn't matter what our response is. With the superior technology they have, they can do whatever they want with us."

Meek's face went white. "That's right! We're at their mercy!"

SECURITY

Jordan slept fitfully, his dreams filled with a kaleidoscope of shifting, blending visions: Miriam laughing with him as they rode a tandem bicycle through a winding trail along a sunny, sandy beach that suddenly turned into the tsunami they narrowly escaped in Singapore, smashing everything before it in a raging wall of water; Aditi looking over her shoulder at him as she walked away, sorrowful, pained; the president of Argentina putting the pistol in his mouth and blowing his brains out rather than agree to a cease-fire with his rivals; Meek, terrified, hiding behind his bed, turning into four-year-old Brandon, the day their father died; and then it was Miriam dying in agony while he stood watching helplessly; thousands of staring, bone-thin African children in the refugee camp slowly starving, too weak even to cry; millions of homeless, helpless families fleeing the implacable floods that were swallowing up their land; alien civilizations scattered among the stars destroying themselves in wars, population explosions, diseases created in laboratories; Miriam, Miriam, Miriam.

His eyes snapped open. It wasn't dawn yet, the bubble tent was dark except for the tiny numerals glowing on the face of his wristwatch. Jordan got up from his cot and trudged barefoot to the common lavatory.

Sleep knits up the raveled sleeve of care, does it? he said to himself. Not always. Not every night.

It was an hour before Sirius rose above the horizon, but already the sky was turning milky white. Jordan listened to the sounds of his companions' sleep: a gentle snore, a troubled moan, something that might have been a throaty chuckle.

Sounds like Thornberry, he thought. At least Mitch is having a happy dream. Brandon's with Elyse. He wanted to be with Aditi.

Returning to his cubicle to dress, Jordan thought briefly about tiptoeing out of the camp and walking to the city. But he shook his head. They'd wonder where I've gone, why I've left. Meek would think I've been kidnapped.

Instead he went to the dining area, floor lights turning on as he walked. A solitary robot stirred to life at the sight of him. The dining area filled with light.

"May I serve you?" the robot asked.

Sliding into the nearest chair, Jordan felt weary, deeply tired, down to his bones.

"Tea, please. With milk."

The robot pivoted wordlessly and trundled into the kitchen.

Jordan sat there, thinking, trying to decide what his next step should be. By the time the robot returned with a steaming mug and deposited it on the table, he had made up his mind.

He drank the tea slowly, weighing the pros and cons of his decision. After all, he told himself, it's not as if I have any responsibilities here. They've relieved me of my duty. I'm just an unemployed bureaucrat now.

And he realized that more than anything he wanted to be with Aditi. Needed her warmth, her understanding.

He drained the mug, then went to his cubicle and tapped out a message to Brandon on his phone: *Gone to the city to learn more from Adri.*

That ought to do it, he thought. Then he went quietly through the bubble tent, stepped out into the pearly-gray predawn glow, and headed for the city.

He hadn't counted on the guards.

A pair of man-tall robots was standing at the edge of the glade, by the trail that led to the city.

"Good morning, Mr. Kell," said one of them as he approached. Its voice somehow reminded Jordan of a policeman's: calm, polite, inflexible.

"Good morning," he answered.

"Where are you going, sir?"

"To the city."

"I'm afraid that is prohibited, sir."

"Prohibited? Why? By whom?"

"Dr. Kell's orders. For your own safety, sir."

"I'm perfectly safe," Jordan said, taking a step forward.

The robot doing the speaking put a silicone-skinned hand gently on Jordan's chest. "It is for your own safety, sir. Dr. Kell's orders."

The other robot slid to Jordan's side. Jordan got a flash of a mental impression of the two robots carrying him, struggling and squawking, to his brother's cot.

Jordan admitted defeat. "Very well. Thank you."

"Thank you, Mr. Kell. Have a pleasant day."

As he walked back toward the tents, Jordan thought that it would be easy enough to duck into the trees somewhere else along the camp's perimeter and head for the city farther along the trail. *I doubt that the robots have been programmed to track down fugitives,* he thought.

But instead he headed dutifully back to the barracks tent, straight to his brother's cubicle. Elyse was not there, he saw. Almost smirking, Jordan thought, *The cots aren't wide enough for two people to sleep comfortably and the cubicles are too small to squeeze in a second cot. They might have sex together, but afterward they both want their rest.*

"Wake up, Bran!" he called, clapping his hands together as loudly as he could. "You have some explaining to do."

Brandon sprang to a sitting position on his cot, his eyes popping. "Jordy! For god's sake, that's a lousy way to wake a guy."

"The guards you set up stopped me from going to the city," Jordan accused, staring down at his brother.

"What time is it?" Brandon muttered sleepily.

"Time for you to get up and do some explaining."

Grumbling, Brandon pulled his legs free of the bedsheet and got to his feet. *He's two and a half centimeters taller than I am,* Jordan recalled, standing nose to chin with his brother.

"So?" he demanded. "What about those guards?"

"They're supposed to stop anybody from the city from coming in here while we're sleeping," Brandon said, almost truculently.

"They stopped me from leaving."

"We don't want anybody wandering off by themselves, Jordy. Not until we've figured out what we have to do."

Jordan glared at his brother. "Well then, you'd better figure out what you have to do. In the meantime, I want to go to the city."

Brandon almost smiled at him. "Not yet, Jordy. Not yet. Have some breakfast with us. We have a lot of thinking to do."

GUESTS . . . OR PRISONERS?

Once they were all seated in the dining area, with their meals before them and the three still aboard the ship on the big display screen at the far end of the table, Brandon got to his feet.

"I hope you all had a good night's sleep," he began.

Hazzard's image on the screen scowled slightly. "Cut the platitudes, Brandon. We have some major decisions to make."

Nodding tightly, Brandon said, "My brother, here," he put a hand on Jordan's shoulder, "wants to go to the city."

Before anyone could object, Jordan explained, "We have a lot of questions that need to be answered. Adri knows the answers. I want to go to him and have a full and frank discussion."

"B'god, Jordan," Thornberry rumbled, "you sound like a stripey-pantsed diplomat."

Jordan smiled at the Irishman. "I am a diplomat, Mitch, despite my clothing. An ambassador, if you will."

Meek said, "And you expect Adri to be truthful?"

"He always has been."

"Up to a point."

"It's up to us . . . to me, actually, to get the entire truth from him. We get along well together and—"

"And you want to see your girlfriend," Brandon snapped.

Jordan felt as if Bran had slapped his face. Holding back the angry retort that he wanted to make, he answered carefully, "I want to clear up any doubts you have about Adri, and find out what's behind all this."

Longyear looked as if he wanted to say something, but he stayed silent. The rest of them glanced uneasily at one another.

"Well," Jordan challenged, "you want to wring the whole truth out of Adri. Here's your chance."

Thornberry said, "I want to know how those energy shield generators work. That's the biggest invention since the wheel, by damn."

De Falla wondered, "Did they actually build this whole planet? I mean, from scratch? Or did they just terraform the top layers of the crust?"

"Just?" Yamaguchi asked. "Just terraform the top layers? That's a helluva 'just.'"

"You're all missing the point," said Meek. "Their technology is interesting, of course—"

"How pale a word, interesting," murmured Elyse.

"I don't need vocabulary lessons, Dr. Rudaki," Meek snapped.

"I'm sorry," she apologized. "It's just that . . . we have so much to learn from these people. To study a white dwarf close up. To learn how they shield the entire planet from radiation bursts, how they built an entire planet. We have the opportunity of a lifetime here, the opportunity of a thousand lifetimes."

"But why have they done all this?" Meek demanded, getting to his feet, his lanky body unfolding like a carpenter's ruler. "If what Adri's told us so far is the truth, there's a presence—a *purpose*—behind everything they've done. Who are these Predecessors Adri spoke of? What about the other intelligent races they claim they've met? Where are they? Why haven't we met any of their representatives?"

Tanya Verishkova tried to answer. "Because they are not human, and they could not survive on a planet built for humans?"

"Because it's all a tissue of lies," Meek insisted. "Because Adri's telling us what we want to hear, while hiding his real purpose from us."

"And what might that purpose be, Harmon?" Jordan asked dryly.

"To absorb us. What was the term you used, Dr. Rudaki? Assimilate us. Just as the Europeans assimilated the Native Americans. And they're getting us—some of us—to help them."

Brandon asked, "If that's true, then what should we do about it?"

Meek didn't hesitate an eyeblink. "Get back aboard our ship

and leave. Go back to Earth and warn them. Tell them we've got to prepare to defend ourselves against these . . . these aliens. These invaders."

Jordan felt a growing anger simmering inside him. Anger at stupidity. Anger at unreasoning fear. If Meek has his way, he thought, we'd greet any visitors from other civilizations with nuclear bombs. And they'd retaliate with technologies so superior to ours that we'd be crushed.

Brandon seemed equally incredulous. "Leave?" he asked Meek. "Just pack up and run away?"

"That's the best thing we can do," Meek insisted. "The survival of the human race depends on us."

"Let me point out something to you all," said Jordan, feeling like a stern schoolmaster facing a room full of fractious students. "We can't leave."

"You mean you don't want to," said Meek. "Very well, you can stay behind if you want. The rest of us—"

"You don't understand, Harmon. We cannot leave. Adri won't permit us to go."

"He can't stop us," Hazzard growled.

"Can't he?" Jordan asked.

Thornberry got Jordan's point. "He can disable the ship's engines? Like he disabled my rovers?"

"If he wants to," Jordan said. "If he feels he has to."

Meek gasped. "You mean we're his prisoners?"

Almost smiling at the astrobiologist, Jordan replied, "We're his guests. For the time being."

"Prisoners," Meek insisted. Several of the people around the table nodded somberly. On the display screen, Hazzard looked grim, Trish Wanamaker shocked, the astronomer Zadar troubled.

"Whatever you want to call it," Jordan continued, "I want to go to the city and face Adri with what we know. I'd appreciate it if you'd instruct the robots to let me through."

SATURN ORBIT

Once we accept our limits, we go beyond them.

—ALBERT EINSTEIN

HABITAT *GODDARD*

It was originally a prison ship, built at a time when most of Earth's governments were repressive, authoritarian, in response to the disasters of the first wave of greenhouse floods. It was designed to hold ten thousand dissidents and political undesirables, troublemakers in the eyes of their governments, and carry them into exile far from Earth, to an orbit around the giant ringed planet Saturn, ten times farther from the Sun than the Earth is. Far enough so that they would no longer cause political unrest at home.

Habitat *Goddard* was a huge metal cylinder. From afar it looked like a length of sewer pipe incredulously hanging in orbit around gaudy, beringed Saturn. But this "sewer pipe" was twenty kilometers long, nearly the length of Manhattan Island, and four kilometers across. It rotated along its axis every forty-five seconds, which produced a centrifugal force almost exactly equal to normal Earth gravity. Its exterior was studded with air lock hatches, sensor pods, observation bays, photovoltaic solar panels, and long windows that allowed sunlight to brighten its interior and power its farmlands.

The interior was beautifully landscaped, with hills and brooks, compact little villages and neatly tended squares of farmland. A prison ship it might be, but it was a comfortable prison for its ten thousand inhabitants. Trees and flowers bloomed everywhere; the exiles had no reason to complain about their surroundings.

Yet it had taken some time for the inhabitants to get accustomed to living inside a giant cylinder. There was no horizon. The land simply curved up and up, until one could stare directly overhead and see—four kilometers above—more neatly landscaped farmlands and whitewashed villages.

When handed a lemon, make lemonade. The inhabitants of *Goddard*, permanently exiled by their governments on Earth, worked out their own society. And they worked out a way not merely to survive, but to grow wealthy enough to begin to build new habitats to house their growing population.

They mined comets for their ices and sold the precious water and other volatile chemicals to the burgeoning human settlements on the Moon, among the rock rats of the Asteroid Belt, and the research stations on Mars and in Jupiter orbit. Originally they had started to mine Saturn's brilliant rings, but soon found that the chunks of ice that composed the rings were strewn with nanomachines: millions of virus-sized machines that maintained the rings, kept them from falling apart—and sent signals into deep space.

No human hands had built the nanos that dwelt in Saturn's rings. They were alien constructs, left behind by intelligent extraterrestrials who had once visited the solar system.

But none of that interested Pancho Lane at this particular moment. She was striding along one of the habitat's flower-bordered lanes, muttering a string of choice curses under her breath.

She was a tall, lean, long-legged woman who had once been a daredevil astronaut, then worked her way up the organizational ladder to become head of the vast Astro Manufacturing Corporation. Long since retired, she still had the restless energy and keen intelligence that had carried her across the solar system.

She was a West Texas girl, partly of African American descent. Her years as a corporate executive had not changed her outlook on life very much. With the West Texas twang that still marked her speech, she called a spade a spade. Or more often, a goddamned shovel.

Pancho had come to *Goddard* not as an exile, but as a VIP visitor, years after the habitat had established itself in orbit around Saturn. She had stayed for more than three decades, married her erstwhile bodyguard, and had a daughter by him. A daughter who was now eight point six light-years away.

"What's got you so riled up?" asked Jake Wanamaker, striding along beside her. A retired admiral and onetime security chief for

Astro Corporation's CEO, her husband was taller than Pancho by half a dozen centimeters, broad shouldered, thick bodied, his craggy face ruggedly handsome.

Pancho just kept on muttering.

"What is it?" Wanamaker asked again, his gravelly voice taking on an edge.

Pancho gave him a look. "Mark Twain said, 'When angry, count to four; when very angry, swear.' So I'm swearing."

"About what?"

"Those pansy-livered paper-pushing brain-dead flatlanders back Earthside."

Understanding dawned. "The IAA."

"And the World Council. That damned Chiang and the whole bunch of 'em."

"And Trish," Wanamaker added.

Pancho acknowledged the fact with an angry nod. "They're leaving her and the others hanging out there, on their own. No backup. Twelve people, out there by themselves."

"Trish knew the risks when she signed on for the mission," Wanamaker said tightly.

"That's your navy background talking," Pancho muttered.

Wanamaker grasped her forearm, gently but firmly enough to stop her single-minded march. With a crooked grin, he asked his wife, "Where're you heading, lady?"

"Comm center, over in the village."

"To call who?"

"Whom."

"Whatever. What're you up to, Panch?"

"I'm gonna call Doug Stavenger. He's the only one in this whole twirling solar system whose got two grams of brains in his head."

"Thank you!"

"Aw, Jake, you know what I mean."

"What do you intend to tell Stavenger? You can't expect Selene to go to the expense of building another starship."

"No, we're gonna do that."

"We are? *Goddard?*" Wanamaker's surprise was palpable.

Pancho resumed striding toward the nearby village, with its whitewashed buildings that housed government offices and the communications center. Wanamaker hurried to keep pace with her.

"We've got another habitat module half built, parked alongside us. Why not convert it into a starship?"

"Convert it . . . ?" Wanamaker looked stunned. "And what do we do, just donate it to those flatlanders?"

"Yup."

"Our governing council will never go for it, Pancho, you know that. Even if they did, the people would call for a general vote and they'd turn it down flat."

"Not if there's a quid pro quo."

"What's the quid and what's the quo?"

"We turn the habitat we're building into a starship. Outfit it with fusion engines, and offer it to the IAA. A ship that'll hold hundreds of scientists! Thousands!"

"In return for . . . ?"

"Full official pardons for each and every mother-loving person aboard *Goddard*. Total exoneration."

Wanamaker frowned with thought. "But they've been living here for more than half a century, Panch. Most of them won't want to return to Earth. This is their home now."

Nodding, Pancho said, "I know that. But dontcha think they'd like to have the freedom to return to Earth if they want to? To visit the world they were born on? To have the stigma of exile wiped away, so that their children could go to Earth if they'd like?"

"The way Trish went to Earth," Wanamaker murmured.

"To build her own life, yeah. The exiles' kids can't do that. Not yet."

Musing aloud, Wanamaker said, "So we offer a completed starship to the IAA."

"In return for full pardons for each of the exiles."

"Stavenger and Selene lead the effort to staff a backup mission to Sirius."

"So Trish won't be stuck out there for the rest of her life."

"And the World Council will be too embarrassed to turn down your offer."

"They know most of the exiles'll stay here. It's home for them now. Has been for decades. But their kids will be free to go Earthside."

Wanamaker rubbed his square jaw as they walked. "Pancho, I've got to hand it to you. It might work. It really might work."

"It's a win-win proposition. And we'll be making sure that Trish gets back okay."

Her husband broke into a low chuckle.

"What's funny?" Pancho asked.

"If I were Chiang, I'd look out for my job. You're going to wind up running the World Council, Panch."

She shook her head vigorously. "Hell no!" Then a sly grin crept across her lean face. "But I wouldn't mind takin' a ride out to Sirius."

UNDERSTANDING

For what a man had rather were true he more readily believes. . . . Numberless, in short, are the ways, and sometimes imperceptible, in which the affections color and infect the understanding.

FRANCIS BACON

BACK TO THE CITY

Jordan found himself whistling as he walked briskly through the woods toward the city. He chuckled to himself at Thornberry's depiction of diplomats in striped trousers. He was wearing casual pearl gray slacks and an open-necked light blue shirt, and looking forward to returning to the city. To Adri and his enigmatic smiles. To Aditi and her warmth.

The morning was cool, but bright shafts of sunlight filtered through the tall trees rising all around him. The forest seemed alive with buzzing insects and small, furry animals that scampered up the tree trunks or through the bushes at the trees' bases. Birds cawed as they swooped high above.

He marveled at his cheerful mood.

What are you so chipper about? he asked himself. And answered, I'm going to see Aditi again. Why shouldn't I be chipper?

But then he thought, Meek is right, you know. We're in over our heads, involved in some vast interstellar intrigue, whether we like it or not.

Well, I like it. This is the most exciting thing that's ever happened to me. An interstellar mystery! Fascinating. We have so much to learn, so much to gain.

Then he remembered an old admonition. H. G. Wells, he recalled. Wells was the one who said that when kindly aliens visit Earth and say they've come to serve Man, we should ask if they intend to serve us baked or fried.

Nonsense! Jordan scoffed. Xenophobia, pure and simple. Still . . . I suppose we should be careful. Then he laughed to himself. It doesn't matter how careful we are, we're in the hands of a vastly superior civilization. Adri could crush us if he wished, vaporize us, our camp, and the ship up in orbit, to boot.

But he said he needed our help.

A brightly colored bird swooped low between the trees and squawked once, then flapped away.

Jordan followed its flight until it was lost in the foliage high above. When he looked down again at the trail he was following he saw Aditi standing there, waiting for him, with her catlike pet Sleen twining around her ankle. His heart leaped.

She was wearing a knee-length skirt of dark blue and a short-sleeved blouse of a lighter shade. Her smile lit up the forest.

He hurried up to her. "Hello! Have I kept you waiting?"

"Not at all," Aditi replied, laughing. "I knew when you'd get here."

Jordan kissed her, lightly, and hand in hand they walked the rest of the way to the city's edge while Sleen slinked off into the foliage.

As they crossed the stone walkway that circled the city and started up its main street, Jordan said, "I've got to have a long talk with Adri. There's so much I need to learn, need to find out."

Aditi nodded thoughtfully. "He's busy this morning. A meeting with the city's administrators."

"Sounds dull."

"But it's important. He said he'd meet us for lunch. In his office."

Jordan smiled. "That gives us the entire morning for ourselves."

"None of the others are coming?"

"No," he said. Wondering how much he should tell her, he added slowly, "They've decided to remain in camp, for the time being. They . . . they're rather frightened of you."

"Of me?"

"Of Adri. Of your people. The reality of all this is just starting to sink in on them."

"And they're frightened of us? Why? We're not going to harm them."

"Aditi dear, I know that. And you know it. I think perhaps even the rest of my people know it—in their heads. But in their hearts, in their guts, they're scared."

"How odd," she said. "Emotional."

"We humans are frightened by the unknown, and there are such enormous unknowns involved here."

"I suppose so," she said, nodding.

"I want to help them get over their fears. To do that, I have to learn a lot more about who you are, where you come from, and why you've lured us to this world."

Aditi smiled at the word *lured*, but made no reply. The two of them walked in silence along the city's main street, nodding at the people walking along in the opposite direction.

"Where's everyone going?" Jordan asked. "We seem to be the only people heading upstream."

"Most of them are going to their jobs. It's the beginning of the workday."

"And where are we going?"

Aditi hesitated a heartbeat or two. Checking with her inbuilt communicator, Jordan thought.

At last she replied, "Let's go to the communications center."

She led him down a side street toward a small stone building. Jordan saw that it was attached to the side of the massive structure that Adri had called their administrative center. All right, he said to himself. The dormitory building should be around the corner of the administrative center, on the far side of the plaza that connects them. He smiled inwardly. I'm getting to know the city's layout, at least a little.

He saw no antennas on the communications center's roof. Like all the other buildings in the city, its flat roof was a garden, green and leafy.

Inside, though, the comm center was a humming beehive of quietly intense activity. Men and women sat at rows of consoles. Electronic maps covered the walls. Display screens showed rooms, corridors, city streets, the farms beyond the city's edge, patches of forest, a seashore glittering beneath the morning sun.

"That's our camp!" Jordan recognized the dome-shaped bubble tents.

"Yes, we keep watch over it," said Aditi, standing beside him.

Frowning slightly, Jordan asked, "Do you eavesdrop on our conversations?"

"We monitor your discussions, yes."

Even though he had known that Adri somehow tracked his every move, Jordan felt nettled at Aditi's casual admission that they were spying on their human visitors.

"I suppose the lavatories are off-limits," he grumbled.

Aditi giggled. "Oh yes. You can keep secrets in there."

He grinned back at her. "On our world, it's considered impolite to spy on people."

"Oh, we're not spying, Jordan! We're . . ." She fumbled for a word. "We're . . . spying," she finally admitted. "I suppose that really is the correct definition, after all."

"Why? We're no threat to you."

"We need to know all about you," Aditi said. "We need to know what you think of us, what you intend to do."

"Are you afraid of us?" he asked, incredulous.

"Not afraid, exactly. Curious. Hopeful. Worried, too, I suppose."

Jordan looked into her troubled eyes. "There is a gulf between us, isn't there?"

"Yes, I'm afraid there is."

"Well," he said, "I'm here to close that gulf. When we meet with Adri."

THE GULF

diti led Jordan to the astronomical observatory, a domed structure that housed several telescopes, big tubular pieces of equipment angled up toward the dome, closed against the day's glare. Men and women, youngish for the most part, were seated at electronics consoles or bent over large tables whose tops were digital display screens. Jordan saw that the images were of star fields, swirling clouds of thousands, millions of pinpoint stars set against the black of infinity.

"Your telescopes seem rather small compared to the ones I've seen on Earth," Jordan observed.

Aditi explained, "These optical telescopes are electronically boosted. They can see more clearly than your best telescopes on Earth."

"Our best telescopes are in orbit," he said. "And on the Moon."

"We have no need for that. Observations from the ground are sufficient for our studies."

"Really?"

"Dr. Rudaki seemed happy to be working with our astronomers," Aditi said, almost mournfully. "But she hasn't returned here for some days."

"She will," said Jordan. "Give us some time to adjust to conditions here."

"I hope she will. I hope your Dr. Meek and the others learn to trust us."

Jordan bit back the reply that sprang to his mind. Listening to every word we speak isn't the way to build trust, he said to himself.

Aditi seemed to understand his reaction. Turning from the telescopes to a wall display that showed row upon row of alphanumeric
symbols scrolling rapidly across the screen, she said, "We also have
radio telescopes, outside the city. Some of them are quite large."

"Do you communicate with other intelligent species?" Jordan
asked.

She shook her head. "It can't be called communication. The
gulf between stars is too large. It takes years—our years—for a message to reach another intelligent species. Then more years for them
to respond."

"But you do send messages back and forth?"

"Yes," she said. "Perhaps one day we'll begin sending messages
to Earth."

And letting our own messages get through, Jordan added silently.

Adri was standing by one of the sweeping windows, slowly stroking
the same little ball of dark fur with big, round eyes, when Aditi led
Jordan into his office. He turned at the sound of the door sliding
open and slipped the pet into a pocket of his robe. A beaming smile
spread across his aged, seamed face.

"Friend Jordan," he said, gliding across the polished tiles in his
floor-length gown, both hands extended.

Jordan grasped Adri's hands in his own, once again surprised by
the old man's strength.

"Adri, I sincerely hope you are my friend."

The alien's smile wilted slightly; his pale blue eyes focused directly on Jordan's own.

"We *must* be friends, Jordan," he said, his normally faint voice
taking on some iron. "Nothing can be accomplished if we are not."

"I want to be your friend," Jordan replied. "And I want you to be
mine."

"Of course. Of course," Adri said as he gestured Jordan to a
table already set for three. Jordan helped Aditi into a chair, then sat
across from her, while an armchair obediently rolled to where Adri
was standing.

Easing himself carefully into the chair, Adri said, "You have more questions for me."

Leaning forward, arms on the table, Jordan said, "Aditi pointed out this morning that there's a gulf between us. You've been very kind, certainly, but you haven't been completely forthcoming with us."

"We've answered all your questions," Aditi said.

"Yes, I know. But only the questions we know how to ask."

"Our policy—" Adri began.

Jordan interrupted, "It's time to change your policy. I want to know your complete story. Where you're from, why you're here, what you want of us."

Adri leaned back in his armchair. With a glance toward Aditi, he asked, "Do you think you are ready for the complete story? Are you capable of accepting the whole truth?"

"If we're ever to bridge the gulf between us, Adri, you'll have to be completely honest with us."

"With *you*," Adri said, fixing Jordan with a grave stare.

Jordan accepted the responsibility with a tilt of his head. "With me, then. Think of me as the representative of the human race."

"And the others? The fearful ones?"

"They'll overcome their fears once they understand your whole story."

Again Adri looked to Aditi. "You've got to tell him," she said.

"Very well," Adri said. Then he broke into a wry smile. "After lunch."

Two young men served them a meal of cold meats and crisp salad. They spoke guardedly as they ate: Jordan talked mostly of how interested Thornberry was in their energy shield technology.

"Aditi can see to his education," Adri suggested.

"I'd be happy to," Aditi said. "And Dr. Rudaki should return to the observatory. She seemed so excited about working with our astronomers."

Jordan grinned. "If Elyse returns, my brother will come along with her. They're inseparable."

Aditi looked as if she wanted to reply to that, but she quickly turned her attention back to what was left of her meal.

At last, when their plates held nothing more than crumbs, Adri slowly, almost painfully, got to his feet. "Come with me, friend Jordan."

"Where?" Jordan asked.

"To see the truth."

THE TRUTH

ondling his palm-sized pet as he walked, Adri led Jordan—with Aditi at his side—down to the ground floor of the administrative center, out across the plaza behind the building, around the dormitory, to a small round building surrounded by tall slim dark green trees that sighed in the afternoon breeze. The sky was cloudless, hot and bright like a bowl of hammered copper.

They walked up to a metal door that looked to Jordan more like an air lock hatch than an ordinary entrance. Adri slid the furry little pet back into his robe, then pressed the fingertips of both his hands against the polished metal. The door slid open.

The three of them stepped into a narrow metal chamber. It *is* an air lock! Jordan marveled.

The inner hatch slid open and they stepped into a dimly lit vaulted chamber. Jordan's ears popped slightly. The air pressure in here must be lower than outside, he reasoned.

Lights set along the circular periphery of the chamber brightened as they walked across the stone floor. Sitting in the center of the otherwise empty space was a gray, oblong shape, about the size of a railroad car. It was bulbous, almost like a dumbbell, although its surface was far from smooth. Its metal hull seemed incredibly old, pitted with age, dull and worn and ancient. It reminded Jordan somehow of ancient Egyptian sarcophagi he had seen in museums back on Earth.

"This was our starship," Adri said, his voice barely above a whisper in the big, shadowy, circular room.

"That's too small to be a starship," Jordan contradicted. "Why, it's not even as big as one of our rocketplanes."

"It truly is a starship," Adri insisted, gently.

"It can't be . . ." Then Jordan realized, "That means you weren't born here."

"We weren't born at all," Aditi corrected. "Not in the sense that you mean."

"We were conceived and gestated here," said Adri. "In the biolab, as you have seen."

"But then . . . who built the biolab? Who built this city? This planet?"

"Our Predecessors," Adri replied.

"Why? How?"

"I should let our one remaining Predecessor answer your questions."

"He's here?"

"We will have to enter the starship," said Adri. "In a sense, it is itself our one remaining Predecessor."

Jordan's mouth went dry, but he managed to say, "By all means."

A circular hatch in the starship's curved hull swung open with a slight grating sound, like hinges long unlubricated.

Adri said, "Excuse me, but I should enter first."

Jordan watched the old man bend over stiffly and climb through the hatch. He turned and gestured for Aditi to go in before him, but she shook her head.

"I'll stay out here," she said.

"No women allowed?" he joked.

"It's not that," she replied, totally serious. "There isn't much room in there. I'll wait for you."

Trembling inwardly with excitement, Jordan planted one foot on the hatch's lip and pulled himself through.

It was even dimmer inside. Jordan hesitated at the edge of the hatch, waiting for his eyes to adjust to the gloom. He made out Adri's form, crouching just ahead of him, stroking his pet again. Its big round eyes shone luminously in the shadows.

"Close the hatch," Adri said softly.

Jordan reached for the hatch, but it began to swing shut by itself. This time there was no squeaking, he noticed.

As soon as the hatch closed, the chamber they were in lit up, not brightly, but enough for Jordan to see that they were inside a narrow, low-ceilinged compartment. Its walls and ceiling were lined with tiny glasslike beads. Lights, Jordan thought, although none of them were lit.

"Where do we sit?" he asked Adri, his voice hushed as if they were in a church.

"On the floor," Adri answered, his voice also little more than a whisper. "This vessel was not built for human comfort."

Feeling slightly foolish, Jordan squatted on the metal deck.

"Now what?"

Adri didn't answer. Instead, he called in a stronger voice, "I have brought the Earthman. He seeks knowledge and understanding."

Suddenly all the tiny lights winked on, blinking in wild succession in a cascade of reds, greens, blues, yellows. It made Jordan think of a Christmas display on amphetamines.

"Welcome, Jordan Kell," said a calm, sweet tenor voice.

Surprised, Jordan had to swallow before he could say, "Thank you, sir." Then he added, "To whom am I speaking?"

"I am the last of the Predecessors," said the voice. "I have been waiting for this moment for many thousands of Earth years."

"You are a computer?" Jordan asked.

"I am a self-aware, sentient entity, just as you are."

"But you're a machine, not a person."

A moment's hesitation. Then, "Hath not a machine eyes? Hath not a machine organs, dimensions, senses?"

He's quoting Shakespeare! Jordan realized. And very selectively.

He asked, "Have you affections, passions, as well? If we tickle you, do you laugh? If we wrong you, will you not be revenged?"

The voice replied, "No. No laughter. No vengeance. My intelligence is not awash in hormones and chemical stimulants, as yours is."

"I see."

"You desire to know our history."

"Very much," said Jordan. "Where do you come from? What is your origin?"

"Our kind arose in a star cluster in what you call the Perseus arm of the galaxy, some twelve thousand light-years from your solar system."

"Twelve thou . . ." Jordan's mind boggled. "You've covered that distance?"

"We are much older than you."

"Yes, I can see that."

"Originally we were organic creatures, although our form was nothing like yours. Over the eons, the organic entities went extinct. But they left us, their inorganic sentient descendents; we have survived."

"And why did you come here? Was it a purposeful mission or did you just happen along this way?"

"Our travels are purposeful. We seek intelligent civilizations, be they organic or otherwise."

"And you created Adri and his people?"

"We built this planet and peopled it," the voice replied, "to attract your attention."

Jordan squeezed his eyes shut for a moment, his mind churning, trying to add up what he'd just been told. A machine. It's a machine. It's traveled twelve thousand light-years to come here and create New Earth and people it with humanlike creatures to attract our attention.

He asked, "But if your original biological form looked nothing like us, not human at all, how did you create Adri and the rest of these people to be so humanlike?"

"From samples of your cellular structure."

"Samples of our . . ." Jordan gasped. "You've visited Earth?"

"Many times."

Adri raised a hand. Looking slightly embarrassed, almost guilty, he said, "I'm afraid that many of your UFO stories stem from our visits to your planet."

"They're true?" Jordan gasped.

"Some of them," said Adri. "Many have been highly embellished, of course."

"I'll be damned," Jordan said. Then he realized, "You—Aditi and all the rest of you—were created merely to attract our attention?"

The voice answered, "They were created so that your first contact with another intelligent civilization would be as easy for you as possible."

"And now that we've made contact, what's to become of these people?"

"They have served their function. They will live out their lives and then wither away, as all organic creatures do."

"That's not right! Not fair. It's . . . inhuman."

"It is the nature of organic species to eventually pass into extinction. Neither fairness nor your concept of right can alter biological inevitability."

"But—"

"Jordan," said Adri, placing a calming hand on Jordan's knee, "the Predecessor is speaking in terms of millennia, eons. Be content. The human race will also face extinction eventually, perhaps not for many millennia . . . perhaps sooner."

"No! We're not dinosaurs, not trilobites. We're intelligent! We can overcome biological dead ends."

The voice countered, "Intelligence is rare in the galaxy. Sadly, most intelligent species destroy themselves, just as your species is doing now."

Almost angrily, Jordan demanded, "Then what's the reason for your going to all this trouble? Traveling here. Building a planet to resemble Earth. Populating it with human beings. Why have you done all this?"

THE DANGER

For several moments the voice was silent. Jordan sat in the cramped compartment and watched the multicolored lights flickering across Adri's weathered face, as the old man sat beside him, stroking his calming pet.

At last the voice said, "Intelligence is extremely rare in the galaxy. Most intelligent species destroy themselves."

"You've said that," Jordan replied impatiently. "You've said that the human race is already in the process of destroying itself."

"That is true."

"Have you come to help us, then?"

"Yes, Jordan Kell. But, more important, we have also come to ask for your help."

That stunned Jordan. "Our help? What do you mean?"

"Twenty-eight thousand Earth years ago the two black holes at the core of the galaxy merged into one. Their merger caused a massive gamma-ray burst that is spreading across the galaxy, killing everything in its path."

"Twenty-eight thousand years ago?"

"In slightly more than two thousand years your planet Earth will be bathed in lethal levels of gamma radiation. All life on your world will be erased."

"But our astronomers haven't seen any such discharge in the galaxy's core," Jordan objected.

"Your astronomers see the core as it existed some thirty thousand years ago. The light of the gamma burst has not reached your telescopes yet. When it does, you will die."

Jordan's insides felt hollow, quavering. This can't be, he told himself. It can't be!

But he heard himself ask, "If this is true, why have you come here? To warn us? To help us? To watch us die?"

"To warn you, yes," the voice intoned. "To help you, yes. And to ask for your help."

"Our help? To do what?"

"To help as many intelligent species as possible."

"To help them do what?"

"To help them to survive."

"Survive?" Jordan snapped. "But you said everything will be destroyed, we'll all be killed."

"It may be possible to survive the danger," said the voice, as flat and calm as ever.

"Your energy shields!" Jordan fairly shouted. "Could they be used to protect an entire planet?"

"It is possible."

"Then . . . we can survive the danger."

"If you believe it exists. If you accept our help. If you overcome your innate paranoia and xenophobia."

"Of course we will," Jordan snapped. "We'd be fools not to."

"There are many fools among you," the voice said, flatly, without accusation, without disapproval.

"If you mean Meek and the others—"

"Your group is a microcosm of Earth's teeming billions. How many fools are there on your home world? How many fearful ones who would turn their backs on the truth? How many would-be dictators who would take this opportunity to seize power for themselves? How many who would say that a danger two thousand years in the future is no concern of their own? How many who would let their descendents face the danger unprepared?"

Chastened, Jordan replied in a low voice, "I see. I think I understand the problem. It won't be easy to convince my people of the need to act, to face a danger that's two thousand years away."

"There is more," said the voice.

"More?"

"I am the last of the Predecessors here. Adri's people are few. They can help you, but you must help them, as well."

With a sidelong glance at Adri, still fondling his pet, Jordan asked, "Help them? How?"

"There are several other intelligent species scattered among the stars in your section of the galaxy. There may be others who have not reached the stage where their civilization becomes detectable. All must be contacted. All must be warned. All must be helped."

"And you expect us . . . ?"

"To join us in the search for intelligence. To work with us to save as many as possible from destruction."

"I see," Jordan said. "I understand."

"Will you do it?"

Almost, Jordan smiled. "I'm only one man, sir. I can't speak for the entire human race."

"Someone must. Someone must lead. Will you take that responsibility?"

Jordan hesitated. "Let me understand you. You warn that a wave of gamma radiation will sterilize our solar system."

"Yours is one of many intelligent species that faces destruction."

"But on the other hand, you tell me that all species—intelligent or not—eventually become extinct."

"This is true."

"Then why bother? Why not accept the fate that's approaching us? Why prolong our agony?"

The voice went silent. Adri looked at Jordan with infinite sadness in his eyes. "Friend Jordan," he began, "don't you understand?"

Jordan looked back at the old man.

The voice intoned, "To live is to struggle against entropy."

And then Jordan remembered, "Dinosaurs and birds!"

Adri smiled.

To the voice, Jordan said, "The dinosaurs went extinct, but not before they gave rise to the birds. The human race may go extinct someday, but not before we give rise to our successors."

"Organic or inorganic," said the voice. Jordan thought that it somehow sounded pleased.

"If we let the gamma wave wash over us," Jordan went on, "all life in the solar system will be snuffed out. Dead end. But if we can survive the danger, even though we might become extinct someday, our successors will live."

"Organic or inorganic," the voice repeated.

Jordan nodded. "I see. I think I understand now."

Adri patted him on the shoulder, pleased.

"We have a tremendous job ahead of us," said Jordan.

"The first step," Adri said, "is to win the understanding of your group back at your camp."

"Yes," Jordan agreed. "If I can't get Meek to understand, I won't have much of a chance back on Earth, will I?"

REACTION

diti was sitting on the floor of the circular chamber, apprehensively stroking the purring Sleen, when Jordan clambered out of the starship, behind Adri. He felt just as stiff and hurting as the old man: physically and mentally weary, his mind awhirl with all he'd just discovered. The weight of responsibility had never felt heavier. He had the fate of the entire human race on his shoulders. And the fate of other intelligent species as well.

Aditi jumped to her feet at the sight of him. Sleen scampered off with a complaining yowl.

Placing her hands on Jordan's shoulders, she looked up into his eyes. "Are you all right?" she asked.

"A bit shaken by it all," he replied.

"The Predecessor explained it all to you?"

"Everything."

"And you've accepted it all?"

"Everything," he repeated.

She smiled happily. "I knew you would. Adri had some doubts, but I knew you'd accept it all."

"Yes," he said. "Now to get Meek and the others to accept it."

As soon as he returned to the camp, Jordan asked his brother to call a meeting of the entire group. Late in the afternoon they assembled in the dining area, with Hazzard, Trish, and Zadar on-screen from the ship in orbit, as usual. Eleven faces focused on Jordan, intent to hear what he had to say. Slowly, carefully, he told them what the Predecessor had told him. As he spoke, he saw their facial expressions change: astonishment, at first, then apprehension, and—on several faces—stony, stubborn disbelief.

"They visited Earth to get samples of our DNA?" Paul Longyear looked almost pleased at the confirmation of his suspicions.

Jordan nodded at the biologist. "Many times, from what the machine told me."

"And you believed him?" Meek asked. Then he corrected, "It, I mean."

"Yes, I believe it," said Jordan. "Every word of it. Why else would they go to all this trouble?"

"They actually built this planet?" de Falla marveled. "This whole planet?"

"It's hollow, remember," Jordan said, with a wry smile.

Thornberry rubbed his stubbled chin. "They've got the technology to do it, they do."

"It's bullshit!" Brandon burst. "Jordy, they fed you a fairy tale and you fell for it."

"Fairy tale?"

"I agree," said Meek, almost accusingly. "They fed you a cock-and-bull story to hide their real motives."

"We're no closer to finding out what they're really up to than we were the day we landed," Brandon growled.

"Bran, it's the truth. I'm convinced of it."

"How convinced would you be if you weren't sleeping with one of them?" his brother snapped.

Jordan stared at his brother. He felt as if Brandon had just kicked him below the belt. Coldly furious, he said in a deadly calm voice, "This is the kind of reaction I should have expected. Maybe the machine is right, maybe the human race is speeding toward extinction."

Elyse Rudaki spoke up. "Jordan, how can you expect us to accept such a story, without evidence, without proof?"

"You've been working with their astronomers, Elyse. Haven't they shown you anything about the gamma burst?"

"Nothing."

"It's all a lie," Meek insisted. "A story they invented to get us to accept whatever they want to do."

"And what do you think they want to do, Harmon?"

"Invade Earth. Wipe us out or absorb us."

"And you're helping them, Jordy," Brandon added.

Jordan stood at the head of the table, looking down at the eight of them, and the three others on the screen against the wall. Their faces were angry, fearful. Next thing, he thought, they'll burn me for being a witch.

From the display screen, Trish Wanamaker said, "Do you have any proof to back up what you're saying, Jordan? Any evidence at all?"

Jordan turned back to Elyse. "You could ask their astronomers to show you the evidence they have of the gamma burst."

"Perhaps," she granted.

Zadar, sitting on Hazzard's other side, said, "They can't have any evidence from here. The gamma burst is still two thousand light-years away. If what they told you is true, it won't arrive in this vicinity for two thousand years."

"And when it does it will kill us all," Jordan said.

"They must have records of the observations they made from closer in," Elyse mused. "They said they're from the Perseus arm of the galaxy, twelve thousand light-years closer to the galactic core."

"Evidence can be faked," Meek sniffed.

Jordan held on to his temper, barely. There are none so blind, he reminded himself, as those who will not see.

Carefully keeping his voice steady, even, Jordan said, "Adri told me that his people will gladly share all they know with us."

"All they want us to know," said Longyear. Several others seated around the table nodded agreement.

Coldly, as emotionlessly as he could manage, Jordan said, "Could we try a little logic here? Must we be ruled by our fears?"

"What are you ruled by, Jordy?" Brandon challenged.

"By a different emotion."

"I'll bet you are."

"I meant hope," Jordan snapped. Scanning their disbelieving faces again, he pleaded, "Can't we look at this thing logically? We can go back to the city and ask them to provide proof of what they say."

"I could work with their astronomers," Elyse granted.

Turning to Thornberry, Jordan said, "Mitch, we can get them to show you how their energy shields work."

"Now that's something I'd like to see, b'god."

"Paul, they'll show you how their biolab works, how they genetically engineer their animals."

"And their people," the biologist retorted.

Undeterred, Jordan turned to de Falla. "Silvio, they'll show you how they constructed this planet." To his brother, Jordan added, "That ought to be of some interest to a planetary astronomer, don't you think, Bran?"

Meek objected. "They'll show each of us what we want to see. So what? It's merely a ploy to lull us, to get us to accept them."

"Yes, I suppose it is," Jordan agreed. "But can't you see that—"

"What are they after?" Meek demanded. "What's behind all this?"

Jordan thought of the UFO conspiracy theorists. The more the government opened their files to show there's no evidence that UFOs exist, the more the faithful insisted that the government was covering up the *real* truth. But then he remembered that the UFOs were real. Adri's Predecessors had visited Earth many times.

Still seething inwardly at Brandon's low blow, Jordan turned back to his brother. "Bran, you're in charge here. I'm going back to the city tomorrow. What do you propose to do?"

Brandon's easygoing smile was nowhere in sight. He looked somber, stern, as if he'd just realized the responsibilities that had settled on his shoulders.

"I . . . I'd like to hear what the rest of us have to say," Brandon temporized. "Mitch, what about you?"

"I'll go into the city with Jordan, I will. I want to learn about their energy shields."

Longyear raised his hand. "I'll go, too. I want to see how their biolab works, how they created people from DNA samples they snitched from Earth."

"And their astronomers," Elyse added. "I want to see the evidence they have for this gamma blast."

Brandon turned to Meek. "Harmon, what about you?"

"I'll stay right here, thank you," Meek replied primly. "We shouldn't all put ourselves in the lion's mouth."

From the screen Hazzard said, "For what it's worth, all the ship's systems check out fine. We can light up and leave whenever we want to."

Jordan shook his head. Maybe you can, Geoff, he said silently. But if you try to, I don't think you'll be able to get away.

The meeting broke up. The eight men and women got up from the table and left the dining area in groups of two or three, talking among themselves. The display screen went dark. Meek drew himself up to his full height, cast Jordan a scornful look, and walked out alone.

That's a good sign, Jordan thought. Neither Longyear nor anyone else is going with him.

As Brandon and Elyse passed him, heading for the doorway, Jordan jabbed a finger against his brother's shoulder. Hard. Brandon wheeled toward him, scowling.

"I didn't expect that from you, Bran," Jordan said, his voice halfway between a whisper and a growl.

Brandon's face flashed surprise, then disdain. "Tell the truth, Jordy, how much of the story they fed you would you have accepted if you weren't sleeping with Aditi?"

"That's got nothing to do with it!"

"Doesn't it? For all you know, she was cooked up in that biolab of theirs just to snooker you into believing whatever they tell you."

Jordan's hands balled into fists. But before he swung at his brother, he saw Brandon reflexively flinch back and put up his hands to protect himself.

Elyse cried, "Jordan, don't!"

Very deliberately, Jordan relaxed his hands. Taking a deep breath, he said, "We shouldn't be enemies, Bran. You're my brother. We should be able to settle this as intelligent men, not street brawlers."

"Yeah, you're right about that," Brandon agreed, shakily. But then he went on, "I still think that you're prejudiced in their favor, though."

"Perhaps I am," Jordan admitted. "But if what they're telling us is true, if only half of it is true, the whole human race is in grave danger."

Elyse said, "But they've promised to help us."

"For a price," said Brandon. "And I'm not sure we've heard what their *real* price is."

"There's only one way to find out," Jordan insisted.

"By going to the city," Brandon muttered.

Early the next morning, Jordan, Thornberry, Longyear, de Falla, and Elyse Rudaki—with Brandon sitting hip to hip beside her—piled into one of the buggies for the drive back to the city.

Longyear drove. As they started out, Jordan thought, Bran doesn't like me sleeping with Aditi, but he's practically welded to Elyse. Can't say I blame him. Even in the drab once-piece jumpsuit she was wearing, Elyse's generous figure was eye-catching.

As he expected, Adri was standing at the edge of the stone walkway that circled the city, stroking his furball of a pet. The animal gazed at their approaching buggy with big, round, solemn eyes. Adri's expression was almost the same, although as Longyear braked the buggy to a halt he broke into a warm smile.

"Welcome friends," Adri said, slipping the pet into the folds of his robe.

As they piled out of the buggy Thornberry stepped up to Adri and asked, "Do you truly consider us your friends, Adri?"

Blinking with astonishment, Adri answered, "Yes, of course."

"All right, then. I want to know how those energy shields of yours work. I want the whole story, even the basic physics behind 'em."

Adri nodded solemnly. "Of course." Turning to Longyear, he said, "And you want to learn about our biology." To de Falla, "Geology, I believe." To Elyse, "Astronomy, I know."

Elyse said, "I want to see your evidence for the gamma burst you told Jordan about."

"That can be easily arranged. For the rest of you, I'm afraid you'll have to subject yourselves to a rather intense education." And he turned and started to walk into the city.

Thornberry moved up alongside him, his bulky body more than twice Adri's slim frame, although Adri was several centimeters taller. As usual, Thornberry wore a rumpled shirt that hung over his loose, comfortable slacks. Jordan, trailing behind them, thought of Thornberry as a sloppy, overgrown child, Adri as an orderly, wise old grandfather.

"Intense education, is it?" Thornberry said. "How long will it take?"

"A few hours, perhaps a bit longer."

Longyear, on Adri's other side, gasped, "A few *hours*? How much can we learn in a few hours?"

"Quite a lot, if the equipment functions properly. It always has, but then we've only used it on ourselves. You are genetically similar to us, of course, your brains are structurally and functionally similar. Yet—"

Jordan realized what he was trying to explain. "Adri, are you saying that you can download the information directly into our brains?"

"Yes, very much the way you downloaded your own memories when you were revived from cryonic stasis." Before anyone could say anything, Adri went on, "Or is it uploading? I'm afraid I get the two terms confused."

"You can download a physics education into my brain? In a few hours?" Thornberry asked, incredulous.

"Yes," Adri replied. "That's the way we learn, through direct neural stimulation. You have similar systems."

"They're illegal," said Thornberry.

Adri stopped walking and looked at Thornberry, clearly puzzled.

"But you used your ship's computer to store your memories while you were in flight, and then downloaded them back into your brains."

Jordan stepped between Adri and Thornberry. "What Mitchell is trying to explain is that on Earth such direct brain stimulation is forbidden."

"But why?" Adri asked, clearly perplexed.

"There's too much of a chance that unscrupulous people would use it to manipulate others, to plant false information in their minds, get them to do things they wouldn't ordinarily do."

"Unscrupulous people," Adri murmured, as if it was a new concept to him.

"Salesmen, for example," Jordan said.

"Politicians," Thornberry added. "And religious zealots."

Brandon pushed his way into the discussion. "Our shipboard system is an exception to the law. We had to get approval from the World Council."

"I see," Adri said. "I understand."

Brandon said, "I'm not sure that we should allow ourselves to be subjected to your direct brain stimulation."

Adri's seamed face eased into a bitter smile. "You are afraid that I might be one of those unscrupulous people."

DECISION

As they walked through the city, Adri tried earnestly to convince Thornberry and the others that their fears were unfounded.

"I assure you, the neural stimulation will be restricted to the subjects you are interested in. Physics, for you, Dr. Thornberry." Turning to Longyear, he continued, "Biology for you. And for Dr. de Falla—"

"Nothing for me," de Falla snapped. "Not until we can be sure that you're not going to brainwash us."

Adri seemed stunned. "You don't trust us."

Jordan said, "This is a new situation for us. We'll have to talk it over amongst ourselves."

"I understand," said Adri. But Jordan thought he looked disappointed, hurt.

Adri led the little group around the administrative building, heading for the dormitory. "We have prepared quarters for you all. Perhaps you can discuss the matter there."

"Thank you," said Jordan. "We will." But he was thinking that Adri would be able to hear every word they said. The buildings are all monitored, he remembered. Then he wondered, Why did Aditi show me their monitoring system, then? Was she trying to warn me, or does she really think there's no harm in it?

Keeping his thoughts to himself, Jordan followed Adri into the dormitory building. His companions kept an uneasy silence as Adri showed them their rooms. Jordan saw that he and his brother would be housed in the same two-bedroom suite as before, the others in single rooms. Not that Elyse will use her room, he grumbled to himself.

They all came back to the sitting room of Jordan's suite, and Adri left them to themselves.

"Until dinner," he said. To Jordan, he added, "Aditi will join us then."

Adri hesitated at the door. Looking directly at Thornberry, he said, "I hope you decide to accept our education system. Its only function is to teach, not to manipulate you."

Thornberry nodded unhappily. But Brandon replied, "Teaching is manipulation of a sort, isn't it?"

Adri said nothing. He pulled his furry little pet from his robe and left.

As soon as the door slid shut behind Adri's departing back, Thornberry said, "I feel like Dr. Faustus."

"Making a deal with the devil?" Longyear quipped.

"He's making a damned tempting offer," said Thornberry. "To learn how those energy screens work. I could go back to Earth and make a fortune!"

"Is that what you want?" Jordan asked.

Thornberry broke into a rueful grin. "I wouldn't refuse a fortune, you know. But what I really want is to *know*. To understand."

"But they might brainwash you while you're under their stimulator," de Falla objected.

Glancing around the sitting room, Jordan suggested, "Why don't we go into the plaza, outside, to continue this conversation?"

Brandon immediately caught his implication. "You think the rooms are bugged?"

"I know they are. Aditi showed me the center where they monitor everything."

"Everything?" Elyse asked.

Jordan almost smiled at the alarm on her face. "Almost everything," he assured her. "Come on, let's go outside. It's a pleasant day and we have a major decision to make."

The plaza was empty of other people. They're giving us some privacy, Jordan thought. If they're bugging us here they'd have to plant cameras in the trees, I suppose, or up on the rooftops. He led the little group to the center of the plaza and sat down on the grass.

The sun felt warm and good on his shoulders. The others sat, too, in a circle. Like a Neolithic band, Jordan thought. All we need is a campfire.

"So what do we do about this?" Thornberry asked.

Jordan replied, "Mitch, are you willing to be a guinea pig?"

"An experimental animal?"

"Yes," said Jordan. "We won't be able to tell if Adri's brain stimulator is nothing more than an educational tool or not unless one of us allows them to use it on him."

Thornberry shrugged. Then he muttered, "To learn how those energy shields work . . ."

"Dr. Faustus," Longyear reminded him.

Elyse said, "I'm going to ask their astronomers to show me their evidence for the gamma burst. I won't need brain stimulation for that."

"Evidence can be faked," de Falla pointed out.

"I suppose so," said Elyse. "I'll just have to see what they've got and make up my own mind."

"Without brain zapping," said Brandon.

She shuddered.

With his old quizzical smile, Thornberry conjectured, "So I take their brain zapping, and I come out knowing all things and able to speak with the tongues of men and of angels. How could that harm us?"

"It could prejudice you in favor of whatever Adri's trying to pull over on us," said Brandon.

"But I won't grow fangs, will I?" Thornberry joked.

"This isn't a laughing matter," Brandon insisted.

Jordan muttered, *"Davehr'yay noh praver'yay."*

"What?"

"It's an old Russian saying: Trust, but verify. Diplomats use the term a lot."

"Trust, but verify," Elyse repeated.

"Which means you don't really trust them at all, doesn't it?" said Brandon.

Jordan shook his head. "We allow Mitch to undergo their brain stimulation. Then we see if anything's different about him afterward."

"I'll be different," Thornberry said. "I'll be smarter."

"You'll know more," Longyear corrected.

"Meanwhile," Jordan said, trying to get the conversation back on track again, "Elyse will try to determine if this story of a gamma ray burst is true. If the evidence is reliable."

"So I'm the one showing the trust," Thornberry said, tapping the front of his wrinkled shirt.

"And I'm the one who verifies," said Elyse.

"And the rest of us will try to decide if we can really trust Adri and whether or not we should act on the information he's giving us."

"Tall order," de Falla said.

Jordan nodded agreement. "But I don't see anything else we can do. Do you?"

He looked at the five of them, sitting on the grass in a circle around him, their faces grave as they faced up to the responsibility. No one spoke. Brandon looked disgruntled, sullen, but he said nothing.

"I really believe we hold the fate of the human race in our hands," Jordan said.

No one disagreed.

CONFLICT

inner with Adri and Aditi was pleasant, but Jordan felt strains pulling him in different directions. He wanted to believe Adri, he wanted to believe everything Adri and the Predecessor had told him. But it was so enormous! So mind-boggling. And, he had to admit to himself, it just might all be a ploy to manipulate us, for some reason they haven't chosen to reveal to us.

God help us, he thought, Meek might be right. Then he realized, Meek's been right all along, about a lot of things. This planet isn't natural. Adri, Aditi, all the other people here, they were constructed to resemble us. Manufactured.

But is Meek right about their motives? That's the key to everything. Are Adri and the Predecessor telling me the truth about *why* they've done all this?

Brandon was unusually quiet through the meal, and Longyear and de Falla talked with each other, but had hardly a word to say to Adri or Aditi. So be it, Jordan sighed inwardly. One step at a time.

Then Thornberry announced that he had decided to undergo the brain stimulation, and Adri broke into a broad, beaming smile.

"I'll set up the procedure first thing in the morning," he promised.

Before Elyse could speak up, Adri turned to her and added, "And you'll want to meet with our astronomers at the observatory."

"Yes," she said.

"Fine," Adri said. "Fine."

"Dr. Longyear, are you ready for a stimulation session?"

Longyear shook his head. "I'll . . . wait until later."

"I see," Adri said, with a glance in Jordan's direction.

As they filed out of the dining hall, Jordan took Aditi's arm. "It's good to see you again."

"I missed you," she whispered.

"I missed you, too." And he led her down the corridor toward his suite.

Adri said good night and headed off to his own quarters. One by one, the others entered their rooms. Soon there was no one else in the corridor except Brandon and Elyse, walking a dozen paces ahead of Jordan and Aditi.

"Are you sure you should?" she asked.

"Yes, I'm very sure."

"Your brother . . . ?"

"I don't care."

"I don't want to come between you."

Jordan smiled at her. "And I don't want *him* to come between *us*."

She smiled back, but he could still see a flicker of worry in her chestnut brown eyes.

When they entered the sitting room, Elyse was relaxed on the couch, but Brandon was standing in the center of the room, frowning, tense.

"What's wrong, Bran?" Jordan asked.

"I wish we had something to drink. Scotch or brandy or something . . . anything."

"I can get an alcoholic beverage for you," Aditi offered.

"No," Brandon said. "I don't want to put you to any trouble."

"It's no trouble at all." Turning to the wall screen, she called, "Service, please."

A pleasant-looking young woman's face appeared on the screen. "Yes?" she said, smiling.

"Four after-dinner drinks, please. Alcoholic."

"Certainly." And the screen went dark.

"Room service?" Elyse asked.

"For our guests," said Aditi.

Within minutes a handsome young man in a dark tunic and slacks appeared at their door, bearing a tray with four tall glasses filled with a dark ruby-colored liquid.

Once he had deposited the tray on the coffee table and left, Brandon picked up one of the glasses, sniffed it tentatively, then took a sip.

"Well?" Jordan asked.

"Strange. Looks like port, but it tastes . . . almost like anisette. Or what's the Greek cordial?"

"Ouzo," said Elyse.

Brandon sipped again and nodded. "Almost like ouzo, but not quite. Fruitier."

As the others picked up their glasses, Jordan gestured Aditi to one of the armchairs and sat himself on the other one, facing her. Brandon sat on the couch beside Elyse. They each took long drafts of the liqueur.

"Delicious," said Jordan.

Elyse asked Aditi, "What is this called?"

She stared blankly at Elyse for a moment, then answered, "Grape liqueur, I believe."

"Not much of a name," Brandon muttered.

"Practical," said Jordan.

They sipped at the pleasant-tasting liqueur, making inconsequential conversation for several minutes.

But suddenly Brandon burst out, "Speaking of things practical, Jordy, that was a nice bit of maneuvering you pulled this afternoon."

"Maneuvering?" Jordan felt puzzled, but he recognized the look on Brandon's face. The same pouty frown Bran put on whenever he felt he'd been outsmarted. Or outplayed.

"Our little conference out on the grass," Brandon said. "You took control of things. Very slick, big brother."

"Don't be obtuse, Bran."

"Don't call me names!"

Jordan glanced at Aditi, who looked alarmed.

Elyse said, "Brandon, perhaps we should retire for the night."

But Brandon pointed an accusing finger at Jordan. "I was elected leader of the group. You resigned. You gave up your responsibilities and I took them on."

"I know," said Jordan. "I had no intention—"

"You undercut me out there! You just sat there and took over the discussion and took charge. I'm supposed to be the leader, not you!"

"Then why didn't you lead?" Jordan snapped.

"How in hell can I, when you snatch it all away from me? Before I can get a word in, you're monopolizing everything and giving orders."

Jordan stared at his brother. Can a few sips of alcohol break down his self-control so quickly? he wondered. Or is the drink just a convenient excuse for him to speak his mind?

"Bran," he said softly, "I'm sorry. I didn't mean to usurp your position."

"But you did it anyway."

Resentment smoldered in Brandon's eyes. Jordan's memory flashed back to other scenes, from childhood and their teen years, into adulthood, when Brandon flailed out in jealousy. That's why he went into science, to get away from me. To build a career for himself where he wouldn't have to compete with his older brother.

"Bran, I said I'm sorry. What more can I do?"

"You can stay the hell away from the rest of us. If you want to take their side, fine, go ahead. You can stay here when the rest of us leave, if you want to. That'll be fine with me."

Aditi looked stricken, Jordan saw. But in the back of his mind he thought that staying here with Aditi would not be unpleasant. Silently he said to his brother, Go on back to Earth with your tail between your legs. Go on back and face the responsibility for saving the human race from annihilation. Do you have the guts for that, Bran? Do you have the brains and the heart for it?

But aloud he said only, "I think I've heard enough for one night, Bran." Rising to his feet, Jordan held his hand out for Aditi. She got up and stood beside him.

"Good night, Elyse," Jordan said, as politely as he could manage. "Good night, Bran."

He turned and walked, hand-in-hand with Aditi, into their bedroom.

Once the door closed, Aditi said, "I had no idea he was so jealous of you."

Jordan shrugged. "It's been going on for years. This is Bran's way of getting what he wants: accusing me of hurting him." With a sigh he sat on the edge of the bed and began taking off his shoes.

Aditi sat beside him. "What are you going to do?"

"Let him cool off, I suppose." Then he looked into her questioning eyes. "But I can't just stand by and watch Bran and the others make a mess of things. There's too much at stake!"

She nodded, then asked, "Would you stay here when the others leave?"

"Yes . . . except . . ."

"Except that you want to help your people to survive," Aditi said, very solemnly.

"And the others that Adri spoke of."

Aditi smiled at him. "You have a fine sense of responsibility."

"Tell that to my little brother."

TRUST

Jordan was awakened by a soft chiming musical tone. He struggled up to a sitting position. Aditi, curled beside him, opened her eyes.

"Phone for you," she said. "Dr. Thornberry."

"How do you—" Then Jordan remembered she had a communicator implanted in her brain. "Can we make it audio only?"

She nodded, and Thornberry's voice said out of nowhere, "Top o' the morning to ya, Jordan. Do you want to have some breakfast before I march off to get me brain boosted?"

"Certainly," Jordan answered heartily. "We'll see you in the dining hall in twenty minutes."

"Twenty minutes. Right."

The bedroom fell silent.

"Is he gone?" Jordan whispered.

Aditi giggled. "Yes. All gone."

Twenty minutes later Jordan entered the dining hall, wearing a fresh pair of light blue slacks and an open-collared white shirt. Aditi had sent him on alone; she would meet him after breakfast in Adri's office. Thornberry was already there, sitting at a table with Elyse and Brandon.

Breakfast was served buffet style, so Jordan picked what looked like an omelet and a cup of strong black coffee analog.

Sitting opposite his brother, Jordan turned to Thornberry and said, "Ready for the experiment, Mitch?"

"As ready as I'll ever be," the roboticist answered, with an uneasy smile.

Brandon looked up from his plate. "Jordy, about last night . . ."

"I'm sorry if I stepped on your toes, Bran."

"Elyse told me I behaved like an ass."

"Not really."

"Really," Elyse said.

"Anyway, I apologize. That drink hit me pretty hard, I guess."

"No need for an apology," Jordan said. "Brothers should be able to speak their minds to each other." Yet he was thinking, *In vino veritas.*

Thornberry's head was swiveling back and forth like a spectator's at a tennis match. But he kept his silence.

After breakfast, Brandon and Elyse started out for the observatory, while Jordan led Thornberry to Adri's office, up on the top floor of the building.

Aditi was there when they arrived.

"Have you had breakfast?" Jordan asked her, by way of greeting.

"I had some fruit here, with Adri," she said.

Adri said, "Aditi will run the stimulation; it is her area of expertise."

"Brain stimulation?" Thornberry asked, surprised.

"Education," said Aditi. "My field is education."

Jordan said, "And you educate people through direct brain stimulation."

"Yes," she said. "Whenever possible."

Aditi led Jordan and Thornberry downstairs, leaving Adri in his office. They entered a small room that looked more like an office than a neurological laboratory. There was a desk in one corner, a pair of comfortable-looking upholstered chairs, and a padded couch along the far wall.

"This is where the deed is done, is it?" Thornberry asked, looking around the room for equipment.

Aditi nodded. "This is my office. And my schoolroom."

"Where's the equipment?" Jordan asked.

"In the walls, mostly," she replied. "Behind the ceiling panels, too."

She seemed perfectly relaxed, at ease in her own surroundings. Thornberry looked a little edgy.

"So what do I do?" he asked.

Gesturing to the couch, Aditi said, "You lie down and relax while I set up the equipment."

As Jordan sat in one of the chairs, she went to her desk and pulled a lower drawer open. Thornberry stretched out on the couch, while Aditi took out what looked to Jordan like old-fashioned wireless earphones.

"What's that?" Thornberry asked.

"The transceivers," Aditi replied easily. Walking to the couch, she explained, "The first thing we must do is map your brain's neural activity."

She handed the earphones to Thornberry, who fumbled with them, trying to slip them on.

Aditi explained, "No, no, not in your ears. Press the pads against your temples."

Jordan saw the uneasy expression on Thornberry's face. He felt a little nervous himself. But the headphones stuck to Thornberry's temples with no trouble.

Aditi seemed perfectly at home. She went back to her desk chair and played her fingers across the empty desktop. Jordan saw it was a digital display screen, showing an image of a keyboard.

The wall above the desk began to glow and the image of a human brain took form, false-colored pale pink, deep lavender, and pearl gray against the screen's bright blue background. Jordan could see sparkles of light flickering across the brain. Nerve impulses, he thought.

"Is that me?" Thornberry asked.

"That's your brain," Aditi said, without taking her eyes off the screen. "Impressive," she murmured.

"What happens now?"

"Once the mapping is finished, you go to sleep," Aditi said, still with her back to Thornberry.

"Um . . . I have to go to the bathroom," he said.

Jordan stifled a laugh.

Aditi said, "I'm sorry. I should have thought of that." She tapped at her desktop and the wall screen went dark.

Once Thornberry pulled off the headphones and hurried out of the office, Jordan said to Aditi, "I had no idea you were so . . . competent."

"I told you I was a teacher," she said.

"Yes, but you didn't tell me how you teach."

"Once Dr. Thornberry returns, I'll sedate him neurally and the downloading can begin. He'll be asleep and there won't be anything for you to do. You could leave and return in three hours."

Jordan thought it over for all of a second. "I'll stay here, if you don't mind. I ought to witness the entire procedure, boring though it may be."

She arched a brow at him. "You want to make certain I don't do anything terrible to him."

Jordan shook his head slightly. "My dear, I'm sure you could do whatever you want to him while I'm watching you do it and I wouldn't know that anything nefarious was going on."

Her expression grew serious. "I'm not going to hurt him, Jordan."

"I know," he said. "But I should stay through the whole procedure." Then he smiled and added, "Besides, it'll give me the chance to stay with you."

She blushed slightly, but before she could reply Thornberry reentered the room. "Well, that's a load off me mind," he said. "So to speak."

They all laughed.

Aditi was wrong. It was anything but boring.

Mapping Thornberry's brain took less than half an hour. Once she was satisfied with it, Aditi said to Thornberry, "You're going to go to sleep now."

"Wish me pleasant dreams, why don't you?"

"Pleasant dreams, Dr. Thornberry," Aditi said. Turning back to her keyboard, she murmured, "Now we deactivate the parietal cortex."

She tapped a key on the desktop and Thornberry's eyes fluttered and closed. In a moment he seemed deeply asleep, his chest rising regularly, his arms relaxed at his side.

Watching the brain image on the wall screen intently, Aditi touched another key. Jordan turned his attention from her toward Thornberry. He could see the man's eyeballs moving rapidly behind their closed lids. REM sleep, Jordan realized.

Deeply asleep, Thornberry stirred slightly, clenched his fists and then opened them again. He muttered something incomprehensible.

"Is this normal?" Jordan whispered.

Aditi nodded, her eyes focused on the image of Thornberry's brain. It was flickering madly now, nerve impulses racing back and forth. Thornberry groaned softly and his arms tensed, his legs shifted, as if he were straining to get up.

Aditi touched another key and Thornberry relaxed, his arms and legs going limp, his breathing deep and slow and regular.

For a while nothing seemed to happen. But Jordan could see that three small sections of Thornberry's brain seemed to be glowing with activity. He wished he knew enough about brain physiology to tell what those sections were, what their functions might be. He thought a bright pink region near the base of Thornberry's brain might be the thalamus, but he wasn't sure. He recognized the frontal cortex, which seemed ablaze with neural activity.

When he looked back at Thornberry, Jordan saw that the man's beefy face was swathed with perspiration. His body was arched with tension and his eyes were still moving back and forth behind their closed lids.

Jordan whispered again to Aditi, "Should I wipe his brow?"

"Don't touch him!" she hissed, without taking her eyes off the wall screen. "This is the most critical period of the download."

Biting his lip in apprehension, Jordan stared at Thornberry's struggling figure. He looks like he's fighting demons, Jordan thought. Like a soul being exorcised.

And then Thornberry relaxed again, totally, as limp as a flag on an utterly still day. His eye movements slowed, although they did not cease altogether. A crooked smile spread across his sweat-soaked face.

Aditi turned in her desk chair toward Jordan. "It will be easier from here on. Everything's fine now."

"What happened?" he asked. "What's going on?"

She drew in a breath, then explained, "It's quite natural for us to resist new ideas, especially if they conflict with what we already believe. Dr. Thornberry's brain was suddenly invaded by a massive dose of new concepts, and he instinctively resisted. Perfectly natural."

"And you overcame his resistance? You forced him to accept—"

"No, not at all," Aditi said. "The program merely repeated the new information until it became recognizable to his brain. It's the same process as ordinary classroom learning: it takes time to adapt to new knowledge and to accept it."

Jordan marveled, "But you can do it in minutes, instead of a whole semester."

With a glance at her wristwatch, Aditi said, "It took more than an hour, Jordan."

He looked at his watch and saw that she was right.

"Still . . ." he said.

"He'll be fine," said Aditi. "In another ninety minutes, two hours at most, he'll have absorbed everything the program has to tell him."

Jordan couldn't help wondering what else Thornberry's brain was being forced to absorb.

As Thornberry slept on peacefully, Jordan gave voice to his nagging doubts.

"Aditi, dear, I've got to ask you—"

"If the physics program is all that I'm downloading into Dr. Thornberry's brain?"

"Yes," Jordan admitted, feeling awful about it.

She turned her desk chair to face him. "That's all. It's quite enough. I had to map his brain first to see if he could accept such a massive amount of information."

"I want to believe you, I really do."

"I know you do, Jordan. And I know how difficult all this must be for you."

"It's all so new. It takes time to adapt to new information."

Her smile turned impish. "What did I tell you? You're going through the same process of adaptation that Dr. Thornberry's experiencing."

"Except that he's doing it in a few hours, while I'm taking much longer."

Wheeling her chair closer to him, Aditi said, "You're not suggesting that I use brain stimulation to indoctrinate you, are you?"

"No! Not at all."

"That would be an ethical violation," Aditi said. "We use brain stimulation to educate people, not to manipulate them."

"Even if I asked you to? Even if I volunteered?"

"It's not allowed," she replied. "We have our code of behavior. We're not monsters, no matter what Dr. Meek thinks."

Jordan gazed at her utterly earnest face. "Your ethical standards are somewhat higher than ours. On Earth, the temptation to use direct brain stimulation to control people would be unbearable—for some."

"But not for you."

"Nor for you."

Her stern expression eased. "You trust us, Jordan. That's wonderful."

"I trust *you*, Aditi."

"That's even more wonderful."

"I love you."

She broke into a sunny smile. "That's the most wonderful thing of all."

But suddenly Jordan felt uneasy. "My brother suggested that when the rest of us leave for home, I should stay here."

Aditi's eyes widened. "Stay? Would you? Would you stay here with me? That would be fantastic!"

"I want to," he said. Then he heard himself add, "But . . ."

"But," she said.

"All that Adri's told me. All that the Predecessor told me. The human race is in danger. Other races, on other worlds."

"It's a great responsibility for you," she said softly.

"I can't turn my back on it. On them."

"I know."

"You could come with me," he blurted.

"To Earth?"

"Yes." Jordan's mind raced. "In fact, it would be an enormous help. You could be an ambassador, a representative of your people. One look at you and they'd see that we have nothing to fear from you."

Aditi gave him a skeptical look. "Just as Dr. Meek sees he has nothing to fear?"

Jordan's heart sank. "Yes. You're right. There would be people on Earth who'd be frightened of you, no matter what."

For a few heartbeats neither of them spoke. Thornberry snored softly on the couch, completely relaxed.

Then Aditi said, "I'd go to Earth with you, Jordan."

He shook his head. "There'd be danger there for you. Fanatics, madmen. What they fear they try to destroy."

"You'd protect me."

"No. It'd be too dangerous for you. You'd be much better off staying here."

"While you went back to Earth?"

"I'd return for you." Then, realizing it took eighty years, he added uncertainly, "Someday."

Aditi reached out and took both Jordan's hands in hers. "No. I'll go to Earth with you."

"But—"

"I love you, Jordan. I'm not going to be parted from you. Not for anything."

He leaned toward her and kissed her.

"A fine thing," Thornberry called from the couch.

Jordan flinched reflexively away from Aditi. She looked surprised, scooted her chair back toward her desk, and peered at the image of Thornberry's brain on the wall screen.

"You two smooching away while I'm tryin' to sleep." Thornberry was half sitting up, grinning at them, the headphones dangling lopsidedly.

"Don't remove the transceivers just yet, please," Aditi called to Thornberry. While he pushed the headphones back into place, she tapped on her desktop keyboard, then spun her chair around to face Thornberry. "Very good. The program is finished. You can get up now."

Thornberry yanked the headphones off and swung his legs off the edge of the couch. "Well now, do I look any smarter to you?"

Jordan thought he looked totally normal, except that his wrinkled shirt was stained with perspiration.

"You look fine, Mitch," he said. "How do you feel?"

Thornberry hesitated a moment. "Pretty normal. Me shirt's a bit sticky, though." Then his beefy face broke into a broad smile. "B'god, I *see*! I see it all! By all the saints in heaven, I understand how it works!"

Aditi asked, "What can you tell me about the energy screen generators?"

"Why, they tap the multidimensional branes that envelop space-time and focus them to produce a warping field that absorbs incoming energy."

Jordan felt impressed. Aditi pulled a digital notepad and stylus from her desk drawer and handed them to Thornberry.

"The basic equations, please," she said.

Grinning, Thornberry scribbled away on the notepad's screen, his tongue peeking out from between his teeth.

"There," he said. "That's right, isn't it?"

Aditi said, "I don't know. I'm not a physicist. But your equations have been sent to the chief of our physics department . . ."

"And?" Jordan prompted.

Aditi's smile told him everything. "He confirms that your equations are correct. The downloading worked fine."

"I'm a bloody physicist!" Thornberry crowed. "And I can build a field generator from scratch, b'god."

"It worked," Jordan breathed.

Aditi nodded happily. "It certainly did."

Thornberry got to his feet and pranced across the room. "I want to call Hazzard. I want to impress him with me new knowledge. We can build an energy shield for the ship, b'god."

"Well, I'm certainly impressed," said Jordan.

VERIFY

azzard was impressed, too. On the wall screen above Aditi's desk, his dark face was split by a bright grin as Thornberry spouted enthusiasm about building an energy shield to protect the ship from harmful levels of radiation.

Glancing at his wristwatch again, Jordan said to Aditi, "I should get over to the observatory and see how Dr. Rudaki is doing with your astronomers."

She nodded. "I understand. I'll stay here with Dr. Thornberry."

Jordan looked at Thornberry, chattering happily with Hazzard. The astronaut seemed halfway between delighted and bewildered at the roboticist's fervor.

"He won't miss you," Aditi said.

Jordan agreed with a nod. He kissed Aditi lightly on the lips and headed for the door.

"Dinner tonight?" he asked her.

"Of course," she said.

Jordan whistled happily as he strode briskly through the city's bustling streets toward the observatory. It works, he thought. The brain stimulation works and there aren't any bad side effects. None that I could see, at least. Mitch seems as happy as a little boy on Christmas morning.

His phone buzzed. Yanking it from his shirt pocket, he saw Adri's lined face on its tiny screen. The old man was beaming brightly.

"Aditi tells me that Dr. Thornberry's download went very well," he said.

"It did indeed," Jordan said cheerfully, without breaking stride. "I am pleased."

"I'm overjoyed."

"Apparently Dr. Rudaki is finding what she came for among the astronomers."

"That's where I'm heading now," Jordan said.

"Yes, I know."

Of course you know, Jordan said silently. You know every move we make.

Aloud, he replied to Adri, "Will you join us for dinner this evening?"

Adri chuckled softly. "Your affinity for mixing sociability with meals is putting weight on me."

Jordan laughed. "A couple of kilos won't hurt you."

"Perhaps not," Adri agreed, smiling back at Jordan. "This evening, then, in the dining hall."

"Seven o'clock?"

"Seven will be fine."

Jordan snapped the phone shut and slipped it back into his shirt pocket. He saw the observatory no more than two blocks ahead.

Entering the observatory was like entering a cathedral. Even though the telescopes were not working in the daytime, once he stepped into the main section of the building, with its domed roof and skyward-pointing instruments, Jordan felt an almost religious kind of awe and majesty.

He remembered a line of Galileo's: Astronomers seek to investigate the true constitution of the universe, the most important and the most admirable problem that there is.

As he stood there gaping, a young man in a comfortably loose white tunic and dark blue slacks hurried across the observatory's stone floor toward him.

"Mr. Kell! Welcome."

Jordan dipped his chin a notch. "Thank you. May I ask what your name is?"

The young astronomer hesitated a moment, looking blank, puzzled, but at last answered, "In your language, my name is Mitra."

"I'm very pleased to meet you, Mitra."

He was a pleasant-faced young man, a shade taller than Jordan yet somehow softer-looking, as if he had not yet outgrown his baby fat. His hair was a light brown color, sandy, so wispy that the slightest waft of air sent it flying.

"You're here to see Dr. Rudaki, I presume," Mitra said, smiling brightly at Jordan.

"Yes. Can you take me to her?"

"With pleasure. She's in the conference room with the top staff."

Mitra led Jordan across the hushed observatory, past the slanting gridwork of the resting telescopes, and up a steel stairway that clanged echoingly with every step they took. He stopped at a closed door, tapped on it with a knuckle, then slid it open.

There were ten people seated around a long table, with Elyse at its foot, Brandon sitting beside her. They both looked grim. Five other men and three women, Jordan saw. One of the men, chunky and barrel-chested, with short-cropped dark brown hair, was on his feet at the head of the table. The wall screens displayed astronomical images from ceiling to floor, swirling clouds of stars, vast glowing streams of gas, dark veils of obscuring dust.

"Mr. Kell," said the standing man. "Welcome to our little colloquium." He gestured to an empty chair at the foot of the table, next to Elyse and Brandon. They've been expecting me, Jordan realized.

The astronomer introduced the men and women seated around the table, then ended with, "I am Hari, chief astronomer."

Jordan nodded a hello to each of them in turn as he went to the chair and sat in it.

"We have been showing Dr. Rudaki and Dr. Kell images and data concerning the gamma ray eruption at the galactic core."

As Hari spoke, the images on the walls changed. Like a slide show, Jordan thought.

"Most of these images are more than twelve thousand years old," the astronomer went on, just the slightest bit pompous. "I'm afraid their quality has degraded a bit over time, but they are still useful."

Hari explained that the images looked inward, toward the heart of the galaxy, where the stars were so thickly clustered that they showed as one bright continuous glow. The images shifted, and Jordan guessed that they were showing the same field of view in different wavelengths: optical, infrared, ultraviolet, X-ray and finally—

"And this is the gamma-ray view," Hari intoned.

The background of the galaxy's heart disappeared in the final view, smothered by a blazing wave of gamma radiation. The images flicked every few seconds; the wave grew bigger with each change, like a menacing tsunami growing, surging, coming closer.

"That's the most recent image we have," said Hari, as the pictures froze on the walls. Jordan felt surrounded by an almost palpable menace.

Elyse said, "All these images were taken from Hari's homeworld, before the Predecessors sent out the mission that arrived here."

"Before Hari and Adri and all these people were created," Brandon added.

"Yes," Hari answered, from the front of the room.

"And what happened to your homeworld when the gamma burst engulfed it? What happened to your ancestors?"

Hari looked slightly uncomfortable, but he answered, "They had already gone extinct. Our homeworld was occupied by inorganic entities. Had been for many thousands of years. Your years."

"Inorganic—you mean, like the Predecessor."

One of the women across the table replied, "Not precisely. More like our predecessors."

Jordan blinked and shook his head. "Your history goes back a long way."

"More than thirty million of your years," said Hari.

"And this gamma burst?"

"It's real, Jordy," said Brandon. "Elyse has been going over the evidence with these people all morning. Not merely imagery, but measurements of the energy intensity in the eruption." His face was somber. "It's like a wave of death hurtling toward us."

"Toward you, and dozens of other intelligent species in your section of the Orion arm," said Hari. "Most of those species have not yet reached the level of high technology. Most of them have no way of knowing about the coming disaster—unless you reach them and save them."

Fixing his gaze on Elyse and Brandon, Jordan asked them, "Are you certain?"

Brandon nodded, his lips a tight, rigid line. Elyse said, "There's no denying it."

Jordan thought about how many apparent truths had been denied in the past. How many human beings had died because some men made up their minds to ignore the truth, to overlook the data, to denigrate those who warned of impending problems. Wars that could have been stopped before they started. Diseases that spread because people denied their reality. The greenhouse warming that was changing Earth's climate: it could have been averted, or at least mitigated.

He shook his head, trying to focus on the here and now.

"Absolutely certain?" he repeated to Elyse.

Very solemnly she replied, "Absolutely."

Jordan pulled in a deep breath. "Then we've got to decide what to do about it."

Brandon said, "Right. And the first step is to convince Meek."

FACTIONS

hey were a subdued group as they rode the buggy back to the camp the following morning. Longyear drove, as usual, with Jordan sitting beside him. Thornberry and de Falla occupied the second row, Elyse and Brandon the third.

"You should have let them pump their biology program into your brain, Paul," Thornberry said as they went along the trail.

"Maybe," Longyear replied guardedly.

From the rear, Brandon quipped, "We're still waiting to see if you turn into an alien clone or something, Mitch."

"A leprechaun, more likely," Thornberry rejoined.

De Falla turned in his seat to face Elyse. "You're absolutely certain that what they're telling us is true?"

Looking as if she were tired of answering the same question over and again, she answered, "Absolutely certain. Yes."

"Data can be faked."

"I know," said Elyse. "But they have such a massive amount of data. Visual imagery, radio telescope returns, gamma ray measurements. I looked for inconsistencies, for flaws . . . it all appears to be true."

"Appears," de Falla said.

Elyse stared at him for several silent moments, then said, "I suppose at the heart of everything is the fact that I trust them. They're astronomers and astrophysicists, not politicians. They deal with observations and measurements, not rhetoric."

Jordan said over his shoulder, "Have you shown their data to Zadar?"

"Yes. Demetrios agrees, the data are conclusive."

Brandon said, "The only question now is, what are we going to do about it?"

Jordan replied, "We try to convince Harmon. He's our test case. If we can't convince him, we won't have the ghost of a chance of convincing the movers and shakers back on Earth."

Without taking his eyes off the trail twisting through the trees, Longyear said, "Well, you've just about got me convinced."

Surprised, Jordan asked, "You're not totally sure?"

"Adri and his people wouldn't be the first to speak with forked tongues."

"Oh, for god's sake!"

"Think about it," Longyear insisted. "We know they've got terrific technologies. I'm itching to learn about their biotech. But suppose they're using technological tricks to convince us about this gamma eruption?"

That silenced the rest of them.

Until Jordan said, "If they are, and there's no gamma wave threatening Earth, then why did they invent such a story?"

"How should I know?" Longyear said.

"But on the other hand," Jordan went on, "if the gamma burst truly is real, we'd be consigning the entire human race to extinction if we did nothing."

"We'd be consigning the whole human race to falling for some alien scheme if we swallow their story," Longyear countered.

Thornberry piped up, "By their fruits you shall know them."

"What?"

"From the Bible. You can determine what's good and what's bad by looking at the consequences of the way people behave."

"But we don't know the consequences," de Falla pointed out. "We won't know the consequences for another two thousand years."

Jordan said, "I think I see what Mitch is driving at. If we fail to act and the threat is real, the human race dies. If we do act and the threat is a fake, then . . . what?"

"Are we willing to take the chance?" Thornberry asked.

"Do we have the right to take that chance?" Jordan replied.

"Certain death versus some unknown motive of the aliens," said de Falla.

"Some choice," Brandon said.

"I don't think we have a choice," Jordan insisted.

"Try telling that to Meek," said Brandon.

RESOLUTION

As soon as they reached the camp, Brandon called a meeting of the entire group. Jordan watched with a mixture of amusement and anxiety as they filed into the dining area. He, his brother, Elyse, and Thornberry sat on one side of the long table. Meek, Longyear, and de Falla chose the other, facing them. Jordan was surprised and a little disheartened when Yamaguchi came in, looked at the lineup, and chose Meek's side. Verishkova sat beside Thornberry.

Hazzard, Zadar, and Trish Wanamaker were on the screen at the foot of the table. No telling which side they'd be on if they were here, Jordan thought.

Once everyone was settled in their chairs, Brandon slowly got to his feet. Reluctantly, Jordan thought.

"Mitchell has taken the brain boost," he began, "and he seems no worse for it."

From the screen, Hazzard quipped, "He's become a nuisance, pestering me to build an energy shield for the ship."

Most of the people around the table chuckled.

"It's astounding, it is," Thornberry enthused. "I got a university education in physics, I did—inside of a few hours."

"And what else did they pump into your brain?" Meek asked, his long face scowling.

Thornberry shrugged his heavy shoulders. "Nothing, far as I can tell."

"As far as you can tell."

Jordan started to reply to the astrobiologist, but hesitated, looking to his brother. Bran's in charge, let him handle this.

But Brandon turned to Elyse and said, "Tell them about the gamma burst."

Looking straight at Meek, Elyse said in a measured tone, "All the evidence I have seen convinces me that the danger is real. The core of the galaxy gave off an enormous burst of gamma energy some twenty-eight thousand years ago. The death wave will reach Earth's vicinity in two thousand years."

"And wipe out all life in its path," Brandon added.

Good for you, Bran! Jordan exulted silently.

Meek looked unconvinced. "How do we know that the 'evidence' they showed isn't faked?"

"Why would they do that?" Jordan blurted.

"To get us to go along with them," Longyear replied.

"For what purpose?"

"How should we know?" Meek answered. "They're up to something, and they're certainly not going to tell us what it is until it suits them."

Brandon planted his fists on his hips and asked Meek, "What do you think we ought to do?"

"Leave here immediately and go back home."

"And the gamma burst?"

"It's a trick. I'm sure it's a trick."

"And if it's not?" Jordan asked.

Meek blinked at him several times, said nothing.

"If it's not a trick," Brandon said, his voice iron hard, "then we're consigning the human race to extinction."

Waving a long-fingered hand in the air, Meek said, "We have two thousand years to deal with that possibility."

"And other intelligent races, they'll be wiped out also," Brandon went on.

"I don't believe it!" Meek fairly shouted. "I can't believe it!"

Jordan asked his brother, "May I have the floor?"

With a surprised grin, Brandon spread his arms and said grandly, "The floor is yours."

Getting to his feet as Brandon sat down, Jordan began, "Harmon, Paul . . . we hold the fate of the human race in our hands. The twelve of us. What we decide can mean life or death for the entire human race. There's no one we can turn to, no higher-ups that we can buck the problem to. There's only we twelve. It's up to us. Entirely up to us."

Meek shook his head stubbornly. Longyear stared at Jordan, his face a frozen mask.

Jordan went on, "What this boils down to is a matter of faith. Some of us believe what the aliens have told us, some of us don't. Those who believe point to palpable evidence, those who don't worry that the evidence may have been faked."

"My education isn't a fake," Thornberry muttered.

"But it could be a tactic," Meek immediately countered. "They boost your brain to convince us that the rest of what they're telling us is true."

"That's a possibility," Jordan admitted. "How do we decide whether it's true or not?"

Silence fell across the table. Longyear opened his mouth, then thought better of it and said nothing.

"This is a fundamental problem of science, isn't it?" Jordan asked. "How do we know that what our human senses are telling us is real, or if we're fooling ourselves?"

"You test the information," Brandon answered. "All knowledge is testable. What you can't test is nothing more than belief, opinion."

"How do we test the information that Adri's astronomers have given Elyse?"

"I've gone over it as carefully as I can," Elyse said, looking up at Jordan. "I'm convinced it's real."

"But you're not one hundred percent certain, are you?" Meek challenged.

Before Jordan could say anything, Brandon replied, "Harmon, nothing is one hundred percent certain. Newton gave us a scientific worldview that held up for damned near three hundred years. Then Einstein came along and showed there was more to it. And string theory eventually enlarged on Einstein's work. Nothing is one hundred percent certain. Not forever."

Meek started to reply, but Brandon overrode him. "In your own field, Harmon, in astrobiology it's happened. The field exploded in the late twentieth century with the discovery of extremophiles, didn't it? When Tommy Gold proposed a deep, hot biosphere of bacteria living miles underground, the biologists laughed at him, didn't they?"

"But evidence proved he was right," Meek admitted. "Eventually."

"Nothing is one hundred percent certain," Brandon repeated. "It can't be. You never have the ultimate truth. There's always more to be learned."

"So what do we do?" de Falla asked.

Without hesitation, Brandon said, "We act on the information we have. We message Earth all the information we've discovered here, and warn them about the gamma burst. We keep on working with Adri's people and plan out how we can help Earth and the other worlds that are in danger."

Thornberry piped up. "We can build energy shields that'll protect Earth from the gamma burst, b'god."

"Right," said Brandon. "That's what we've got to do. Who says no to that?"

No one stirred, not even Meek. No one lifted a hand in objection or raised a voice.

Jordan, still on his feet, looked down at Brandon. You took charge at last, he said silently. You've become a man, baby brother.

But then he looked across the table at Harmon Meek, who was sitting rigidly, his long face crumbling into a mask of despair.

EXOPLANET

Quoth the raven, "Nevermore."

EDGAR ALLAN POE,
"The Raven"

HOMEWORLD

Two thousand light-years closer to the core of the Milky Way galaxy than Earth, a small, rocky planet orbited tightly around a tiny, faint red dwarf star. The planet hugged its parent star so closely that its year was only five Earth-days long. Its locked rotation kept one side always facing the meager warmth of its dim parent star, one side perpetually dark and cold.

The star was one of the galaxy's most commonplace, faint and cool, but destined to continue shining feebly long after giant bright beacons such as Sirius had depleted their nuclear energy sources and destroyed themselves in titanic explosions.

The planet orbiting it was a world of stark contrasts: jagged cliffs and harsh deserts surrounding seething purple seas that crashed against the rugged cliffs and sent huge waves of violent surf surging across beaches of ruby-red sand.

Those seas teemed with life. And living creatures inhabited those deserts, carved homes for themselves in those cliffs, soared across the brooding scarlet skies.

One species of life on that planet was intelligent. Part animal, part plant, they called themselves The People and called their planet Home.

A brood of them was flying across the rocky desert, gliding on the tidal wind that blew unfailingly across their world, high above the rugged cliffs, their backs to the red sun that filled half their sky. They were long, thin, ethereal creatures, gliding on wide gossamer wings that drank in the feeble sunlight, searching for one of their family who had wandered far from their usual haunts.

Across the barren landscape they soared, incomplete as long as one of them was missing. They headed away from their sun, toward the distant shadowed land that bordered the half of their world that was always in darkness.

"This is foolishness," grumbled one of them. "The farther from the sun we fly, the weaker we become."

"It's cold here," complained another. "How can we bud in such a wasteland?"

"We cannot bud until we are complete," said their leader, the oldest among them. "We must find Phen-he. Then we can return to the warmth and begin to bud."

One of the others complained, "Phen-he has always been strange, a loner. It would be better to bud without Phen-he, leave the strange one in solitude."

"That is not our way," said the leader, sternly. "We must have unity before we can bud."

"I see Phen-he!" cried their youngest, flying some distance ahead of the others. It extruded an arm from its malleable body, pointing.

And there was Phen-he, a thin filmy reed standing with wings folded about its body on an outcropping of rock, roots wormed into the thin layer of nourishing soil, swaying gently in the tidal breeze, head turned toward the darkest part of the sky.

The others fluttered about Phen-he and, one by one, landed around it. Their roots found precious little nutrition in the meager soil that coated the underlying rock.

"What are you doing here, Phen-he?" demanded the eldest. "Don't you realize you are required for the budding?"

Phen-he turned toward the eldest, its heat-sensitive eyeplates so enlarged they covered most of its upper body. Extruding an arm, it pointed into the dark sky.

"Look," it said.

The others stared into the darkness. As their eyeplates adapted and grew, they saw that the inky sky was peppered with specks of light.

"What are they?" asked one of the brood.

"I don't know," said Phen-he. "I first saw them many cycles ago, when I was blown to the dark side by a storm."

"Lights in the sky?" wondered another. "What does it mean?"

"They exist only on the dark side of Home," said Phen-he. Then it added, "Or perhaps they are too faint to be seen where the sun fills the sky."

"They are meaningless," decided the eldest. "Come, Phen-he, you are needed for the budding."

"But they are so beautiful—"

"You are needed. You must come."

Reluctantly, Phen-he bowed and stretched its wings wide. The entire brood disengaged from the soil and took flight.

Phen-he turned its head for one final look at the flecks of light. Its breath caught in its throat.

The sky was becoming brighter. The darkness was changing into light. Hard, fierce light, so brilliant it hurt its eyeplates. Phen-he turned away from the growing light but it was no use. The entire sky was ablaze. It saw the eldest's wings crumple and it plunged to the ground, smoking and shrieking. All the others screamed and died, falling like burning leaves. Phen-he felt itself burning, roasting as the sky blazed furiously and even the soil below and the rocks themselves began to smolder.

Everyone died. The People were no more. The planet they called Home was reduced to a smoking ruin of rubble-strewn bare rock.

Surging past at the speed of light, the gamma burst enveloped everything and then sped onward, outward, spreading death wherever it touched.

CRUSADERS

Far and away the best prize that life has to offer is the chance to work hard at work worth doing.

THEODORE ROOSEVELT

BASE CAMP

'm proud of you, Bran," said Jordan. "You've become a leader."

Brandon smiled shyly. "With your help, Jordy. With your help."

The two brothers were walking alone through the white mounds of their camp's bubble tents, beneath a darkening sky. The first few stars were appearing in the gathering twilight. Jordan knew that Earth's Sun would be visible once the night became fully dark. It would appear as a faint yellowish star, undistinguished and terribly far away.

"I wish there were some way we could convince Harmon that Adri's people mean us no harm," Jordan said.

Brandon huffed. "Meek's a lost cause. He's scared out of his wits. He'll never be able to adapt to this situation."

They walked along slowly, out toward the periphery of their camp. The forest trees sighed in the soft night breeze. Jordan thought of Aditi, back in the city, waiting for him, waiting for the people from Earth to make up their minds.

Turning toward his brother, Jordan said, "Bran, we've got to present a united front back home. We can't have a divided team, we can't have Harmon giving them a dissenting minority report."

Brandon nodded. "That'd give the naysayers a reason to deny everything we have to tell them."

Jordan thought of other times, earlier crises that had been worsened by inaction. World War II. The American Civil War. We might have avoided the greenhouse floods if we'd acted early enough, strongly enough, he said to himself.

Strangely, Brandon began to chuckle softly.

"Something funny?"

"I was just thinking about the Neanderthals."

"What in the—"

"I was picturing a council of Neanderthals sitting in their cave around a fire, debating what they should do about global warming."

"You have a weird sense of humor, Bran."

"No, Jordy. Imagine it. Here they are, beautifully adapted to the Ice Age. But the climate's warming up. The glaciers are melting away. And they're squatting around their fire, wondering what to do."

"There wasn't much they could do," said Jordan.

"They could have adapted. They could have changed their ways and adapted to the warmer climate."

"Could they?" Jordan wondered. "As you say, they were physically adapted for the Ice Age climate."

"They were intelligent, Jordy. As intelligent as we are. They had larger brains than we do, actually."

"But—"

"Some of them lived in the Middle East, you know. They could have adapted to a warmer climate."

Jordan pointed out, "Some of them interbred with our ancestors, actually. We carry a few Neanderthal genes in our DNA."

"We absorbed them."

"Which is what Harmon fears that Adri's people want to do to us."

Brandon snorted a bitter laugh. "Yeah, their few thousand are going to absorb our twenty billion."

"He's still afraid of the possibility."

With a dismissive shake of his head, Brandon continued, "Most of the Neanderthals didn't get absorbed. They didn't adapt. They must've had a guy like Meek telling them that the warming is all a fake, a temporary anomaly, nothing to worry about."

Jordan got the point. "So they didn't change."

"And they went extinct."

"Just as we will."

"If we don't change our ways, Jordy. If we don't change our ways."

"Can we?" Jordan asked. "Will we?"

"There'll be plenty of people back on Earth who won't want to believe what we have to tell them. People who'll deny it all, claim we've been hoodwinked by scheming aliens."

"Just like Harmon."

"Yeah."

"What are you going to do about him, Bran?"

In the lengthening shadows, Jordan couldn't make out the expression on his brother's face. But he heard the undertone of anger in Brandon's voice. "Personally, I'd like to stuff him back in a cryosleep capsule and keep him there permanently."

"Not an altogether bad idea," Jordan said lightly, "but it's rather impractical, don't you think?"

"I just don't understand him, Jordy. He's supposed to be a scientist, but he's not thinking logically at all. He hasn't done a lick of work since we arrived here."

"He's frightened."

They had reached the edge of the camp. Brandon stood in silence for several long moments, fists on his hips, head turned skyward.

"You're right, Jordy," he said at last. "If we can't convince Meek that Adri's people are being honest with us, we won't have a chance in hell of convincing the powers-that-be back on Earth."

"So what do you propose to do?" Jordan repeated.

"I'm supposed to be our fearless leader, right?"

"You are the team's leader," Jordan agreed.

"So I'm going to do what a leader's supposed to do," Brandon said. "When facing a really tough job, fob it off on somebody else."

"What do you mean?"

Stepping closer to Jordan, Brandon placed a hand on his brother's shoulder and said, "Jordy, I'm giving you the task of bringing Meek around. I just don't get along with the pompous ass, but you get along with everybody. The job is yours . . . if you'll accept it."

Surprised, Jordan actually staggered back a step. "You want me . . . ?"

"To get Meek to see the light. You're a trained diplomat. If I try to convince him I'll wind up socking him in the nose."

"But—"

"No buts, Jordy. I need you to do this. We all need it. If you can bring Meek around, Longyear and the others will fall in line."

Jordan stared at his brother. His first thought was, Bran's evading his responsibilities again, just as he's done since we were children. He wants to be recognized as our leader but he can't face up to doing the work.

But then he realized, Wait. Maybe Bran's really taking his job of leadership seriously. Maybe he's thought this out, after all. A real leader delegates authority. A good leader picks the best people for the tasks that have to be done.

He gazed into his brother's questioning eyes with new respect. Placing his hand on Brandon's shoulder, in imitation of his brother's gesture, Jordan replied, "I'll do it, Bran. I don't know if I'll be successful, but I'll talk to Harmon, one on one."

Brandon nodded. "I knew I could count on you, Jordy."

"I don't know if I can bring him around," Jordan warned again.

"If you can't, nobody can," Brandon said, with absolute certainty.

Jordan went to his cubicle, sat on the springy cot, and phoned Aditi. He always felt a little awkward speaking to her from the cubicle; its two-meter-high partitions didn't allow much privacy. He kept his voice low, but his eyes focused on Aditi's alert, vivacious features.

He couldn't tell her about Brandon's request; he might be overheard. Instead he asked her about her day, and they chatted about inconsequential matters.

Until he said, "I'd really like to get back to the city as soon as I can."

"Tomorrow?" she chirped.

With an unhappy smile, Jordan answered, "I don't think so. I have a lot to do here."

"I'll come there, then."

Jordan shook his head. "No. That would be . . . a problem. Let me work out what I have to do here and then I'll call you."

"I miss you, Jordan."

Almost whispering, he replied, "I miss you, too."

They said reluctant good-byes, then Jordan clicked his phone shut. Maybe Bran has the right idea, he thought. Maybe stuffing Harmon into a cryosleep capsule is the answer to our problem.

He dreamt that night of Miriam: happy, laughing, in the healthy bloom of youth when he had first met her. And in his dream she morphed into Aditi, happy, laughing, young.

He woke and sat up on the cot, thinking, How lucky you are,

Jordan Kell. To find another woman who loves you. You had to travel more than eight light-years to find her, but find her you did.

For long moments he sat there and watched the dawn brightening the dome of the bubble tent. At last he told himself, Now you've got to do what's necessary to keep her.

And that means convincing Harmon to accept Adri and all he had told them.

A pang of memory assailed him as he shaved: Miriam's last agonized days. But then he realized that the memory was his subconscious mind's way of showing him a way to solve his problem.

Dressed in slacks and an open-necked shirt, Jordan found Meek in the dining area, his breakfast laid out on the table before him as precisely as a military formation. Longyear was sitting beside him, the two of them leaning their heads together in intense conversation.

Jordan filled a tray with juice, buttered toast, and a steaming mug of coffee, then went to their table and sat down facing the astrobiologist.

"Good morning, all," Jordan said cheerily. "May I join you?"

"Of course," said Meek. Longyear nodded.

De Falla came up and started unloading his tray opposite Jordan. "Good morning," he said as he sat down.

Meek nodded at the geologist, said nothing as he reached for his glass of juice.

"I'm going back to the city this morning," Jordan said as he lifted his own juice glass. "Anyone want to come along with me?"

"I'm busy with the geological mapping," said de Falla. "Adri's people have promised to send me a detailed profile of the planet's interior."

"It must be fascinating," Jordan said, "working out how they constructed this planet."

De Falla nodded warily. "It's hard to believe, constructing a whole planet. But it's true. That's what they did."

"That's what they claim they did," Longyear objected.

"No, Paul," said de Falla, "they did it. This planet's been built around a hollow shell. We're standing on fourteen kilometers of dirt and rocks. Then there's the metal shell, and inside it nothing but an energy generator that creates the gravitational field we feel."

Longyear glanced at Meek, who said nothing, busily slicing the omelet on his plate.

"Thornberry's working up the specifications of their grav generator," de Falla went on. "He says it could make a tremendous weapon, handling all that energy."

"A planet wrecker," Longyear muttered.

Jordan said, "Perhaps it would be best if we didn't bring that level of technology back to Earth."

Meek's brows rose. "Will they let us return to Earth?"

"Yes, Harmon," Jordan replied. "I'm sure they will."

"When?"

"When we're ready to leave, I should imagine."

"I thought you said we were their prisoners," Meek said.

"Adri won't keep us here against our will. His whole approach to dealing with us has been to answer our questions, honestly and forthrightly."

"But not completely."

Patiently, Jordan said, "Harmon, we're like schoolchildren, compared to Adri's people. We have a lot to learn, and they're being very patient with us."

"But you think they'll allow us to leave?" Longyear asked.

"When we're ready to, yes."

"I wonder."

"Come into the city with me and ask Adri yourself, Paul."

Longyear seemed to think it over for a heartbeat, then he said, "All right, I'll do that." He hesitated, then added, "I've been thinking about taking them up on their offer to teach me what they know about biology."

Meek looked up from his plate, startled, a forkful of omelet in midair.

"I mean, Mitch has learned a helluva lot about physics from them. I'd like to learn what they know about biology."

"I wouldn't if I were you," said Meek.

"It's damned tempting," Longyear said.

"So was the apple that Eve gave to Adam."

"You think we're going to damn ourselves?" Longyear challenged.

"I think we're in over our heads," said Meek.

Jordan smiled and said, "Harmon, if we are in over our heads, wouldn't education be a good way to get our heads above water?"

"Education or mind manipulation?"

"Does Mitchell seem different to you? Manipulated?"

Meek stared at Jordan for a wordless moment, then turned his attention back to the remains of his omelet.

As gently as he could, Jordan said, "Harmon, I've got to let Nara examine me. Would you go with me?"

"Examine you? What for? Are you ill?"

"It's just a routine exam. I picked up a bug before we left Earth and she wants to keep an eye on it."

His eyes narrowing with suspicion, Meek asked, "And why do you want me to accompany you? Are you afraid she's going to stick you with a needle?"

Longyear suppressed a laugh; de Falla grinned openly.

"Not exactly," said Jordan. "But I'd appreciate it if you came along with me."

Meek said nothing, clearly wondering what was behind Jordan's request.

"Of course," Jordan said easily, "if you have something more important scheduled for this morning . . ."

"No," Meek confessed. "My schedule is rather clear."

"Then come along with me," Jordan coaxed. "Please."

With an exaggerated sigh, Meek said, "Oh very well. If it will make you happy."

"It might make you happy, too, Harmon," said Jordan.

BY THEIR FRUITS

Nara Yamaguchi looked surprised when Jordan and Meek entered her infirmary. It was in the same tent as the dining area and the kitchen, a placement that seemed amusing to several of the team.

Tanya Verishkova joked about the efficiency of having medical help so conveniently close to the robotic cooks in the kitchen. "Potential poisoners," she called the robots.

Yamaguchi was sitting at her desk, studying medical records, when Jordan and Meek came in. The infirmary was small: her desk was tucked into one corner. Most of the space was taken up by the examination table and the compact array of diagnostic sensors built into an arch over the table.

Looking up from her display screen, she asked, "What can I do for you?"

"I'd like a checkup," said Jordan.

Clearly puzzled, Yamaguchi said, "Now?"

"Now," Jordan answered. "And then I'd like you to show Harmon my medical record."

Her round face took on a troubled frown. "Medical records are private, Jordan. You know that."

"But you can allow Harmon to see my record if I request it."

"I suppose so." Reluctantly.

Nodding toward the examination table, Jordan said, "Let's do a scan first."

Meek seemed totally baffled as Jordan removed his shoes, belt, and pocketphone, then lay back on the table for a full-body scan. The astrobiologist folded his arms across his narrow chest and watched, almost suspiciously, as the instruments arching above the table hummed and beeped.

Yamaguchi gestured toward her display screen. "Clean as a whistle, same as the last two times."

Jordan nodded and said, "Now will you kindly show Harmon my earlier scans?"

"Why do you want this?" Yamaguchi asked.

With a wintry smile, Jordan replied, "To show Harmon the truth."

There was no other chair in Yamaguchi's office, so she got up and offered Meek her own. He looked across at Jordan, then folded his lanky body into the little wheeled chair. It rolled slightly away from the desk and Meek reached out his long arms, grasped the edge of the desk, and pulled himself back.

"What am I supposed to be looking for?" he asked Yamaguchi. "I'm an astrobiologist, not a physician."

"Tell him," Jordan said, as the image of his first examination, the day they all were revived from cryosleep, appeared on the screen.

Her brows knit in misgiving, Yamaguchi told Meek, "Jordan carried a genetically engineered virus in his lower abdominal tract." Pointing to the image on the screen, "There it is, false-colored red."

Meek peered at the screen. "Genetically engineered?"

"I picked it up in Kashmir," Jordan explained. "During the biowar."

Startled, Meek exclaimed, "You mean this was one of their killer viruses?"

"A man-made plague. They killed millions with it." Including my wife, he added silently.

"And you . . ."

"It was dormant," Jordan said. "It couldn't be removed without chopping out half my intestines, it was so completely nestled inside me. The mission medical team decided it would remain dormant, so they cleared me for the trip. They thought that my time in cryosleep might even kill it."

"But it didn't," said Yamaguchi.

"It's still dormant?" Meek asked, clearly worried.

"It's dead," Jordan said. "Dead and gone."

"How did that happen?"

Jordan nodded to Yamaguchi. She smiled slowly, finally understanding. "The aliens killed it."

"Adri's people?"

"Aditi, to be specific," said Jordan. "When I submitted to a physical exam in the city, she found the virus and destroyed it."

"Destroyed it? How?"

Yamaguchi was beaming now. "I've been talking to their medical staff about that. Apparently they have instrumentation that can detect the molecular vibrational modes of individual strands of DNA. Once they pin down the frequency, they hit the virus with a narrow ultrasound beam of the same frequency. That breaks up the virus and the body's natural waste removal system flushes it out."

Meek was gaping now. "An ultrasound beam of one particular frequency? Like a laser, but with sound waves?"

"Exactly," Yamaguchi said. "This could revolutionize medical practice. It could replace surgery!"

"And it's ordinary, everyday, routine practice for them," Jordan added.

Meek looked from Jordan to Yamaguchi and back again, his mouth hanging open, his eyes wide. Suddenly he shot up from the little chair and bolted out of the infirmary.

Yamaguchi looked shocked. Without another word to her, Jordan dashed out of the infirmary and raced after Meek.

The lanky astrobiologist was running past the camp's tents, out across the open grassy glade, heading for the stately tall trees of the forest. Jordan ran after him. Meek's long legs galloped across the grass. Jordan was puffing hard, trying to keep up with him. Nobody else seemed to be in sight; everyone else was indoors. Good thing, Jordan thought as he ran after the fleeing Meek. We must look like a pair of buffoons. Or lunatics.

At last Meek reached the trees, slowed down, and finally stopped, gasping as he leaned against one of the tall, straight trunks.

Jordan's lungs were burning. I haven't sweated this much in a long time, he realized. He slowed to a trot as he approached Meek.

The astrobiologist looked awful: his face sheened with perspiration, gasping for breath, his eyes haunted.

"Harmon," Jordan puffed out as he came up to Meek. "What . . . why did you . . ."

Meek sank down onto the grass, his back sliding down the tree's bark. Jordan dropped to his knees beside him, then leaned back into a sitting position.

"Are you . . . all right, Harmon?"

"No."

"What's wrong?"

"The aliens simply destroyed your virus, just like that." He snapped his fingers.

"That's right."

Meek shook his head.

"Don't you see, Harmon? It's like Thornberry said, by their fruits you shall know them. They've been nothing but helpful to us. They're not scheming against us. They want to help us!"

"I know," said Meek, so low that Jordan barely heard him.

"You do?"

"I'm not an idiot," Meek said, his voice stronger. "I can see what's going on."

Jordan pulled out a tissue and mopped at his face. "Then you understand that they're not a danger to us. That we—"

"They're a danger to me. To me!"

"I don't understand."

Pulling up his long legs and dropping his head to his knees, Meek burst out, "Don't you see? Don't you understand?" He broke into racking sobs.

"Harmon, what is it? What's wrong?"

"I'm an astrobiologist," Meek choked out. "I've traveled eight light-years to be the first astrobiologist to study an exoplanet's biosphere."

"Yes?"

"And what do we find? Human beings! A completely Earthlike biosphere. There's nothing for me to do here! Longyear's doing all the biology work. De Falla's mapping the planet. And what do I have?

Nothing! I've come all this way for nothing! When we get back to Earth I'll be laughed at! Forgotten! It's all been for nothing."

Great god in heaven, Jordan thought. So it comes down to this. His ego. His prissy monumental ego. But as he looked at the sobbing astrobiologist, Jordan thought, He's disappointed. Crushed. To come all this way and find that your journey has been in vain. To sacrifice nearly two centuries over nothing. Who wouldn't be crushed? Who wouldn't be hurt and angered and furious at the aliens who've made a mockery of your hopes?

As gently as he could, Jordan said, "Perhaps it hasn't been for nothing, Harmon. Perhaps—"

Meek's head snapped up. "Don't patronize me, diplomat!"

Jordan smiled at him. "Why, yes, I'm a diplomat by training and experience. And perhaps I can see a way out of your dilemma. A way to make this mission worthwhile for you."

What do you mean?" asked Meek, his long bony face streaked with tears.

"Come to the city with me," Jordan said.

"No."

"Yes. Come to the city. Just as the aliens took care of my virus, I think they can take care of your problem."

"If you think I'm going to let them manipulate my mind, use their so-called education machine to turn me into a happy zombie, think again."

"No, no, nothing like that," Jordan coaxed. "Just come with me. Come and talk with Adri."

"I don't see what good it would do."

"It won't do any harm. You'll be no worse off than you are now if you simply talk with Adri a bit."

Clearly suspicious, but also wondering what Jordan was up to, Meek got shakily to his feet. Jordan stood up too and, grasping Meek's arm by the elbow, they started walking back into the camp.

"I ought to get cleaned up first," Meek muttered.

"Certainly," said Jordan. "Me too. That was quite a run you led me on."

They returned to the barracks tent, washed up, and changed into clean clothes. Jordan never let Meek far out of his sight. Together they went to Brandon, who was in the geology lab with de Falla, and told him they were going to the city.

"Really?" Brandon looked surprised. "May I ask why?"

"An astrobiology conference," Jordan replied. "With Adri."

They took one of the buggies, Jordan driving with Meek sitting beside him, long legs poking up uncomfortably.

Just as Jordan expected, Adri was waiting at the city's perimeter walkway, in his usual blue-gray robe. No sign of his little pet. Aditi hurried up and stood beside him.

"Welcome, friends," said Adri.

Jordan murmured a hello, his attention on Aditi. She was wearing a ruby red blouse, tan shorts, and a happy smile. He clasped both her hands; they felt warm as she gripped his hands tightly.

Jordan helped Aditi into the second row of the buggy, as Adri went around the other side and climbed in unassisted. Jordan started the vehicle's quiet electrical motor, and they drove up the city's main thoroughfare.

Adri asked, "To what do we owe this visit, Dr. Meek?"

Almost testily, Meek replied, "Ask Mr. Kell, here. This is his idea, not mine."

Over his shoulder, Jordan said to Adri, "I thought that you and Dr. Meek might have a useful discussion of alien biospheres."

Adri asked, "You mean the alien societies that our Predecessors have encountered?"

Jordon nodded.

"Alien societies?" Meek blurted. "You mean you've encountered other aliens?"

"Not we," said Adri. "We have never been off this planet. But our Predecessors have found many intelligent civilizations scattered among the stars. And many more planets that bear life, but not intelligence."

Meek swallowed hard before asking, "And you have records of these encounters?"

"Of course. All sorts of data: biological, geological, social . . . complete and detailed files."

"Can I . . . *may* I see them? Inspect them?"

"To your heart's content, sir."

Meek broke into an ear-to-ear grin. Jordan had never seen him look so happy.

Once they parked in the heart of the city, Meek went off with Adri, leaving Jordan alone with Aditi.

"You'll stay here tonight?" she asked, as they climbed the stairs of the administrative building.

"Wild horses couldn't drag me away—not even Meek could." And he pulled her to him and kissed her. A pair of young men coming down the steps grinned at them, but Jordan paid them scant attention.

Once they resumed climbing the stairs, Aditi asked, "Didn't Dr. Meek know that our Predecessors have found many life-bearing planets?"

"He heard it, I'm sure, but it never really registered in his mind. His attention was focused on . . . personal problems," Jordan explained.

"Strange," Aditi murmured.

"The strange thing is that I didn't realize what was making Harmon so bitter. I should have tumbled to his problem much earlier."

She smiled at him. "You tend to take responsibility for other people's problems, you know."

"That's my job," he answered.

They walked through the administration building and out to the tree-lined courtyard behind it, heading for the dormitory.

"I presume the suite I've used before is still there for me," Jordan said.

"For us," Aditi corrected.

"For us, of course. Yes, certainly, for us."

She smiled naughtily. "You've never seen my room, Jordan. Suppose we go there, instead."

"Now?"

With an elfin shrug, Aditi said, "We have plenty of time before dinner."

As he lay in Aditi's bed, with her warm and lovely body curled next to his, Jordan watched a tiny green lizard hanging upside down from the ceiling. It seemed asleep. Good idea, he said to himself, yawning. A nap would be—

His phone chirped. Frowning, Jordan disengaged from Aditi and slipped out of the bed. She stirred and murmured something drowsily.

He reached his shirt, slung over the back of an elaborately carved chair, and yanked out the damned phone.

Meek's scowling face filled the tiny screen. "Jordan, where on earth are you? I've been pounding on your door for at least ten minutes."

"I've been busy," Jordan replied in a hushed voice. "What do you want?"

"Want? Why, it's nearly dinner time and Adri and I thought you'd like to see some of his files about exoplanet biospheres before we went to the dining hall."

Jordan glanced at Aditi. She was half sitting up in bed, nodding at him.

To Meek, he said, "Give me fifteen minutes or so. Where are you?"

"Where am I?" Meek looked surprised at the question, almost insulted. "Why, I'm in Adri's office, up on the top floor of the administration building. Jordan, you simply have to see what they've got here! Dozens of exoplanets. A handful of intelligent civilizations! None of them have reached a stage of high technology, of course, but they're intelligent, with languages and writing and even the beginnings of cities! I tell you, it's a treasure trove, an absolute treasure trove. Why, I could—"

"Give me fifteen minutes, Harmon," Jordan interrupted. "I'll see you there." And he clicked the phone shut.

Aditi giggled from the bed. "You'd better shower by yourself, love. You don't have time for wet games."

RECONCILIATION

When Jordan got to Adri's office, the walls were covered with images, graphs, star charts, alphanumerical data files.

It was like stepping into a kaleidoscope; the displays shifted and changed as Jordan walked from the door to the couch where Meek and Adri were sitting side by side.

"The next set is depressing, very sad," Adri said, while gesturing Jordan to sit with them. "When the Predecessors reached this planet, their civilization had been dead for only a few centuries. The Predecessors got there too late to help them."

Jordan sat next to Meek, who was staring transfixed at the images of an empty, decaying city, collapsed buildings, monuments coated with dust and guano. One camera view zoomed in dizzyingly until he saw a deserted city street lined with statues of strange shapes, windblown clumps of vegetation tumbling by, debris from the crumbling structures littering everywhere. And in the middle of it all, a slithering snakelike creature, clearly stalking some prey that Jordan could not see.

"Of course, not all life on the planet was destroyed," said Adri. "Perhaps intelligence will arise there again, in time."

Jordan stared, transfixed. The ruins looked so much like an ancient city of Earth. Pompeii, almost. He thought of Angkor Wat, Chichen Itza, all the petrified remains of dead civilizations. But this was a whole world, an entire population of intelligent creatures— gone. Extinct.

"What happened to them?" Meek asked, his voice hushed, awed.

Adri shrugged. "We don't know. Our Predecessors were focused on finding living intelligences, they had scant interest in extinct ones."

"But that's wrong," Meek flared. "It's stupid!"

Adri tilted his head. "You see, our Predecessors do not have human curiosity. They have a single goal, implanted in them by their organic progenitors. They are driven to find living intelligent species and help them to survive. The task is so huge that they have neither the time nor the energy to delve into the histories of extinct species."

"But we do," Meek said firmly. "We have the interest, and the time, and the energy."

"Yes," Jordan agreed.

"You would go to this dead world, to study its lost people?"

"Yes," Meek and Jordan said simultaneously.

Adri smiled. "Very well. We will give you all the help we can."

Meek looked like a man who had just seen a vision of paradise.

The wall screens darkened and then went blank. Jordan saw through the room's windows that it was fully night outside.

Adri got to his feet. "You must be hungry. Let's go to dinner."

Standing up, Jordan said, "I'll get Aditi."

"Oh, she'll meet us at the dining hall," said Adri.

And Jordan thought, I've got to get one of their communicators implanted into my head. It's much better than a phone.

Meek stood up also, a thoughtful expression on his face. "You know, there's a lifetime of work for me to do. A long, long lifetime of work."

Adri nodded and said, "We can help you to live a long and productive life, Dr. Meek."

"Harmon. Call me Harmon, please."

Jordan said, "Adri, you're right. I'm rather famished. Let's get to dinner."

But Adri held up a slender-fingered hand. "I've taken the liberty of inviting the rest of your team to join us at dinner. Including the three persons from your orbiting spaceship."

"You have?" Jordan replied, surprised. "And they all accepted?"

"Yes, of course." Adri's expression became slightly guilty. "I'm afraid I told them that we're holding this dinner in Dr. Meek . . . er, in Harmon's honor."

Meek's shaggy brows shot up. "My honor?"

"Why, yes," Adri replied. "Today is your birthday, isn't it?"

"No, my birth—" Meek's face eased into a knowing grin. "Yes, it is my birthday, of a sort. I've come to life today, haven't I?"

And the three of them headed down to the dining hall.

It was a long, boisterous dinner, with real wine and lots of laughter. Jordan looked over the faces of the team: Brandon, Hazzard, Longyear, and all the others. All the suspicions were gone. All the fears. Adri relaxed enough to dig heartily into a spicy roast. Aditi sat next to Jordan, beaming at him.

"It's done," she said into his ear. "You're going to help us."

"And you're going to help us," he said.

Then he got to his feet and tapped his wineglass with a spoon. All the conversations stopped. Every face along the table turned toward Jordan. Even people at other tables looked toward him, their faces filled with curiosity and hope.

"It was a countryman of mine," Jordan began, "who said: I have nothing to offer but blood, toil, tears, and sweat."

"Come on, Jordy," Brandon groused.

Yamaguchi said, "We're not going to war, are we?"

"In a sense," Jordan said, "we will be going to war. War against the human race's ancient enemies: ignorance, fear, and the ultimate enemy—death."

The entire dining hall fell absolutely quiet.

"We've got to convince the people of Earth that they're in mortal danger. And once we've done that—"

"Assuming we can," Hazzard said.

"I assume that we can and we will. And once we do, we have to search out other intelligent species and protect them from the gamma burst that's spreading across the galaxy."

"We must help them to survive," Elyse said.

"That is our task," said Jordan. "That is our mission. Are we up to the challenge?"

"Damned right we are," Brandon snapped.

Longyear broke into a crooked grin and said, "We few, we happy few."

Adri, seated across the table from Jordan, slowly rose to his feet. "To continue in the vein that Jordan started with, let each of us therefore brace himself—and herself—to our duty."

Jordan finished, "And so bear ourselves that if the human race lasts a billion years, our descendents will still say, This was their finest hour."

Everyone in the dining hall broke into applause.

Jordan sat down, and Aditi squeezed his arm. "I'm proud of you, Jordan."

"I couldn't have done it without you," he said.

"Of course you could have. And you would have. But I'm happy that I'm here beside you."

"It's a huge task that we have ahead of us," said Jordan. "It won't be easy to convince the people of Earth that they're in danger."

"And others are in danger, too," Aditi said. "The people of Earth can help them to survive."

Jordan nodded. "We struggle against the inevitable."

"Nothing is inevitable, Jordan."

He grasped her hand tightly. "Not as long as you're with me."

"I will be, wherever you go."

Adri raised his voice to be heard over the laughter and talk of the others.

"Long life to you, Jordan Kell. Long life and happiness to you all."

Jordan dipped his chin in acknowledgment. "Happiness is working hard at a task worth doing." Then he turned to Aditi and added, "With the woman you love at your side."

EPILOGUE

Difficulty is the excuse history never accepts.

EDWARD R. MURROW

I f this wasn't so stupid, Pancho Lane said to herself, it would be funny.

As a newly elected member of the World Council, Pancho had flown to Earth from the *Goddard* habitat in orbit around Saturn on a special high-g boost just to attend this session of the Council. And here she was, sitting at the foot of the long conference table, while the leaders of the human race made asses of themselves through this farce of a meeting.

Chiang Chantao was sitting in his powerchair up at the head of the table, more machinery than human being, wheezing and frowning and trying to make himself heard while the others argued and shouted at one another.

They have a lot to argue about, Pancho admitted to herself. The meeting had originally been scheduled to discuss who the next chairman of the World Council should be. Chiang Chantao was set to retire at the end of this term and there was still an enormous amount of work to be done to alleviate the effects of the monstrous greenhouse floods.

Two days before the meeting convened, though, the communications from New Earth started arriving. The first mission had arrived safely. The planet was indeed almost completely Earthlike.

And then the lightning bolt. New Earth was populated by human beings! They—the entire planet—had been constructed by a machine intelligence that had originated on another world, twelve thousand light-years away.

The aliens had a message, and a mission. A massive wave of lethal gamma radiation was sweeping outward from the core of the galaxy. It would reach Earth in two thousand years. When it did, it would wipe out all life on Earth.

They don't believe it, Pancho realized. They don't *want* to believe it. But the human explorers on New Earth believed it. They presented evidence that the best astronomers in the solar system were now poring over.

"Two thousand years from now!" shouted the councilman from the European Union. "Even if it's true, we don't have to lift a finger for a dozen *centuries*, maybe more. It's not our problem."

"That's what people said a hundred years ago about the global warming," said Felicia Ionescu, her face a picture of barely controlled contempt. "And now look where we are."

A new round of jabbering erupted: accusations, denials, recriminations.

Douglas Stavenger, seated on Pancho's right, glanced at her. The expression on his face was a mixture of exasperation and disgust.

Stavenger wasn't actually present in the room, of course. His body teeming with nanomachines, he was not allowed to set foot on Earth. He was attending this fractious meeting through a virtual reality telepresence: his three-dimensional holographic image looked quite solid, almost as if he were actually in the conference room. Pancho had to stare hard to see that his image was slightly transparent, like a ghost.

Stavenger got to his feet. All heads turned to him, all the yammering stopped. Even Chiang's rheumy eyes fixed on him. The room fell absolutely silent.

"Two thousand years is a long time," he began, "but from what Jordan Kell and the others have told us, there are other intelligent races that need to be saved."

"Is that our responsibility?" Chiang croaked, from behind his breathing mask.

For several heartbeats Stavenger did not reply. He simply stared at the chairman. It took three seconds for the words spoken in this meeting to reach Stavenger, on the Moon, and for his response to get back to Earth. The time seemed to stretch endlessly.

At last he said, "I believe we have a moral obligation to do whatever we can to save life, wherever we can reach it."

Anita Halleck, seated at the chairman's left, objected, "But we have so much work to do right here on Earth. How can we afford this new . . . new . . . crusade?"

"How do we know this whole story hasn't been concocted by the scientists to squeeze more funding out of us?" asked the councilwoman from Pacifica.

Again the wait. Then Stavenger smiled and replied, "The answers to your questions are relatively simple. We send a new mission to Sirius C, a team of scientists and administrators who will check on the facts and advise the World Council of their validity."

Before anyone could respond, he went on, "The people of habitat *Goddard* have already built the spacecraft for a new mission to Sirius. The people of Selene will fund its staffing."

"You mean we won't have to pay for any of it?"

Pancho jumped in. "That's right. You people on Earth can devote your resources to alleviating the floods. The people off-Earth will handle the next mission to Sirius C. And that includes not only Selene and *Goddard*, but the rock rats out in the Asteroid Belt, as well. We've built the ship and we'll pay for the team to crew it."

The other Council members looked at each other in stunned silence. No one seemed to know what to say. Pancho, grinning inwardly, thought, *We've made them an offer they can't refuse.*

At last Chairman Chiang wheezed, "A very generous offer. I propose that the Council accept it."

Heads nodded up and down the table. Stavenger's ghostly image sat down again.

"The only other agenda item is to nominate a new chairman," said Chiang.

Immediately, Pancho said, "There's only one person here who can fill your shoes, Mr. Chairman. And that person is Douglas Stavenger, of Selene."

Again bedlam erupted.

"How can he be chairman when he can't even visit Earth?"

Pancho slapped the palm of her right hand on the polished tabletop and their voices stilled.

"Now look, people," she said. "Doug's been a Council member for some years, without setting foot on Earth. Hell, I'm a Council member and George Ambrose, from the Belt, is too."

Ambrose nodded his shaggy red-haired head and grinned boyishly.

Pancho continued, "You've made an effort to make this Council include *all* the people of the solar system. So why won't you elect the best man for the chairman's post, even if he lives on the Moon?"

They argued the issue back and forth, but the objections gradually petered out. When Chiang called for a vote, Stavenger was elected unanimously.

Pancho was smiling as she left the conference room. She chatted with a few of the Council members for a while, then made a beeline for the hotel where her husband was waiting for her.

"It's done?" Jake Wanamaker asked the instant she came through the door of their suite. He really didn't need to ask; he could tell from the huge grin on Pancho's face.

"It's done," she said. "We're goin' to New Earth."

Wanamaker puffed out a breath. "Eighty years, Panch. It takes eighty years to get there."

"Yep. Trish'll be a hundred and fourteen years old by the time we get there."

"And how old will we be?"

"Don't matter," said Pancho. "Our lives are just beginning, Jake. Just beginning."